LITTLE DOORS

Also by Paul Di Filippo

Lost Pages
Fractal Paisleys
Ribofunk
The Steampunk Trilogy

LITTLE DOORS
PAUL DI FILIPPO

Four Walls Eight Windows
New York/London

Copyright © 2002 Paul Di Filippo

Published in the United States by
Four Walls Eight Windows
39 West 14th Street
New York, NY 10011
http://www.4w8w.com

U.K. offices:
Four Walls Eight Windows/Turnaround
Unit 3, Olympia Trading Estate
Coburg Road, Wood Green
London N22 6TZ, England

First printing November 2002.

Library of Congress Cataloging-in-Publication Data

Di Filippo, Paul 1954-
    Little doors / by Paul Di Filippo
        p. cm.
        ISBN 1-56858-241-2
        1. Science fiction, American. I. Title.

PS3554.I3915 L58 2002

813'.54—dc21   2002069292

The stories originally appeared in the following publications:

"Little Doors," *Night Cry* (1987); "Billy," *Pulphouse* (1988); "Moloch," *Journal Wired* (1990); "The Grange," *The Magazine of Fantasy and Science Fiction* (1991); "Sleep Is Where You Find It," *The Magazine of Fantasy and Science Fiction* (1993); "The Horror Writer," *Nova SF* (1994); "My Two Best Friends," *The Thirteenth Moon* (1996); "The Death of Salvador Dali," *The Edge* (1996); "Our House," *The Edge* (1998); "Jack Neck and the Worrybird," *Science Fiction Age* (1998); "Stealing Happy Hours," *Interzone* (2000); "Singing Each to Each," *Interzone* (2000); "Rare Firsts," *Realms of Fantasy* (2000); "Return to Cockaigne," *Interzone* (2001); "The Short Ashy Afterlife of Hiram P. Dottle," *The Magazine of Fantasy and Science Fiction* (2001); "Slumberland," *Fantastic Metropolis* (2002); "Mehitabel in Hell," *Dead Cats Bouncing* (2002).

10 9 8 7 6 5 4 3 2 1

Printed in Canada

Book design by Joel Tippie

CONTENTS

To Deborah Newton: a volume of moonbeams from her mooncalf.

Special thanks to: Susan Cafferty Moore for her keyboarding expertise, cinematic enthusiasm and all-round panache; and to the inimitable Dan Pearlman: "scanners do not live in vain."

LITTLE DOORS

Once upon a time . . . began the story Jerome Crawleigh was trying to read but couldn't.

Squeezing crocodile tears out from his eyelids' tender embrace, Crawleigh pinched the bridge of his fine Roman nose. Good God, was there no end to the books to be devoured and digested before he could begin to write his own latest? And his field—children's literature—was comparatively empty. What if he had chosen some other, older byway of literature, more crowded with primary texts and execrable exegeses? Wouldn't that have been just dandy?

Ah, exegesis—such a resounding, academic word. When in doubt, explicate. Extricate yourself from words with more words, analogous to some hair of the dog on the morning after. Something of a self-perpetuating cycle. But what the hell, give it a go. Perhaps penetrate the thicket of cliché that hid the elusive hare of fairy-tale truth. . . .

Once: Not twice or thrice, but once. Singular, not-to-be-duplicated experience. Yet by implication, if unique wonders happened once, others might again.

Upon: What other preposition would do so well here? During, in, on? Definitely not! We need the connotation of "in the course of," indicating simultaneous progression and fixity in a particular milieu.

A: Here, a neat touch of vagueness and remoteness. Not "the" time (as of a certain king, perhaps), but "a" time, nebulous and mistily distant.

Time: Ah, yes, the most loaded word in the language. Not its counterpart, space, an intuitively graspable dimension, but time, breeder of paradox, reviver of hopes and loves. If the tale to be told were merely distant in space, how easily discounted or disproved. But "dis-placed" in time, what power it gains!

So—

Once upon a time . . .

But Crawleigh's professorial spell, although woven by a past master, was not strong enough to get beyond this initial obstacle. Something was wrong with his brain today. Dropping the offending book upon his littered desktop, where it snapped shut with a dusty clap, he pushed blunt fingers through curly greying hair, as if to palpitate the reluctant organ. Was it the office itself that was to blame? Dark wood moldings waxed by generations of janitors; shelf upon shelf of accusatory books, their spines stiff as soldiers'; yellowing framed diplomas on cracked plaster walls, constricting his life as surely as if the frames had been dropped like hoops over his head and around his arms.

Possibly. Quite possibly the office was at fault. He ought to get out. But where would he go? Not home. No, definitely not home. Upon his unexpected arrival, there would be unpleasant questions aplenty from Connie to greet him. He would face her usual endless prying into his affairs, her tirades about his meager pay and her lack of status among other university wives. Not the faculty lounge either. At the moment, the company of his fellow pedants was least attractive to him.

Suddenly he thought of Audrey. How many days had it been since his last tryst with audacious Audrey, queen of the copiers, Zenobia of the Xerox shop? Just the tonic for his blues, just the girl he'd hate to lose. Audrey it was.

Crawleigh emerged from behind his desk, moved to the coat rack and snatched his modified safari jacket from its hook. With his desert boots and cords and jacket, he thought he looked rather rakish, explorer of an intellectual terrain.

And besides, he felt more comfortable with Audrey, dressed so.

Crawleigh left his office behind.

Out on the quad, under the elms, Crawleigh began to feel better almost immediately. Seeing the students idling in the young shade of the newly leafed trees recalled his own youth to him, reminding him of a time when he had had dreams and hopes and desires similar to theirs.

And were such things gone now entirely from his life? he wondered as he traced a diagonal across the grassy square. Or had the simple wants and plans of his youth merely been transmuted into mature shapes? Was loss involved, or only metamorphosis?

Crawleigh tried to put by such ponderous puzzles. He was in search of forgetfulness right now, not answers. The anodyne of Audrey was augury enough.

As Crawleigh approached the big arch that framed one entrance to the campus, his gaze was attracted by a bright dab of colors down by the ground, at the foot of the marble gateway. Intrigued, he stopped to investigate.

My, my, the art students had been busy with their guerrilla activities again. Not content with formal galleries, they had recently taken to creating public displays that would ostensibly reach more people.

This piece seemed more whimsical than strident.

Painted on the marble surface of the arch was a tiny *trompe l'oeil*. Starting at ground level, a flight of stairs led up to a little door. The golden knob and black hinges were rendered in minute detail. The whole thing looked quite convincingly like an entrance into the solid marble structure. But the only creature that could have used such a door would have been small as a mouse.

And in fact . . . why, yes, there were words below the painting that said—so discerned Crawleigh while bending down without regard for propriety—"The Mouse Collective."

Straightening up, Crawleigh found himself smiling. His fancy was tickled. As students' conceptions went, this wasn't too sophomoric.

Moving under and beyond the arch, out into the public street, Crawleigh kept his eyes open for further works by the Mouse Collective, and was not disappointed.

A painted ladder ran up a retaining wall and into a drainpipe.

A curtained window big as a playing card mimicked the human-sized one set beside it.

Small steps made of wood were nailed in a spiral on a tree. Up in the branches, Crawleigh thought to detect a tiny treehouse.

At the base of a stop sign was painted a mouse-sized traffic light, glowing perpetually green.

A nail-studded, wood-grained, rusty-ringed trap door was illusioned into the sidewalk.

After noting these fanciful brainchildren of the Mouse Collective, Crawleigh began to grow bored with the project. As usual, no one knew when to stop. Just because once was clever, twice was not twice as clever. Crawleigh ceased looking for the little paintings, and in fact soon forgot about them.

In a couple of minutes he came to the Street, which cut perpendicularly across his path. Traffic was thick today, car horns blaring as drivers jostled for parking spaces.

Paul Di Filippo

The Street was the commercial heart of the town's university district. Here, around the university bookstore, dozens of businesses had gathered over the decades. A dry cleaner, a liquor store, two ice-creameries, clothing stores, shoe stores, a Store 24, an Army-Navy surplus outlet, jewelry and lingerie boutiques, several restaurants, a deli, a grocery, a hardware store, a toy store, a computer vendor—

—and, of course, those invaluable adjuncts to exploding and processing information, rival copy shops.

In one of which worked Audrey. Disarmingly simple, naive urchin, waif, and savior of overcivilized senses, thought Crawleigh. Be there today, when I need you.

Arriving at the door of the copy place, Crawleigh saw her through the window and let out an involuntary relieved sigh. Then he went in.

The interior of the shop was hot and noisy and smelled of obscure chemicals. Automatic feeders sucked in sheets to be copied faster than the eye could follow. Light blasted the images off them onto blanks, and copies and originals were spat out by the insatiable machines. Workers scurried to collate paper and placate the crowd of customers.

Audrey unwittingly presented her profile to Crawleigh. She was copying pages of a book. She left the copier lid up during the process, so that her form was bathed in a garish green light as each page was zapped, transforming her visage into something from another world.

She was small and skinny. Her tight blue-and-white-striped stovepipe pants revealed her legs to be without any excess flesh, from thigh to ankle. (How unlike cloyingly constant Connie's chubby calves!) She wore ankle socks, white high heels. Her black hair was teased on top and short except where it feathered her neck.

Finishing the task at hand, she scooped up the copies from the out-tray and turned toward the counter.

Her features were plain, perhaps sharp, but not homely: simply undistinguished by any great beauty or vitality. To compensate, she wore too much makeup. Dark eyeliner, glossy lipstick, lots of blush. A few stray arcs of hair cut across her forehead. She was twenty-two years old.

Crawleigh had never seen anyone so outlandishly attractive to him. That wasn't precisely right. (And we must have precision mustn't we?) Audrey was so quintessentially like a thousand, thousand other young women her age that she affected Crawleigh like an archetype. When he made love to her, he felt he was tapping into the essence of a generation, pinning a symbol to the mattress.

4

Every litcrit's wet dream.

Crawleigh saw Audrey's face pass through three or four distinct emotions when she spotted him. Surprise, anger, interest, a determination to play the coquette. She was so delightfully transparent!

"Hello, Audrey," Crawleigh said.

As usual, she was chewing gum. Ringing up the sale, she snapped the elastic fodder deliberately, knowing he couldn't stand it.

"Oh, Professor Crawleigh. What a surprise. I thought you moved outta town or something. Haven't seen you in so long."

Crawleigh experienced the delightful thrill that came from bantering with double meanings, trying to maintain at least a surface of innocence, yet also trying to get across the rather salacious things he intended.

"Ah, well," Crawleigh replied, "you know how busy life becomes around midterms. I barely get to leave the department. And I just haven't needed your services till today."

"Izzat so?" Audrey studied her polished nails as if they contained infinite secrets. "Next!" she called out, and stuck out her hand for something to be copied. Receiving a loose page, she turned as if their conversation were over.

Crawleigh was not discouraged, having played this game before. "If I drop something off later this afternoon, will you attend to it personally? I need it quite desperately."

Audrey spoke back over her small shoulder. "Okay. But don't make it too late. I'm done at three."

"Wonderful," said Crawleigh, meaning it.

When Audrey smiled then, she was almost special looking.

And when she stepped into Crawleigh's car at three, he was smiling too.

* * *

The book—if it was ever started, let alone finished—was going to be burdened with one of those weighty titles complete with colon that assured academic immortality.

The Last Innocents: Children's Fantastic Literature in America and Britain during the First Decade of the Twentieth Century.

The projected text that Crawleigh had in mind—the Platonic ideal that always outshone the reality—was going to concentrate on two authors of genius.

For the sake of glorious symmetry, one of the geniuses would be British and female, the other male and American.

The envelopes, please.

Edith Nesbit.

Lyman Frank Baum.

Through the carapace of Crawleigh's cynicism and jadedness, these names still sent a thrill along his nerves. Simply to hear or read them was to be propelled back in time to his youth, when, as a solitary sort of kid, he had hid on many a summer day in the fantasies of these two, who—he knew even then, as a ten-year-old surrounded by the insanity of a world orgasming in its second great war of the century—had been special voices from an era far, far away and utterly unreachable.

What was it about the first decade of this mad, bad century that made it so luminous and special in Crawleigh's mind? He was not fool enough to imagine that life then had been Edenic, nor human nature other than its frequently rancid self. No, he knew the litany of facts as well as any other educated person. Child labor, endemic diseases running rampant, bigotry, hunger, outhouses, colonialism, jingoism, the Armenian genocide, illiteracy, poverty, fires that would decimate wooden cities, and of course, lurking just around the corner, The War to End All Wars. . . . Taken all in all, not an objectively pleasant time to live.

But if one tried to understand the era in the only way one could ever apprehend the past—through its art and artifacts—then one was forced to conclude that the decade had been possessed of a certain uninhibited innocence that had vanished forever from the globe.

The Wizard of Oz. The Five Children and It. Queen Zixi of Ix. The Story of the Amulet. The Magical Monarch of Mo. Gone, all gone, that unselfconsciously delightful writing. Current fantasy was produced mainly for adults, and the little bit Crawleigh had sampled was a botched, stereotyped, unmagical mess. And what of juvenile literature today? Full of drugs and pregnancies, child abuse and death. Jesus, you could practically see each author panting to be hailed as the next Balzac of the training-bra set.

His book would illuminate this whole fallen condition, and the glory whence it had descended. The outline had him starting back with the Victorians for a running jump. Thackeray, Lang, Stockton, MacDonald, certainly Carroll. Then land in the era of his main concern, and spend the largest portion of the book there. Perhaps with a digression on fantasy in early comics: Herriman's *Krazy Kat* and McCay's *Little Nemo.*

Yes, a fine ambition this book, and certain to be widely appreciated. The culmination of a life of reading.

If only he could just finish these last few texts.

Crawleigh had gotten through the book that had stumped him the other day. A minor work, but useful as one more citation. Now he was ready to read one last critical work that had just reached him.

The book was by a colleague of Crawleigh's whom he had often met at numerous literary conferences. Judd Mitchell. When he and Mitchell last talked, the other man had let slip a bit of his newest thesis, and Crawleigh had grown nervous, since it touched peripherally on Crawleigh's own. But now Mitchell's book was in hand, and a quick riffle through it had shown Crawleigh that it certainly didn't poach on his territory to any great extent.

Feeling quite relieved and even generous toward Mitchell for hewing to what was expected of him, Crawleigh settled back in his office chair to study the book at greater length.

A couple of hours passed. Crawleigh stopped only to light a stenchy pipe and discharge clouds of smoke. He found himself enjoying the book. Mitchell had a certain facileness with facts. Nothing like Crawleigh's own witty yet deep style, of course. Too bad about the man's personal life. Crawleigh had recently heard rumors that Mitchell had lit out for parts unknown, abandoning wife and family. Something about accumulated gambling debts coming to light.

Midway through the book, Crawleigh came upon a passage that affected him like a pitchfork to the rear.

> Perhaps one of the most curious books for children that has ever been written is the neglected *Little Doors*, by Alfred Bigelow Strayhorn. Published by the once-prestigious but now defunct firm of Drinkwater & Sons, in 1903, the story concerns the Alicelike adventures of a girl named Judy, who encounters a surprisingly mercenary cast of characters, including a Shylockian shark and a racehorse who escapes the glue factory by gaining wings. Judy's encounter with Professor Mouse, who explains the theory of little doors, is particularly well-done. But the cumulative effect of the narrative is vastly more unsettling than the sum of its parts. . . . Of course, it is most fruitful to read the book as a sustained attack on capitalism and its wastage of human souls . . .

Crawleigh abandoned Mitchell's book and puffed contemplatively on his pipe. Once one discounted Mitchell's inane socialism, the man seemed to have stumbled upon an undeniably exciting find. In Crawleigh's own extensive searches of the literature, he had never encountered the book cited by Mitchell. (And why did that queer title strike him so deeply?) Now he knew he had to track it down, though. If he failed to incorporate it into his study, everyone would soon be making unflattering comparisons between his book and Mitchell's, in terms of completeness.

To the library, then! Descend like the Visigoths on Rome! Pillage the stacks, burn the card catalog, smash the terminals, rape the librarians. . . .

One shouldn't start thinking in such violent sexual imagery on a hot April afternoon, of course, unless one was quite prepared to act on it, Crawleigh reminded himself.

So up he got and went to seek Audrey's awesomely attractive and appreciated little arse.

* * *

Which now reared under the sweaty sheets like two little melons.

It was Audrey's lunch hour. Crawleigh had cajoled her to come with him back to her apartment, which was not far from the Street.

Audrey lived in a single room with a kitchen alcove and bath and one window. The shade there was pulled down now, an ebony oblong framed by hot white light on top and two sides. The room was plunged into that peculiar deracinating artificial darkness that could only be found when you shut out the sun in the middle of a bright day and retreated inside from the busy world with its bustling billions. Crawleigh felt simultaneously ancient and infantile. He was sated, yet not bored with life. On the other hand, he felt no immediate impulse to get up and get busy. Simply to lie here beside Audrey was his sole ambition for the moment.

Crawleigh rested on his back; Audrey on her belly. Turning his gaze on his little nymph, Crawleigh saw that Audrey's arms formed a cage around her head, while her face was buried in the sheets.

This was most unlike Audrey. Usually after sex she was quite talkative, regaling him with really amazingly funny anecdotes about her daily travails and accomplishments. It was astounding how much drama she could extract from such trivial situations, and Crawleigh always listened with gleeful indulgence.

Something must be wrong now. Crawleigh experienced a mortal shiver as he considered the possibility that perhaps his performance had been below par.

Crawleigh laid a hand on her sheet-covered rump and squeezed with what he hoped was proper affection.

"Was it all right today, dear? I really enjoyed it."

Audrey's mattress-muffled voice drifted up. "Yeah. I came."

Crawleigh grew slightly miffed at her easy vulgarity. Such talk was fine during the act itself, but afterward things should be, well, more romantic. Connie, for all her other faults, was never so coarse.

"For heaven's sake, then, why the sulking? You'd think I just tortured you."

Audrey whirled around and pushed up, coming to rest on her haunches, looking down on naked Crawleigh with the twisted sheet pooling around her thin waist. In the half-light, her little pink-tipped breasts reminded Crawleigh of apples. Her face was really angry.

"It *is* torture!" she cried. "*Mental* torture. I really like you, Jerry, but I can only see you whenever you have a lousy minute to spare. And when we're together, we never leave this stinking room. There's more to life than sex, you know. When are we gonna go someplace exciting, do something different? I gotta come back to this room every day after work as it is, without spending lunchtime here too!"

Crawleigh was unprepared for the vehemence of this outburst. He had had no sense of mistreating Audrey, and he was taken aback by her accusations.

All he could think to say was, "You must have had an awful day at work to get so upset, dear."

"So what if I did?" Audrey shot back. "I always have an awful day at that place. You know what it's like—people shouting and insulting you, standing over those hot stinking machines for eight hours, making twenty-five cents over minimum wage— I hate it! I really hate it! Do you think that's what I wanna do with the rest of my life?"

Crawleigh had never given the matter any thought at all, so he was quite unprepared to answer. Trying to divert the argument back to safer ground, Crawleigh said, "Well, perhaps I have been neglecting to give you the proper, ah, stimulation. But you must realize, dear, that it is not easy for us to be together. You know how small this town is. Everyone knows everyone else. If we were to go places together, my wife would soon learn. And then where would we be?"

"Why don't you ditch that old cow?" Audrey demanded.

Crawleigh smiled as the mental image of Connie as a cow in a dress was conjured up. "It's not so easy as all that, Audrey. You're an adult. Surely you know how such things work. We must give it time. Listen, I have an idea. The very next out-of-state conference I have to go to, you'll come along."

For a moment Audrey seemed mollified. But then, without warning, she threw herself down on Crawleigh and began to weep. Crawleigh wrapped his arms around her shaking body. Her skin felt like a handful of rose petals.

"Oh, I'm so ordinary," Audrey wailed. "I'm so plain and ordinary that no one could love me."

Patting her, Crawleigh said, "That's not true. You're my princess. My princess."

Audrey seemed not to hear.

* * *

O, frabjous day, they'd found the book!

Crawleigh stood in the English Department offices. He had just opened the little door on his mailbox and withdrawn a slip that reported on his request for the volume mentioned by Mitchell. After failing to locate it in any of the university's collections, he had initiated the search of associated facilities. And wouldn't you know it, his fabulous luck was holding. It was available right here in sleepy old College Town, at a private library Crawleigh had often passed but never visited. It would be delivered by a campus courier later that day.

Crawleigh could barely contain his excitement when he returned to his office. Why, he even felt charitable toward Connie, who that morning had unexpectedly gone to the trouble of rousing herself from bed before eleven and sharing breakfast with him.

To pass the time until the courier arrived, Crawleigh idly picked up one of his favorite novels not written by The Illustrious Pair. *Look Homeward, Angel*, set in the period Crawleigh worshipped, had always struck him as somehow akin to fantasy, concerned as it was with the mysteries of Time and Space.

Crawleigh flipped open the book to the famous preface.

> . . . a stone, a leaf, an unfound door . . . the unspeakable and incommunicable prison of this earth . . . the lost lane-end into heaven . . .

The words filled him as always with profound melancholy, and he became so lost in the book that hours passed. When a knock sounded at the office door, he emerged reluctantly from the text.

The courier demanded a signature for his package, and Crawleigh complied. Taking the plainly wrapped parcel with trembling hands, Crawleigh shut the door on the messenger and the world.

Peeling off the old-fashioned brown paper and twine, Crawleigh settled down to look at this obscure book, whose title had so profoundly affected him.

The book was a hardcover, about ten by twelve inches, and fairly thin. Its cover was the kind simply not made any more: the burgundy cloth framed an inset colored plate. The plate depicted a curious scene.

Stretching away to a horizon line was an arid, stony plain. Standing in the foreground of the picture was a door and its frame, unattached to any building. Its knob was gold, its hinges black, and it was open. Within this door was an identical one, but smaller. Within the second, a third, within the third, a fourth, within the fourth . . .

Crawleigh couldn't count the painted doors past twenty. There was a small pinprick of green in the very center of the stacked doors, as if the very last portal, however far away and miniscule, opened onto another, more verdant world.

The title was not given on the cover.

Intrigued, Crawleigh opened the book. Inside, beneath the copyright information, was the colophon of the publishers, Drinkwater & Sons: an eccentric house with gables, turrets, chimneys and at least a dozen doors in it on all levels.

Here at last, on the facing page, was title and author:

LITTLE DOORS

by

Alfred Bigelow Strayhorn

Crawleigh flipped to page one and began to read.

> Once upon a time . . . began the story Princess Ordinary was trying to read but couldn't.

Odd opening, thought Crawleigh. He had expected to be introduced right away to the heroine mentioned by Judd Mitchell, named Judy. Oh well, auctorial intentions were not always immediately fathomable, even (especially?) in children's literature. On with the story.

Princess Ordinary finally gave up and tossed the book of fairy tales down with a pettish sigh.

"Drat it all!" she exclaimed, and kicked her satin hassock with her pretty little velvet-shod foot. "Why can't I enter these old tales as if they were my own dreams, as I once did when I was a child? Surely one doesn't lose talents as one grows older, but only gains new skills, moving on from strength to strength. At least that's the way things *should* be." The Princess paused for a moment. "At least they should be that way for princesses, who are special, even if they're as ordinary and drab as I fear I am."

The Princess stood up then, and moved to a wood-framed mirror that stood across the room from her. (The Princess was to be found this morning in her luxurious bedroom, for that was where she liked best to read, and lately she had taken to staying in the one room almost all day.)

At the mirror, she pirouetted with rather more abandon than she felt, holding out her full skirts with one hand to add a little extra graceful touch she had seen her mother employ at royal dances. But in spite of all her airs, Princess Ordinary was forced to admit that the reflection greeting her gaze was that of a young woman whom no one would ever call beautiful. Her hair was an awful coal-black — everyone in this kingdom thought only golden hair was to be admired — and her nose and chin were sharp in a way that betokened a certain sullenness. No, the Princess was just what her name implied: a common sort of girl who, except for the accident of her royal birth, might just as easily have been found waiting on customers in a shop; which of course is not to say that she hadn't a good heart and soul that were to be cherished as much as those of a real beauty, but only that they could not be so easily inferred from her appearance.

Princess Ordinary spun the mirror — which was mounted in a frame on pins through its middle — so that the glass faced to the wall. Now, curiously enough, the wood used for this mirror had once been a door (there was a shortage of lumber at the time) and it still retained its handle on the back side. Seeing the silly handle to a door that could never be opened, the Princess laughed, but only for a moment. She was soon sober again.

"Not only am I ordinary," she cried in a fit of pique, "but the whole world is quite unimaginative and boring! There isn't a single thing in it that interests me any more, and I wish I could leave it all behind!"

At that exact moment, the Princess's tutor appeared in the door. He had come looking for her for her daily lesson (for the Princess wasn't so old that she had quit learning, nor should any of us ever be), and when he heard the Princess's wish, he was moved to let out a blast of steam.

The tutor, you see, was a mechanical man named Steel Daniel, and had been constructed especially to be Princess Ordinary's companion. Consequently, he had great affection for her and did not like to see her upset.

"Is that really what you desire, Princess?" asked Steel Daniel. "To visit another world where things are perhaps more to your liking, but definitely not as they are here?"

"Yes," said the Princess, stamping her foot (the one that had not kicked the hassock, for that one was a trifle sore). "Any world must be better than this one. I'll go anywhere that extends a welcome."

The Princess did not stop to think about how she would be leaving her mother and father and Steel Daniel behind, and truth to tell, she didn't precisely care just then.

"Well, in that case," said Daniel, "I have no choice but to obey your commands. I will tell you whom you must visit to satisfy your wish. It is Professor Mouse, who lives far away, over much treacherous terrain. You must journey to him on foot, disguised as a commoner, and no one can help you. The only aids I can proffer are these."

Steel Daniel opened a little door in his chest and took out a magic stone and a magic leaf. Princess Ordinary took them, and, before you could say tara-cum-diddle, she was clothed like a peasant girl and marching down the path leading from the castle gate, without so much as a fare-thee-well . . .

Perplexed, Crawleigh shut the book. Where were the characters itemized by Mitchell? Except for Professor Mouse, they were nonexistent. Had Mitchell gone over the edge at the end, beset as he was with personal troubles? Did Crawleigh even have the same book?

Whatever the explanation, Crawleigh would have to proceed as if this were the text to be dissected. What else could he do? He would take Xeroxes (Audrey's job, that), and use them to refute anyone who sided with Mitchell's version of the book.

But for now, he had had enough of *Little Doors*. The reading had left him with an unexplainable headache, and he resolved to go home for the day.

* * *

When Crawleigh arrived to pick up Audrey, he found her still packing. The shade was up today, letting Saturday sunlight spill in, and Crawleigh found the room foreign-looking. Audrey was frantically rummaging through her dresser and closet, tossing clothes into an open suitcase. Her cheap turntable was spinning, and loud music filled the air.

"Oh, Jerry," she cried when he let himself in after knocking. "What am I gonna pack? What kind of restaurants will we be going to? What kind of people am I gonna meet? Oh, Christ, why didn't I buy that goddam dress I saw on sale last week?"

Crawleigh refrained from telling Audrey that she wouldn't be meeting any of his colleagues if he could help it. The MLA conference— held in San Francisco this year—was just the place where news of his perfidies would disseminate the fastest. Audrey would have to stay in the hotel room until he was free to be with her; or otherwise amuse herself inconspicuously during the day.

But time enough to tell her this when they were on the plane.

"Listen, dear, just take what you consider to be most stylish, and I'm sure you'll look fine. We don't have much time, you realize, if we're going to make our flight."

Audrey frantically stuffed loose shirttails and sleeves and legs into the battered suitcase. "Jesus, I'm gonna forget something important, I just know it."

While Audrey finished, Crawleigh moved idly about the room, still bemused by how strange it looked to him today. He picked up the empty cardboard record-sleeve lying by the turntable and studied it. It was good to know a few names in the rock and roll world to drop in front of students, and Crawleigh relied on Audrey for this knowledge, in addition to the carnal variety.

This particular record cover showed a fuzzy close-up photo of a katydid, and said:

STEELY DAN
Katy Lied

As Crawleigh read the title, the singer's words leaped into sonic focus.

> *A kingdom where the sky is burning,*
> *A vision of the child returning.*
> *Any world that I'm welcome to,*
> *Any world that I'm welcome to,*
> *Is better than the one I come from.*

A shiver ran down Crawleigh's spine with the velocity of chilled honey.

How in the hell—? What synchronicity could account for the close parallel of this song with Princess Ordinary's lament? Was it simply that these pop-prophets had somehow read the obscure book he was currently researching, or was it all coincidence, a mere common concatenation of certain sounds, simply a new linguistic shuttle bringing up the same sequence, after nearly a century?

Crawleigh probably would have let the mystery bother him if Audrey hadn't yelled loudly then, and begun to swear.

"Yow! Oh, Christ, I broke a frigging fingernail! Why the hell aren't you helping me Jerry, if we're so late?"

Crawleigh hastened to Audrey's side and together they got the stuffed suitcase closed and locked.

Aboard the jet, Crawleigh tried a dozen times to find a way to tell Audrey of the peculiar conditions that bore on her accompanying him. But she was enjoying her first air-journey so much that he hadn't the heart right then.

In the middle of the flight, as their plane crossed a seemingly limitless desert, she turned a radiantly excited face toward him and said, "Oh, Jerry, this is all just like a dream. I feel like—I don't know. Like the princess in that book you let me read a year ago."

Crawleigh's stomach churned.

In the lobby of the hotel, he had a nervous fifteen minutes as they registered together, fearing that some acquaintance would surely see them. Crawleigh's luck held, however, and they got up to their room without being accosted.

Audrey threw herself down on the queen-size bed, bouncing and squealing.

"What a palace," she said. "This room's bigger'n my whole *apartment.*"

"Glad you like it," Crawleigh said, fiddling nervously with the luggage where the bellhop had set it. "I picked it with you in mind."

With this as an opening, he plunged ahead and told her.

Crawleigh had always thought that *crestfallen* was just a word. But when Audrey's face underwent the transformation he witnessed and her whole body seemed to cave in on itself, he knew the reality behind the word.

For a minute, Audrey sat as if devoid of breath or spirit. Then she shot to her feet and faced Crawleigh quivering with rage.

"You—you fucking liar!"

She pushed past Crawleigh, elbowing him in the gut, and raced out the door.

Crawleigh sat on the bed, an arm across his sore stomach. His free hand—behind him for support—felt that the cover was still warm from Audrey.

Well, this was not turning out as he had planned. But perhaps he could still salvage the star-crossed seminar somehow. Audrey had to return to the room. He held the plane tickets and all the money. And when she did, he would have an eloquent speech ready that would soothe her ruffled feathers and have her falling all over him.

When Crawleigh's midriff felt normal, he got up and unpacked his bag. Lying on top was *Little Doors.* He had hoped to get some work done amid everything else this trip, and he had still not finished the book.

After pacing anxiously a bit, Crawleigh determined to read to pass the time until Audrey came back. He settled down in a chair.

> When the Crow approached Princess Ordinary, she was nearly dying of hunger.
>
> The Crow, fully as big as a human, alighted beside the famished Princess in the midst of the desert she was then traversing. His appearance was quite frightening, and Princess Ordinary wished she still had either the magic stone or the magic leaf to protect herself with. But the

stone had been used up saving her from the Jelly-Dragons, and the leaf had crumbled up after expanding into a flying carpet and carrying her over the Unutterable. Consequently, lacking either of these two tokens, she had to hope that the Crow possessed a nature belied by his exterior.

"Oh, help me, please, good Crow," cried out the Princess. "I am dying in this wasteland, and will surely end my days here unless you come to my aid. Let me mount you so that you may carry me away."

"That I cannot do," said the Crow, "for I can support only myself in the air. However, I can bring you sustenance that will enable you to make it out of the desert under your own power."

"Oh, please do then."

The Crow flew away with mighty beats of his wings. Princess Ordinary found herself disbelieving his professed inability to carry her, but what could she do about it? Soon he returned, bearing a bright red berry in his beak.

"Eat this," Crow said, speaking around the fruit.

"It won't do anything bad to me, will it?"

"Of course not!" replied Crow indignantly.

The Princess took the berry then and swallowed it. It was the sweetest food she had ever tasted. But as soon as it hit her belly, she knew she had done wrong. She was revitalized, but another thing had also happened. Placing a hand on her belly, the Princess cried out:

"Now I shall have a baby! You lied to me, Crow! You lied!"

But the Crow just laughed and flew away.

Crawleigh felt sick. He threw the book across the room, hoping it would hit the wall and fall to pieces. But it landed safely atop a pile of shirts.

Audrey came back around midnight. She crawled naked into bed beside the sleeping Crawleigh and woke him up by straddling him and rocking against him until he was erect. Then she made love to him as if possessed.

      * * *

The semester was over. Normally Crawleigh would have felt an immense relief and excitement at the prospect of a summer's worth of free time stretching ahead of him. But at the close of this semester he felt nothing but trepidation and unease. Nothing was going right, in either his personal or his professional life.

Regarding the former, Audrey had refused to see him since they got back from San Francisco and their aborted vacation. He missed her more than he had ever imagined he would.

And for his current project—he was impossibly stumped by that damnable *Little Doors.*

He had finished reading the book. But he still didn't know what to make of it. That it was important—perhaps pivotal—to his thesis was no longer in doubt. He simultaneously blessed and cursed the day he had learned of it. But exactly what it meant was not clear.

The central nugget of mystery was contained in a single speech, at the very end of the book, by the one constant character in both Crawleigh's and Mitchell's versions of the story.

Professor Mouse.

With late May breezes blowing into his office, Crawleigh took the irritating book down from its shelf. It was long overdue, but he ignored the notices mailed to him. He couldn't give it up till he understood it.

Opening to a well-thumbed page, Crawleigh studied the central passage for the hundredth time.

> "You claim," said Princess Ordinary, rubbing her swollen belly, "that I can leave this world only through a little door. Well, I would be glad to follow your advice—for this world has not treated me well of late, and I am anxious to reach another—but I am at a loss as to what a little door is. Do you mean something like the tiny door by which I entered your burrow? Am I in another world already?"
>
> Professor Mouse curried his snout with his paws before answering. "No, my dear. I am afraid you have misunderstood me. A little door is not a physical thing, although it may very well manifest itself as one to your senses. A little door is more a twist in the universe that results from a state of mind occasioned by certain special everyday things which most people have come to take for granted, but which are really quite special."
>
> "Such as what?" asked the Princess.
>
> "Oh my, there are so many I could hardly name them all. But I'll tell you a few. February 29th is a little door, of

course, just like New Year's Eve and the First of May. So are the four hinges of the day: midnight, six A.M., noon, and six P.M. Certain books are little doors. Special smells and tastes that reach back to your childhood are little doors. Shifting dapples of sun and shade in the forest are little doors. Mountains are little doors, although to be sure they are quite big. Your birthday is a little door, and I daresay a full moon is one too. Cats with double-paws are little doors. So is the call of a hunter's horn. A trunk full of memories in an attic could be a little door. And it is indisputable that love is a little door, as is memory. My goodness, I could go on and on."

Princess Ordinary tried to understand and did indeed feel herself trembling on the verge of some new knowledge. But still she had a question.

"You say all these common but uncommon things are little doors to somewhere else. Why then, I could have encountered any number of little doors back home, without ever having to undertake this dreadful, tiresome journey. Why have I never been able to, say, step through my mirror, as I have often wished?"

"Ah, you lacked the key to a little door," the big mouse said patiently. "You see, little doors do not always open when you wish. You must approach them with the proper state of mind. Your emotions and attitude are the key, and they must be strong. Serenity or desperation, desire for or aversion toward—these are some of the states during which a little door may open. I say 'may' since nothing is certain in this world, and many have wished for little doors to open and never been so lucky. And of course there are those rare instances when the last thing a person thought he wanted was to enter a little door, but it opened up and swallowed him anyway."

"So on this journey," said the Princess slowly and thoughtfully, "what I did was refine my desires until they were pure and intense enough to open a little door."

"Exactly," agreed Mouse.

A light broke upon the Princess then, making her look quite beautiful. "Then the quest was its own goal, wasn't it? And now I can leave your burrow and find my little door."

"Of course," said Professor Mouse.

And so she did.

Crawleigh looked up.

Audrey had walked in silently, and now stood looking at him.

Crawleigh felt two polar emotions. He had told her never to come here. But he was glad she had. Finally he adopted a cautious neutrality.

"Well, Audrey—what can I do for you?"

For a long second she studied his face, at last saying. "You've knocked me up. I forgot to take my pills with me to California, and now I've missed a period."

Crawleigh felt the world billow around him like a sail in the wind. He grew nauseous, then unnaturally calm. What a stupid little slut, he thought. But I'll take care of her, out of the goodness of my heart.

"I'll pay for the abortion of course," Crawleigh said. "We'll have it done out of state, if you want, so no one will ever know. And I'll even come with you."

Audrey was silent. Crawleigh thought she hadn't expected him to take it so calmly.

"That's all you have to say?"

"Yes. What else could we do? Certainly not—"

"Damn you!" Audrey shrieked.

She ran out the door.

For a moment, Crawleigh sat shocked.

Then he followed.

Out on the quad, Crawleigh spotted her, still running. She was headed toward the arch.

Heedless of onlookers, Crawleigh took off after her.

"Audrey! Wait!"

She kept running.

Crawleigh gained slowly.

When Audrey got to within a few feet of the arch, the world inverted.

Crawleigh saw the huge arch shrink into insignificance.

At the same time, the painted door and the painted stairs at the base of the arch assumed solidity and reality as they swelled larger than lifesize. The stairs projected out into the quad, a luminous flight of veined marble. At the top, the hammered-silver door with its golden knob and iron hinges beckoned like a distillation of every forbidden door in every fairy tale ever written or narrated.

From far, far away, Crawleigh heard the campus bells chime noon. A car horn sounded long and loud, dopplering away as in some dream.

Audrey had stopped. Crawleigh did too. They seemed the only people in the world. Crawleigh felt ageless.

Confronting Crawleigh, Audrey said, in a voice hushed with reverence, "It's happening, Jerry, it's really happening, isn't it? The big, good thing I always wished for. I guess I finally wished hard enough, or was scared enough, or something . . ."

Stupefied and fearful, Crawleigh could not bring himself to share Audrey's delighted childlike awe.

"Don't be a fool, Audrey, it's only some hallucination or delusion. I can't explain what's happening, but I know it's not real. There's no escape from this world. Stop running, and let's confront this problem like adults."

Crawleigh felt insane and deceitful, arguing so prosaically in front of this magnificent apparition. But he didn't know what else to do.

His imagination had failed him.

Ignoring her former lover's advice, Audrey moved to the first step. She placed one foot delicately on the surface, testing its solidity. When it held her, she brought the other foot up too.

She looked beseechingly back at Crawleigh, who averted his eyes.

Slowly at first, then with more and more confidence, Audrey climbed all the stairs until she stood at the top.

She gripped the golden knob.

Crawleigh heard the click of her painted nails on its metal. He raised his eyes to watch whatever would come next.

Audrey opened the little door.

A world too marvelous to be trapped in words revealed itself beyond. Its sky seemed to be gloriously on fire, and the radiance that spilled out the door made Audrey lambent. Crawleigh winced, and flung up his hands as if blinded.

Audrey turned to face Crawleigh. The sight had transfigured her plain features into something otherworldly.

She spoke softly. "It's so wonderful. Just what I always dreamed. Come with me, Jerry. Everything will be okay there."

Crawleigh shook his head, mute.

Audrey stepped through—
—and pulled the door shut.
Crawleigh fainted then.
And when he awoke, with the campus medics bending over him,
he said:
"Audrey—"
But no one could tell him where she was.

BILLY

Billy's father was in the delivery room when Billy was born. Billy's father stood by his wife's white-gowned left shoulder, holding her hand, as the Doctor and nurses worked to deliver the baby boy everyone expected. To Billy's father, the operating room lights seemed those of another world, and the air smelled like the inside of a medicine cabinet. His wife's face was covered with sweat. She seemed to be having a difficult time.

The first moment Billy's father suspected that something was wrong was when one of the nurses blanched and averted her face. Then the Doctor paled, and seemed to fumble between Billy's mother's legs. Recovering, the Doctor continued the delivery.

Billy's father wanted to ask what the matter was. But at the same time, he didn't want to alarm his wife. So he kept quiet and only continued to squeeze his wife's hand.

In the next thirty seconds, his wife screamed, a young nurse retched and rushed off, clutching her stomach, the baby emerged, its cord was cut, and, inexplicably, before Billy's father could get a good look at the infant, it was rushed from the room.

Billy's father leaned down to his wife's ear and whispered, "You did wonderful, dear. I'll be right with you. I've got to see the Doctor now though."

Billy's father walked over in his green antistatic slippers to the Doctor.

The Doctor said, "Please step outside with me for a moment."

In the corridor, his mask now dangling around his neck, the Doctor said, "I'm afraid I have some bad news for you. Your son exhibits a grave congenital deficiency."

Billy's father nodded, not knowing what to say. The Doctor seemed to be having a difficult time finding words also.

"He's—anencephalic," the Doctor finally managed to say.

"I don't understand," said Billy's father.

"Your son's skull never fully developed. It's open. In fact, it ends approximately above his eyes. Consequently, his brain never developed either. Such specimens—ah, children—usually possess only a small portion of gray matter above the spinal cord."

Billy's father thought a moment. "I take it this is a critical problem."

"It's normally fatal. Children with this trauma usually don't live beyond an hour or so."

"This is bad news," said Billy's father.

"Yes, it is," agreed the Doctor. "Do you want me to tell your wife?"

"No. I will."

Billy's father went to his wife's room, where she was resting. She looked angelic and fulfilled. He told her what the Doctor had said.

When Billy's mother was done weeping, her husband left her to inquire what forms he had to fill out in connection with their son's death, or stillbirth.

He found their Doctor surrounded by a group of his fellows, all conferring with animation and wonder.

"I can't understand it—"

"Not in the literature—"

"Autonomic functions are being supported somehow—"

"Do we dare attempt a bone graft?"

"I doubt it would take."

"He surely can't live his life without one."

"The possible infections alone—"

"Not to mention the cosmetic appearance—"

Billy's father interrupted politely. "Doctor, please. What kind of paperwork is there to be done before my son can be buried?"

All the doctors fell silent. Finally, Billy's Doctor spoke.

"Well, you see, it hasn't happened yet."

Billy's father's brain hurt. Once more he was forced to say, "I don't understand . . ."

"It's your son. He hasn't died. He's breathing normally. His EKG is fine. No brain activity, of course. Not surprising, since he hasn't got one. Doesn't respond to visual stimuli either. But he's alive. And he gives every indication of continuing to live for an indefinite period."

Billy's father considered long and hard. "This is good news, then. I guess."

"I suppose so," the Doctor agreed.

"I'll go tell my wife."

Billy's father returned to his wife's bedside. He told her the news.

Billy's mother seemed to take the new development in stride.

"We'll call him Billy," she said when they had finished discussing what this meant for their lives.

"Of course," said Billy's father. "It's what we planned all along."

* * *

Billy came home from the hospital a week later.

It had turned out that he did not need any special equipment to survive. As the doctors had finally concluded, he possessed just enough gray matter to insure the continuation of his vital functions.

Billy's mother was thus able to carry home her child, who was wrapped in a gay blue blanket, on her lap in the car, while her husband drove.

Once home, Billy was installed in the nursery his parents had prepared before his birth. It was a very nice and pleasant sunny room, with popular cartoon pictures on the wall.

Unfortunately, Billy could not appreciate these decorative touches. When he wasn't sleeping he lay motionless on his back, his dumb, passive, blank eyes—which, however, were a beautiful, startling green—fixed implacably on an unvarying point on the ceiling.

He stared at the point so long and hard that Billy's father began to imagine he could see the paint starting to blister and peel under his son's unfathomable eyes, slick and depthless as polished jade.

In addition to this fixity of vision and lack of interest in his surroundings, young Billy exhibited few of the gestures or reactions of a normal baby. He seldom moved his limbs, and had to be rotated manually to avoid bedsores. This chore his parents performed conscientiously and tenderly, on a regular schedule.

Also, Billy made no noises of any sort. He was utterly silent. No gurgles or whimpers, cries or primitive syllables, ever issued from his lips. Billy's parents knew he possessed a complete vocal apparatus, but assumed correctly that the neural controls need to operate it were missing.

They had been ready to put up with sleepless nights due to their baby's wailing. Instead, their house seemed somehow quieter than it had before Billy's birth.

Sometimes at night Billy's mother and father lay in bed, awake, tensed for a cry that never came.

Since it never came, after a while they stopped listening.

One instinct that Billy possessed to a sufficient degree was that of suckling.

Billy's mother had decided while still pregnant with Billy that she would breast-feed her infant. When she came home with Billy, she remained determined to follow this course. Several times a day, then, Billy's mother would hold him to her tit and Billy would take her sweet milk eagerly, his tiny lips and throat working silently. After feeding, he never even burped. Neither did he exhibit colic.

Thus was Billy able to take the nourishment necessary for his survival and, indeed, his growth.

While nursing Billy, his mother would gaze down at her child with a complex mixture of emotions. She would note how the bony pink ridge of his cranial crater—below which grew a smattering of fine hair like a monk's tonsure—was hardening and changing color, from roseate to peachy. She refrained from looking inside.

The doctors had decided that no cosmetic repairs were possible for Billy's tragically grave prenatal malformation. They admonished his parents to keep the interior of Billy's partial skull free of foreign objects (the exposed backs of the eyes were particularly sensitive), and to wash the rim daily with a mild solution of hydrogen peroxide and water, being most careful not to allow any of the solution to come in contact with Billy's tiny, yet hard-working brain fragment. (Truth to tell, the doctors felt that Billy would not survive for long, so they were reluctant to expend much time and energy on him, when there were so many other more curable patients demanding their skill and attention.)

Billy was supposed to wear a protective surgical cap, but his mother felt that it would do Billy's skull good to receive fresh air, and so she soon abandoned this practice.

Indeed, Billy's appearance quickly came to seem so natural to his parents that they almost forgot his unique condition. After supper each night they would stand by Billy's crib, holding hands and gazing down on their silent, motionless son, speculating wordlessly about his future.

One night Billy's father said, "I imagine that we'll always have to care for Billy. He won't ever be normal, will he?"

"No," admitted Billy's mother, "he won't ever be special, as we had hoped. But I don't mind. Do you?"

"No. But we must never try to have another child."

"I agree."

* * *

When Billy was sixteen years old, his life changed forever.

Billy had attained the normal stature of an average sixteen-year-old. His unlined, emotionless face was attractive in the manner of a well-designed mannequin. His narrow crescent of hair, kept neatly trimmed by his mother, was a common brown. His eyes remained the same empty mint-green pools.

Each morning Billy's mother removed him from bed. She took off his pajamas, bathed him, dressed him in pants and shirt, socks but no shoes, and fed him. (Billy had progressed to solid food at the appropriate stage in his development, mastication apparently being as instinctive as suckling, and within his limited capabilities.) Then she sat him down in a comfortably padded chair and left for work. Billy's muscles were kept well-toned by a series of exercises which his father put him through each night, and he would maintain whatever pose he was arranged in.

Billy's mother knew she could leave her son safely alone while she worked, for he would make no movement of consequence to endanger himself. The only thing she worried about was a spontaneous fire of some sort, in which case Billy would continue to sit until consumed. (Billy's reaction to even a pinprick was nil.) But after installation of an elaborate fire alarm system and a machine that would automatically dial 911, she managed to rest easy.

Occasionally Billy's mother would leave the TV on for him, knowing full well that it made no difference, but somehow feeling better for doing it.

On this fateful day, the television was not on. Therefore Billy sat in complete silence. Time passed. Morning shadows lengthened into those of the early afternoon. Billy sat as his mother had left him. He did not stir, save to blink now and then. His heart beat. His lungs worked. The few neurons he owned discharged in their efficient, albeit limited fashion.

Directly above Billy's head, a spider was attached to the ceiling by her thread. She was a rather large black spider, of a mundane household species, but about the size of a ping-pong ball. Although Billy's mother was a good housekeeper, she had somehow missed this spider in her weekly cleaning.

The spider was very intelligent, as were most members of her species. Contemplating Billy's gaping skull below her, the spider reached the conscious decision that the inside of Billy's head represented a safe and attractive place to build a web.

The spider began to descend, letting out silk in her judicious way.

She paused a few inches above Billy's open pate. From this vantage, the place still held its appeal.

The spider entered Billy's skull.

When her legs touched Billy's bare brain, Billy's limbs twitched.

The spider cut her silk. She looked around. The place was pleasantly confined, yet open to passing insects.

"This is a good place to build a web," she said aloud, to herself.

Then she began to spin a web, parallel to the base of Billy's brain, and anchored to the sides of his skull.

Since the spider did not again touch Billy's brain, he did not move.

When Billy's mother returned that night, the spider's web was complete.

Billy's mother did not notice, since she had long ago ceased to look inside Billy's head.

When supper was ready, Billy's mother brought him to the table.

The spider was initially somewhat alarmed when her new home began to move. But since the movements were gentle, and her web was not threatened, she eventually accommodated herself to the notion that her web was now mobile. It seemed an advantage, in that more territory would be open to her predations.

Billy's father, massaging and exercising his son's limbs later that night, also failed to perceive the new occupant of his son's skull.

Thus a new symbiosis was achieved with little difficulty.

For the next few weeks, the spider lived a pleasant life, alone in Billy's skull. She caught bugs. She ate them. She slept.

Billy's exterior life did not change.

One day the spider heard an unusual noise outside her home. It resembled the sound of claws digging into the fabric of Billy's chair. The spider looked nervously up at the rim of Billy's skull.

The next instant two pink paws appeared, followed by a whiskered snout.

A moderate-sized rat, his hind legs on Billy's shoulders, now peered into the spider's home. His black eyes were like twin chips of marble.

"What're you doing in there?" asked the rat.

"This is my home," answered the spider.

"This is a human. A strange human, for it doesn't notice us. But it's still a human. You can't live inside a human."

"But I do."

The rat considered this reply. "No one bothers you?"

"No."

"Is it dry in there?"

"Reasonably so."

"Then I'm coming in to live too."

"You'll break my web."

"I don't care."

The spider in turn considered this assertion. She doubted she could dissuade the rat. And not being poisonous, she had no defense. So she resolved to give in.

"Just let me rework my web. I'll have the rear, and you can have the front."

"Good enough. Hurry up though, before someone comes."

The spider ate her web and restrung it smaller. Then the rat clambered in.

"Don't step on that lump down there," warned the spider. "It makes the house jump."

"Oh, really?" said the rat. He probed Billy's miniscule brain with a claw.

Billy stood up. The rat, growing nervous despite his bravado, retracted his claw. Billy remained standing. The rat lay down with his soft furry stomach across Billy's brain. This caused no further response on Billy's part.

That evening Billy's mother returned to find her son still standing. Although puzzled, she was not overalarmed, but rather proud, as if a new milestone had been reached.

Billy's father did not know what to make of the event either, when told. His reactions were rather similar to his wife's.

"Perhaps Billy is changing."

"Maybe so," said his wife.

Neither thought to check the inside of Billy's head, having been conditioned by years of inactivity to expect no development there.

Another week passed. The rat left on nocturnal forays, but always returned during the day. It was good that he was absent at night, for, with Billy supine, he would have rolled to the back of the skull and crushed the spider's web.

It was a warm summer's day. Billy's mother had left a screenless window open. The rat and the spider were sleeping inside Billy's skull when they were awakened by a raucous voice.

"Hello, folks! What's up?"

Perched on the rim of Billy's skull was a smallish parrot. This parrot had escaped from a neighbor's house, and had been flying rather aimlessly, yet happily about since.

"What do you want?" the rat asked.

"You look so comfy, I was wondering if I could join you," replied the bird.

"No," said the rat. "Go away."

"Come now," said the spider. "You're not the original owner, you know. Why can't the parrot join us?"

"Birds are messy. He'll leave droppings in here."

"I would not," the parrot proudly said. "No more than you would."

"What can you offer us?" continued the rat.

The parrot thought a moment. "I can speak human."

This seemed to intrigue the rat. "Say, that is a handy talent. Okay, you can move in."

"Great!" said the parrot.

And so he did.

* * *

One morning Billy spoke.

His mother was lifting a spoon of cereal to his lips when Billy said, "I can do that myself, thank you."

Billy's mother dropped the spoon. After her heart stopped racing, she managed to say, "Why, Billy—you've learned to talk."

"That's obvious, isn't it, Mother?" said Billy.

Billy's mother was so mesmerized by the sight of his moving lips that she failed to notice that the squawky voice was emerging from the top of Billy's head. Of course, it was the parrot speaking while the rat and the spider in concert caused Billy's lips to move with expert probes into his primitive gray matter. The trio had been practicing for some days past while alone, and now had complete mastery over Billy's body.

Billy now picked up the fallen spoon from the tabletop and began to feed himself. Without visual feedback, the controlling trio made a mess. Still, to his mother the achievement was miraculous.

After eating, Billy said, "I'd like to go out now, Mother, but I need a hat."

Billy's mother found an old fedora of her husband's and placed it on Billy's head, without looking in.

"Thank you. Have a good day at work, Mother."

Billy's mother left the house in a stupefied way.

When she was gone, the rat chewed two small holes in the hat so the parrot could look out to guide them.

"Left, right, around the chair, grab the doorknob, now straight ahead down the walk!"

The adventurers in their stolen puppet set out to explore the world.

Downtown, the trio walked Billy up and down the commercial district. They found it vastly stimulating to masquerade as a human. They felt instantly superior to all their kind, having gained entry to the world of humanity.

The two animals and the arachnid found themselves after some time outside the very hospital where Billy had been born. They stopped to contemplate the building, feeling some strange kinship with it, though they had no idea of its true significance.

At that moment the Doctor who had delivered Billy—and given him yearly examinations since—stepped out the door.

When he saw Billy standing there, he scrabbled at his chest and fell to the ground.

People began to scream and cluster around the Doctor. The parrot got nervous and said, "Quick! We must go back to the house!"

They hurried home.

When Billy's father met his wife at the door that evening, he was soon informed of the startling change Billy had undergone. News of Billy's delayed maturation did not seem to alarm Billy's father as much as it had his wife. Perhaps this was because he was learning of it secondhand.

"Well," said Billy's father, "I guess we were mistaken when we said our son would never turn out to be anyone special."

"It appears we were," agreed Billy's mother.

"Where is he now?"

"In his bedroom. He's been there since he came back from his walk."

"Well, let's bring Billy out to share supper with us. We're a real family now."

The table was laid, steaming food was brought from the kitchen, and Billy was summoned.

The inhabitants of Billy's skull had been hiding with Billy in his room ever since their precipitous return from their first excursion abroad. They had been rather alarmed by the human world, especially the confusion at the hospital.

Now, though, they mastered themselves enough to bring Billy's body to the table when called.

"Hello, Father," said the parrot from within Billy's head. Its voice was somewhat muffled by the fedora through which it peeked.

Billy's father did not seem to care or notice. He looked inordinately proud. "Hello, Billy. I heard you gave your mother quite a shock today. But that's all water over the dam. Let's eat."

The rat and the spider manipulated Billy's synapses, causing him to sit. With the parrot issuing directions, the trio was able to feed Billy more efficiently than earlier in the day.

(The parrot's commands to his compatriots, of course, were uttered *sotto voce* in his natural language. Therefore all Billy's movements were accompanied by a low series of trills and whistles, which Billy's parents chose to ignore.)

After their meal, the family retired to the living room to watch television.

The animals knew all about television, from having inhabited human households all their lives, and enjoyed watching it when given a chance. Now, with Billy sitting undemandingly, they could take turns at the hat's eyeholes. (The rat and spider were already beginning to feel a little put-upon, forced as they were to labor over Billy's brainstem in the dark beneath the hat.)

The local news was on. The lead item was about Billy.

First, the Doctor appeared. He had survived his heart attack. He explained that he had been shocked by Billy's appearance in public. An old photo from the hospital's files was shown: baby Billy's empty brainpan. The Doctor claimed that if Billy had really regenerated enough brain tissue to become aware and move about, then it promised great hope for solving all sorts of neurological disorders.

No sooner had the doctor faded from the screen than the phone began to ring in Billy's house.

It didn't stop all night.

Around three in the morning, Billy's father turned to his wife and said, "Well, it seems as if our little Billy is on his way to becoming famous."

Billy's mother sipped some coffee. "I hope it's for the best."

"We'll soon see," replied Billy's father. "But I'm afraid it's out of our hands now."

The spider, rat and parrot, at first confused by the ruckus they had caused, were soon enamored of their new status, and began to discuss how best to exploit it.

By morning, they had a plan.

The first person to arrive was the Doctor. He was barely recovered from his mild heart attack, but insisted on being the person to examine Billy.

Soon the Doctor was alone with Billy in the boy's bedroom. Like everyone else, after the initial shock he seemed quite accepting of Billy's new abilities.

"Now, Billy, if you'll just let me have a look beneath your hat . . ."

"All right, Doctor," squawked the parrot.

While the Doctor's back was turned in the process of taking an instrument from his bag, the rat, spider and parrot quickly scrambled out and hid behind furniture.

The Doctor, lifting the battered fedora, was given pause by the unchanged poverty of Billy's mental equipment.

"Why, there's nothing but an old spiderweb in here! This is an even greater miracle than I suspected."

The Doctor left the room, and the three squatters returned to Billy's skull.

A crowd of cameramen and reporters from various media was assembled on Billy's front lawn. The Doctor held an impromptu press conference to explain his findings. The reporters clamored for Billy, but the Doctor, being shrewd, denied them. He explained that Billy would be making his first scheduled appearance on a national morning television show that had paid a lot of money to have him.

That same day, Billy and the Doctor and Billy's parents left for New York.

The secret inhabitants of Billy's skull reveled in their new role. They enjoyed being the center of attention, and fooling all these dull humans who fancied themselves better than other species. The three anticipated much fun, and began to hatch many schemes.

For starters, knowing it would disconcert the humans, they made Billy drink several glasses of liquor. Naturally, this had no effect on the real masters, who maintained the semblance of a startling sobriety in their puppet. Emboldened by their success, the parrot directed the rat to have Billy insert tidbits of food under the hat when no one was looking. All in all, they had a splendid flight.

Soon they were in New York. A waiting limousine whisked everyone to a hotel. Billy's party spent the remainder of the day sightseeing, then retired early, since they had to be up around four A.M.

Almost before they knew it, they were onstage. The talk show host was a very pleasant young woman in a pretty dress who shook hands politely with Billy. After some chitchat, the cameras came on.

The woman explained about Billy's history, and his amazing post-pubescent changes. At one point she said, "We wish we could show you Billy's empty head and undeveloped brain, but the network standards forbid it, since it is quite repulsive-looking." The Doctor spoke up then, testifying to the minuteness of Billy's brain. His air of authority was very convincing. Billy's innocent looks—his face blank as cheese, his placid green eyes—and his unnatural voice, lent further credence to the miracle of his being.

Soon the show was over.

Billy's parents breathed a sigh of relief.

But it was only the first of many telecasts.

Over the next few weeks, Billy appeared on every show of consequence. The culmination of his television career was the *Oprah Winfrey Show*. Ms. Winfrey assembled the parents of other anencephalics—whose children had of course all perished at birth—to accompany Billy and his folks in a discussion of the problems related to having such children.

It was not long after this that a disturbing fad began to manifest itself.

Teenagers were seeking to emulate Billy and his mystical serenity through surgical procedures.

It was uncertain who first conceived of the operation. All that was known was that initial attempts were not successful, resulting in death or total catatonia. However, after some experimentation, surgeons learned just how much of the brain they could safely excise to leave the patient in a prelapsarian condition of mental diminution that approached Billy's state.

Part of the conversion involved leaving the top half of the skull off, so that the person's newly diminished brain would enjoy the atmosphere just as Billy's did.

Sales of the type of hat Billy wore also skyrocketed. So did the sales of a special antibiotic ointment for anointing the wounds.

At first this phenomenon caused much parental concern. Parents fruitlessly forbade their children to spend their allowance or discretionary income on the operation. Campaigns were started to outlaw it. Preachers and role models spoke against it. However, all the anti-Billy sentiment could not contend against the real desires of youths to emulate their new hero.

Clinics specializing in the operation opened to accommodate the swelling demand for "Billyization." More and more people—not just the young—signed the consent forms allowing the removal of their gray matter. Recognizing the futility of their fight against the tide of disavowal of sentience, all but the die-hard protestors gave up.

Two years passed. Hundreds of thousands of Billys had been artificially created. Billy himself turned eighteen. The parrot, rat and spider, fat and confident from two years of high living, embarked on the next step of their master plan.

Billy announced that he would run for the House of Representatives to become a voice for his people. He established residency in a district where anencephalics were a majority. He won handily.

In the next few years, Billy, under the direction of his cranial riders, managed to push through much legislation granting special privileges to anencephalics, claiming that they needed extra dispensations due to their unique disability, self-administered though it was.

Many people began to envy the anencephalics their easy lot. However, unlike elites of the past, it was easy to gain entry to this class. Billy's final legislation in the last year of his first term was to establish public clinics where anencephaly was produced free of charge.

Billy did not neglect his parents in this busy time. Like a good son, he brought them to Washington and established them in a luxurious Georgetown house, where they arranged entertainments that served to advance Billy's career.

Billy won re-election to his seat easily.

At the end of his second term, Billy stepped down to campaign for the presidency. He had previously succeeded in lowering the minimum age for that office.

Billy had his own political party now, the Decorticates.

The campaign was very grueling, more so than the three creatures inside Billy had anticipated. The parrot was kept busy making speeches, and found sometimes that he had to talk faster than he could think. The rat had improved his synaptic manipulations to the point where he no longer needed the spider to assist him. This freed the spider to sit in her web and plot the details of the campaign.

It was touch and go in the polls right up until election eve.

But when election day itself was over, Billy had won.

On inauguration day, the celebratory cortege featured a squad of a hundred Billy-boys and Billy-girls, newly decorticated for the occasion, attempting precision marching. They blundered into each other, and the parade had to be stopped while they were untangled.

Billy's career had reached its apex.

One day well into his third term, Billy sat alone in the Oval Office.

He had removed his hat, so that the inhabitants of his skull could enjoy light and fresh air.

The parrot was fat as a pigeon and had developed the habit of continually puffing out his chest feathers and preening.

The rat was sleek as a guinea pig, his cheeks always bulging with food.

Only the spider, being something of an ascetic, retained her old proportions, albeit in a self-satisfied manner.

They filled the confines of Billy's skull nearly to bursting.

The parrot said, "We must begin to think about the next election. Perhaps we could just do away with it. I'm getting tired of masterminding these things."

"*You're* getting tired!" demanded the rat. "What about me? You have no conception of how hard it is to goad this lump properly. I'm the one who really suffers during these campaigns. I think I deserve the lion's share of the credit."

"Come, come," the spider admonished. "Don't argue. Remember, if I hadn't discovered this place and invited you both in, you'd be nowhere today."

"Oh, shut up," said the parrot.

"Yeah," chorused the rat. "Listen to Fathead and go back to your spinning."

"Who are you calling 'Fathead'?"

"You, you second-rate ventriloquist!"

Enraged, the parrot bit the rat's tail.

The rat responded by sinking his teeth into the parrot's wing.

The parrot sought to escape by beating his free wing wildly. He managed to half-flutter, half-fall out of Billy's skull, dragging the rat with him.

They rolled on the floor, clawing and biting.

The spider emerged and walked across the floor. Attempting to act as mediator, she was crushed to death by her co-conspirators.

In a moment, the parrot's beak had sunk through the rat's eye to his brain. At the same instant, the rat managed to bite out the parrot's throat.

The three corpses lay cooling on the rug.

After many hours, the Decorticate advisors summoned up the initiative to enter the chief's office.

They failed to notice the insignificant corpses on the carpet. They went up to Billy and peered curiously into his skull.

"It's empty," said one.

"So it is," agreed another.

MOLOCH

1

The car was a '73 Marauder the color of dried blood, and showed all its age. Its driver's side door was unopenably buckled by some ancient impact, revealing the harsh metal beneath the cosmetic paint. The rust pitting the steel corrugations nearly matched the paint, as if nature had sought to hide the damage in a kind of protective mimicry. The car's hood was partially sprung, its trunk secured with clothesline.

The sound of its big engine as the car ascended slowly up Mount Tophet, in western Pennsylvania, was a deep but sickly roar, like thunder heard by a man in a fever. The car seemed to have muffler problems as well as engine troubles.

The car was alone on the road. The sky overhead was a seamless, variegated grey, like felted lint from a dryer vent.

Inside the car on the rear seat, riding backwards, strapped into a child carrier which was in turn held down by a seat belt, was a male infant. He wore a blue acrylic sweater, cap and leggings, and white booties. The cushioned pad of his carrier was patterned with anthropomorphic cartoon sunfaces, each smiling in a corona of spikes. Regarding the landscape he swiftly left behind, the infant rode placidly, apathetically, like a small bored commuter.

Andrew Stiles was driving, his wife Dawn beside him. Each wore jeans. The extra material inside Dawn's pant legs at the hem had been let down without restitching, and was now coming unraveled. Andy wore a grey hooded sweatshirt; Dawn a patchwork rabbit fur coat.

Andy's brown hair was longish, and brushed the hood of his garment. His beard was adolescently sparse. Dawn used no makeup, and her skin was clear.

"Look at that sky," said Dawn. "Something's going to happen."

Andy said nothing. The concentration he exhibited while driving was immense. Dawn tried a different topic.

"Do you think your parents will mind? I mean, we never even called. I know I'd mind if some relative just dropped in and said they were staying for a few weeks. Although maybe it's different when it's your son. It's hard to imagine Peter really grown up, so I can't say. He's too new to me yet. Don't he feel too new to you too, Andy?"

Dawn smiled timidly at the unintentional string of assonant sylla-bles. She turned to look back over the seat at the baby, then swiveled back to her husband.

"I mean," she continued, "it ain't like we got a choice. When you can't pay the rent, you got to move on. We got to live somewhere till you find a job. It's no fault of yours you got fired, nor of mine that I got to stay home with Peter. Your folks will understand that, won't they, Andy?"

"Do you know what it is, Dawn?"

"What what is?"

"That sky."

Dawn ducked her head to peer intently at the sky through the wind-shield. "Some storm brewing, I guess."

Andy shook his head. His knuckles on the wheel were bloodless, the color of quartz. "No, it ain't no storm. That sky is too empty. There ain't nothing behind it, Dawn. No stars, no sun, no moon, no weath-er. That sky is the sky of hell. Plain and simple, it's the sky of the devil's kingdom. Somehow we took a wrong turn. I been thinking it for some time now. We're lost, Dawn. We are trammeled in Satan's snares. This ain't Mount Tophet. We are in hell."

"Andy, please, don't start talking that way again. Not now—"

"It's right for you to be scared, Dawn. There's plenty to be scared of in this world. But you done good to notice what happened. When you mentioned the sky, I knew my feelings was right. There's no point in trying to hide what you noticed. Maybe it's not too late. Maybe we can get away. If we just drive fast enough—"

The car had reached the summit of Mount Tophet. Off to Dawn's side, far below an unrailed edge, the land spread away in forested chaotic acres broken by the infrequent incongruous geometric insults of civilization, all illumined by a dull stoic light which seemed to have no source.

Beginning its descent, the car entered the first switchback.

Andy pressed the accelerator to the floor.

Dawn was forced back into her seat by gravity's deific hand.

Andy's arms were braced straight and rigid, locked at the elbows. "Hold tight, Dawn. This is the only way out."

The car swayed back and forth between lanes, its cranky steering linkage fighting commands, its engine running fit to burst. Veering far to the right, its front tire bit gravel, seemed at times almost to hang suspended, spinning uselessly, and clipped runty saplings and weeds. Veering to the left, its front fender scraped crumbling escarpments.

Entering the first curve, the car barely slowed. It smashed a headlight on the rockface, which went by in a blur, before rebounding.

Dawn screamed. The baby began to cry.

Andy said nothing. He seemed barely conscious of the road, his eyes fixed on the sky.

The speed of the car seemed a manifestation of Andy's will, an impulse which flowed out of him, down his rigid arms and into the vehicle.

Dawn shut her eyes and crumpled to the seat. This did not stop the car. The baby's carrier jerked back and forth, fighting the restraint of the seat belt like a wild thing caught in a trap.

Andy said, "Dear Lord, I'm listening, just tell me what to do. We're weak, but we can serve." It was not apparent if he received an answer.

The child wailed, Dawn sobbed, brakes squealed.

Eventually they reached the end of the steep and treacherous road, having encountered no other cars, nor plunged over a precipice.

Andy stopped the car in the middle of the road, slewed across the yellow line. He crawled over Dawn to get out on her side. He stood on the pavement, feet spread, arms raised.

"It's a miracle!" he shouted. "Lookit that sky! We did it! We out-raced hell!"

Dawn forced herself to stop crying. She sat up and looked out.

"Andy," she said, sniffling, "that sky ain't changed at all."

2

"Andy," Dawn said, "you got to take the boys out. They are driving me right up the wall."

Andy lay on the couch, staring up at the ceiling. It was a false ceiling, dirty grey acoustical tiles suspended below older hidden plaster. The acoustical tiles seemed to hold an infinity of tiny pits, each horrible in its circular perfection. Andy was trying to count them. His lips moved.

In one corner of the room the tiles were stained a dingy yellow, like an old bandage on a leaking wound, where the upstairs neighbors' overflowing toilet had leaked through. Andy was saving those for last.

Andy's booted feet rested on one arm of the couch. Over the

months they had worn the fabric away, revealing dirty white stuffing that was surely nothing natural.

"Andy," said Dawn, "are you listening to me?"

"I'm listening."

"Will you take the kids off my hands for a few minutes then? Supper needs fixing."

Andy turned his head away from the tiles. Dawn stood in the kitchen doorway. Peter, three years old, was holding one corner of her stained apron. Simon sat in a swing suspended from four wobbly aluminum legs. The swing had a small windup motor which propelled it back and forth like a metronome. It made a monotonous ratcheting click which neither Andy nor Dawn heard anymore. Simon's bare feet brushed the matted pile of the rust-colored rug in two parallel tracks.

"All right," said Andy, "get 'em dressed. I'll take 'em to the park."

Dawn dressed the boys in light jackets for the seasonable April afternoon. She shod Simon and stuffed him into a collapsible stroller. Andy had swung his feet to the floor and stood up. Peter had transferred himself from Dawn's apron to his father's shirttail, which hung outside the man's trousers, a pair of green work pants.

Dawn saw the trio to the door. She seemed to remember something then.

"Did you take your medicine today, honey?"

"Yeah."

"That's good. You can't forget now, not one day. That's what the doctor said."

"You been telling me that for six months now."

"Well, it don't hurt. And Andy—"

"Yeah?"

"While you're walking with the boys, will you think some more about getting a job? Your benefits are gonna run out soon, and even if they wasn't, it might do you good to be working. You know, meet some people, make some friends . . ."

"I'll think about it."

"Good." Dawn kissed him on the cheek. Andy left with the boys. Dawn watched him as he bumped the baby's stroller down three front stairs rather roughly and set off down the cracked walk.

There was one steel mill left in the town, out of the many that had once offered employment. It was enough to fill the place with a seeming infinity of soot and cinders, piles of clinkers and ash. When there wasn't a strike, there was a layoff. Surprisingly, they were actually hiring now.

Andy thought about applying. It seemed like an impossible chore, a task for Superman. But then again, since that day when he and Dawn had outraced hell, on through the long stay in the hospital, right up to the present, so did any little chore, from getting up in the morning to tying his shoes to brushing his teeth at night.

Maybe he would do it. Lord willing, he'd try. It might make Dawn happy. He wanted her to be happy. But she had to realize that sometimes it just wasn't possible, here in this vale of tears. . . .

The park was half an acre with a duck pond, a few vandalized benches and a children's playground where the swings either hung uselessly from one chain only, or were wrapped around the crossbar in inextricable snarls of rusty links.

Andy wheeled Simon in his carriage to the edge of the pond. He brought it to a stop and removed his grip on the handle. The carriage began to inch forward, and Andy realized the ground sloped away, down to the water. He halted the carriage and set the brakes. The carriage stayed put. Peter bent clumsily down for a pebble, which he shied at the ducks who had already swum over, anticipating bread. Andy did not attempt to stop his son when he reached for another stone, and another after that.

The grass was very green. The trees were very green. The shrubs and hedges were very green. The color began to hurt Andy's eyes after a while. It was too aggressive. He sat down and closed his eyes.

After some time, he felt Peter by his side. The child must have wandered off before returning, because Andy could not remember feeling him standing there before. Andy opened his eyes.

Peter said, "Daddy, come look at what I found."

Andy got up and let Peter lead him to the base of an oak.

The squirrel must have died during the harsh winter and remained buried under the snows. With the coming of spring, it had begun to decay. The corpse lay on its back, split open. Some sort of scavenger had cleaned most of the meat and organs from it, and it was little more than a furred shell. It was missing its tail and a leg. Ants crawled among its ribs. The squirrel's small teeth were exposed in a rictus, and they were amazingly white.

"What's the matter with it?" asked Peter.

"Nothing's the matter. It's just dead, Petey. It comes to all of us, sooner or later, death does. It's the way the good Lord made life work. Look at it up close. Go ahead. Don't be afraid."

Peter obediently squatted and stared.

"Now touch it."

Peter extended a pudgy finger. An ant in its single-minded travels immediately crawled onto this bridge from dead squirrel to living boy. Peter jerked his hand away.

Andy grabbed the boy's wrist and brought it back into contact with the small corpse. "No, I said touch it."

Peter tried to jerk away. Andy squeezed the back of the child's neck with his other hand and immobilized him.

As he held the boy's hand there, a steady stream of ants followed the first, vanishing up the boy's jacket sleeve.

3

The union rep tapped Andy on the shoulder while he was waiting for the blow to end.

"Let Jerry watch it and come with me," he shouted in Andy's ear.

Andy turned away from the huge dark furnace, out of whose open top refulgent light gushed, born of 330 tons of molten metal. He followed the rep across the busy mill floor and into an office. The rep sat down behind an empty desk with a green rubberized top and indicated that Andy should sit too. Andy did.

Andy wore thick brown Carhartt coveralls, work boots and gloves. From a breast pocket, held by an alligator clip, hung his photo identity badge. In the photograph, Andy looked bewildered.

Andy's face as he sat uneasily in the chair was blackened with soot. His hair was mussed. He wore protective goggles over his eyes. Removing one glove now, he lifted the goggles atop his head and waited for the rep to speak.

"Listen, Stiles, your probation period is almost over, and I gotta make some kinda report."

Andy nodded, but said nothing.

"Now, you're a decent worker. You punch in on time, you don't miss no days, and you pull your weight. But as far as sociability goes, getting along with your coworkers . . . well, hell, you just don't."

Andy continued to sit mute, staring at his hands in his lap. They looked funny, one gloved, one ungloved. The ungloved one was plainly his, but the gloved one seemed to belong to someone—to something—else.

"Like now for instance. Just look at you. You can't even talk to me. It gives some guys the creeps. And then there's the other thing."

Andy looked up from the puzzle of his hands. "What other thing?"

The rep seemed embarrassed. "What your coworkers claim. That you, uh, talk to it."

"To what?"

"To the furnace."

Andy looked back into his lap and mumbled something.

"What?" demanded the rep. "What's that? If you got something to tell me, tell me."

Still with bent neck, Andy said, "It started talking first."

"Oh, shit," said the rep wearily.

There was mutual silence for a full minute. Then Andy spoke.

"I didn't believe it myself at first, you know. I wasn't, like, looking for something like this to happen. But the universe is weird, Mister Ptakcek, it really is. The Lord filled it with marvels and wonders, for our edification. And if He chooses to make the furnace talk to me—for I surely believe it's His doing—then I ain't got no choice but to listen, and to answer when I'm asked a question. Do I now? Have a choice?"

"Kid, you got bad chemicals, I know that. Are you still following your doctor's orders?"

"You sound like my wife."

"Yeah, yeah, but are you?"

"Sure."

"Let me see 'em."

Andy fished inside a pocket, took out his prescription bottle and exhibited it to the rep.

"Okay. Put 'em away."

Andy did so.

"Now listen up close. You know it's impossible for the furnace to be talking to you, don't you?"

"The Lord spoke to Moses out of a burning bush . . ."

"That was then, for Christ's sake, in prehistoric times. This is now. Jesus Christ, I'm a good Catholic myself, but the Lord don't make no more personal appearances nowadays. Maybe the Virgin, once in a while, but not God Hisself."

The rep paused for thought. "It ain't the Virgin, is it?"

"No, I don't think so . . ."

The rep seemed disappointed at this foreclosure. "I should just give you your notice now, Stiles. But I know you got a family, and I don't feel like training someone new. So I'm giving you one more shot. You got a week left before I gotta make my report. If I don't hear no more about this crazy stuff, we'll just forget you ever done it."

The rep stood. Andy stood. The rep conducted him to the door. On the point of stepping out, the rep said, "And Stiles—maybe you should see your priest about this too. It couldn't hurt."

"I don't have one."

"Well, find one then."

Andy went back to his post and relieved Jerry. The twenty-minute blow was just ending, completing the forty-five-minute cycle. The watercooled oxygen lance was withdrawn, prior to the tilting of the furnace and the decanting of the molten steel through a tap hole in the top of the furnace.

As the liquid metal began to flow, the furnace spoke. Its voice was as supple, rich and thick as the river of smelted ore.

"You did not listen to Ptakcek, did you, Andrew?"

The thing that startled Andy most was that the furnace knew the rep's name. It was the first time it had exhibited such knowledge. Looking to left and right, Andy whispered, "No, I didn't."

"Good. He is ignorant, an idolater. It is wrong to heed such men."

"I won't," Andy said. "I won't, Moloch. I promise."

4

The house of the Very Reverend Wade Demure sat in a hollow down by the tracks. It was a three-story structure clad in asphalt siding which simulated bricks. Porches scabbed to each level sagged dangerously, seeming to compress the columns that held them up almost beyond their tensile strength.

The structure sat on a lot full of used car parts. Engines and trans-missions, air filters and wheel rims, brake shoes and mufflers, axles and batteries, all were threaded with weeds, goldenrod poking through machined casings, Queen Anne's lace dancing above spark plugs scattered like dragon's teeth.

Every Wednesday night there was a midweek assembly of the rev-erend's small and eclectic congregation. The members of the informal church met in Reverend Demure's parlor. The parlor was furnished with a dozen chairs, no two of which were alike. Straight-backed and cane-bottomed, sag-cushioned with threadbare armrests. Wooden fold-ing chairs stenciled with the names of previous institutional owners, aluminum dinette chairs with ripped padded seats. In their variety, the chairs mimicked the parishioners.

The chairs rested along three walls atop several overlapping carpets which served to hide the worn floorboards, but which were themselves almost as disreputable in their aged condition. In the middle of the room was positioned a long table whose veneer was incised with meaningless scratches.

Andy sat between a fat black woman and a thin neurasthenic fellow. The fat black woman had a face whose left side was collapsed, from surgery, accident or stroke. The eye on that side was missing, gummed permanently shut with an exudation that resembled pine resin. Her cheek was deeply puckered, as if she were continually biting down on the inward-drawn flesh. Part of her jaw seemed to be missing. The man on Andy's other side carried a big boxy hearing aid in the pocket of his plaid shirt. The cap of the plug in his hairy ear was big as a quarter. A tic twitched at the corner of his mouth like a creature leading an independent existence.

The reverend stood at the end of the table farthest from his audience. A big Bible was splayed open on the table to aid the reverend in his interminable sermon, although he seemed not really to need it, so thorough was his mastery of its contents.

Andy was not really listening to the reverend's words. He was too nervous among these strangers to concentrate. It was his first time at the reverend's church. He had come to ask one simple question, and now awaited the opportunity. While waiting, he stared at the reverend.

Demure was a bulky man with a big nose and skin spotted with blackheads. His dark hair was slicked back with pomade whose scent carried to Andy across the room. He wore a red shirt, a wide white tie with a waffled texture, and a brown suit-coat of some synthetic material. He seemed full to bursting with words, which he had to vent for his health. Andy failed to listen to any of them. They went right through him without registering, like wind through a bed of bullrushes.

At last the reverend finished. He closed the Bible with a mighty thump and folded his arms across his chest, as if daring any of the congregation to challenge him. None accepted the challenge. The people rose and began to file out, each meekly shaking the reverend's hand and offering a word or two of praise or agreement.

Andy stood back from the "Amens" and "Praise the Lords"—which seemed to hang around Demure like a cloud—until everyone had left. Only then did he approach the preacher.

"Well, son, did the spirit move you tonight?"

Andy declined to answer. "Reverend Demure, I got a question I'm hoping you can answer for me."

"Shoot."

"Who is Moloch? I been trying to find out for myself outa the Bible, but the way I read it, he seems like two different things. One time, it's like he's God, and other times it's like he's Baalzebub or something."

Reverend Demure cupped his chin in one hand and his elbow in the other, signifying the ponderous nature of the question. "Well, boy, you have hit upon a conundrum all right. You see, Moloch was the name the ancient Jews invoked when they was preparin' to sacrifice one of their offspring, immolatin' the infants upon Tophet Hill, as they continued to do elsewhere right up to the Middle Ages. Now, the word 'Moloch' don't mean no more than 'king,' and as such was just another name for Yahweh, Him of the Old Testament. So in one sense, Moloch was the Lord. However, later prophets done renounced Moloch, twistin' the way they pronounced his name so as to sound like 'shame,' and claimin' he was some heathen god like the Golden Calf. As near as I follow it, the jury's still out on who was right."

Andy thought a minute. "So you're telling me that Moloch is just another name for God."

"Well now, boy, you wasn't listenin' right. I said that was one interpretation of it—"

Andy thrust out his hand with some excitement and the reverend bemusedly took it. "Thank you, sir, thank you very much. You told me all I need to know."

5

Since the night when the Reverend Demure had confirmed Moloch's identity, Andy had found he no longer had to speak aloud for Moloch to hear his reply. Just as Moloch's voice resonated in his head—and perhaps nowhere else, Andy was now forced to admit—so did Andy's replies seem to find reception in the sun-hot stomach of Moloch without actual utterance.

This was all to the good. Andy was able to preserve the appearance that he had abandoned his "delusion" while still conversing with the being who called himself Moloch. Andy's coworkers were less leery of him, and the number of taunts they sent his way diminished slightly, although they were never what could be called friendly to Andy.

In addition, Mister Ptakcek was happy. He gave Andy a good report. Dawn was happy too, since she had heard rumors from other wives during the period when Andy was speaking aloud to the furnace, and had worried. Now she was gratified to see that Andy's latest "spell" appeared to be over.

The only one who was not happy was Andy. Neither was he unhappy, however. He was merely puzzled, intrigued, and even somewhat flattered.

Why, out of all humanity, had Moloch chosen to speak to him, Andrew Stiles? It was a question without easy answer. Andy sometimes tried to imagine what, if anything, he had in common with the famous Biblical prophets of yore. Some figures were simply beyond him, he knew. Moses, Saint Paul, Saint John—these were mighty individuals deserving of dealing directly with God. Others, though, seemed rather common folks, not unlike Andy. Lot, Job—these were more his kind, simple working men. Andy supposed that if God had chosen to speak to such men in the past, then He could still choose to do so today.

Whatever the answer, Andy definitely had a lot to think about. And the conversations with Moloch certainly made his shift pass fast.

One day Mister Ptakcek switched his assignment from the basic oxygen furnace—where the already molten ore was further purged of contaminants—to the blast furnace, where the ore was initially melted.

Andy was worried. Moloch had always spoken to him from the basic oxygen furnace. Would he speak from the other as well?

Positioning a wheeled container beneath the outlet from which the worthless slag flowed, Andy jumped when the voice of Moloch rumbled out. The hot air around the furnace seemed to pulse in time with the words.

"You wait upon my presence. That is good."

Andy voiced his reply inside himself. "I wasn't sure you could talk outa this one too."

"My body is many, and yet one."

"Are you the whole mill then?" Andy asked.

"I am the mill and the town, the earth and the trees, the sky and the stars. I am everything that ever was or will be."

"Why didn't you ever speak to me then, till I come to this mill?"

"You were not ready. And there were barriers. Even now, I find it hard sometimes to talk to you."

"How come?"

"The medicine you take."

Andy let the conversation drop then. He was afraid that Moloch would order him to abandon his pills, and he did not know how to refuse.

Another time, Andy was telling Moloch about the day he and Dawn had outraced hell.

"How do you know you truly succeeded?" asked Moloch.

"Cuz the sky. It changed—"

"Did it, though? Your wife said it did not."

Andy had not told Moloch anything about that comment of Dawn's. Yet he knew, just as he had known Mister Ptakcek's name. . . .

"You're telling me I might still be in hell then? How can I be sure I'm not? How can a man be sure of anything in this world?"

"There is one way to determine if this is hell or not."

"What is it?" asked Andy suspiciously.

"In hell, no one has free will. They must do what they are told. If you exercise your birthright as a being made in My image, if you show initiative, do something unexpected—only then will you be sure this is not hell."

"What could I do? What would be enough to prove it?"

"Do not look to Me for orders," said Moloch sternly. "Simply following My commands would prove nothing. I could be Satan in disguise."

"I don't want no orders. Just gimme some suggestions."

"All right. If you sincerely wish Me to."

"I do."

"Do not listen to your wife or Mister Ptakcek."

"Okay."

"Do not take your pills."

"Oh, Jesus Christ, Moloch, I don't—"

"Do you wish to live in hell?"

"All right, 'don't take my pills.' What else?"

"Bring Me your sons."

6

The car was a '78 Thunderbird, in fair shape. Andy and Dawn had come up in the world since he got the job at the mill.

It was a Sunday. The car was alone on the road. The sky overhead was a seamless, variegated grey, like felted lint from a dryer vent.

The car passed through the center of town, heading west on Highway 61, away from the mill. About a mile beyond the last house, it made a U-turn and headed back. It detoured through the hollow where the Reverend Wade Demure kept church. Sounds of ragged singing issued from within the asphalt-clad tenement, a dismally joyful noise that sought to rise heavenward but only filled the hollow like clammy fog. The woman with the disease-wracked face contributed a recognizable gargle.

The car navigated through residential streets, uphill and down, wandering aimlessly. Like a dog chained to a stake, however, its movements were bounded by a central pull, an almost gravitational force at the heart of its existence: the mill.

Simon and Peter were in the back seat. Peter sat on a little bolster apparatus of molded plastic. Simon still used the infant carrier that had once been his brother's. The passage of time, the friction of its two passengers, had worn the smiling faces off the multiple suns, restoring them once more to a frightful primeval obscurity. Both boys were carefully belted to keep them safe from accidental injury.

Dawn said, "Let's be getting home, Andy. It's almost lunchtime, and the boys must be hungry. We had enough of a holiday drive." Dawn turned and hung one arm over the seat. "Ain't that so, boys?"

The boys said nothing. They seemed stupefied, bemused, almost drugged.

Andy's grip on the wheel was tetanus-tight. "Just one more stop, Dawn. I want to show the boys where their daddy works."

"Aw, honey, they ain't old enough to appreciate the mill. 'Specially little Simon." Dawn reached over the seat to adjust Simon in the carrier. Her position was awkward, and she succeeded only in pushing Simon's bonnet down over his eyes, so that his backward view of the objects they flew from—the landscape which seemed almost to push them away, to hurl itself in retreat from the car—was cut off.

Andy did not reply, but simply drove on.

The vast parking lot of the mill was empty, save for the lone car of the security guard, who, sitting bored in his gateside booth, waved the Stiles family through when Andy explained what he was about.

Andy parked the Thunderbird near the main door of the mill.

Dawn said, "Aw, Andy, why you stopping? The boys can see the mill good enough from here. Can't you, boys?"

Andy did not reply to Dawn because he did not hear her. Moloch was speaking to him. This was unique. Moloch had never spoken to him outside the mill before. It must be because he had stopped taking his pills.

"You have brought your sons to Me, Andrew. This is good. You exhibit strength of will. You are almost assured of learning a very important truth: your whereabouts. But you are not quite done. You must bring the boys inside, to see Me."

"What about Dawn?"

"She cannot come."

"What'll I tell her?"

"You must decide."

Andy levered open his door. He stepped out and opened the rear door on his side. He unbuckled Peter and pulled him out. Then, leaning in, he removed Simon from his carrier.

"Andy," said Dawn, "what's going on?"

"I got to take the boys inside for just a minute."

"I don't know, Andy. Is that smart? It could be dangerous in there for a child . . ."

"Everything's shut down. Ain't nothing that can hurt them."

"Oh, all right," said Dawn. "One minute." She moved to get out.

"No, honey, just me and the boys. It's—it's personal. Man to man. I want to show them what they got to look forward to when they grow up."

Dawn settled back into her seat. "Of all the silly notions," she said, although she seemed rather pleased. "I hope our boys'll be doing better than working in a mill."

Carrying Simon, holding Peter's hand, Andy walked to the main door of the mill. It was locked.

"The side entrance is unsecured," said Moloch.

Andy went to it. Moloch had spoken true.

Once inside, Andy locked the door. He walked to the basic oxygen furnace where Moloch had first spoken to him. It was cold.

"You are a good and loyal listener," said Moloch. "Give Me the boys."

Andy knew it was much too late to argue. He activated the motors of the cold furnace, which whined like animals whose legs were pinioned in traps. The pear-shaped vessel tilted to a point where Andy could just reach its lip.

"Put the boys in."

Andy lifted first Peter, then Simon, dropping them both in, where they rolled to the canted bottom. They were curiously mute, almost sedated.

"Leave the vessel in the charging position, and go to the blast furnace."

Andy did as he was told.

"Melt some ore."

Andy moved quickly and efficiently. He knew that once he started the blast furnace, people would soon become alerted to the unwonted activity at the mill. Luckily the furnace caught easily, almost unnaturally so. Cans on a conveyor carried the raw ore to the top of the furnace. Soon Andy had tapped molten metal. This metal was a substance at 2,370 degrees Fahrenheit, or 1,300 degrees Centigrade. In the basic oxygen furnace, under the inrush of that life-sustaining gas, it would soar to 3,000° F, or 1,725° C.

There came a banging on the main door. Andy wondered why the watchman didn't just use his keys. Possibly in the confusion no one remembered. Such things happened. Possibly Moloch was preventing them.

At the receptacle that held the boys, Andy stopped with the charge of molten iron.

"Now?" he asked, already knowing what Moloch would say.

"Yes."

Luckily it normally took less than five minutes to charge the furnace, and that was with a much larger draught.

There was no noise from inside the kettle as Andy worked. Only a titanic inrush as of breath when the vessel was full, which Andy knew came from Moloch.

Andy righted the vessel and lowered the oxygen lance. This was a steel tube fifty feet long and ten inches in diameter. It descended like the finger of God.

Andy stood watching, listening to the flow of oxygen and to Moloch's keening exaltations. Then Andy felt hands grabbing him. "Moloch," he called aloud, "Moloch, now I know!"

But Moloch did not answer.

THE GRANGE

"Look," said Lucy, "the moon—"

Edward laid down his newspaper and looked up in the sky, where his wife was pointing. A waxing crescent moon, pale as a mermaid's face, thin as a willow whip, was visible in the translucent blue heavens, trailing the noontime sun by some twenty-five degrees.

"Pretty," said Edward, making to lift up his paper again.

"Pretty?" Lucy demanded. "Is that all you have to say?"

"What else should I say?"

"Well, what's it doing up there now? Isn't that weird? I mean, look, the sun's still up. It's only lunchtime."

Edward slowly folded his newspaper into quarters, stalling for a few seconds. His mind was disordered; his fine intellect, complex as a cat's cradle, had come completely unknotted in an instant. Lucy did this to him. Even after fifteen years of marriage, she still did this to him. All it took most times was a single utterance winging unexpectedly out of the conversational blue, or an idiosyncratic action. The day she had asked him what ocean Atlantic City fronted on. . . . Her puzzlement about why one had to apply the brakes when going into a curve. . . . The hurt incomprehension she had exhibited when she destroyed the microwave oven by trying to warm up a can of soup. . . .

It was at such times that Edward found himself utterly speechless, baffled by the unfathomable workings of Lucy's mind. She was quite clever in many ways. That much must be granted. And it wasn't a lack of logic she exhibited. Far from it. It was a kind of otherworldly, Carrollian logic she possessed, something utterly alien to his rational method of thinking.

He had believed he understood her before their wedding. They had, after all, known each other for most of their lives. Had been the traditional high school sweethearts, in fact. Surely such a long intimacy should have bred comprehension.

What a naive and pompous young idiot he had been! He realized quite fully now that he did not understand her at all, not in the slightest. Would never understand her. But he loved her, and that, he supposed, would have to suffice.

Trying to come up with a rational response to Lucy's objections to the moon's sharing of the sun's domain, Edward studied her where she lay. Reclining on a folding, towel-padded aluminum lawn chair, she wore the smallest of two-piece swimsuits. Her graceful limbs and slim torso were thoroughly oiled and buttered. Her small tummy resembled a shining golden hill, her sweat-filled navel a mysterious well or spring atop it. She was levered partway up on her right elbow and forearm, her eyes shaded with her left hand, facing Edward expectantly.

Knowing full well that it was all in vain, Edward tried to explain.

"There is no reason why the moon cannot be up at the same time as the sun. Because of the special way the sun and the moon and the earth spin around each other, the moon rises at a different time each day—"

"The moon rises?"

"Yes."

"It isn't just always there, but you see it only when the sun goes down?"

Edward sighed deeply. "No. Now pay attention. If, one night, it rises at, say 11:00 P.M., the next night it will rise later. Pretty soon it will be rising during the day, like now. Eventually it will go back to rising at night."

"Why should it work in such a complicated way?"

"Gravity—"

"Stop right there. You know I don't understand that word."

"Well, then, you'll never understand why the moon can be up during the day."

Lucy flopped back onto the lawn chair. "Maybe I don't want to understand. Maybe you're wrong. Maybe this is a once-in-a-lifetime occurrence, and you just think you've seen the moon in the daytime before."

Edward started to get irritated. "Listen, I know what I know. The moon is often up during the daytime. I've seen it a hundred times, if I've seen it once."

"You're pulling my leg."

"No, honest, I'm not."

"Well, I've never seen it before."

"You've seen it now."

"Now is not always. Like you keep saying, 'One item does not make a series.'"

"Look for it tomorrow, then, if you don't believe me."

"Just forget it, then."

"Maybe I'll do just that."

Edward tried to resume reading his paper. For some reason he had lost all relish for it. In the back of his mind was a nagging uncertainty. Had he ever seen the moon by day before . . . ?

Lucy spoke sleepily. "Why don't you take off that silly hat and get some sun?"

"I don't want to burn."

"You stayed blanched all those summers we lived in the city. You should enjoy our new country life."

Edward had just received tenure at an urban-campused Ivy League college in the Northeast, where he taught philosophy. He and Lucy had promptly bought an old farmhouse forty-five minutes south of the city, in a sparsely populated district where cows outnumbered humans. Their property included five acres, one of which was lawn, the other four being scrub growth.

The time of the year was the first week of June.

"I can't see the sense of getting all greased up to lie mindlessly for hours in the sun."

"It feels good."

"I suppose."

"In fact, it feels so good that I'm taking off my suit. It's silly to wear it, out here in the middle of nowhere."

"Lucy, I don't know—"

But it was too late. In a mere second, Lucy had skinned out of her bikini. The twin white premises of her breasts and the conclusion of her pale pubic delta formed a wordless syllogism whose validity was unsusceptible to proof.

Still, Edward felt professionally compelled to try.

Later that afternoon, after a lunch of curried chicken-salad sandwiches and Chardonnay, Lucy said, "You know what? I think I'm going to start a garden. It'll give me something to do."

"A garden? You've never grown anything before."

"That was when we lived in the city. Things are different now."

"What kind of garden? Flowers or vegetables?"

"Both."

"How will you even know where to begin?"

"Oh, I don't know. I'll ask around. Maybe there's one of those whatchamacallits around here."

"I have absolutely no idea what you're talking about."

"Don't be obtuse. You know what I mean."

"I do?"

"The place where the farmers get together for their hoedowns or hootenannies or whatever."

"A Grange."

"Yes, that's it. A Grange."

* * *

It was odd, this living in the country. Very strange and disturbing to the intellect. Nature had an effect. Yes, it must be admitted. The mind, much as it might like to think it was sovereign and independent, was hooked up to the body; and the body, in turn, was merely a quivering antenna receptive to a bewildering variety of sensory inputs. And out here, away from the city, amidst a wild profusion of growing things, of hidden, scurrying animals, of running water and blind stones migrating upward through the soil, the inputs were different. More persuasive in a subtle way—although perhaps less blatant—than car horns and advertisements, sirens and the smell of restaurants.

But there was more to it than individual stimuli, or even the sum of the novel sensations. There were the underlying patterns to consider, the ancient cycles and the total ecology of nature. Take just the seasons, for instance. In the city, they passed almost unnoticed. Street trees donned and doffed their cloaks of leaves, and no one paid any attention. Pigeons did not fly south for the winter. Any river big enough to notice was too big to ice over. Flowers were something one bought already cut and bundled.

Out here in the country, though, it was different. In just the couple of months that they had been living here, Edward had become attuned to the progress of the summer. In a way that was almost sly and sneaky, things changed. Plants that, a few weeks ago in May, had been tiny shoots were now monstrous weeds, bearing heavy, randy blossoms never bred by man. Where there had once been a clear line of sight from the front porch to the mailbox, there was now an impenetrable greenness. The sun now rose above that ancient oak, whereas formerly it had crowned that other. (Elm, sycamore, ash? How could one tell?)

And the way the discrete elements of the environment related to each other. . . . When the trumpet vine that climbed the tumbled stone wall along the eastern edge of their land had blossomed, the hummingbirds had materialized from nowhere. How had they known to come? The ants that stripped the chewed carcass that might have been a possum—what had summoned them? The cloud of delicate dandelion parasol seeds—what fitted them to be carried by the wind?

There was a kind of mindless fecundity behind it all, an inexhaustible and exuberant organic experimentation. What was it the writer Annie Dillard had said? That nature was "wasteful and extravagant of life. . . ." That seemed about right.

Edward had noticed unmistakable changes in himself since their residency here. For one thing, his attention was more liable to drift from his work. He had fall-semester classes to prepare, scholarly papers to write, a book to outline. (It was to be a volume of philosophy for the layman, hopefully very popular, like what Sagan and Gould had done in their fields.) Despite these demands, he found himself spending useless hours outdoors, wandering along the game trails that threaded the adjoining woods, his mind wandering likewise, unable to focus on the work at hand.

(But was it totally empty during these walks, or rather, working in a different way, examining different, wordless topics . . . ?)

And then, of course, there were the changes in Lucy. Back in the city, during his untenured years, she had done part-time librarian work to supplement his pay, and spent most of her free time as an expert shopper. Since the increase in his income and their subsequent relocation, she had quit her job and completely lost interest in the local stores or the more distant, inevitable mall. All it seemed she wanted to do was vegetate in the sun. That, or cook these intricate, peasant-type meals for them. Supper might be a big pot of thick stew and a crusty whole-grain loaf, still hot from the oven. Breakfast an omelet round and golden as the sun accompanied by cornbread made with white meal and cooked in a cast-iron skillet in the oven, emerging like a scorched harvest moon.

Edward found himself putting on weight, like some country squire.

And now there was this matter of a garden. It was the last thing Edward would have predicted Lucy would want. (Of course, when had he ever been able to guess what she would do next?) It was certainly a harmless enough hobby. Maybe she would find some local folks who might provide her with company on days when he was working.

As for his own inability to concentrate—well, there was bound to be a period of adjustment connected with such major changes in their lives. Edward was certain that any day now he would be back to his old self.

Meanwhile, though, perhaps he'd just go out for a stroll. . . .

*   *   *

Car tires chewed noisily on the gravel in the drive. Edward looked up gratefully from the disorganized pile of papers on his desk. Splotchy sunlight, filtered by the leaves of the large oak just outside the window, carpeted the varnished floor of his study with a pattern of shadow. The house had seemed empty without Lucy. Maybe now that she was home, they could go for a walk together. It wasn't as if he were accomplishing anything sitting here. . . .

Stepping beyond the wooden screen door onto the wide porch that wrapped itself around three-quarters of the old house, Edward was met by Lucy bounding up the steps from the verdant lawn. She grabbed him and whirled him around in a crazy little dance.

"I found it, I found it, I found it!"

Stepping back dizzily when released, Edward said, "My God, it could only be Leibniz's universal calculus—"

"No, dummy, the Grange."

Edward took Lucy's hand, and they went into the cool indoors.

"I stopped in at the Blue Label feedstore and asked the man there. He said there was a Grange in town. It's one of the oldest branches, in fact. They meet in that brick building with the waterwheel that we wondered about. It used to be a real flour mill hundreds of years ago, even before World War I."

"That old, huh?"

"Yes. And tonight there's going to be a meeting that the public can attend. At least the first part. The Grange is a society, you know. You have to be members before you can go to every meeting and function. But if we go tonight and show some interest, I think they'll ask us to join. The feedstore man said that most of the members were pretty old, and that they were always looking for younger people to belong."

"I guess we qualify, then. Anyway, I know you make me feel pretty young."

Edward grabbed Lucy's ass.

"About sixteen years old I would estimate," she said.

"You should remember."

"Oh, I do."

Later Edward was motivated to pull down the proper volume of the Encyclopedia Americana and look up:

"GRANGE, one of the general farm organizations in the United States, formerly known as the Patrons of Husbandry. It is a secret, ritualistic society. Established in 1867 in Washington, D.C., by Oliver Hudson Kelley and six associates, its officers bear the titles of Grange Master, Overseer, Chaplain, Secretary, Treasurer, Steward, and Gatekeeper. . . ."

Neat, thought Edward. Each of the original seven founders got to be an officer. That's my kind of club. . . .

Evening filled the woods with twilight. The tall trees surrounding the farmhouse—where the porch light defined a small circle of artificial day—had become towering, shadowy masses, rustling in a light breeze, seeming to exhale waves of moist coolness. Crickets chirruped. A chorus of falsetto frogs peeped cheerfully in a distant swamp. Stars began to burn through the canopy of night. The scent of new-mown grass filled Edward's nostrils as he and Lucy walked to the car. The crew of locals that maintained their property had been by that afternoon.

Just where the lawn met the gravel of the driveway, Lucy stopped. "Edward, look at this."

Edward saw an irregular ring of beautiful white mushrooms, each about three inches high, phallus-capped, rearing proudly above the mower-shortened blades of grass. They limned a hollow moon.

"The men must have missed it," he said, knowing even as he said it, as he stared unbelievingly at the cut grass beneath the ring, that he was not speaking the truth.

"No," Lucy said, "these things can sprout up fast. I've heard about them."

"In a couple of hours?"

"There it is."

"Well," said Edward, "Maybe they're good to eat."

"Oh no, we can't pick them—"

Edward decided not to mention that the landscapers would decapitate them next week.

Lucy drove them into town. She liked driving; Edward didn't. He tried to restrain his foot from pressing an imaginary brake pedal each time she took a curve.

The car radio played softly, a pop song sung by a nasal Australian voice:

> I have the moon in my bed,
> I have the sun in my heart,
> I have the stars at my feet. . . .

There was a sizable parking lot attached to the old mill. Normally vacant those few times Edward had driven by, tonight it was nearly full. Lucy found an empty slot. The cars were those models Edward associated with his parents' generation: conservative Buicks, Oldsmobiles, Chevys.

Edward could read the bumper sticker on one, in the illumination of a streetlight:

HOWDY, STRANGER!
I'M A GRANGER!

"Corny."

"Be nice. These aren't academics. They're a different kind of people from any we know."

At the door to the mill, they were not far from the grassy banks of the stream that had once spun the wheel that had turned the grindstones in their immemorial embrace. The water flowed with a serene chuckling over weed-draped rocks and between reeds and rushes, its clean odor lying lightly on the night air.

The interior of the mill had long ago been subdivided into offices and meeting rooms. Here and there, portions of the original pegged beams showed through, like the skeleton of an old, old narrative poking its elbows through its modern dress. Everything was freshly painted and well-lit with modern fixtures. Edward and Lucy made their way down a corridor—corkboard hung with notices of farm equipment for sale, a table holding ag-school bulletins and a box full of food coupons for exchange, a forgotten pair of galoshes under the empty coat hooks—toward a room from which voices drifted.

The hall held fifty wood-slatted folding chairs, nearly all occupied. Edward and Lucy slid into a pair of empty seats at the back in what they hoped was an inconspicuous way.

Looking toward the front of the room, Edward saw a wooden dais bearing a table and seven chairs. The chairs were occupied by four

old women and three old men. Each wore a yellow-and-white satin
sash across their elderly chest. Their average age seemed about seventy.
The woman in the middle, although remarkably unwrinkled, had to be
in her nineties. . . .

The backdrop behind the Grange leaders was a green cloth on
which was stitched a golden stalk of grain.

The meeting was already under way. One of the officers was detail-
ing the status of the treasury in exquisitely tedious detail. Edward settled back into his chair, quite prepared to be very bored.

The next forty-five minutes didn't disappoint him. Accounts of
planned fund-raising activities, the success of a recent dance, news of
crop prices, the formation of a committee to do political work for the
Grange-backed candidate in the upcoming presidential election. . . .

Edward was just drifting off to sleep, when he was reprieved.

"This concludes the first half of tonight's Grange meeting," said
one of the officers. "We will break for ten minutes. I must remind the
general public that the second half of the meeting is closed to them."

Chairs scraped as people got to their feet. Edward stood. One leg
had gone to sleep and now prickled painfully.

"Can we go now?"

"In a minute. We want to introduce ourselves first."

"We do?" Looking to his wife for an answer, Edward was taken aback.

Lucy's eyes were shining, as if the boring meeting had been some
kind of rapturous experience for her. She seemed drawn to the people
on the stage.

Edward shrugged and accompanied her up front.

From old-fashioned wall-mounted Seeburg speakers issued barely
discernible music. Edward thought he recognized the old English bal-
lad "John Barleycorn Must Die."

The officers had descended from the stage and now stood among
the respectful crowd, softly conferring among themselves. Lucy
approached the nearest, one of the men.

"Hello," she said, extending her hand. "My name's Lucy Pastorious,
and this is my husband, Edward."

The white-haired man shook first Lucy's hand, then Edward's, and
introduced himself. "Calvin Culver. I'm the Grange's Sower."

Had that been one of the Grange titles? Edward couldn't be sure,
but he didn't think so.

"We're new residents of the town," continued Lucy, "and we're
interested in joining the Grange."

Edward had an impression that he and Lucy were being instantly appraised, and found not too alien. Culver seemed honestly pleased at their interest. "We're always glad to see some young faces round here. The Grange can't go on without new blood. I don't think there'd be any problem about you two joining. Let me just introduce you to the rest of the sashes."

Culver turned toward his fellow officers and named them one by one.

"This is Betty Rhinebeck, our Attendant.

"Roger Swain, our Presbyter.

"Alice Cotten, our Thresher.

"Edwin Landseer, our Plowman.

"Nancy Rook, our Sluicekeeper."

When Edward had finished shaking the fifth papery, dry old hand and making his fifth polite hello, he was certain of one thing. None of these titles were the same as the ones he had earlier found in the encyclopedia. Was this Grange a chapter of the Patrons of Husbandry, or was it a branch of some different organization? Had the titles changed with time? Or were false ones given to the public? If the latter, it seemed a needlessly mysterious practice. . . .

Edward suddenly realized that there remained one officer left to be introduced: the most senior woman, who had sat in the middle of the others. It occurred to Edward now that she had been the only one to remain unspeaking throughout the meeting.

Culver shepherded Lucy with evidence of great respect up to the small, trim woman. "This is Sally Lunn, the Grain Mistress."

Grain Mistress . . . ? What had happened to Grange Master?

Edward watched Lucy extend her hand. The woman took it, her simultaneously old and young face broadening into a smile showcasing perfect teeth. "So pleased to meet you at last, Mrs. Pastorious," said Sally Lunn.

Lucy's lips were slightly parted, as if she had started to speak but had her thought processes short-circuited. Sally Lunn released Lucy's hand, which continued to hang for a moment in midair.

Before he knew what was happening, Lucy had staggered back, and Edward had been invited forward.

"Edward," said Sally Lunn, "my pleasure." Then she took his hand.

His mind was somewhere deep under the earth. The rich smell of soil filled his nose, and cool clods sealed his eyes. He could blindly sense a twinned presence high above his head, calling him up. He struggled upward through the clinging loam, grew taller, taller, until he burst forth, into the ecstatic light, mingled gold and opal—

His hand and self were his own again. Somehow they were at the exit to the mill, having been escorted there by Calvin Culver.

"Sorry you folks have to leave now. But something tells me there won't be any problem about you joining. No siree, none at all."

* * *

Edward contemplated his breakfast. Lucy had cooked a pot of Wheatena with raisins. She had mounded a hill of the gritty golden cereal into a bowl, deposited a dollop of honey into the center of it, and splashed a moat of milk into the bowl.

The golden hill and white ring around it had Edward mesmerized, as if it were an intricate mandala containing infinite depths of meaning.

Reluctantly, he jerked his attention away from the absolutely mundane image. Picking up his spoon, he broke through the dike containing the honey, let it runnel away into the milk, a golden thread. He stirred the whole mixture up into an amorphous mess and began to eat.

The cereal tasted especially sweet this morning, the day after they had attended the Grange.

Lucy sat down at the table, picked up her spoon, and dipped it into her own cereal. "Well, what about it?"

Edward was taken aback. He hadn't expected Lucy to beard him so soon about what they had agreed last night to postpone discussing. But he should have known, given her obvious excitement at the Grange meeting, that she would wait only the barest minimum of time.

Edward feigned ignorance. "About what?"

"Don't be an ape. What about us joining the Grange?"

Edward looked sheepishly down into his bowl. There was no way out of it now. "I don't think I want to."

"Let me guess why. You've got no time?"

"Well, yes, there's that. . . ."

"You aren't interested in the kind of things they do and talk about?"

"I suppose you could say that. . . ."

"You don't like the people? You think they're clodhoppers?"

"Well, now, I wouldn't go that far. . . ."

"You had the stuffing scared out of you by Sally Lunn?"

Edward said nothing. He looked up to find Lucy entreating him with shining eyes.

"Don't be scared, Edward. I felt it, too. I don't know what it was, but it was nothing to be frightened of. It was something entirely natural and good. I think maybe it was just some kind of saintliness or wisdom that comes, if you're lucky, when you get as old as she is. Maybe it has to do with her living out here in the country all her life. Whatever it was, I liked it. It made me feel good, like I understood for the first time what the world is all about. Sometimes I don't, you know. Sometimes, in fact, I think everyone but me knows the secret of how things work. You with all your talk about gravity, the way the plumber yelled at me that time I put the plaster down the drains— I get tired of feeling like such a big dope all the time. So I'm going to join the Grange. And that's that."

Edward struggled to speak. Lucy's words had made him sad. Did she really feel like that? Was he partly responsible?

"Lucy, I want you to be happy. Do whatever you want. I'll be glad if you join the Grange. But I just can't. You see, when you touched that old woman's hand you felt confirmed in everything you knew. But I felt just the opposite. I felt as if a pit of quicksand had opened up underfoot, as if the whole world I had known and accepted as solid and rational were a sham—which can't be true. The old woman twisted my vision somehow and showed me everything in a new, unreasoning light. All the careful work I've put into explaining the world to myself and others was undone in a second. Maybe it was just momentary self-hypnosis. But I can't go through that again."

"And what," Lucy asked, "if she was showing you the truth?"

"I think," said Edward, "that I'd rather not accept that as a possibility."

Lucy scraped the last of her cereal up methodically and swallowed it. "That's fair, I guess. Will you at least help me with my kitchen garden?" She licked the bowl of her spoon sensuously like a big, lazy cat.

"Unfair tactics, and not strictly necessary. Of course I will."

"Good. I'm going into town and look up Mr. Calvin Culver, our Sower and tell him I'm in if they'll have me. You can work off a little of the spare tire you're accumulating by getting the grass up from that plot I marked near the back steps."

And with that, Lucy was gone.

Spare tire? And who had been feeding him such rich meals, as if fattening him up for a sacrifice? Was there no justice?

Edward did the breakfast dishes and went outside.

Even this early in the morning, the June sun was overpoweringly hot, a celestial bonfire. Soon Edward had his shirt off. The sharp, untried, shiny blade of the pointed shovel easily severed the ancient turf demarcated by stakes and string. Edward picked up each heavy clod by its green hair—disturbingly like a severed head—shook the moist earth from its roots, and tossed it aside. Fat and juicy flesh-colored earthworms, some truncated by his blade, wriggled away into the earth.

After some time, Edward had exposed a square of black earth some twenty feet on a side to the sun's curious stare. The gaze of the deity was already turning the soil a different, lighter shade as it dried. The pile of turfs made a small warrior's barrow.

Edward was resting on his shovel, his back glistening with sweat, when Lucy called out. "Hello! Come help me!"

Rather wearily, Edward went around to the front of the house. Lucy was struggling with some handled device sticking out of the car's trunk.

"I rented a Rototiller," she explained. "It'll save us some work."

"Us?"

"We're a team, aren't we?"

Edward wrestled the machine to the ground. "And your role on the team is—?"

"I'm the fructifying force."

Edward stopped in midmotion, astonished. "'Fructifying'? Where the hell did that come from? Good old Calvin Culver? Are you sure you don't mean—"

"Don't say it. You've got a filthy mind. Just do a good job, and you'll get your reward.

"Oh, by the way," she added as he wheeled the machine off, "I'm a Grange member now."

The Rototiller, despite its noise and stink, did make the job easier. Still, there were what seemed to be thousands of stones to bend over for and pluck from the newly turned earth. In a couple of hours they formed a companion cairn to the sod barrow.

When it was over, Edward had never felt so tired in his life. Every muscle in his arms and legs and back ached. So this was the pastoral life. Ah, Arcadia! The city had never looked so fine. . . .

"Edward," called Lucy from the back porch. He turned, hoping she had brought something cool for him to drink.

She wore a circlet of daisies in her hair. And nothing else. Her body glowed white and tan as if lit from within. She stepped down the stairs with a motion like water falling. The air around her appeared to shiver. She crossed the lawn, her bare feet seeming to imprint the grass with a brighter greenness.

Edward was mesmerized. He felt hot and cold at once. Then his unknown wife, her eyes filmed with a cool light, was upon him, unbuckling his pants, finding him unsurprisingly ready, and pulling him down to the broken soil.

The earth was cool and moist beneath his knees and palms. He wondered briefly what it felt like to supine Lucy. Then there was nothing left of him to wonder.

When it was over, Edward had never felt so refreshed in his life. Every muscle in his arms and legs and back throbbed with vitality. So *this* was the pastoral life. . . .

"You don't pay the lawn-maintenance guys this way, do you?"

Lucy wasn't listening to him. She was looking up into the infinite sky. Edward cast his own gaze over his shoulder, and saw the moon watching them.

"Now it will blossom," Lucy said.

That same evening, Lucy announced she was going out.

"There's a Grange meeting tonight."

"So soon?"

"It's an emergency. We have to deal with the gypsy moths."

"You mean those stupid caterpillars that are chewing up all the trees? I thought there was nothing that stopped them short of spraying. And the town council's voted against that."

"Sally has a plan."

Lucy was gone till after midnight. When she crawled into their bed, beneath the down comforter the country nights still made a necessity, Edward came half-awake.

"How'd it go?" he murmured sleepily.

"Shhh, go back to sleep. I'll tell you in the morning."

But in the morning there was no need to ask, for the gypsy moths lay dead in heaps everywhere.

* * *

All work on his book had gone by the board. Edward found he couldn't concentrate on what had once seemed so important to him. It wasn't the environment that was distracting him anymore, though. At least not firsthand. He had realized with a start, soon after the wild coupling with Lucy on the garden bed, that his senses had become harmonized to the natural world somehow, had achieved a rapprochement with the forces of sunlight and soil, leaf and limb. These forces did not make the same demands on his attention as they had when they were new to him. He found he could go about his daily life without paying much attention to the bewitching, continually varying play of light and odors around him.

Not that nature had vanished or retreated from the back of his mind or the depths of his gut. No, that had not happened, no more than one's heart or lungs had ceased to function, simply because they went hourly unheard.

No, what preoccupied Edward now was trying to find out what Lucy had gotten herself involved in.

What exactly was this organization known as the Grange?

Here and now, in mid-June, this question—along with its corollary, Was the Grange good or bad for his wife?—filled all of Edward's mind. He attacked it the only way he knew how, short of confronting the Grange members themselves (something he was surprisingly reluctant to do), and that was through research.

Every morning, Edward set out for the city, leaving Lucy behind to tend to her garden. He worried about what she might be getting up to, picturing her reenacting their fructifying ritual, only with other partners. Then he would admonish himself for a fool. Lucy, despite her newfound interest in matters horticultural, was still the same woman he had always known, and she wouldn't do that to him. Besides, any such activity would surely crush the tiny seedlings that now sprouted where Edward and Lucy had tumbled, and even the sturdier shoots of the transplanted tomatoes, and Lucy wouldn't stand for that. The garden seemed to be her whole life lately. In the end, there was nothing Edward could or would do if she wanted to rut all day, so he dismissed it from his mind as best he could.

On the campus, moving from stack to dusty stack in the various familiar libraries where he had spent so much time—and which now seemed so alien—Edward sought answers to the meaning of the Grange and what it stood for.

He confirmed in detail the brief encyclopedia entry he had read on that day, seemingly ages gone by. The Grange, if this was indeed the same one, had been the brainchild of Oliver Hudson Kelley in 1867. (The word "grange" came from the same Latin root as "grain," *granum*, and meant merely a storehouse for grain.) He dug into Kelley's past. The man had been an immigrant, his father Irish, his mother French. There the personal trail petered out. Edward switched to the public practices of the Grange.

On the surface, the Grange's history was one of promoting solidar-

Paul Di Filippo

ity among farmers, for the benefit of both individual farmers and farmers as a class. Antitrust, transportation, and education laws were agitated for, cooperatives established, research promoted. There was a social side to the Grange, too. Dances, harvest suppers, lectures. It all seemed extremely innocuous today—although, of course, at the time, it had been considered quite radical and dangerous.

But through all his readings, Edward began to accumulate the feeling that this surface level of activity was not everything, was not even the most important reason for the Grange's existence. There was something unspoken beneath the primary texts of a century ago, half a century ago, even two decades ago, something that popped up only now and then, as if it were too powerful to keep completely submerged, rearing its massive green head like the crown of an ancient thick-boled oak bursting full-grown and -leafed through the bland surface of the earth.

And the unspoken secret seemed, Edward slowly realized, to revolve around a woman—or women—known as Sally Lunn, and how she was . . . well, there was no word for it but *worshipped*.

From a privately printed, anonymously authored book titled *Gleanings and Chaff: An Amateur Agriculturalist's Experiences with the Patrons of Husbandry*, 1879, whose spine was broken and pages flaking:

> *Sallie Lunne was present that night, for the first time since I had attended the Grange, and I was told to show all proper respect and deference to this old dame, although how she differed from any farmer's elderly wife I could not immediately apprehend. I was told by the Grange's Thresher that Dame Lunne was not her baptismal name, but an appellation given to the woman who filled the role of Grain Mistress, and that therefore each branch of the Grange boasted its own Mistress Lunne, simultaneously in attendance all across this broad land—nay, even the globe.*
>
> *Mistress Lunne seemed a taciturn, even dull, sort, and spoke not a word during the Grange meeting itself. But afterward, when I was brought forward to be presented to her, I was forced to revise my hasty first impression.*
>
> *Her exact words I do not recall, but know with a cer-*

tainty that they most favorably impressed me with her strength of character and Demeter-like vitality. She seemed a veritable fount and wellspring of pastoral virtues, her high office having caused her to transcend herself, and her touch was correspondingly galvanic. It is hard to overstate her effect on those made of lesser stuff.

Even more difficult of relation is the aspect she dons during certain private Granger rituals. But I can say no more. . . .

One morning, prior to leaving for the city, Edward took his coffee out to the back porch. Lucy was still in the shower. Edward hadn't told her what he was doing on campus each day; she thought, he believed, that he was working on his book.

His eyes drifted toward their vegetable garden. It was nine days since he had turned the soil with such backbreaking labor, and he hadn't paid much attention to it in the interval.

The tomato plants were spilling over their wire cages, heavy ripe fruit bedecking their leafy sprawl. Peas were ready to pick, as was an abundance of lettuce, eggplants, cucumbers, and zucchini.

Lucy emerged, barefoot, robed, and toweling her hair. "Oh, I'm sorry—did I scare you?" she asked.

Dabbing ineffectually at his coffee-soaked shirt, Edward said, "Just clumsy, I guess." He set his empty cup and saucer down noisily on the porch rail. Then his eyes caught on what was nailed above the back door.

Lucy followed his gaze. "It's a sprig of touch-leaf," she explained. "Saint John's wort. Aren't all those golden flowers beautiful?"

"Beautiful, yeah, they are. I guess. Why's it there?"

"To guard against thunder, lightning, and fire. There's a spray over the front door, too."

Lucy regarded her husband as if waiting for him to inquire further, or contest what she had said. Edward didn't bite. He was just waiting for what came next. Something had to come next. It was in Lucy's eyes. They were floating in that same opalescent light as on the day the two of them had consecrated the miraculous garden.

"Saint John's Eve is just a few days away, you know. Midsummer Night. It's an important day for the Grange. There'll be a lot going on. Do you think you might come?"

"I—I'll see. Listen, I've got to be going now. A lot of research to finish—"

Lucy kissed him chastely good-bye. "If you call, I might be out. There's a red tide on the coast, and we're helping the local Grange there deal with it."

"I see," said Edward.

The car radio confirmed that one of the nuisance-making algal blooms had just been spotted that morning. Edward didn't give it a snowball's chance in hell of lasting more than a day.

Edward had run into a dead end investigating the Grange itself. Nowhere were the more arcane practices he suspected them of described in detail. He was forced to turn to anthropological and mythological works, notably Graves's *The Greek Myths*, Frazer's *Golden Bough*, and Campbell's *World Mythology*.

In the Frazer, he found that the ceremony he and Lucy had participated in was old, old, old, as old as agriculture itself. Fucking in a field, by couple or community, to ensure fertility, was a ritual found from Central America to New Guinea to Central Africa to the Ukraine. Edward could now personally testify to its efficacy.

There were a hundred, a thousand other bizarre and not-so-bizarre practices connected with raising crops. An activity so central to civilization could not have failed to accumulate myriad superstitions over the millennia, contributions from every ethnic and racial group known to history. Druids, Gauls, Bantu, Aztecs, Greeks, Romans, Seminoles, Apache—Edward wallowed in the descriptions till his head reeled. Intercourse with trees, beating recalcitrant crops, supplicating the rain and sun, chastising the moon, sacrificing animals and humans—

Which of these did the Grange practice?

Sacrifice?

Human sacrifice?

Yes, Edward was suddenly convinced. He was the intended victim for the Saint John's Eve festivities. Coinciding with the summer solstice, after which the days began to shorten and vegetation implicitly to die, the archaic holiday was marked with propitiations to distant winter. In Russia, a straw figure was drowned in a stream. The Druids burned their sacrificial king in the Midsummer bonfires. This was why Lucy had been fattening him up, like some hapless Hansel. Oh Lord, what was he going to do?

Almost blinded by tears of fear and disappointment at the treachery of his wife, Edward continued to flip uselessly through the pages of the book before him. A phrase leaped out at him: . . . *known as soleil lune.* He backtracked.

> *A large, round cake was baked from the summer's first harvest of grain and consecrated to the Sun and the Moon, twin tutelar deities of husbandry, by whose radiant beneficence the crops ripened, and by whose phases propitious times for sowing and reaping were determined. This cake was ritually broken and shared among the community. Known as* soleil lune *in France, this symbolic body of Ceres was, due to misunderstanding of the original phrase, called Sally Lunn in England. . . .*

* * *

The flames soared high. Edward could see them from across the field in the night. A circle of leaping bonfires, they ringed a small wooded hill. The air was thick with their smoke, and with the richness of the Midsummer vegetation.

Lucy handled the jouncing car well on the rutted dirt road. She whistled as she drove. Edward, slumped miserably in his seat, thought he recognized again "John Barleycorn Must Die."

In the end, he had agreed to accompany Lucy to the Grange's ceremony. What else could he do? If Lucy wanted to get rid of him, then there was no reason for him to go on living. He had never quite realized what she meant to him until now. Only her apparent abandonment of him as a sacrifice to her new religion had showed Edward the depths of his ties to her. She had been everything that had supported him in his work, his bastion during hard times, his joy during good. If their life together was at an end, he'd at least be loyal to her up to the ultimate moment, for all they had shared, even if she had betrayed him.

The car came to a stop amidst others, the same old models that had been parked outside the Grange hall. The early arrivals, Edward saw, were standing near the fires, lit with gold, partly shadowed.

Lucy levered open her door and stepped nimbly to the sweet-smelling, trodden hay grass. Edward dragged himself out of the car.

"Are you O.K., dear? Are you sure you want to be here tonight?"

Edward nodded dumbly. How could she be so appallingly blithe at his imminent demise?

They walked toward the crowd. Sally Lunn was not visible. The other six elderly officers separated themselves and approached. They were wearing their sashes and nothing else, their old carcasses somehow not pitiful or funny, but immensely dignified and potent. They carried archaic flails and scythes.

"Is your husband ready?" one asked. Edward thought he recognized Roger Swain, the Presbyter.

"Yes."

"We will escort him. You must remain behind." Swain took Edward by the elbow. The six officers and Edward began to walk uphill.

Looking up as he ascended, Edward stared full into the beaming face of the moon. Where had it come from? A moment ago it had been nowhere in sight. . . . He stumbled, and was forced to drop his gaze. When he looked up again, there were only innumerable stars.

By the time he reached the top, he was winded, more from fear than physical exertion. Under the dark trees, away from the flames, he could hardly see. They stopped to let his eyes adjust. Edward thought he saw an open work structure, like a giant wicker beehive. They moved toward it.

The structure was an airy hut woven of willow withes. Sally Lunn sat cross-legged inside it, clothed in a robe. Edward could feel her presence from six feet away.

"Happy Saint John's Eve, Edward. We're glad you could make it."

The other officers had faded respectfully back and left him alone with Sally Lunn.

Edward collapsed nervelessly to the earth. He thought he could hear the gentle purling of a stream or spring nearby.

"Do you know who I am now?" asked Sally Lunn.

Edward shook his head no.

"I think you do. I am the Sun and the Moon and the Earth. I am Ceres and Gaea and Demeter, Persephone and Hecate. I am the force that through the green fuse drives the flower. I am burgeoning and fecundity, blossom and fruit. Do you acknowledge this?"

Edward's lips were very dry. "Yes," he whispered.

"Do you know why you are here tonight?"

"Not really. But I can guess."

"It's because of your wife."

"I know that much—"

"Quiet. You know nothing. Your wife is a very important person. Look at me. This body I inhabit is one of a few special ones, receptive to me. I come into it only from time to time. I am immortal. But although I can lend it a few years, this body is not immortal. In fact, it will soon go to feed the soil. This chapter of the Grange will be without their Sally Lunn. The important work they do would falter without guidance. But your wife—"

Revelation burst on Edward then, and he dared to get to his feet and interrupt. "You mean to possess her."

"I already have."

The officers had drifted back silently during Edward's audience, and now stood outside the door of the hut. Sally Lunn spoke softly.

"It only remains for you, as Lucy's husband, to marry me."

Edwin Landseer, the Plowman, was helping Edward to remove his clothes, while Betty Rhinebeck, the Attendant, was slowly pulling the robe off Sally Lunn's wrinkled shoulders. The Presbyter was aspersing them both with crisp water, while Alice Cotten, the Thresher, plumped up a bed of fragrant herbs and ferns. As Edward stared, Sally Lunn's robe pooled about her waist.

She was no longer old. She was young as spring, a nymph with unmottled skin and abundant flesh, supple as a reed. Her hair was as thick as wheat in a field. She looked like Lucy and like every woman he had ever coveted. A heady perfume rose from her loins, indistinguishable from the earth.

Nancy Rook, the Sluicekeeper, was behind Sally Lunn, lowering her backward to the bracken. The goddess dug her heels into the ground and arched her back off the ground so her robe could be removed from underneath her, then finally pulled off her uplifted feet when she settled back down.

Calvin Culver, the Sower, guided Edward between her legs.

It was infinitely more intense than what Edward had experienced with Lucy in the garden. And that had been the headiest sex he had ever had.

He rose to meet the sun.

He answered the moon's pull.

He tasted the earth.

He was a long, hot root in the soil.

He found the spring, the honeyed well on the hill, and drank deeply.

The act felt as immemorially old as the grinding of one stone against another, with the grain being crushed between.

Then he flowered whitely, like an anemone.

When it was over, he lay for a time in Sally Lunn's arms, eyes closed. He dared not look whether she was young or old again.

"Would you die for me right now, Edward?" she asked.

"Yes."

"I am pleased to say it won't be necessary. But someday I might ask again."

After a quiet interval, he somehow knew he was expected to get up and redon his clothes, so he did. The sashes came to lead him back downhill. He looked over his shoulder once, like Orpheus. The hut was empty.

The fires were dying down, the people dispersing. He found Lucy. Her hair was crazy, and her shirt hung out of her pants.

Driving back home, he was too baffled at being alive to be able to talk.

But in bed, holding the wife he had never known, whom he had so recently remarried, he found his voice and asked, "What I did tonight—it doesn't bother you?"

Sleepily, Lucy said, "But why should it, dear? She was only me."

SLEEP IS WHERE YOU FIND IT

[co-written with Marc Laidlaw]

1

Sunday Morning in Manhattan

Down in the Lincoln Tunnel, alone with his headlamps and the dashboard's glow, he hears a voice and thinks for one second that it's the police dispatcher. "Tonight's the night," it says, a tiny little voice.

Weegee scowls to himself and answers back, "What do you know? Tonight's always the night."

But the radio is mute; really. Under the river there's hardly even static. He looks around and discovers a girl fading in like another station, her own signal getting stronger and brighter as he nears the end of the tunnel. For a lingering moment she's nothing but a silvery glow condensing out of darkness, pure potential, and then suddenly she's flesh, sitting half-naked on the fabric-covered seat, her grimy right elbow on the passenger's armrest.

Not bad, Weegee thinks to himself. *The Darkroom's being nice to me tonight.*

He's used to far worse, and it's hard not to squirm when he thinks of all the things that have appeared next to him on other occasions, messing up the seat covers. The Mob hits that insist on talking with half their faces blown away; the weary-looking accident victims, stanching bloody noses; the roasts, with their skin so crisp and blackened that it crackles as they reach out wistfully for a puff off his cigar. Why they hound him, Weegee doesn't know. It's as if they consider him responsible somehow. But then this whole nighttime city, and everyone in it, has a haunted look.

It's a relief not to share his car with something that makes him want to puke or scream or bawl his eyes out; but even so, Weegee has made it a matter of principle not to speak to the spooks. With the worst of them, he stops at the mouth of the tunnel and makes them get out and walk . . . or crawl. But tonight—well, he's tempted. Strongly tempted.

The kid must be about twelve. Glossy black hair pulled back with a Li'l Orphan Annie clip to reveal the delicate whorls of one perfect ear. Rosy lips and dark eyes, slightly Spic or Portagee features. She wears only a black skirt and incredibly filthy white bobby sox. In her lap, she's got a gray tiger kitten gripped so tightly by its throat that the creature can't even mew.

Her adolescent breasts are obviously new as a Brooklyn dawn and twice as pretty—not to mention almost as rare a sight to Weegee. The nipples are pink as frosting flowers on a birthday cake, so pink—

Weegee tears his eyes off the girl's chest and puts them back on the road. The end of the Lincoln Tunnel has appeared ahead, although out there is only another order of darkness.

Now he recognizes her, remembers where he caught her. He hasn't thought of her in . . . how long? It was a sweltering summer night, and leaning from his tenement window you could see, all up and down the side of the building, whole families out sleeping on their fire escapes. He'd spotted her by the faint light from the street, the oldest of nearly a dozen kids sprawled on the bars below. A brief flash from his camera, the secret glow of infrared, and he pulled back inside to develop the image and study it in secret. He could still remember the voyeur's thrill on discovering that she was almost naked, an innocent bud cloistered in the safe darkness, never knowing he'd been watching. He had never been quite sure how he felt about that. That's why she's come for him, isn't it?

She's an unresolved tension, a fragment of undigested guilt, in her way more troubling than the corpses.

He has seen girls her age hooking, sure. The places he goes, you see everything after a while. But in his mind, in his photographs, he'd always thought of the girl as kept safe somehow, fixed in that innocent moment, protected not only by the other children but by his photography, as if the infrared flash were an angel's halo hanging over her.

Obviously she isn't safe anymore. She'd slipped down from that fire escape, unknit herself from the limbs of her brothers and sisters, and found her way to him in the darkness, in the tunnel, where everything found him eventually, each with its fresh burden of unwelcome thoughts, its chain of unsavory associations. . . .

She's only a girl, but she reminds him of a woman—reminds him of all sorts of things he can never really have, thanks to the camera.

When was the last time I had a woman, one I didn't have to buy like a dancehall hostess? Weegee asks himself. *Can't get close to one with this damned camera always in front of my face, hanging at my hip, keeping me up all night without sleep. . . .*

Weegee shakes himself out of his self-pity. Aloud—he's a talker, Weegee, loves to talk to anyone, high or low, young or old, and in a pinch his own forlorn forty-five-year-old self will do—Weegee says, "Oh, shut up, you rummy old bastard. If you wanna cry, go buy yourself one of those heartbreak pillows at Lewis and Conger's, fer chrissakes."

He looks reproachfully at his warped reflection in the windshield. The cigar ember flares orange in the corner of his distorted mouth. Out of the corner of his right eye, he sees the girl coolly watching him, saying nothing.

As he drives from the gas-fumed tunnel and out under streetlamps again, both car speakers kick in at full volume, a loony Rossini overture tinkling from one while the other crackles with the police dispatcher's voice. (It's illegal for the average citizen to have one of these rigs in his jalopy. But Weegee has special dispensation from the police, who always welcome the '38 Chevy coupe with license plates 5728Y, its trunk stuffed full with cigars, film, flashbulbs, flashlights, a pair of fireman's hipboots, disguises, even a typewriter and a ream of paper, for quick captioning of photos, notation of who, what, and where, of disaster, death, and—too rarely—laughter.)

The dashboard clock says one minute past midnight, but for Weegee the night is just beginning.

Neon light from a hundred signs—HORSEFLESH SOLD HERE; ROOMS 35 CENTS & UP; TROMMER'S WHITE LABEL—slides liquidly up the maroon hood of the big car. A salami rolls across the seat as he takes a corner. He wolfs down an oily slice of meat he's slightly surprised to find in the fingers of his free hand. He can't remember cutting it. Can't, in fact, remember where he was headed before the tunnel. Consciousness is fragmentary, a sign of exhaustion. When was the last time he slept? He tells everyone—himself included—that he sleeps in the day, but when was it ever day?

Weegee wipes his greasy fingers on a wad of teletype notes that poke from his jacket pocket like a stiff handkerchief. Idly, pointedly ignoring the girl, he uncrinkles the sheets, holds them up at eye-level, so he can still scan the street.

They're blank, except for salami grease.

"What's this, Mister?"

The girl's voice startles him. It's the voice that had said, "Tonight's the night."

Weegee looks to where she's pointing. It's the camera resting on the seat between them. Always between him and everyone else.

2

Camera Tips

The camera is a 4 x 5 Speed Graphic with a Kodak Ektar lens in a Supermatic shutter, all American made. The film inside is Super Pancro Press Type B. A flashbulb is always used, since most pictures are taken at night. But even when shots are made by daylight, the flash is still used. A Graflex flash synchronizer is employed. Exposure is always the same: 1/200 of a second, stop f/16. That is, at a distance of ten feet. At six feet, it may be stepped down to f/32. Focusing is always at either ten or six feet.

There is no time for anything else on a story.

3

The Curious Ones

The girl releases her cat's neck, her hands still arched around its belly, ready to grab. The animal inches forward to sniff the camera.

Ignoring her question, which lingers in the air like a prostitute's recriminatory perfume, Weegee continues to drive down Forty-second Street, past crowds outside theaters and bars, idlers and gawkers, lovers and fighters, musicians and sailors, the people of a sleepless New York poised on the precipice of another Sunday morning hangover. He's wondering just how seriously he'll have to take this phantom.

It's a slow night, though still early. Weegee is jumpy, anxious for distraction, despite the fact that something always happens, and he always turns up just in time to capture it. It's the girl making him nervous, isn't it? He reaches forward and twiddles the Rossini to soften it slightly, then turns up the police radio, alert to any news that might concern him. The radio gives out a soft babble, like the voice of a crowd, teasing him with the sense of speech but no actual words. But he rarely needs the police; he gets his instructions from somewhere else.

The car slides over the streets like the planchette on a grimy Ouija board, spelling out clues he's too close to read, rolling over letters in ripped-up broadsides, smashing the labels on bottles and cans; ghost fingers move him this way and that, from "Hello" to "Goodbye." Sometimes he thinks that if he takes his hands off the wheel, the car will keep driving, taking him to another crime's aftermath, another dark scene that is his alone to illuminate. Something is coming, something developing in this Darkroom the size of Manhattan. He's at the mercy of forces that make him feel small and alone. Ghost fingers tickle the back of his neck.

But it's the kitten's whiskers. The creature comes crawling over the back of the seat, hunting for the salami. Instinctively he reaches for the camera, pulling it toward him, as if the cat had any interest in it.

"Where did you get it?"

Against his better judgment, Weegee answers her question with another.

"Get what?"

"The camera."

The question makes no sense. He's always had the camera. There was never a time without it, this appendage vital as his hand, foot, or balls. So baffled is Weegee that all he can do is repeat her last words.

"The camera?"

The girl unselfconsciously lifts one arm and scratches her downy pit. The breast on that side flattens, the pink nipple rising slightly up her ribcage.

The kid yawns, and Weegee thinks, *Kinda late for her to be up. Kids need their sleep. . . .*

Finished with her yawn, she says, "You don't remember, do you? Here." She reaches out and touches his face.

Spirit fingers, driving him. . . .

4

Harlem

Arthur Fellig dozes one night under newspapers in Bryant Park, behind the library. It's his favorite midtown spot. Normally, the cops don't bother anyone flopping here. But tonight is different. Fellig is rousted by a nightstick-wielding bull who sends him and all the other homeless bums out to wander the sidewalks of this gay and heartless burg.

The night before last, he was in the Municipal Lodging House down in the Bowery. Five nickels a night, but he ran out of nickels. On the way out, he noticed for the first time the big sign posted over the desk.

Paul Di Filippo

DEPOSIT CASH
AND VALUABLES
WITH THE
CASHIER
BEFORE GOING DOWNSTAIRS

Fellig began to laugh insanely, till tears coursed his stubbled cheeks. "Cash!" he choked. "Valuables!" He imagined a wall-safe full of pocket lint and bottlecaps.

Now, heading uptown, bracing himself against the winter winds, Fellig feels like ratshit. His stomach is gnawing itself, his mouth tastes like sour apple wine, his feet inside shoes whose soles flap with each step are starting to burn. He has no prospects, no skills, no friends.

He's standing outside a furniture store window. The sight of a bed with white sheets is almost enough to drive him crazy. It looks like the most desirable thing in the world.

Tearing himself away, he strides madly off, bumping solid citizens without concern.

He finds himself at the Hudson. The water looks as inviting as a woman's spread legs. Fellig pictures himself jumping, the splash—

Just then, a squad car cruises by, inserting its unwelcome presence into his morbid fantasy. The cop hears the splash . . . he jumps out, takes off his hat, his coat, his shoes, then his pants, which he rolls up in a bundle to hide and also protect his gun . . . places all of them on the edge of the pier . . . and jumps into the icy water in his shirt and underwear, cursing. After a rescue the cop always has to take the trip to the hospital along with the would-be suicide to get thawed out . . . they have equal chances of catching pneumonia.

"Move along, buddy."

Fellig pushes on, heading north along the West Side.

At 127th Street, he turns east.

He's in Harlem now.

Fellig's always gotten along good with coloreds. He's got no beef against them. Discrimination seems so stupid and ugly to him. They're all human, ain't they? They can all laugh, all cry.

He wonders, But can they sleep?

He feels a little more at ease up here. The people around him seem content somehow, despite a grinding poverty almost as bad as his. Fellig's spirits lift a bit. Might be a chance of a handout somewhere here. . . .

Fellig passes a church. A huge banner reads:

AFTER DEATH—WHAT?
REVIVAL MEETING

He hits Lenox Avenue, stopped short by a store at the corner.

(ALLEGED)
YOGI AND PROF. NIGER
ALL HINDU COSMETICS, OILS AND INCENSE
6TH AND 7TH BOOKS OF MOSES
LODESTONES—DREAM BOOKS
SPIRITUAL ADVISER—RELIGIOUS ARTICLES
7 KEYS OF POWER

It's the "alleged" that piques Fellig enough to make him enter, tickles the ragged remnants of his sense of humor.

There's a rack of colorful pulp-paper dream-interpretation books. Many shelves hold two-quart Mason jars with handwritten labels: Hindu Commanding Incense, Hindu Magnet Incense, Hindu Conqueror Root. . . . Tinted apothecary bottles are filled with any-colored liquids. A framed portrait of a turbaned swami hangs next to one of Father Divine.

The black man behind the counter sports a crop of white hair beneath his tasseled fez, but his thin mustache is still dark as coal. His large nose supports a pair of pince-nez glasses.

"How may I help you, son?" asks the proprietor in a serious, resonant voice.

Fellig flips a thumb up and back, indicating not the punched-tin ceiling but a spot outside, above the door.

"You the 'alleged' Professor Niger?"

The black man lets out a booming laugh. "At your service. And you must be the 'alleged' Weegee. I'd know your face anywhere."

Fellig takes a step backward. The name sounds familiar, but in a way that frightens him. A long-buried memory nudges its way to the surface, floating up from a grave of old newspapers, broken tarmac and wornout tires.

(Small fingers brush his cheek . . . come out tonight, come out . . . remember . . . ?)

"My name's Fellig," he says sharply.

Niger narrows his eyes and reaches under the counter. For a minute Fellig thinks he may be going for a gun; he tenses, backing off, spreading his hands to show he means no harm.

"Then this isn't yours?"

The Professor lays a camera on the counter. Fellig stares. Almost remembering. Before the nights of rambling, before the drunken sleepless bouts of twisting on pews in the Bowery Allnight Mission, there was another time. Another name. . . .

And a camera. This camera.

His?

His attention is caught in the burnished aluminum reflector that surrounds the empty socket where the flashbulb will fit. All the meager light in the store suddenly seems concentrated in the polished bowl, with his warped reflection at the center instead of a bulb. Fellig is blinded, as if he had been staring at the sun, as if the nonexistent bulb had just gone off in his face.

When he recovers his eyesight, all is as before.

Except that his hunger and aches are gone.

How had he ever forgotten? How had he spent all this time wandering in a dark city? When had they become separated?

"Got any money on you, son?"

He checks his pockets, wondering if there's anything else he might have forgotten. But they're empty. He shakes his head.

"Sheeit. Well, I promised to hold this till you come for it, without no word of no payment, so I'spect you can have it anyhow."

Professor Niger pushes it toward him, across the counter. He reaches for it, hesitant, wondering how much more he can remember.

"Take it, alleged Weegee."

"My name's Fellig," he mumbles, voicing his last doubts; but as soon as he touches the camera he knows that's not true anymore. All doubt is gone.

He's Weegee now.

Carrying his moments of split-second light forever through the city of never-ending night.

5

Psychic Photography

The camera takes the pictures.

The camera makes the pictures.

Weegee is convinced of this.

Whatever it is, wherever it came from, whether crafted by hands angelic or satanic, the Speed Graphic is more than just metal and glass. It, not he, is the doer, the actor, the Prime Mover. Weegee is only the instrument, the vessel, the driver and hustler who delivers the camera to its chosen sites; his hands cradle but cannot really even be said to point the thing.

Without the camera's presence, the incidents he "photographs" might never happen, or would happen differently.

It is a heavy burden, especially when he considers all the death he has photographed.

Death. He is known for death, yet death is only part of what he knows. Can't the camera see there's more to life than its climax, must be more!

The shots of lovers on the beach, the children sleeping peacefully on the tenement fire escapes, the happy barflies and lushes, the hot jazzmen, the Village artists and their free-spirited babes, the nurse pushing a carriage, the baker delivering bagels—

Weegee weighs all these shots against the others, the charred corpses, the burning buildings, the gutshot crooks, the suicides with brains blown out, the hit-and-run victims, the drowned secretaries, the murdered bocce ball player, the crushed stampede victims—

Which way does the balance tip? He's afraid he knows.

If Weegee has any training in photography, he can't remember it. And it would be irrelevant. The camera knows what it needs. He suspects that even his primitive alteration of the aperture makes no difference.

Yet he continues to put his eye to the viewfinder, as if it might take him somewhere, show him a way out of the darkness.

And it's always dark in there, always a vagueness and a seethe of unstoppable motion and form, until suddenly he senses the flash quivering, the lens lusting. At this point, Weegee becomes one with the camera. He has teamed to estimate the forms of darkness, a kind of divination prior to the fulfillment of the flash. A struggle of forms, a tangle of shadows. He moves toward the heart of it, waiting until the sounds and movements reach such a peak that he knows he's at the center of the blackest moment. And then, his one (perhaps needless) contribution, he thrusts the camera into the formless sprawl and tries to press the already self-descending button. Too late. There it is, the unchangeable result of his photography, limned in the unforgiving light, a revelation to him as much as anyone. The most fleeting possible light, yet the subject's fate has been fixed forever.

Often he doesn't know what he's seen until later, after development. And then he feels the guilt—or, more rarely, the joy—attendant on aiding the scene's real creator. For he is at best a collaborator, along with darkness, light, and above all else the camera. His flash has created the moment by isolating it—a moment that might have gone another way, been forever lost in the rush of time and in the dark, its syrupy edges blending in with the rest of the night, as if it had no special value save that which he gave it.

Even the seemingly neutral shots—a stack of newspapers on the sidewalk; a car covered in snow, its lines resembling a woman's haunches; his favorite skyscraper, Sixty Wall Street Tower, hanging at the lingering edge of a dawn that never comes—press down on his conscience, as if by putting them on film he has ineluctably tampered with their true selves.

Once he set the Speed Graphic down on the bar at Sammy's, needing both hands to pick up an overstuffed ham on rye from the free dinner platter. He turned to find Sammy joshingly aiming the camera at him.

Sammy, bearing no grudge, poured drinks for the next month with a splinted forefinger.

6
Sudden Death

The girl eyes Weegee with a look he's seen before. It's the look a high-society dame lays on her diamonds, the one a gal at Coney Island gives the boyfriend who just managed to win her a stuffed owl; it's the look a Death Row hood turns on the electric chair at Sing Sing. A look of total possession and absorption, subject and object merging into one, fatalistic but underpinned with dread.

Dread of the inevitable loss time brings: loss of the boodle, the boyfriend—specifically, of life.

"You remember now?" says the girl. Ribs of light and shadow slide across her face like the bars of a portable prison.

"Yeah, I remember."

The girl pets her cat thoughtfully, no longer regarding him. Weegee takes the opportunity to ask, "So—what's your story?"

"It's part of yours."

He expects a mischievous smile, but she looks serious, even grim.

"I mean, what's your name?"

"Tara."

"Like *Gone with the Wind*, huh?"

"No."

Before Weegee can question Tara further, the police radio dispatcher, speaking plainly for the moment, broadcasts the code for the discovery of a fresh stiff (Weegee knows all the codes), along with an address down in the Bowery.

Luckily, Times Square lies just ahead, bright as the shine on a salesman's shoes. Weegee whips the big Chevy onto Broadway in a screech of tires and roars off downtown.

The lights and traffic are all with him. The other cars seem to give way around him, letting him pass, knowing he has pressing business, as if he were a cop car with siren wailing. He's never had a run quite like this, and he's had doozies. His car melts away hindrances like Sinatra mows down teenagers.

It seems like only seconds before he's nudging the curb with his wheels, nosing in behind two cop cars. He bolts out of the Chevy, camera in hand.

The corpse lies on the granite sidewalk, in a pool of congealing gutter-bound blood. A cane he'll never need again waits patiently by his limp hand. The corpse is conveniently situated in front of a meat store. The fire escape above the store is draped with an NRA banner:

TIME IS SHORT
EVERY MINUTE COUNTS

There's a crowd of spectators—there's always a crowd of spectators—held back by cops. Weegee recognizes several flatfoots.

"O'Malley, Johnson, how about letting me through?"

"Sure thing, Weegee."

Somehow, Weegee senses that Tara's trailing along behind him. The cops make no move to stop her.

When Weegee breaks through into the charmed circle, he spots the corpse.

He's seen him somewhere before, another shabby figure roaming the streets, at the edge of the crowds, maybe watching a fire or bumming change. So familiar is the dead man that Weegee even imagines he's some former public figure fallen from favor, some guy who once towered on the courthouse steps years ago, but has long since been consigned to a wino's belly-dragging existence.

But then the sight of some of the man's spilled wares fixes his ID.

It's Tobacco Jack, the pencil-seller. The chaw that gave him his nickname now contributes a brown runnel out of the corner of Jack's slack lips to the larger flow of blood.

Weegee's attention is suddenly drawn to half a dozen pencils still poking from the inner pocket of Jack's coat. Their erasers are a shiny pink, brand new, so unlike the weather-scoured, blood-dappled gangrenous gray of Jack's own flesh—

The camera is tugging at his arm, insistent. Shaking himself, Weegee tries to move in closer, thrusting aside all memories of Jack as a once-living individual, now eager only to get the demanded shot.

A sergeant shoves him back. "Not this one, Weegee. Detective Trevino don't want no press on this one."

"Whadda ya mean?" demands Weegee. "It's just another bum murdered for his spare change. . . . Ain't it?"

An ambulance has arrived. Stretcher-bearers are now approaching the corpse, along with a useless priest from the parish church that towers across the street.

The sergeant's attention is diverted by the newcomers.

Weegee seizes his chance.

Going below the cop's broad back, Weegee kneels along with the bearers in the brutal street, oil or blood soaking into his pants leg. He lifts his lens and sights through it numbly, letting the camera have its way. It's dark inside the viewing glass—even darker than the street. Then he sees a cop's flashlight roving the crumpled body, snagging on its features, isolating bits of the corpse, giving them an importance they might actually deserve.

The stretcher-bearers move in closer, as if to cradle the man in their own arms, to bear him away in his old tweed coat like ascending angels. One of the bearers lays a hand on the stiff's hip and rolls it onto the stretcher.

A cop shouts, "No, not that way!"

The crowd sucks in a collective gasp of horror.

Weegee shoots.

His flash freezes everything.

The body is tumbling into the stretcher.

But Tobacco Jack's head remains behind, rooted to the sidewalk.

There it is, fixed forever by Weegee's intervention, the ultimate violation.

The cop who warned Weegee off breaks the spell. He drags Weegee to his feet, pushes him away, yelling, "Geddoutta here, you snoopy bastid! I should smash that goddamn camera of yours!"

Weegee needs no further prod: scramming is all he wants to do.

The crowd and the cops now close in around the corpse, shutting out the sight, spinning Weegee blinded into the night.

He leans against his car, gasping, winded, frightened, still seeing Jack's head like the trophy of some saloon Salomé. His feelings of revulsion and pity are tremendous, even greater than when he shot the woman watching her daughter and granddaughter perish in flames. Yet at the same time, with a deep sense of shame and disgust, he wants to study the image more carefully, to see the moment he captured on film. He wonders if he should open the trunk and get to work developing the neg. Before he knows it, he's halfway there, the key out of his pocket.

Then Detective Trevino strolls up.

The dick wears a weary face. The brim of his fedora looks mashed, like he's been working it between his hands.

"Weegee. How's tricks?"

"Not bad. Till just now."

Trevino sighs. "I know. This is a nasty one. Ever heard of the Human Head Cakebox Murderer?"

Weegee feels a sickening pang, deep in his gut. Another memory is wrenched out of the cold muck and freezing mire like a week-old drowned man being hauled from the East River—hardly recognizable. He can't let on that the name alone makes him nervous. Something fearful is developing but it's nothing to do with him.

He forces a grin for the cop's benefit. "Nope."

Trevino smiles wryly. "Finally, a case we managed to keep secret from Weegee the All-knowing. I'm pleased as punch, as you can tell from my joyful mug. Well, you just saw some of his handiwork. Appears he was interrupted before he had a chance to stuff the head into a cakebox like he usually does. But his signature's all over the job. Not only that, but the description given by the witnesses who spooked him tallies with what we already knew. The nutcase who does this wears some kinda weird getup, a regular ten-cent comic book villain."

Trevino pauses. Weegee suddenly notices Tara sitting on the hood of the Chevy, legs splayed immodestly, her cat beside her. Absentmindedly, Trevino reaches back and strokes the kitten. Weegee almost chokes on the dead butt of his stogie.

Trevino stops petting the cat and sighs. "We can't let you use that shot, Weegee. At least not right away. Number one, we don't want to encourage any copycat killers. Number two, we don't want any false confessions, so the fewer details out there the better. Number three—"

"That's enough numbers, Tony, I get the picture."

"That's what I'd expect from the famous Weegee."

"Ha. You know *Life*'s paying thirty-five bucks for a good murder, don't you?"

"You want it outta my pocket?"

"Just thought I'd mention it."

"Yeah, well, you'll get it eventually, just not right now. Be patient. Listen, I gotta move. Jesus, I don't know how the fuck I'm gonna get to sleep when my shift's over."

"At least your shift's got an end."

Trevino looks at him nervously, as if Weegee has just brought up something forbidden. "Of course it does. Of course. . . ." But there's a question in his voice.

As soon as Trevino turns away, Weegee tosses the Speed Graphic down on the seat and climbs in. Tara's already there. He jabs the starter button, twisting the key, and the car rumbles to life.

Moving again, he feels oddly at ease, as if he's on a barge drifting effortlessly with the current. Forget about ghosts, or strange powers pushing him. No need to reach for wild explanations. The fact is, Weegee knows this night city better than the inside of his eyelids. Prop the camera on the dashboard and let it scout the streets, let it do the driving. If he were to go blind, he would never be lost; he could probably keep driving with both eyes poked out.

Or with his head missing.

7

The Bowery

At 267 Bowery, sandwiched between missions and quarter-a-night flophouses, is Sammy's, the poor man's Stork Club. There is no cover charge nor cigarette girl. Neither is there a hatcheck girl: patrons prefer to dance with their hats and coats on. But there is a lively floor show . . . the only saloon on the Bowery with a cabaret license.

After midnight, some odd types always drop in for a quick one. There's a woman called "Pruneface," a man called "Horseface" . . . Ethel, the queen of the Bowery, generally sports a pair of black eyes nature did not give her. A gent with a long white beard continually claims he is looking all over for the man who stole his wife forty years ago. Old-timers wonder whether, when thief and victim meet, the wife-stealer will get beat up or thanked.

Tonight, as on many nights, Weegee is one of the early morning drop-ins.

On the stage, in front of the gallery of framed photos, some of them Weegee's, a 250-pound woman named Norma, in yards of satin and pounds of makeup, belts out "Don't Sit under the Apple Tree." A tuxedoed man is drunkenly nuzzling a live pig lying on a tabletop. Two female imposters have picked up an unwitting sailor.

There's a burly dwarf standing at Weegee's left, dressed in nothing but a paper hat and grubby diaper while quaffing his foamy draft brew. There were numbers on the hat once, 1940-something, but now only the peeling "1" remains. The costume is a leftover from a New Year's Eve party, but here it's always the stroke of midnight, always the edge of the same old New Year, and even that turns stale and flat, like the blackened confetti trodden thick as sawdust underfoot.

Although the floor is a throng of bodies packed cheek by jowl, and although all the seats at the gingham-covered tables are taken, no one moves to occupy the spot at Weegee's right where Tara stands, her chin barely clearing the bar. No one acknowledges the presence of the half-bare waif either.

Sammy brings Weegee his customary boilermaker.

Reaching for the beer stein, Weegee finds his hand quivering.

Over the hubbub, Sammy says, "Take a photo with those jitters, and it'll look like ya shootin' an earthquake."

"Tell me something new."

Sammy's face grows concerned. "Ya okay, Weegee?"

"Yeah. I just need some rest."

"Well, what's stoppin' ya?"

"My camera."

"Ha! That's a good one!"

Weegee downs his shot. Then he rests his head on the bar.

Behind his back, the raucous life of the saloon continues. Sounds convey the scenes he knows so well. Two old broads, Mabel and Flo, are hoofing it on stage, decked out in dresses that were old when vaudeville was young. Pretzel and hot dog vendors have entered, making their pitch.

Weegee feels half dead. Is the only time he's alive when he's looking through his camera? He's forgotten what he does during the day. Sleep, mostly. . . . Or does he? Maybe he just goes into some kind of Buck Rogers suspended animation when the camera doesn't need him. He can't be sure. . . .

From his right elbow comes a too-familiar voice.

"What would make you happy?"

Weegee raises his head. Tara's standing on the brass rail, bobby-soxed feet arched over it. Her cat's drinking slops on the mahogany bartop.

"I just wanna sleep," he says.

"So why don't you?"

"Do you do whatever you want? For instance, did you ask to show up on my front seat tonight?"

She shakes her head solemnly. "You did."

"Me?"

She leans forward and touches his hand, speaking more urgently now. "Why can't you sleep, Weegee?"

"Jesus, what do you think? It's the goddamn camera!"

Everyone stares at him for a second; Sammy's should never be so quiet. He sinks into his shoulders, embarrassed, while the sound level creeps back up again.

"I'm sorry I yelled," he mumbles, close to the girl's pretty pink ear. "I don't mean to snap at you. It's just . . . the camera won't let me stop. Ever since I got it, I feel like I'm its damn slave. It wants shots, you know? Vivid, heartstopping, bloody, tragic shots! If only I could find the ultimate shot, then maybe it would let me be. Maybe then I could rest."

"I know what it wants," she says, with such confidence that he believes her instantly.

"How could you?" he says.

"Because I came out of it. Just like you."

"You came—what are you talking about?"

"What if you could photograph the Cakebox Murderer? Catch him in the act?"

Again, at that name, Weegee feels revulsion like vomit rising up in him. Something horrible is being invoked—a murderer, out there, wandering the city, severing heads. Nothing to do with him—but then why does he take it so personally?

"I know where to find him," she says.

"You're full of shit."

"No I'm not."

Despite himself, Weegee finds himself believing her. After all, she's a spook, isn't she? In touch with the night city. One of them.

"Why are you doing this?" he asks. "Why are you here? What do you want from me?"

"I'll tell you when you screw me," she says flatly. Weegee cringes and glances around nervously, but no one looks their way. He might as well be standing at the bar talking to himself.

Weegee hangs his head again. When he lifts it, he prays Tara will be gone.

She isn't. And in her eyes is something that makes her look very old, as old as the eternal city, the endless night. As if this childish form is not her true one, but only a facet of it, something to win his confidence.

"Well . . . I know a place," he says.

8

Subcellar Ball

Two walls of the basement are brick; two are raw, unfinished rock. Gurgling waste pipes run across the walls like cell bars. In one corner crouches the huge bulk of an asbestos-clad furnace, giving off a stink of heating oil like Manhattan's own minor Moloch. The furnishings of the basement consist of some tin pails and bushel baskets, an old steamer trunk and a water-spotted mattress.

Weegee can't bring himself to take Tara to his cheap apartment. Instead, he drags this ghost of his own sick mind to this cellar, where a friendly building superintendent frequently lets jazz musicians hold a jam.

He tries to rationalize what he's doing by reminding himself that she's only a phantom.

But the hot touch of her hand rips this last defense away.

Under her skirt the girl wears white cotton panties hand-embroidered with pink roses around the waist. Weegee worries they'll get dirty when they hit the floor, especially when the kitten curls up on them.

She kneels on the mattress in front of him.

Weegee pauses behind her momentarily, his own wool pants around his knees.

"You're not real," he whispers. "You aren't, are you?"

Tara looks backwards over her shoulder. "No. But you aren't either."

"You got things mixed up, kid. I'm Weegee. I'm famous."

"You're the 'alleged' Weegee. You're only supposed to be him." She turns toward him. "Take that off."

He looks down. He's still got the camera slung over his shoulder, bumping against his bare waist. She moves to touch it, but he stops her hands. "No."

"You have to. Please."

He relaxes slightly, helps her lift the thing, her small hands moving under his own. They set it gently on the floor, and at the last moment she turns it so it faces away from them, the lens looking into a corner, oddly forlorn for an inanimate object. Weegee feels guilty relief. He's tempted to reach out, to stroke it again—but she catches his hand and brings it toward her, placing it on her breast. Her lips tremble and her eyes lock onto his, young again, innocent.

"I—I can't do this," he whispers. "You're young enough to be my daughter."

She moves closer, pressing against him, her lips against his ear. "I am your daughter."

Weegee struggles, but his ankles are caught in his pants, he can't move away. Her arms lock around him, holding with a gentle pressure.

"And your sister. And yourself," she says. "We're the same stuff. I had to get close enough to tell you, without the camera between us."

"Tell me . . ." he gasps.

"You're safe—this is all we have to do. We're neither of us whole, alleged Weegee."

"Why do you keep calling me that?"

"Because you're not the real Weegee, no more than I'm a real girl, or this is the real New York. We're both photographs, don't you see? We're pictures the real Weegee, whoever he was, took. This is his city."

"You're crazy!" he says.

"Don't be afraid of me. Don't be ashamed. It wasn't you who caught me sleeping—it was Weegee. He caught you, too! None of this is our fault, but we're stuck here until somehow we undo it."

"Photographs! This is insane! I don't know what you are, but I'm alive. I've got things to do, pictures to take, unfinished business—"

"You think it's the camera driving you, Weegee, but really it's you. You're the one with the power. The one full of need. Have you looked at yourself, Weegee? Have you ever really looked at yourself?"

She lets go of him now, and he stumbles back, grabbing for his clothes, his camera. She snatches up a chipped piece of mirror lying in a corner, and holds it out to him.

"Look!" she says.

"Get away from me!"

But he's already seen. . . .

A face bent and bubbling like a Coke bottle melted in a bonfire, the left eye huge and endlessly gaping, the other forever squinting as if through a viewfinder; his nose squashed and flattened. It's not a horrible distortion, but it's undeniable. He snatches the mirror from her fingers, hoping it's the fault of the glass. Smashes it down on the bare floor. Staring down into the shards, he sees the same thing. He's a twisted joke, a self-portrait taken in a carnival mirror. . . .

Cool small fingers slide in among his own.

"Now you've met yourself, you're ready to meet him," she says. "He's one of us, too. Part of you and me. Something incomplete we need to finish with."

Weegee—the "alleged" Weegee—can't argue with her. He knows all too well who she's talking about:

That evil, out there in the night. The one with a practical joker's name.

"Where?" he says numbly.

"Not far. Right down here in the Bowery, under our noses. Up on the El."

9

The Best People Go to Heaven

There's no rearview mirror in the coupe, and now he knows why. He must have glimpsed himself once, long ago, and torn it out, starting in on the hard, steady labor of denial.

He speeds along a black and almost empty street, past boarded-up liquor and Optimo cigar stores, decrepit brick tenements, shuffling figures wrapped is rags, a few startled souls picked out in his headlamps as if his is the first light they've ever seen, blinding them like cave creatures.

Suddenly, Tara issues an order.

"Turn here."

He throws the wheel hard to the right into a sharp, spiraling turn that takes him down some impossible concrete chute, his headlights scraping down and down over a dead gray wall that looks like raw dirt, with twisted strands of roots or maybe frayed electric cable poking out of it. After an implausibly long time the spiral straightens out, depositing him on a long dark avenue, and he finally spots something he recognizes.

Skeletal metal rises ahead of him, black columns lining the avenue, joining overhead.

The El.

Odd, there's no moon or stars tonight, only a weird light the likes of which he's never seen. The whole city seems to be melting, shimmering beneath the humid sky that's like the moist ceiling of an underwater cavern pressing down.

In the morning, he knows, the sun will shine through these tracks in beautiful black and gold patterns, giving meaning to the lives of forgotten men. He'll be asleep then, in the morning, but it means something to him to know that others will see it.

If that morning ever comes. . . .

Now he's zooming through the aisle of metal columns; they're like corroded iron trees lining the avenues of an eerie, broken-down industrial estate. The complicated ironwork seems to continue overhead and on either side for an infinite distance.

The police radio has been dead for a while, though Tara is guide enough. But suddenly the classical station, barely a whisper anyway, dies out too. The signal is lost under so much metal, so much earth. Ugly static pours from the speakers till Tara turns it off. He finds her movement reassuring, because it has occurred to him that he might lose her too.

"Just up ahead." Weegee spots a staircase, iron treads rising up to the level where the trains ride the trestles.

He brakes the car alongside the stairs, still in the shadows of the girders.

He quickly loads the Speed Graphic. Then he gets out.

Tara follows silently.

There are no cars, no people. Where are the inevitable spectators he's so used to? Nowhere to be seen. He longs for the vapid parties he occasionally covers, socialites and dancers, smiles and fast friends, quick kisses in the dark, the simultaneous pop of the flash and the cork, as the champagne spills from the stem of the bottle, spills like the light from his bulbs, or the flood of images pouring through his mind as he slows his step and hesitates at the foot of the staircase with its switchbacks.

The camera draws him upward.

At the first switchback, Weegee looks down. A column blocks his sight of the car. The street seems wreathed in a newly risen mist. Weegee grows dizzy on the stairs. Gravity always claims you in the end. The dead fall down, death doesn't move, it lies down forever while other crimes scurry off into shadows, fugitive, leading to pursuit and threatening shouts, guns fired, all that busy activity of life. That's how he knows he's alive, that whatever this long night is, it isn't death. Maybe Tara's right after all. Maybe this place is just a photograph or a heap of them, collaged together, linked only by the eye that took them. Wherever that eye may be now, the images live on.

"Go on," chides Tara. "Up."

Yes, up. Don't pause to look back. Up to the open air, the stars, the bustle of trains and life. Leave the car behind, catch a homeward train and be out of here, recover the disguises and the rubber boots another time. . . .

At last, after many turns, he gains the platform.

It's dark, striped with shadows, empty. Except for something pink resting on a bench.

Weegee moves closer.

The focus is always six or ten feet, even for close-ups. . . .

The pink object resolves itself into an innocuous cakebox. That's all. An innocent thing, tied up with a string, left behind by a sleepy purchaser. Just a cakebox, whether forgotten or abandoned. Weegee's curious about what it contains. Maybe it's canoli or creampuffs or crunchy *chruscik*. Anything but a human head.

Approaching the box, Weegee imagines calling the cops to announce his find, without telling them of its innocence.

How they'll laugh, opening the box to share the pastry right here on the tracks in the dark! Now that'll be a picture, a bunch of cops with crumbs and frosting, or powdered sugar on their faces and fingers, caught in his flash like guilty kids raiding an icebox.

At the box, Weegee defiantly, resolutely snaps the string and lifts the lid.

It's empty.

The weighted wooden shaft catches him slantwise across the neck and skull and sends him crashing down.

The Speed Graphic—his talisman, his demon, his identity—skitters away, across the platform. He feels all his power going with it.

Despite the immense pain lighting up the inside of his skull like God's own flashbulb, Weegee manages to crawl a few feet and turn, but he's never felt so vulnerable, so lost. Without his camera, what can he do? He's nothing without it. Sights come and go in the darkness—he illuminates none of them, understands and communicates nothing.

It is his time to die, isn't it? He's outlived his usefulness.

His right eye is swimming in blood, the left one bulging as if ready to pop from the socket. He looks up to see how it will end.

Evil stands at the edge of a shadow, half in darkness, half in light. There's something of each of them in the figure and something that just looks wrong.

The Cakebox Murderer wears a fantastic suit contrived of mismatched odds and ends. On his head is an air-raid warden's metal helmet fastened under the chin. His face is swathed in thin muslin. His eyes are covered with welder's goggles. His torso is bulked out with layers of cloth, canvas, and rubber. Several pairs of pants balloon around his legs. Strapped to his shoes are blocks of wood wrapped in cloth to make him look taller and to soften his steps. But none of this is the strangest part.

In one rubber-gloved hand he holds his nail-studded bludgeon.

In the other, a crusted hacksaw.

But those are easy enough to believe in.

It's something else that mystifies Weegee.

He struggles to rise, but slumps back, dizzied and weak.

The Cakebox Murderer slowly advances. As he separates fully from the shadows, Weegee figures out what it is that looks so damn strange about him.

Everything about him is reversed. Where his hacksaw should reflect highlights of the platform lamps, it throws off black sparks. Where the folds of his absurd costume should gather in shadow, instead they envelop faint dustings of light. He drinks in the light and turns it to darkness, and casts back darkness like another kind of light. This is a creature that vanishes in daylight—a monster that glows in the dark.

The sort of thing that would haunt a photograph.

Weegee murmurs helplessly, "Tara. . . ." He looks painfully around for her form—

There she is.

The Speed Graphic is in her hands.

Somehow he can tell that the stupid kid has the focus set on infinity.

Tara's expression is invisible beneath the camera poised expertly in front of her face. But Weegee knows she's smiling for the first time that night.

"Say cheese!"

The Cakebox Murderer spins and hurls himself at her, a blur of reversed edges, moving faster than she's prepared for. Weegee cries out, but too late. The bar crashes down, crunching into the camera, shattering the bulb and the metal reflector, totaling the case, turning the lens to crushed ice, wrecking the film inside. The twisted metal drops from Tara's bleeding hands. She stares down at it, her face blank with terror, absorbed in the loss. He remembers her saying, *I came out of it.* And now that God is dead. . . .

But the Human Head Cakebox Murderer lives. He raises his bar again, covering her in his luminous shadow. She stares up in paralyzed submission—

And Weegee screams. Not with his mouth, but with his eyes.

Searing white light pours over the monster. Shadows leap into sudden intensity, seeming to set the platform on fire. The murderer's hue shifts from light to dark, dark to light, searing in places. The creature turns, throwing up its arm to ward off the flash that comes pouring out of Weegee's eyes. But the light ignites the smoked-glass lenses; they focus the rays inward, cooking out the sick brain, cauterizing whatever vile impulses drive him—

The monster howls, its shadow now a stain of almost total blackness, down in the depths of which Weegee barely sees Tara cowering—but safe.

The light fades slowly from Weegee's eyes, and he thinks, *She was right. It was me all along, and not the camera.*

The camera is a small pile of slag but he doesn't need it now. It can't rule him. And the creature cannot frighten him or anyone now. It totters blindly about, groping at air, its costume in rags, seared to ashes, blistering, blackened.

Weegee finds the strength to stand. He pushes past the creature, intending only to grab Tara and run, but Weegee misjudges his force and the murderer trips on his clumsy clogs, falling sideways, flailing. The madman catches the railing with his gut and goes over.

The sound the body makes hitting the street is a familiar one. Still, Weegee leans over the railing to make sure of it.

It's dark in the depths beneath the track, and he's somewhat blinded himself. Hard to tell exactly what he's seeing. But somehow it's not nearly as dark as it's been. A subtle light is growing all around him, buzzing between the girders, as if the light from his eyes had leaked into the sky and set off a chain reaction.

He backs up laughing. "Dawn!" he shouts. The trestles and tracks and ironwork angles are threatening to turn to gold. He turns to find Tara, to share it with her. Dawn is coming to the city!

But he's alone on the platform. Nothing remains of the struggle but a small sprinkling of shattered glass. He kneels and touches a finger to it, sees the stuff glisten with the imminent light; on an impulse, he puts it to his tongue, and grins. Not glass.

Sugar.

It tastes the way he feels. It tastes like the pictures he'll take from now on.

Right then and there, he resolves to cut the wires of the police radio in his car. He's through with chasing ambulances, through with being haunted. He's been saturated with the tears of women and the sight of impoverished children sleeping on fire escapes. From now on, he'll do all his shooting by daylight. He'll sleep only at night.

He looks up through the girders at the pinkening sky, and wonders.

What if night never comes?

THE HORROR WRITER

There were figures in the yellow wallpaper.

Moving figures.

He *knew* it, despite what anyone else said they saw. The wallpaper was in his bedroom. His wife had chosen it. Today a contractor was coming over to give an estimate on repapering the room.

The doorbell rang. Its chimes resounded in his skull like the bells of a Black Mass. His wife had chosen the chimes too. They played the theme from the first movie made from one of his novels. He would ask the contractor about also replacing those.

The man on the doorstep was one of those hideously inbred locals, his features a sludge of genetic debris. Hardly able to keep his eyes on the man, the Horror Writer fixed his gaze on the tall wrought iron fence in the distance that surrounded his property.

"Mister Prinze . . . ?" said the contractor, obviously a bit confounded. It was not that there was any mistaking the Horror Writer's famous face. No, it must be the intensity of his certitude. Yes, that was it. The Horror Writer's unswerving moral vision in the face of the terrible evil around him—evil that would have overwhelmed a lesser mortal—must have impinged, however dimly, on the contractor's dull mind.

"You okay, Mister Prinze?"

The Horror Writer roused himself. This was no time for hesitation or inaction. If he was ever to surmount the accursed forces that had gripped his world, he would have to move fast.

"I'm fine," he said gruffly. "Let's look at the room."

Opening the bedroom door with the contractor by his side, the Horror Writer recoiled in shock.

The figures were much more pronounced today, their warty faces contorting into obscene leers at his presence as they scampered around in their two-dimensional space. If they were ever to escape into the world of mankind—

"This the room?" said the contractor, brushing past the Horror Writer, his primitive senses oblivious to the menace contained within.

It was all the Horror Writer could do to step into the bedroom with the ignorant local. He had to take the risk, though—

"Ayup, I remember when Miz Prinze picked this pattern out. We didn't spare no expense, no sir. Seems a shame somehow to change it now, while it's practically brand-new. . . ."

What a fool he had been! How could he have forgotten? This was the very same dupe who had hung the original wallpaper. Dupe? No, of course not! This man was in collusion with his wife! Together, they had conspired to paper his bedroom with this transdimensional portal, knowing that at the proper cosmic moment it would open, sucking him through to an eternity of torture!

The Horror Writer resolved to test his theory, although he had no real doubts.

"I want this paper stripped off. Not a shred of it must remain."

"Stripped? That don't seem strictly necessary, Mister Prinze. Mighty big job, and a waste of time to boot. We'll just put the new paper up on top of it—"

"Get out! Get out of my house right now!"

The Horror Writer hustled the stunned man down to the front door.

"What kind of fool do you take me for? I can read your every thought! Get back to your bestial otherworld masters! Tell them I won't be taken so easily. I've got powers! I know who to contact! I'm not alone against you!"

The contractor picked his cap up off the ground and dusted it before repositioning it atop his head.

"I know you're busted up about your wife, Mister Prinze, but that ain't no reason—"

"Get out! There are still places beyond your reach!"

The contractor shook his head, climbed into his truck and drove away.

The Horror Writer would sleep on the couch from now on.

There were many other steps he could take.

* * *

His cat was missing.

He had called it for an hour that morning, but it had not come.

He knew his enemies had taken it, to use against him.

Hostages to fortune, that's all loved ones were.

Or what was worse—traitors!

Now, against nigh-insurmountable odds, he was forced to search for the animal.

He wondered if he should dig a grave for it in advance.

Arming himself with a stout walking stick and a long sharp kitchen knife, the Horror Writer began a search of his property.

The cat was not in the garage. Nor was it in the barn. But in this latter place, the Horror Writer detected signs of a struggle: some clawed wood, disturbed straw, the half-eaten corpse of a field mouse. Yes, his enemies had taken the cat. Somehow they had gotten past his pentagram and abducted it, probably while he slept and his will was weakened. The animal was probably beyond his help now. Yet still he had to search. He owed it to the dumb beast. Often, they deserved more loyalty than your fellow humans, who would stab you in the back as soon as you looked away.

Haunted woods loomed on three sides of his property, their trees gruesomely contorted like gassed Jews at Auschwitz. He avoided getting within the grasp of their limbs.

By the fence, on the southern side that bordered a neighbor's lot, he found the talisman under a Druidic oak, and knew his doom was closer than he had thought.

The fetish was a small bundle of rabbit fur. Inside were bones and gristle. Probably the remains of his cat—

"Those owls are amazing, aren't they?"

The Horror Writer shot erect with his heart pounding.

Beyond the fence stood his neighbor. By the man's side was his dog. The beast was a huge sheepdog. Its eyes gleamed with more-than-canine intelligence. Saliva drooled from its curled lip. Its teeth looked razor-sharp.

A strong offense would be his best defense, he knew.

"Owls? What owls? Kind of strange to be talking about *owls* in the broad daylight, isn't it?"

His neighbor gestured toward the fetish. "That's an owl's leftovers you've got there. They always wrap it up in a neat bundle. Really something, nature, huh?"

The Horror Writer tossed the bundle down as if it had burned him. "That's what you'd like me to believe, I'm sure."

His neighbor shrugged. "Just the truth." The man turned to go.

At that moment the dog whined and made a move toward the fence.

The knife leaped into the Horror Writer's hand. "Keep that hell-hound away from me! I know what she's done!"

The neighbor patted the dog's head as it scratched behind one ear. "Old Tina? She wouldn't hurt a fly? What's the matter with you, Stefan? Get a grip on yourself. You've been acting kinda crazy lately. . . ."

A stab of pain like a hot poker some evil imp had just thrust into his ear shot through the Horror Writer's head at the mention of the dog's name. "You bastard. Naming that dog after my wife. I hate your fucking guts."

"I've told you a hundred times, Stefan. We owned Tina before you ever moved here. The way you never listen, I swear you think you're the only human on the planet."

The Horror Writer whirled on his opponents and stalked off. The charms he had hung on the fence—weather-stained pages torn at random from his many books—would keep them from following.

The only human— How accurate such a statement sounded now. . . .

All the way back to the house, the Horror Writer could hear the subliminal *thump-thump* of his cat's disembodied spectral heart.

Back in the driveway, something protruding from beneath his car caught his eye.

It was the cat's tail.

He should have guessed. The car had been acting funny lately, almost as if it had a mind of its own. Possession wasn't limited to living beings—

An engine backfired!

The Horror Writer slowly began to retreat from his car. Mustn't let it pin him against the wall—

The mailman's Jeep puffed up the drive. It came to a stop, its engine backfiring once more as the postman turned the key.

"Sorry to bother you, Mister Prinze, but it's a special delivery letter. Need your signature."

With relief, the Horror Writer took the letter without looking at it and signed.

From beneath his car his cat emerged, coming up to the postman and rubbing on the official's ankles.

"Nice kitty," said the postman, bending to pet the cat.

It was then that the Horror Writer noticed.

The postman's back, visible where shirt and trousers gapped, was inhumanly hairy!

Werewolf!

The Horror Writer looked at the letter in his hand.

It was from his wife's lawyer!

Tricked!

"You goddamn son of a bitch!"

The mailman straightened up. "What's the matter, Mister Prinze?"

"Look at those fucking nostrils of yours!"

"You've been working too hard, Mister Prinze. You need a day off."

"I don't take any fucking time off! I'm always ready for trash like you!"

"Everybody needs some time off, Mister Prinze."

"Get the fuck off my land! I'll see you in hell, you Satan-spawn!"

When the mailman had gone, the Horror Writer considered the traitorous cat.

Perhaps he would stake it out for the owls.

*   *   *

There was no other way out.

He would have to physically confront his wife, the spider at the center of the web.

Then maybe this splitting pain behind his eyes—he could envision the doll of him she had fashioned, then repeatedly pierced—would stop.

That evil bitch! Never since Morgan Le Fay had there been a woman as wicked as her!

But it wasn't really her fault, the Horror Writer reminded himself. She literally wasn't the same woman he had married. No, an uncaring universe had stolen that woman away and put in her place a cruel imitation.

He wanted to wear his lucky shirt to the showdown, the old flannel shirt with the Led Zep emblem sewn on, in which he had composed his first novel, back when he had been a harried schoolteacher, writing nights and early mornings, living in a trailer—

That halcyon period before his wife had died and been replaced by the sadistic succubus.

But the lucky shirt was in a closet in the bedroom, and he couldn't go in there.

So on the day he had chosen—the *Farmer's Almanac* had revealed it to be a new moon, when the succubus's power would be at low ebb—he began the fateful journey without that particular shield.

At first he had been planning to take his car. But then the memory of the day it had crushed the cat flooded back on him, and he knew he couldn't trust it. So he had phoned for a taxi. Cleverly—oh so cleverly—he had arranged without giving his name for it to meet him at the Dairy Mart down the road. No one would suspect it was him calling!

He trudged down the deserted country road, away from his mansion. In his guts he felt he wouldn't be returning. Just as well. The place held nothing for him anymore.

At the Dairy Mart, the taxi was waiting.

"Oh, hi, Mister Prinze. I figured it'd be you. No one else out this way ever uses us. How was your walk?"

The Horror Writer stopped in shock. The driver's teeth, long and pointed—! A vampire. All the citizens of the innocent town had been turned into vampires!

Luckily, the Horror Writer was prepared.

The garlic, the mirror, the cross, the silver—

You had to get up pretty fucking early to catch his balls in a nutcracker!

He got into the taxi.

"Take me to my wife's apartment. The Salem Arms. And don't try any funny stuff."

The driver smiled obscenely. Was that *blood*—? "You've lived here as long as me, Mister Prinze. I think you'd know if I was taking the long way 'round."

In the town, the Horror Writer marveled at the simulation of life being carried out by the vampires. Anyone less perceptive than him would be completely taken in. The last real human in a world of fiends! What a fate.

There was no sense in running out on the fare and giving the driver an excuse to call the vampire police. He wasn't sure how many of these damned souls he could fend off simultaneously. So he tossed some bills in the cab driver's face.

"Let's put an end to this farce, shall we?" said the Horror Writer debonairly.

"Fuck you too, Jack," the vampire swore. "You and your fucking millions can go hang."

The Horror Writer paid no attention to the insults, and the driver roared off. His mind was concentrated now on one thing.

His wife.

Stealthily, he took the stairs up the three flights of the Salem Arms. No way was he going to be trapped in the elevator!

At his wife's door, he paused.

There was the sound of running water from inside. Excellent! It would cover his entrance.

He tested the doorknob.

Unlocked! His spell had worked!

Inside, the bathroom door was half ajar. Steam poured out as if from the gates of hell.

He crept to the door.

Then banged it open!

The corpse of the woman lay in the tub. It was bloated and reeked, despite the heavy odor of bath salts. Plainly she had been dead for days. Some enemy of the succubus stronger than herself. . . .

The corpse shrieked!

"Jesus Christ! Stefan, you asshole! You scared the shit out of me. What the hell do you want here?"

So, it had been an elaborate ruse, and he had nearly fallen for it. Imagine if he had touched her—! Well, he would not let her gain the upper hand.

"We've got to talk," stalled the Horror Writer.

The succubus began to unconcernedly soap herself with a scrap of rag. What gall!

"There's nothing more to talk about. You can talk to my lawyer from now on."

"Lawyer! What's the lawyer know about our private life?"

"Plenty. I've told him all about your fucking insanity. Don't look so shocked, that's what it is. Oh, it might have started as eccentricity, but you're way past that point now. The charms for the insomnia, lighting candles in front of your computer, the washing rituals . . . I tried to get you to let up on yourself, cut back on the self-induced stress. We didn't need the extra money. But you wouldn't, would you? Oh, shit, I suppose it wasn't your fault. You were fucked up way back there somehow. But you only aggravated it by what you chose to write about. As if the whole world were nothing but some plot against you."

The demon was spouting filth. His hands ached to close around her throat. He inched closer as the succubus unconcernedly scrubbed her polluted flesh.

"Not that it matters now anyway. My lawyer's got plenty. There isn't a court in the country that wouldn't give me anything I asked for. To think of all the shit I've put up with. Well, no more, buddy! Maybe your fans think it's cute. But they don't have to live with you."

He was within reach now. Another second, and her vile speech would be silenced forever—

"Oh, Stefan, stop with the Boris Karloff stuff already!" said the succubus.

And she lashed out with the wet washcloth across his face!

The water stung like acid! Demon liquid! He couldn't see! He stumbled back, his defenses crumbling, at her mercy—

A whole minute passed. Amazingly, he was still alive. Fumbling for a towel, he cleaned his face and opened his eyes.

The succubus was dressed and waiting for him in the door.

"If you're done fooling around now, clear out. I've got errands to run, and I don't want you hanging around."

The Horror Writer didn't know why he was being spared, but he took advantage of the demon's momentary lapse and made his escape.

On the stairs down, he made a silent prayer of thanks to whatever gods there were.

But out on the street, surrounded by vampires, with no place to go, an empty sky hanging like a shroud above him, he knew the truth.

Whoever was scripting his life, probably the Big Horror Writer up above, just wanted another chance to twist the knife.

MY TWO BEST FRIENDS

Chris used to be my best friend.

Until I discovered that he was cursed.

We were sitting in the company cafeteria, having a coffee. The place was pretty empty. I was talking about a hike that we had been planning, up to an AMC site in New Hampshire. Chris was unusually silent.

"So how about it?" I said. "We've got that long weekend coming up."

Chris sighed. "I was afraid that was what you were going to suggest. I'm sorry, but it's out of the question."

I was a little hurt. "How come?"

"It's a full moon that weekend."

I started to laugh, but the expression on Chris's face stopped me.

"You're serious. I can't believe this. All right, I'll play along. What's so special about the full moon?"

"I change."

"Oh, right. Don't we all. Okay, I'll bite. Into what? A wolf? That's the traditional animal, isn't it?"

"This isn't a traditional change."

"Panther?"

"No."

"Dragon, fish, horse, cow?"

"None of those."

I was getting a little tired of this nonsense. "What then?"

"A woman."

I set my coffee cup down gently. "A woman?"

"Yes."

"A human woman?"

"Is there another kind?"

Now Chris was pissing me off a little with his nonsense. "So you're telling me that you're a werewoman. All the years we've known each other, and this suddenly comes out?"

"You never wanted to do anything during a full moon before. After all, it only happens thirteen times a year. The odds were against my ever needing to mention it. So I never did."

"Chris, if you don't want to go on this trip, just say so. I'll understand."

"But I do. It's just that it can't be the weekend you picked. It would be—inconvenient."

I started to get up from the table. "Listen, I'll talk to you later—"

"You don't believe me."

"What sane person would?"

"Let me show you something."

"Please, not here."

Ignoring my feeble joke, Chris took out his wallet. From it he removed a photo.

I could see that the woman in the photo was plainly Chris. The facial features were somewhat softened, but I attributed that to some trick of makeup and lighting. The rest of the changes were obviously padding and a wig.

I handed the photo back. "You're a transvestite. Why didn't you just say so? It's kinky, but I could live with it. I wouldn't even mind if you wanted to use the ladies' tee when we golfed."

Now Chris got mad. "I'm not a transvestite. How can a woman dressing as a woman be called a transvestite? It's not like I do it anytime except when it's a full moon. If I dressed like a man when I was a woman, then I'd be a transvestite. I mean—"

"Chris, old buddy."

"Yeah?"

"You need some serious help."

Needless to say, my relationship with Chris was different after he made his revelation. In fact, it became quite cool. I started sharing lunch with some other guys, not excluding Chris, but always making it a point to be with him only in a crowd. I never went out for drinks with Chris after work anymore. We saw each other at the company bowling league, but didn't share a ride.

I was kind of sad about the changes, and I guess Chris was too. But there didn't seem to be any alternative, after Chris had shared his delusion with me.

One night I decided to go to a club. Alone. In the past, Chris and I would have always made the club scene together. It felt weird to be going without him.

I was standing at the crowded, smoky bar, feeling kind of blue. A band was wailing away, but the music didn't do anything for me. I couldn't even get interested in drinking.

A woman squeezed in next to me, pressing closer than perfect strangers should.

It was Chris.

He wore a dress that revealed several acres of highly non-artificial breasts.

"I knew you'd be here," said Chris in her new voice, which reminded me of my sister's. "Well, do you believe me now? Or do you need to see the rest?"

"I can't believe this. How many years has this been happening?"

"Since I was thirteen. Wanna dance?"

"I guess so. You're the best-looking one here."

After a dance or two, Chris said, "Well, I've got to go now. The night is young and I've got a lot to do."

"See you at work—I guess."

"Oh, you will."

"Chris?"

"Yeah?"

"Be careful, okay?"

Chris laughed. "What kind of girl do you think I am?"

After that night, I felt a little better about Chris. At least I knew he wasn't a liar or a nut. We started doing things together again, not quite as many as before, but enough that I could honestly call him my friend again. His being a werewoman didn't seem to matter that much, and I made sure never to ask him exactly what he did during "that time of the month."

Sometimes I'd catch him looking at me funny. Sometimes he'd catch me. But basically, we were pretty comfortable around each other.

It was shortly after this period that I fell in love with Jo.

Jo worked in Legal. I had seen her around before, but never really gotten to talk much with her. Now we had ended up working on a project side by side. We started putting in a lot of overtime together. I found out she was a really great person. Smart, funny, passionate, all the qualities you could want in a woman. One thing led to another, and before you could say "office romance," we were an item.

I started doing less with Chris again, so I could spend more time with Jo. It wasn't so sad this time, since Chris knew I was happy, and I wasn't avoiding him out of disgust or anything crazy like that.

Jo and I did everything together. We went hiking and swimming, to the movies and to clubs. I met her family and she met mine. Things were really serious.

About six months into the affair, I showed up unannounced at Jo's apartment. I had a little box with me.

When we were sitting on the couch, I said, "Close your eyes," and she did.

I took the ring out and slid it on her finger.

She opened her eyes and gasped. "It's beautiful!"

"It was my mother's. A jeweler fashioned it special for her. There's not another one like it in the world.'"

"But does it mean—"

"Let's just say for now we're best friends."

It was late autumn. I approached Chris one day at the office.

"Charley and Phil just got word that they've gotta fly to the West Coast immediately."

"And?"

"And so they gave me their tickets to the Jets game on Sunday."

Chris whooped. "Goddamn!" Then his face fell.

"What's the matter?"

"Lunar disturbance."

"Oh, the hell with that. Women go to football games, too."

"I know. But is it wise for us to be seen together? What if we meet someone from the office? What if Jo finds out?"

"Screw that. This is a sold-out game."

"All right. But Dutch treat."

"Sure."

For some reason, I didn't tell Jo what I was really doing on Sunday. I guess I thought she'd want to come too, and there was no way I could explain Chris's presence, especially since Jo knew the male Chris from work. But she didn't make any fuss about our separate plans, and seemed sincerely happy that she and I were mature and stable enough to spend an occasional weekend apart, no questions asked.

The full moon hung in the afternoon sky as Chris and I entered the stadium.

The first two quarters were some of the best football I've ever seen. I had to keep cautioning Chris not to stand on her seat. Not only were her high heels dangerous, but looking at her lovely calves at such close range proved rather unnerving.

At halftime I volunteered to go for beers and dogs. "Thanks," said Chris. "My feet are killing me."

Standing in line, I thought about how it didn't really matter what sex a person was. As long as you shared certain interests with them, you could have a good time. Sex didn't have to come up at all.

The guy ahead of me turned around too fast with his overfull plastic cup of beer and sloshed a little on me.

"Hey, buster, watch it—"

I caught a glimpse of his left hand.

"Jo!"

My fiancée was wearing ripped jeans, a flannel shirt and work boots. She smelled of Brut, but she needed a shave.

"I can explain—" she began.

"Don't bother. Just come with me."

"Where are we going?"

"You need to pee."

"I do?"

"You do."

After we got out of the men's room, I was kind of in shock.

Jo looked contrite. "I was going to tell you eventually."

"I believe you."

"You see, it all started when I was thirteen—"

"I know."

"You know? How could you know?"

"Never mind. Just come with me. There's someone I want you to meet."

Chris was just finishing touching up her lipstick.

"Chris, meet Jo. Jo, Chris."

At first they acted embarrassed. After all, they were both in the habit of moving undetected and unrecognized during such times. But after a while, they were chattering away as if they had known each other all their lives.

Which, in a sense, I guess they had.

I get invitations now and then to dinner at Chris and Jo's house, and since I still like them both a lot and they put on a swell meal, I usually go.

Unless it's a full moon.

THE DEATH OF SALVADOR DALI

Salvador Dali, the century's finest madman, the Great Masturbator, the Holiest Goof, the Critical Paranoid, Saint Salvador the Supreme Surrealist, is dying at last.

In the converted castle in Pubol that was one of his last gifts to Gala, twenty miles outside Figueras, the small town where Dali was born, the old painter lies in bed, attended by his court.

He wears a white satin gown. Around his neck on a blood-red sash hangs the Grand Crown of Isabella, an enormous medal given to him by Franco. Across his withered lap lies one of his favoured canes, the one with the gold head that he always maintained once belonged to Sarah Bernhardt.

Sad to say, Dali looks like hell.

The grand rampant moustaches, once lovingly waxed each day, are no more; a few wispy grey hairs, sparsely planted across his upper lip, are the only token they ever existed. Dali's hair, always worn long, is greasy and lank. Dali's face, ravaged by the persistence of time, has collapsed. It now resembles a premonitory soft watch, or perhaps the weathered rocks of Cape Creus, not far from Port Lligat, where so much of his best work was done.

A clear plastic tube blocks one nostril and descends down his throat: it carries nutrients and vitamins, for Dali can neither chew nor swallow.

Dali's court no longer consists of fellow simpatico artists, poets and bizarre nonpareils, but only of museum curators and administrators of his estate, seated or uneasily standing. He has outlived all his old cronies. Breton, Eluard, Picasso, Tanguy, Ernst, Man Ray, Magritte, Gala . . .

Most especially Gala.

Gala: wife, "sister," muse, model, protector, companion of fifty years. "Gentle Gala who is also the beautiful Helen of the golden apple . . . Gala is the one who devours for me, my teeth being very small and feeble . . . Gala is Trinity . . . the woman whose glance pierces walls . . ." Gala the indispensable, the vital, the lost . . .

One final real friend, however, is still present. Antonio Pitxot, who has been Dali's companion since Gala's death. Pitxot is a much younger man than Dali, with a head full of dark curls. The Pitxots and the Dalis were neighbours since before little Salvador's birth. Pitxot is the only one now who can interpret Dali's feeble Catalan utterances.

The assembled company unanimously stirs at this moment in their vigil, as if blown by an extradimensional wind. They know intuitively that these are Dali's final minutes of life. The atmosphere in the room is thick with forebodings of transition. The harsh Spanish light the colour of sand streaming in through the thick embrasures is quanti-fied with particles of mortality. The mundane features of the commonplace articles in the room are transfigured as if by a patina of paint.

Dali shifts his head on the pillows, eyeing the seated witnesses to his less than grandiose passage from this world. His dry lips stir, and Pitxot lowers his ear to Dali's mouth.

"What does he say?" asks a timid goateed man in a conservative dun suit. (This is the local Pharmacist of Ampurdan, invited according to Dali's express and inviolable—albeit inexplicable—wishes.)

Pitxot replies, "He says, 'A chair can even be used to sit in, but on the sole condition that one sits on it uncomfortably.'"

The crowd nods solemnly, as if enlightened.

Dali whispers again. Pitxot straightens up and says, "Dali wants us to know that the quicksands of automatism and dreams vanish upon awakening. But the rocks of the imagination remain."

Once more the deathbed spectators wag their heads sagely.

Dali beckons a final time. Pitxot patiently receives this last message, which is a long one, and passes it on.

"The glove of myself is edible, and even a little gamy. I am the most generous of painters, since I am constantly offering myself to be eaten, and I thus succulently nourish our time. Every morning I experience the supreme pleasure of being Salvador Dali, and wonder what prodi-gies I will accomplish today."

After allowing enough time for this stubborn assertion of his stature and of his old will to be digested, Dali waves to an old-fashioned phonograph. Pitxot, knowing full well what Dali wants, gets up and moves to the phonograph. On the turntable sits a record whose label is long gone, and whose grooves are worn down by countless playings. Pitxot turns on the machine and sets the needle on the record.

An irritating storm of white noise—which Dali has said resembles "the most beautiful sound in the world, that of sardines frying in oil"—fills the room.

Pitxot returns to Dali's side.

The old man's face has relaxed, losing some of its lines of pain. The white noise seems to be facilitating his departure from life.

Dali reaches out. Pitxot grabs his parchment hand—has the man become canvas itself?—and squeezes. The witnesses cease to breathe, as if, drawn by the force even of Dali's waning charisma and wishing to follow him beyond life, they are ready to commit a kind of spontaneous mass yogic suicide.

"Gala," says Dali, plainly enough for all to understand. "Gala, Gala—"

Then Dali dies.

* * *

Everything is black. There is confinement. The universe seems infinitely small, like Hamlet's walnut shell, its bounds located just a few inches beyond Dali's skin, as he floats in foetal suspension.

The air is stale, and smells of a sun-dried tidal pool in which things have died.

This situation is not without interest. What is going on? Where is he? How does he exist, if exist he does? He remembers dying . . . Is this heaven or hell, or something else? For once, Dali has no ready answers.

But, being Dali, this does not deter him.

It is amazing how well he feels. Not for decades has his body radiated such healthy messages. He feels like a forty-year-old again. Dali flexes his limbs tentatively in the enclosure. No, make that a twenty-year-old!

The new bodily vigour inspires him. He must escape this prison—assuming it is not the whole of his new existence.

Dali pokes hesitantly at the walls of his unseen shapeless box. They reveal themselves to be rubbery, organic, slimy. Dali thrusts a foot into the shell and extends his bent leg straight out. He can feel the membrane wrap his foot, mimicking its shape. But it refuses to tear.

The resistance frightens him—is he doomed to spend post-mortal eternity in this confinement?—and he begins to flail wildly. He grabs handfuls of the wall and pulls, he butts his head into the shell, deforming it to his own personal contours . . .

Something finally gives.

Dali's right hand juts through the shell, into what feels like open air. He extends the rip, producing a crack that propagates with a noise like rotting fabric tearing.

A shaft of light, accompanied by fresh air, enters, spurring Dali on. His arm is free to the shoulder. Somehow, though, in his haste to escape, his head has become enfolded in the membrane. He cannot see the new worlds beyond his shell yet. Desperately, he pulls free of the pliable material, and falls through the crack to the ground.

Dali stands.

He looks around. He has emerged from an egg-shaped globe on which the familiar continents stand in impasto relief, Tierra del Feugo melting off, and the Cape of Good Hope levitating away. The globe rests on a white cloth. Above it floats a curdled shadowed canopy. Dali's destruction of the globe has caused it to bleed: an unchanging bright crimson globule lies on the cloth, connected to the globe by a viscous thread.

Dali smiles. How droll. Of all possible afterlives, that he should find himself here . . . Impossible to say if such a fate is heaven or hell. Or is this all only the phantasm of his dying mind, an illusory eternity in a few milliseconds . . . ?

"Are you ready now?" says a voice behind Dali.

Dali turns.

It is—as he instantly knew it must be—a naked little boy with a shaved head: Geopoliticus Child. The child watches Dali with calm unconcern.

"Ready for what, tiny avatar of my magnificent self?"

"You mistake me," says the child. "But no matter. Ready to travel, of course."

"Where?"

"To Gala."

Dali feels faint. Vertigo overwhelms him, and he falls backward against the egg, his hand smearing Barcelona and all of Spain. Amid all the excitement of being reborn, he neglected to conceive this possibility. If this is indeed the true world beyond death, then Gala must be here also. To be reunited with his beloved—! It seems too rich a possibility.

Yet faced with this intimate landscape, what alternative does he have but to believe, and act on that belief?

"Are you going to guide me?" asks Dali.

"Yes," says Geopoliticus Child. "For part of the way. The journey is not long, but neither is it easy."

Dali reaches up instinctively to preen his moustaches. They are there, splendid in their stiff glory! Sensitive feelers aquiver to the numinous passage of pi-mesons! Yes, he is his old self, Dali the invincible! He is ready to travel indeed.

Pushing himself boldly away from the globe, Dali notices for the first time that he is naked. However, he does miss his old favourite red felt hat.

"We must attempt to find some headgear for me," says Dali to the child. "The painter must officiate with headgear, preferably a model which conceals an electronic and cybernetic apparatus by means of which televised information could be communicated."

"We shall see. Meanwhile, let us be off."

"With a will. I am ready to encounter all phantasms of deification which my own deluded brain may project. But be forewarned: the only difference between a madman and myself is that I am not mad."

Dali steps off the white cloth that lies beneath the World Egg, and onto the gritty, hard desert floor where Geopoliticus Child stands. The glossy bead of blood has not altered, and seems pregnant with a hematinic foetus, ready to give birth to bloody terror.

With the Egg no longer obscuring the foreground, Dali is able to take in the landscape.

The desert stretches away, uninterestingly featureless, to the western horizon. A square tower, dark with shadows on its northern side, looms some distance away in the east. Beyond the structure are mountains. Between the mountains and tower, across the illimitable plain, are scattered mystic figures of indescribable half-humanity, engaged in alchemic conversations and cryptic intercourse. The sky is grey.

"Marvelous," exclaims Dali. "Although I have never been here, I remember so much!"

The child takes Dali's hand, and they set off for the tower.

The plain is hot and pebbled beneath Dali's bare soles, but he does not object to the discomfort, so enthralled is he with his renewed youth and this translation to the scene of his most private imaginings.

"How is it, dear child, that life after death resembles the peculiar prophetic visions of one Salvador Dali? I always realised that, as a genius, I was exalted and privileged in my communications with alternate planes of existence, but even I never dared conceive that heaven's architecture would spring from my brush."

The little hand of Geopoliticus Child is warm and alive in Dali's own. "What makes you so sure you are dead?"

This reply gives Dali pause. He recalls his intuition upon first stepping from the egg that this was only the final hallucination of a cooling brain, a time-shifted pseudo-life that would unravel and disintegrate along with his expiring neurons . . . Can this be what his diminutive Virgil means?

As if sensing Dali's hesitation, Geopoliticus Child says in his sweet voice, "What if you have been spirited away by superior beings? Taken from your deathbed to another world? The agents of your fate might be a race other than man, whose members wish to preserve your life amid familiar and reassuring scenery."

Dali snorts. "Wellsian nonsense! Even I, the great Dali, know that such talk is piffle, fit only for hypergonadic adolescents."

"I merely propound the theory. Believe what you wish."

During their talk, the two travelers have drawn closer to the lonely tower by means of strange and disconcerting physical and temporal shifts. Stopping now a few feet from its walls, Dali can see that the structure's doorless base is cracked, the stucco crumbling, revealing the sand-colored bricks beneath. Above, the sky has gone hyperxiological: composed of some colloidal substance, infolded and wrinkled on itself in a non-Euclidean manner, studded with nails, coral and teeth.

In the upper floors of the tower are square openings. A single iron rod extends across the middle of each.

In one opening, leaning on the rod, is a naked woman.

Her left forearm rests on the rod, while her right hand clasps her left bicep, thus framing her pendulous full breasts, the nipples of which are perfectly round cherry-colored marbles that float above the skin. Her hair resembles that of Botticelli's Venus. The iron rod cuts athwart her pubis. She is not entirely naked, for she wears seamed black nylons and scuffed brown loafers. Her left leg supports her weight on the ball of her foot, raising that foot from her shoe. Her right knee is bent, the tip of the right shoe balanced on the stones of the tower floor. Around her in a cluster float bulbous phallic horns.

Her joints are curiously configured, almost as if her limbs could be detached.

The tantalizing woman calls down to Dali. "Come up here, Painter, and consummate our alchemical wedding, the union of mercury and sulphur."

Dali feels a creeping paralysis and a desire to submit to the beckoning of this siren. At the same time, he wants to turn and flee. But he is aware that this is the first obstacle on his path to Gala, and must be conquered.

Suddenly Dali realizes that his head is level with that of the Geopoliticus Child. He has shrunken to a child himself, clothed in a blue sailor's suit, clutching a hoop and thighbone. Ah, the Spectre of Sex Appeal!

Dali summons his innermost strengths and addresses the woman. "Young Virgin, autosodomized by your own chastity! You can lean on and play with the unicorn horns morally, as was practised in the time of courtly love! But to embrace the fiery Dali would result in your destruction!"

The woman postures invitingly. "I am unafraid to try it. What of yourself? Climb between my legs, Painter, and see what happens—if you dare!"

Dali quivers with a wash of lust, fear and anguish. He stirs toward the tower, ready to scale its walls with bloody fingers to reach this artifact of his own devising, supreme attractor crafted to his own tastes. Images of rolling her detachable nipples between his fingers inflame him.

At the last moment, however, through some deep access of resolve, Dali instead hurls the thighbone at the temptress.

It hurtles end over end through the space between them, finally smiting the Young Virgin upon the forehead.

At the instant of contact, the woman and tower vanish.

Dali looks down at himself; he has regained his adult stature and nudity. He turns to share his triumph with Geopoliticus Child.

The child is gone.

In his place is a giant black ant fully as large.

Dali notices that he and the ant now stand on a beach lapped by a broad sea. Wedged into the sand is a canted wooden crutch holding a black telephone receiver, which trails a wire that ends in midair.

Before Dali can question the ant about the disappearance of Geopoliticus Child, the phone begins to ring.

Dali lifts the receiver off the crutch. "Hello? Yes, who is it?"

Gala speaks. "It is I, Salvador, she who veils herself and walks in mystery."

"Gala, Gala, my dearest, where are you, how can I reach you? Tell me."

"You are doing wonderful, Salvador, without any instruction from me. Just remember the paranoiac-critical method."

"Of course! A spontaneous method of irrational knowledge founded on the critical interpretive association of the delirious phenomena will see me through, as always! Thank you, Galutschka, thank you! Once again, you have put me in touch with my true self!"

"Goodbye for now, Salvador. If you just persist as nobly as you have been, we shall be reunited soon."

There is a click, and a noise like the sound of sardines frying fills the earpiece.

Dali turns to the magnificent ant. "I assume you are to lead me in place of the child."

"Yes," answers the ant. Its voice, unlike that of Geopoliticus Child, is a harsh rasp.

"Onward, then, Admirable Atta!"

The ant and Dali begin to walk along the subtle sands.

Soon, they come upon a scene of frantic activity.

The conquest of the tuna.

In the marine shallows a party of heroic unclothed figures struggle with enormous glaucous tuna fish. The men are composed of golden and silver whorls of energy. Some have visible brains like coral. They grapple with the slippery dying fish, stabbing them with knives and spears. Blood runs from the fish, and from the hemolactic nipple of one of the men, staining the water. On a headland, a group of reserve fishermen watch complacently; a naked woman balances on one leg, like a stork, and hides her face. Gulls screech overhead.

Dali pauses to admire the barbaric commotion. After a while, the ant speaks in its mordant rasp.

"How appalling men are! Why can they not be as the noble ant, and scavenge for their sustenance?"

"Both ants and men make war, as I indicate by their conjoined presence in *Autumn Cannibalism*. Therefore, ant, do not preach. Remember: the hard and the soft must be equivalent in classic work."

"Let us agree to disagree. Meanwhile, we must continue."

The pair leave the ferocious fishers behind.

For some time, they walk along the vacant shore in silence. Dali becomes preoccupied with his thoughts. Assuming he does reach Gala, what will happen? What is the purpose of existence here in this new dimension? Is it all some lugubrious game? Is —

Suddenly, without warning, an enormous pair of lips forms and opens in the sand beneath Dali's right foot. His leg plunges into the gullet up to the thigh, before finding purchase on the palate.

At once the teeth and lips close, severing Dali's leg.

Dali screams in pain.

The mouth vanishes, leaving Dali lying on the beach with an amputated leg.

Slowly the pain diminishes to a barely tolerable level. Dali looks reluctantly at his shortened limb. There is no blood. The leg looks as if it has been missing for years, ending in a scarred nub.

"The real shadow of a lion threatens me," says Dali through his grimace of sustainable pain. "But I will persist."

Dali notices then that the ant has deserted him. Helpless, he decides to await its return for at least a while.

He is not disappointed. The ant soon reappears, bearing in its mandibles a crutch. Gratefully, Dali takes the crutch and uses it to lever himself up.

"I have always maintained that for slumber to be possible, a whole system of crutches in psychic equilibrium was needed. But I never thought I would require one in reality."

"We must continue," says the ant unsympathetically.

Dali stumps awkwardly onward.

They pass a row of sharks with their snouts out of the water. Each second, a flounder leaps from the water and slides down the throat of one shark or another like a letter down a letterbox.

"The sharks of time eat the soles of memory."

"Possibly. Possibly not."

Reaching a huge cliff whose spill of wave-slapped boulders blocks further progress both along the beach and in the brine, Dali and the ant turn inland. Soon the sea is but a memory.

They reach a stagnant pool, flanked by ochre buttes, as storm clouds begin to congregate overhead. A huge decomposing stone figure sits in the pool, head bowed. A marble hand rises from the earth beside the pool, bearing an egg from which sprouts a white flower. Small ants crawl upon the hand.

"One moment," says the oversized ant. "I must speak with my brothers."

The large ant moves off to rub antennae delicately with the small ones. While Dali waits, he notices a lean dog chewing a portentous bone. He attempts to pet it, but is repulsed with a growl.

"We all complacently savour the narcissistic odours of every one of our drawers," muses Dali ruefully.

The ant rejoins Dali. "I have the information I need. We can go on."

"Where?"

"To see the Christ."

"But of course!"

Detouring around the buttes, Dali is led onward by the ant.

The heat of the desert is suddenly overwhelmingly oppressive. Dali wishes he were again by the sea. He wipes sweat from his brow and continues.

Pausing to look up, Dali sees a mirage—what he fervently hopes is a mirage—high in the atmosphere.

Gala, naked, lies on her back upon a flat blue rock. Snarling tigers leap through the air toward her, and the bayonet of a hovering rifle seems ready to pierce her flesh. The total effect is one of menace constrained only by the thinnest of threads.

"Quickly, ant! I feel Gala is in some danger!"

"Let us take this car then."

Dali becomes aware that they have halted by a low free-standing rock formation. Projecting from the rocks, its rear bumper fused into the granite, is an open-roofed touring car, a 1931 Packard. The car is overgrown with flowers and greenery.

"How, ant, how? The car is one with the rock!"

"You must free it."

Dali moves hopelessly to the rear of the car, inserting himself partly between it and the rock wall. Planting his crutch and single foot firmly into the friable earth, he leans his left shoulder against the vehicle, and strains against it. The car does not move. Dali pushes harder. His guts feel ready to spill out, like those of the crucified tuna. He releases a deep rumble of simultaneous frustration and denial of failure.

With a crack the car comes free of the rock, intact.

Dali falls forward with its release. When he picks himself up, the ant is already seated behind the wheel.

"Lacking a foot, you cannot drive."

"That is incontestable."

"Then I shall."

"Very well," says Dali, and climbs into the passenger's seat.

The ant engages the clutch and they move off.

After some miles, a gigantic floating figure becomes visible low on the horizon. As they near it, it comes to fill the whole sky above them.

It is the Christ pinned to a hypercube. His body floating above the bronze geometry and taking the place of the essential ninth cube, according to the precepts of the mystic, Raymond Lull. Christ is surrounded by antimatter angels, as befits his status.

The plain is now an onyx checkerboard shadowed by the immense figure. The car's tires hum smoothly along the pavement. The ant is forced to brake far in advance of where it wishes to stop, so frictionless is the surface.

At last though the car is motionless, below the feet of the Christ.

Looking upward, the only features of the Saviour's face that Dali is able to see are the Saviour's titanic underlip and nostrils.

A resonant voice that vibrates the whole world thunders out: "Who disturbs me?"

Dali stands up in the car, cranes his head backwards and shouts upward, in pitiable imitation of the voice of Christ.

"It is I, Dali, your humble explicator, and glorifier! I have come seeking Saint Gala."

"Leave me alone with my suffering. Your quest is trivial compared to mine."

Dali becomes angry at these words. "You pompous clod! How dare you deny Dali! What did you ever accomplish, compared to my work?"

"Don't blaspheme," warns the ant. "His mercy is strange and unpredictable."

"This is my universe!" roars the angry Christ. "I brought it into being with my suffering. It is a cognate of my Father's creation. You are here only because I opened a crack for you at death."

"What nonsense! I would rather believe in aliens! Look about you! Everything here has sprung from my splendid brain. Even your agony is depicted according to my conception."

The Christ is silent for a moment. "You have a point there," He says at last. "I must think about this."

"Think all you like. But in the meantime, tell me how to reach Gala."

"Oh, very well. Simply follow the elephants."

"That's it?"

"That's all. Now, begone!"

Dali cannot resist asking one more boon. "Oh, great Jesus, I do not wish to meet Gala so disfigured. Can you not heal me?"

"It is done," says Christ.

Dali looks. His leg is indeed restored.

However, a new weight drags down his body. He peers over his shoulder.

His buttocks are exaggerated sacs of flesh, yards long.

"These monstrously long buttocks must have a deep significance, I admit, but it escapes me just now!"

Restored sunlight falls over Dali. Christ and his antimatter entourage have vanished from the sky.

Dali realises he is now standing on the black and white pavement, his flabby fundament dragging on the cold tiles. The car and the ant have been subsumed back into the texture of this universe, and Dali is alone. Bereft of a guide for the first time since his arrival, hindered by his new deformity, he reasserts his devotion.

"I make the most abysmal subconscious avowal that I shall forge onward to a final accommodation of my desires, symbolised by a stone almond: the illumined pleasure of clasping Gala to my bosom!"

Feeling somewhat better after this assertion, Dali begins to walk on, encumbered by his flabby ass.

At the end of the tiles, the granulated desert floor reappears.

Dali's buttocks leave a trail like that of a sledge.

In the middle of nowhere, Dali comes upon a living green eidolon with wild hair, standing on a pedestal. The figure's eyes and mouth have been overgrown by the substance of its body. A locust crouches on the membrane where the mouth should be.

"Have you seen any elephants lately?" asks Dali.

Wordlessly, both the eidolon and the locust point in the same direction. Dali obediently directs his gaze thither.

A herd of elephants dominates the near distance. Their huge bodies are elevated half a mile above the earth on spindly stork legs which are jointed uncountable times. They carry palanquins occupied by obscure forms. The troop is rapidly approaching.

"Thank you," says Dali. "By the way, would you have the time?"

The mute produces a soft watch rimmed in gold with a blue face, and displays it for Dali.

"Metabiotically speaking, a soft watch represents DNA, the cell's memory. I take this as a good omen that Gala, my soul's DNA, will soon be mine."

Dali advances to meet the elephants.

Soon the first ones are atop Dali, their splay feet, attached to ridiculously thin shanks, sending up dust from the plain. Each stride of theirs covers half a kilometer. Dali realizes that they will soon outpace him. How is he to follow? He begins to trot desperately, dragging his posterior painfully.

"Stop, stop, you must lead me to Gala!"

It is no use. The elephants continue on their way, heedless.

Just as Dali is about to give up, he feels a trunk encircle his waist.

Up, up, up, seemingly miles high he is lifted, until he is placed inside a palanquin.

The canopied bower is filled with madmen, their clothing besmeared with excrement, their faces bloody with self-inflicted wounds. They hoot and holler at Dali.

"Fishermen of Port Lligat! How wonderful to meet here again! Let me shake all your hands—"

Dali and his old friends spend the time talking gleeful nonsense, while the elephants stride spaciously on.

After an unknown time, Dali finds himself submerged in clouds. It becomes hard to tell whether or not he is still moving. Finally, Dali decides that he is indeed stopped. He steps from the palanquin onto a cloud.

It upholds him.

Again Dali is alone.

He moves through the clouds until he emerges into an immense luminous cloud cavern. High up near the roof is a fragmentary arch of classic design. Occupying the arch is a naked male figure whose face and genitals are swathed in mist.

The man thrusts a hand out, as if to ward off something evil. The flock of antimatter angels that attended the Christ reappear.

In their midst, riding a swan, is Gala, clothed in a white robe that falls charmingly from her beautiful shoulders.

"Leda Atomica!" shouts Dali ecstatically. "Gala, my own! Fly down to your Castor, Pollux! Let us engender progeny worthy of our loins!"

Gala smiles, and begins the descent on her feathery steed.

The empyreal notes of an average fine and invisible harp fill the air.

As soon as the pi-mesons from Gala's smile strike him, Dali feels his most recent deformity vanish. He is made whole for the arrival of his celestial bride.

The swan alights. Gala steps off. Dali rushes into her embrace.

Instant ecstasy overwhelms him. He feels their flesh fuse in a metabiotic mesomorphic alchemical union. One androgynous soul is born from the crucible of their love.

Gali/Dala is home at last.

* * *

The officious Pharmacist of Ampurdan stands up in the bedroom in the castle at Pubol and moves to close the lids of Dali's dead eyes.

But before he can lay a finger on the chilling flesh, the body is transformed into a carpet of roses which distill the odours of a woman's sex.

Antonio Pitxot, Catalan, smiles knowingly.

OUR HOUSE

The three of us—I, my wife, and the realtor—stood on the sidewalk, amid broken glass and candy wrappers, crumpled cigarette packages and bottle caps, looking up at our house.

Even though my wife and I had never been inside, you see, I already had the habit of referring to the place as "our house."

From the moment I had first seen it, driving past one evening on a new route home from the office, I knew we would one day own it. Its strange proportions and unique charms attracted me as no other structure ever had. It seemed to promise a certain domestic serenity to anyone lucky enough to live in it, a kind of natural ease, as if it could mold itself to its inhabitants, becoming an extension of their bodies, rather than a stiff shell or clumsy carapace, like most houses. Perhaps this was entirely fancy on my part. All I really knew was that the house attracted me.

Our house was situated in a rough section of town that was now undergoing the early stages of gentrification. At one time this neighborhood had been several square blocks of Victorian and Edwardian respectability and pomp. (How they had loved their cluttered neatness, their elaborate classifications, the people of that age!)

Now, however, the area enjoyed a status barely above that of a ghetto. There were many empty, fire-blackened lots. The houses that had survived were mostly shabby. Youths with bad intentions congregated on corners. Liquor stores did a thriving business. Still, here and there a building stood out, either having been maintained throughout the years of general neglect, or now being renovated.

Our house was one such.

Despite being surrounded by a weed-filled yard, it was in decent shape. I could see that its slate roof was intact. Its clapboards were sound, if in need of paint. Its foundation appeared firm. I have already alluded to the uniqueness of its overall appearance. Three stories tall, our house was a whimsical structure—what I believe is called a "carpenter's gothic"—reflecting the unknown intentions of its long-dead architect. (In a way, its lines, from certain perspectives, seemed almost arbitrary, as if the edifice had grown willy-nilly, an organic thing, rather than having been planned and constructed deliberately. An evolutionary sport, perhaps.)

Our house sported gables and towers, gingerbread and scrollwork, stained glass and leering wooden gargoyle bas-reliefs. At moments, it seemed almost like three separate houses jammed together. At others, its disparate elements were miraculously fused into a whole that, as I have said, struck one—struck me at least—as very appealing. I hoped, of course, that my wife, seeing our house for the first time, would feel the same way.

Turning to her now, I tried to gauge her reaction to our house.

Her brow was wrinkled, her lips composed in a straight line, her gaze a bit remote. Not a face of disapproval, I thought, but merely her familiar abstracted look of weighing and evaluating, which often settled on her appealing features when she was working on a case at home, prior to writing a brief. Her judgment was still in suspension, and I could only hope it would eventually be made in favor of our house. Wishing to sway her, I turned to the real estate man, the third member of our party.

"What's the asking price?" I inquired.

He named a ridiculously low figure, and I nodded sagely.

"It's the neighborhood, of course," he continued. "Puts quite a few people off. But I can see that you two wouldn't be bothered by that. You look like folks who enjoy being on the cutting edge of things. That's just the situation we have here. This whole district is turning around. The smart people are buying into it now. Pretty soon you won't be able to touch a house like this for even twice the price. And believe me, this would be a lot of house at even twice what they're asking."

I caught my wife's eyes, now focused again. She nodded slightly to me, and I knew that the outside of our house, at least, had not put her off. I wasn't sure if her feelings were as intense as mine, but at least she didn't dislike it. In time, I was sure, her enthusiasm would grow to match mine.

"Well," I said, "we won't learn any more standing out here. Shall we go in?"

At this point, the real estate man grew nervous. He absentmindedly ground a bottlecap into the concrete with the tip of his shoe, as if trying to expunge something distasteful.

"There's a slight problem," he said. "We won't be able to see the whole interior. Oh, the bulk of the house is perfectly accessible. Very nicely remodeled too, all the modern conveniences . . . It's just the third floor and the basement that we can't inspect."

"And why is that?" I asked.

The agent ground the cap down more forcefully. "It's the tenants."

"Tenants!" interrupted my wife. "The reason we're buying a house is to escape tenants. We're tired of renting, we need more room, a house of our own. We plan to have a child in two and a half years, and we were going to devote the third floor to it. Part of the second floor has to be my home office "

"They're very good tenants," the agent temporized. "Always pay their rent promptly, never make any noise. Why, their rents will almost completely cover your mortgage payments . . ."

Before my wife and the agent could further antagonize each other, I interceded.

"Do they have leases?"

"No, I don't believe so. Nothing actually signed, anyway. But they're tenants of long-standing. From what I've heard, they've always lived here, even before the current owners."

"Still, without leases, they're in something of a precarious position, wouldn't you say? Times are changing, and if we should see fit to raise the rents above what they could afford, I can't imagine what alternative they would have, except to move."

My wife smiled. The agent just shook his head. He seemed unusually tenderhearted for someone in his profession.

"This is really nothing for you to worry about," I offered. "Why not just show us the portion of our house that's open, and let us make a decision based on that?"

The agent acquiesced. We began to move up the front walk, crushing the weeds that grew up between the flagstones.

"I won't have people living in our cellar and in our attic," said my wife forcefully, as if demanding the death penalty in a murder case.

"Don't worry, dear," I said, not really bothered by the prospect of evicting the unseen tenants. For she had said the words that let me know she was as much in love with the place as I.

"Our cellar. Our attic."

* * *

It was a weekday evening. We were idling in the cozy parlor on the first floor of our house. We had been living in our house for three weeks. Already, as I had anticipated, it felt as if we had always lived there. Our house seemed a natural layer on our existing personalities, a kind of second skin, comfortable as a wrinkled pair of favorite jeans. With our house as a refuge to retreat to, away from the pressures of the daily world, both my wife and I were functioning more efficiently at work. We really couldn't have been happier.

Except, of course, for the matter of the tenants.

I had discovered, by making careful inquiries among the neighbors and at City Hall, the names of our unwanted lodgers.

Huddling cravenly in the basement, a Mr and Mrs Ab.

Perched insouciantly on the third floor, a Mr and Mrs Meta.

Illegal immigrants both, I was certain, with names like that. It was an angle I was willing to exploit, if necessary. No pressure seemed too unethical to apply, if it would force them to leave. Why, they probably didn't even belong in this country, much less in our house. Every time I thought of them, practically trespassing on our property, I became as angry as I ever did. I knew my wife felt the same way. Tonight, I had resolved, was to be the occasion of my speaking sternly to at least one set of these disreputable squatters. And I had decided, rather arbitrarily, to buttonhole the Abs first.

Although it might seem queer, I had not confronted either couple previously for several good and sufficient reasons.

First, I had had to contend with the expected, but nonetheless taxing exigencies connected with uprooting oneself and transporting all one's possessions to a new home. This had been very debilitating. (Not that the stress hadn't been worth it, in order to possess our house. Quite to the contrary . . .)

Second, the unwanted couples were—to be fair about the matter— so innocuous, so quiet, so hidden, that they slipped my mind for days at a time. No noise ever intruded from above or below, and we had yet to witness our tenants coming or going.

Third came my natural reluctance to cause a scene, even knowing that by all civilized standards I was absolutely within my rights as the new owner of the house.

In any case, these hindrances were no longer operative. Tonight, I had finally overcome them all.

This very evening I was determined to venture downstairs, into the terra incognita of our basement, and break the news to the Abs that they had better think about moving, and soon.

I rose from my chair and turned toward my wife.

She was sitting in a rowing machine on the floor. The ultramodern and slightly diabolical-looking apparatus appeared absolutely incongruous amidst our heavy Victorian furniture, which we had been accumulating for years in anticipation of one day living in just such an immaculately restored house. I marveled, not for the first time, how the old and new managed to coexist in our society . . .

Clad in a blue Lycra stretchsuit, she faced the television set, which was on and tuned to PBS. (I had not been watching, instead sitting pensively, anticipating the various possible objections the Abs would raise, and how I would counter them.)

"I'm going downstairs now," I said to my wife, who pulled vigorously on the oars, rowing to nowhere.

"Great," she huffed. "Give 'em hell."

I hesitated, suddenly reluctant to confront the Abs. "What's that you're watching?" I asked, seeking to delay the inevitable moment.

"*Nova.* Something about the brain. Three-part structure. Cortex, cerebellum . . . I don't really know. Not paying attention, I guess."

Then she began to stroke harder, effectively precluding further talk. With no additional excuse for delay, I left the parlor.

In the hallway, I abruptly stopped. A thought had occurred to me: where exactly was the entrance to the cellar?

There was no exterior door or bulkhead set into the foundation. I had mowed the weedy lawn just yesterday, making a complete survey of our house's perimeter, and would surely have noticed any possible exit. Such a lack could mean only that the entrance to the basement was within the house.

This seemed incredible. How could the prior owners have consented to this kind of arrangement? Who would want one's tenants trooping daily in and out through one's own private quarters? I couldn't conceive of such a setup. Yet what alternative was there? There had to be some sort of access to the cellar, and if it wasn't outside, it had to be inside. The Abs must come and go while we were sleeping or at work . . .

I set out to find the hidden door below.

After much opening and closing of hitherto undiscovered closets, I came upon the door I sought in a shadowy corner of the kitchen. It was secured with a rusty nail hammered into the doorframe then bent at an angle and rotated into the body of the door. The nail had bitten so deeply, and for so long, that I had to use a claw hammer to remove it . . .

I opened the door onto a Stygian stairwell, a benighted shaft. The light from over my shoulder illuminated only the first four or five steps. After that the darkness was complete.

I looked for a light switch on either side of the door.

There was none.

I found a flashlight in the kitchen junk drawer. Its batteries were dead, a corroded and fused acidic mass. Perhaps, I thought, I should postpone this encounter until I caught the Abs venturing upstairs . . . But then, imagining what my wife would say if I told her I had failed to confront the Abs, I knew such a course was out of the question.

Reluctantly, my left hand on the railless wall on that side, my right hand extended out into the blank abyss in the other direction, I began the descent.

The stairs seemed to go on forever, with many twists and turns. The wall beneath my left hand changed from plaster to stone. The stone became damp, then actually wet. I could feel the movement of small rills. My right hand encountered nothing. A reptilian smell filled the air, as at the snakehouse at the zoo. I shuffled on, carefully lifting each foot and seeking out the next step.

Eventually I reached the bottom. Beneath my shoes, the floor seemed made of stone and lightly scattered with sand.

So: this was our house's cellar. It seemed somehow fitting that such an impressive edifice should have a correspondingly deep and solid foundation. I was not alarmed. In fact, I was rather proud.

My eyes having adjusted to the gloom, I noticed a faint, reddish, lambent glow emanating from one direction.

I moved toward it.

After navigating several bends, I realized the glow must be the familiar radiance cast by naked flames. My shadow, in fact, now danced behind me.

One last turn brought the source into sight. The corridor opened out into a cave, at the center of which was a small crackling fire. Its smoke spiraled upward and vanished into the gloom that hid whatever ceiling—our floorboards?—there was. The cave walls—much dryer here—were decorated with primitive yet affecting drawings, consummated in charcoal and organic paints: mammoths, giant sloths, sabertooths, and the outlines of hands, created, I knew, by blowing powdery pigments through a hollow reed as the actual digits lay splayed against the wall. There were various implements of bone and stone arranged around the cave: spears, fishhooks, knives . . .

By the fire crouched a lone figure. It looked up as I entered the circle of light.

I instinctively recognized Mrs Ab.

Moving closer, I lifted my empty hand in a greeting. Mrs Ab did likewise.

At first I thought she was clothed in the fur of some animal. Then I realized the covering was her own dense pelage, and that she was naked. Her dark rubbery nipples poked through the fur. The short, thick, not unappealing pelt covered even her massive brow. Her brown eyes were those of an innocent beast.

I squatted by the fire. For several moments neither of us said anything. I was unsure of Mrs Ab's ability to converse at all, and did not wish to embarrass her. Yet what alternative did I have? I had to say something to explain my presence. The musky, primeval smell I had noticed at the head of the stairwell was incredibly pungent here, I realized, and it was beginning to make it hard to concentrate. I had to speak, before I forgot how to.

"Uh, Mrs Ab," I began. "Is your husband home?"

"Ab hunt," she replied, coarsely but intelligibly.

Well, that was a relief. At least she could speak. I felt on more solid ground.

"I hope I haven't come at an inconvenient time," I said. "Allow me to introduce myself. I'm the new owner of the house below which you dwell. Your landlord, so to speak. As such, I have come here to make new arrangements regarding your tenancy. To put it plainly, Mrs Ab, my wife and I do not wish to have lodgers sharing our house. Nothing personal, you understand. I'm certain just from seeing your home that you and Mr Ab are fine folks, decent hardworking members of the lower middle class. And to be sure, you haven't made any disturbance that would be cause for complaint. It's just that we desire our privacy, you see, and the arrangements that exist now—the exit through our kitchen and all— Well, it just can't continue."

Mrs Ab cast a hairy hand behind her, indicating the depths of the cave. "Ab go that way, not your way."

Aha, that explained it. There was another entrance to the cavern. I pictured Mr Ab, spear in hand, exiting from between, say, two boulders in the city's park at night, hunting squirrels, dogs and cats. Amazing. Still, they had to go.

"Mrs Ab, I'm afraid you and your husband must find different lodgings as soon as possible. It's as simple as that. My wife and I plan to finish off the basement. Perhaps we shall install a Jacuzzi. No prejudice involved, I assure you. The Metas will be receiving their notice next."

Mrs Ab shivered charmingly. "No. Ice. Too much ice. We almost die once. No go again."

"Mrs Ab," I countered reasonably, "you're prevaricating. There is no ice outside. In fact, it's been one of the hottest summers on record. No, I'm afraid the old 'ice' excuse won't cut it. You must make plans to leave . . ."

Mrs Ab lay back on the floor. Bracing her feet, she spread her legs. Her inner thighs were hairy all the way to her genitals, which the firelight illumined in flickering detail.

I felt myself becoming aroused. The thick air seemed a primal aphrodisiac.

"Mrs Ab, get up," I begged. "This is not the way to behave . . ."

Still offering herself, she said, "No move. Please no move. We mate. No move."

"Mrs Ab," I faltered, "what you're proposing— I simply couldn't— It's out of the question."

Mrs Ab reached between her legs and spread the wet lips of her vagina.

It was more than I could withstand. Before I fully realized what I was doing, I was naked and atop her.

Our mating was the coupling of wild animals, brief but all-consuming, like a storm or wave.

When we were done, lying together, naked flesh against furred skin, Mrs Ab whispered over and over, "No move, no move . . ."

I must have dozed. When I awoke, the fire was low and Mrs Ab was gone.

I dressed and sleepily made my way back to the foot of the stairs. I went up. The journey, once made, seemed shorter the second time.

Upstairs, once more in our house, I shut the door and poked the nail into its old hole, so that the door would look permanently shut, yet allowing me easy entrance if I wished to return.

My wife had gone to bed. I took a shower to rinse away the ancient odors that clung to me, then joined her.

* * *

It was several days before I was able to contemplate with any equanimity the events that had transpired on my uncanny visit to the Abs, our intrusive and unwelcome basement-dwelling tenants. (If only they would just pack up their chipped flints and scraped mammoth hides and depart voluntarily, how wonderful everything would be! Our house would begin to assume the homogenous, unified nature we so desired . . .)

During this period my wife maintained a continuous inquiry as to how I had made out. Employing all the legalistic tricks of her trade, she probed and cross-examined me at breakfast and each evening on the reaction of the Abs to my demand that they depart.

Feeling as if I were on the witness stand, I grew tongue-tied and hesitant, and was unable to answer her questions satisfactorily.

"Well, just tell me: did they agree to vacate or not?"

"It's not as simple as getting a yes or no. There was, ah—a slight communication problem. As I suspected, they turned out to be, um—foreigners. It was hard to make myself understood . . ."

"We'll see if they have any trouble understanding the police enforcing an eviction notice!"

Naturally I couldn't tell her the truth of my seduction by the hirsute Mrs Ab and the awkward position of acquiescence it had placed me in, so I temporized, just as the realtor had done—and probably for the same reason.

"There's no need to take such a step yet. Just give me a little more time. I'm perfectly capable of handling this little matter."

"All right. But I won't put up with living this way much longer. And don't forget, you still haven't tackled the Metas yet."

Ah, yes, the Metas . . .

I had managed to push those unknown upstairs upstarts to the back of my mind. My wife's mention of them now brought them forward. Suddenly they seemed less like a hurdle than a convenient excuse to postpone revisiting the Abs.

"Good idea, dear. I'll deal with them tonight."

"It's about time!"

That evening I rose from my chair—where I had been pretending to read the newspaper while actually worrying about the upcoming encounter—and regarded my wife once more.

Dressed in her blue exercise suit, she was hanging upside down in a set of padded inversion cuffs attached to a braced chrome framework similar to a chin-up apparatus. She had detached the antenna from the television and inverted the set, so that she could watch it in her bat-like position.

I was momentarily overwhelmed by a strange sensation as I contemplated both her and the image of the documentary narrator standing on their heads. For an instant I was convinced that the whole world had flipped over, and that I alone was left wrong side up, falling, falling, falling—

When the queasy feeling dissipated, I asked, "What are you watching?"

"It's all about Freud and his theories. Id, ego, superego—you know."

I nodded, wondering what the mundane gesture looked like to my wife, from her novel perspective.

"I'm going to speak to the Metas now," I said.

She grunted a wordless reply, reminding me of Mrs Ab during her bestial climax. I left her thus.

Wandering throughout the second floor's many halls and rooms (our house was much bigger than it looked from the outside, due to many convolutions and curious folds), I pondered the problem of how to secure entrance to the third floor, where the Metas resided.

Just as there was no exterior access to the basement, so was there no outside flight of stairs that would lead to the Metas. Entrance, therefore, had to be made from somewhere within. Yet the main staircase ended at the second-floor landing.

But just as I had located the inconspicuous cellar door, I finally found the hidden way upward, in a dark corner at the end of a hall.

Obeying a nameless impulse to look up, I detected the hair-thin outline of a square trapdoor in the high ceiling. Fumbling about in the shadows, I discovered wooden rungs set into the wall.

Grasping an upper rung and lifting my right foot to the first, I began to climb.

It seemed to take an inordinate amount of time to reach the ceiling. When my head was nearly touching the trapdoor I placed a hand against it and pushed. The panel resisted slightly, as if long disused, then yielded.

As soon as the smallest crack showed, the panel was yanked away by unseen inanimate forces, a torrent of white light flooded out, blinding me, and I was snatched bodily, as if by suction, up and through the square hole in the ceiling.

I found myself standing in a medium-sized white room, lit by a harsh, pervasive light whose source was hidden. The walls and floor of the place were padded in a substance that seemed both organic and artificial, giving way slightly under pressure, like skin, yet firm and tough as plastic. There was no furniture, nor any door. And the panel in the floor, by which I had hoped to return to the familiar portion of our house, had been in some manner seamlessly closed. I could detect no trace of it.

As I stood, baffled, contemplating my prison, I sensed a presence behind me. I turned.

There had somehow appeared a man clothed in a form-fitting white jumpsuit of some synthetic material that merged imperceptibly with white boots. His head was completely bald. His features were smoothly regular and extraordinarily placid, as if he surveyed the world from a lofty perch, far removed from any of its foibles and cares. He looked utterly imperturbable.

This, then, had to be Mr Meta.

Before I could quite recover my equilibrium, he spoke.

"What are you doing here, sir? You really don't belong up here."

Mr Meta's voice was a sensible, rational monotone that completely infuriated me. To suffer such treatment in our own house—! It was too much. I'm afraid I lost my temper, and began to rant.

"You listen to me, Meta, it's you and your wife who don't belong here. I'm the new owner of this house, with clear and incontestable title. If anyone belongs here, it's my wife and me. We're sick of having half our house occupied by oddball tenants. We want it all! We're the owners, goddamn it, and we're serving notice! You've got no lease, and no right to live here without my sufferance. It's out on your ass, Meta, as soon as physically possible! Go try to find another landlord who'll have you!"

Mr Meta's face remained unmoving throughout my tirade. He failed even to cross his arms on his chest, as any normal person might do when confronted with hostility. Instead, those somehow arrogant limbs continued to hang, relaxed yet competent-seeming, by his side.

When I finally spluttered down, and the silence began to grow discomfiting, Mr Meta spoke.

"We'll have to discuss this with Mrs Meta. Please follow me."

Then he disappeared. As cleanly as vacuum imploding to nonexistence.

"Meta!" I called. "Mr Meta, where are you? Damn it, Meta, I can't follow like that. Don't leave me here, you bastard. Meta!"

Mr Meta's head and shoulders poked neatly through one wall, so that he looked like a mounted trophy.

"Please don't bellow, sir. Keep calm. We cherish our even-temperedness on this level. Please try to maintain an objective perspective on affairs, sir. Put yourself beyond emotions. It's the only way."

Mr Meta extended a hand through the wall, as in a Cocteau film.

Instinctively, I grasped it.

He pulled me through.

We were in another room identical to the first, save for an antiseptic white couch. On the couch sat Mrs Meta.

She was dressed identically to her husband, and was just as hairless. Her skull resembled a china egg. Save for a few different contours, she and Mr Meta could have been twins.

"My husband tells me you wish us to vacate our residence. May I ask why?"

Mrs Meta's voice was, if anything, even more disconcertingly rational than her husband's. Once again I was put off, and could speak only haltingly.

"Well, it's just that the wife and I need the space you're occupying. We're going to have children someday, you see . . ."

I faltered. It all sounded so lame and insignificant and somewhat bestial, in the presence of the noble sexless Metas. Still, now that I was here, I had to press on.

"Besides, it's unnatural, the kind of life you lead. I've never seen either of you leave our house. Who knows what you two do up here all day? How do you even survive? No, it's too creepy. We want you out."

Mr and Mrs Meta exchanged a glance pregnant with meaning. Then one of them—I confess to being so confused by now that I could hardly tell them apart—said, "Well, if we show you how we spend our time, will you reconsider?"

"I don't know. I, I—"

"Here, sit down with us."

Seeing no reason not to comply, I took a seat on the white couch, between the Metas. Mr Meta then gripped my right hand, Mrs Meta my left. I felt a strange sensation race up my arms. Then the Metas linked their free hands across my lap.

The room vanished. Disembodied, I was in a place filled with cold equations and numinous symbols, all gold and silver, pure and instantly apprehensible, yet infinitely deep. Totally disoriented, I tried to grasp the meaning of this new world. After a dimensionless time spent probing the symbols, I realized what I was viewing. It was a complex schematic representation of our familiar universe, all the people and objects and relationships therein, a structured, scientific version of our familiar jumbled mess of emotions and ethics, desires and compulsions, needs and wants. I could even distinguish the icons that represented the Metas and me, and our relationship. Their import was unmistakable: I was acting like an irrational idiot.

I felt utterly humbled and minuscule. For an indefinite period I remained in this pitiless abstract world, face to face with my own insignificance. In a stern kind of way, it was rather bracing. Finally, I returned involuntarily to the Metas' couch. They had broken the circle of hands.

"Now you see how we spend our time," said Mrs Meta. "Perhaps, in some slight fashion, you now understand why we cannot be disturbed."

I was speechless. I allowed Mr Meta to lead me back through the wall into the original room. There, he bent over, grabbed my ankles, and effortlessly lifted me up, so that I hung suspended in the same position my wife had occupied when I left her.

Then he pushed me headfirst through the floor.

Somehow, without having landed heavily, I was lying on the carpet in the hall outside our bedroom door. All the lights were off. It took a moment for my eyes, dazzled by the illumination of the Metas' apartment, to recover.

When I felt that I could make my way without stumbling, I stood and entered the bedroom. My wife, again, had gone to sleep without awaiting my return.

Exhausted, I crept into bed beside her, still clothed.

* * *

After my failure to evict the Metas, my wife's importunings became unbearable. When I couldn't stand them anymore, I burst out: "If you think you can handle the Abs and the Metas then go to it!"

"I will!" she feistily replied.

That night, descending the long staircase, she visited the Abs. I went to sleep before she returned, feeling not one whit guilty.

In the morning, she looked unnaturally disheveled, and had nothing to say. A male musk permeated her hair.

Two nights later, somewhat recovered, she set out for the Metas. I generously pointed out the location of their trapdoor.

Sometime around three A.M., I sleepily sensed her fall into bed beside me.

Over breakfast, I asked, "Did you convince the Metas to seek new lodgings?"

"Shut up," she wearily replied, as if embarrassed and confused.

After this, there was no more mention of our inherited tenants.

     * * *

Our life settled into an easy routine. Months passed.

We adapted quite nicely to sharing our house. Despite being excluded from cellar and third floor, we felt the house mold itself to our personalities like a favorite set of weekend clothing. We still planned to have children, but had resigned ourselves to housing them on the same floor as our bedroom. It would probably be more convenient anyway.

The Metas had, of course, been right: the house was big enough for all of us.

I have just said that we were excluded from the basement and the upper story. This was not entirely true.

There grew a pattern of visits between the levels, with my wife and I acting as solo intermediaries. (Naturally, the Metas never went slumming down with the Abs, nor would the Abs ever have dared to visit the Metas. In fact, I doubt whether the cave dwellers even knew or could possibly conceive of the existence of the Metas, beings so far removed from the life the Abs experienced.)

By far the majority of our separate visits were made downstairs, to the Abs. Their company was simply much more congenial than the chilly hospitality of the Metas. Far down below our house, sitting mutely for hours in the damp cave around the flickering flames that alternately disclosed and hid the painted walls, rolling on the gritty floor in animal passion, Mrs Ab's hairy legs locked behind my back, I felt utterly connected with my roots, cast backward in time to a more primal, aboriginal existence, where words and abstract concepts meant nothing, failed even to exist.

I believe my wife experienced the same sensations in her unaccompanied visits to the Abs. I knew, from the apish scent that clung to her the mornings after, that she regularly had carnal relations with Mr Ab (whom I had met one night, when heavy rains kept him from hunting; a fine fellow, the salt of the earth). But I wasn't jealous. How could I be, considering what I did with Mrs Ab?

No, my wife and I both gained from our separate visits below, and our own relationship was only strengthened.

Even the much rarer visits we made to the Metas were beneficial. The mental jaunts to the land of symbols, made with the Metas as guides, were as frigidly character-building as a January dip off the coast of Maine. Still, it was not something one cared to do every day, whereas visiting the Abs was. But alas, this happy coexistence was not to last forever . . .

One night I was taking my leave of Mrs Ab. We rose from the cave floor, I dressed, and, as was now her habit, Mrs Ab kindled a piney torch from the flames and accompanied me back to the foot of the stairs, lighting my way.

At the base of the wooden stairs, Mrs Ab was overcome with lust. (I believe her physiology included an actual period of estrus.) Dropping the torch, she ripped my clothes to shreds with her sharp nails and tripped me to the floor. Soon we were coupling as if we had not done it for weeks.

Unnoticed, the torch passed its flame to the staircase. The ancient wood quickly accepted the gift, and just at the climax of our union, I became aware of the spreading conflagration, which now lit the rocky walls with an awesome radiance.

The way upstairs was impassable. And fire was climbing two steps at a time toward the first floor.

I jumped up and managed to wrap a scrap of fabric around my loins. Grabbing Mrs Ab's furry hand, I raced back down the tunnel and out the exit I had never ventured down.

As I had once speculated, the tunnel emerged in a public park not far from our house, occupied during the day by addicts and drug peddlers, winos and children. Mrs Ab and I hurried through the deserted city streets back to our house.

The entire building was ablaze, a hopeless pyre lighting the night. On the lawn stood my wife and the Metas, looking bewildered. Yes, even the imperturbable Metas were reacting in their subdued fashion to the destruction of our beloved house.

Mrs Ab and I joined them. As we watched, Mr Ab slunk forlornly out of the night, dragging a club.

The six of us, huddling together, watched in silence for a time. Sirens began to fill the night.

"Ab cold," said Mr Ab at last.

"I'm heartsick," said my wife.

"There's just no making sense of this," said Mr Meta.

Further silence, save for the crackling of the flames.

In the end, I felt compelled to speak.

"Don't worry," I said. "There are other houses in this neighborhood just as nice. We only have to stick together, exert ourselves, and we'll surely find one. The important thing is not to split up."

"New safe cave?" inquired Mr Ab tentatively.

"Enough room for my office?" asked my wife.

"Privacy to meditate?" ventured Mr Meta.

"Yes," I said. They were all watching me hopefully. "Yes and yes. Something for everyone—

"All in our house."

JACK NECK AND
THE WORRYBIRD

On the western edge of putty-colored Drudge City, in the neighborhood of the Stoltz Hypobiological Refinery ("The lowest form of intelligent life—the highest form of dumb matter!"), not far from Newspaper Park and Boris Crocodile's Beanery and Caustics Bar—both within a knuckle-bone's throw of the crapulent, crepitant Isinglass River—lived mawkly old Jack Neck, along with his bat-winged and shark-toothed bonedog, Motherway.

Jack Neck was retired now, and mighty glad of it. He'd put in many a lugubrious lustrum at Krespo's Mangum Exordium, stirring the slorq vats, cleaning the lard filters, sweeping up the escaped tiddles. Plenty of work for any man's lifetime. Jack had busted his hump like a shemp to earn his current pension (the hump was just now recovering; it didn't wander so bad like it used to), and Jack knew that unlike the lazy young and fecund time-eaters and space-sprawlers whom he shared his cheapjack building with, he truly deserved his union stipend, all 500 crones per moon (except once a year, during the Short Thirteenth, when he only got 495). Why, it had taken him a whole year of retirement just to forget the sound of the tiddles crying out for mercy. Deadly core-piercing, that noise was, by Saint Fistula's Nose!

But now, having survived the rigors of the Exordium (not all his buddies had lived to claim their Get-gone Get-by; why, his pal Slam Slap could still be seen as a screaming bas-relief in the floor tiles of Chamber 409), Jack could take life slow and easy. During daylight hours, he could loll around his bachelor-unclean flat (chittering dust-bunnies prowling from couch to cupboard; obscurantist buildup on the windows, sulfur-yellow sweatcrust on the inside, pinky-grey smogma on the outside), quaffing his Anonymous Brand Bitterberry Slumps (two crones per sixpack, down at Batu Truant's Package Parlor) and watching the televised Motorball games. Lookit that gracefully knurltopped Dean Tesh play, how easily he scored, like a regular Kuykendall Canton pawpaw!

Ignoring his master's excited rumbles and despairing whoops, Motherway the steel-colored bonedog would lie peacefully by the side of Jack's slateslab chair, mostly droop-eyed and snore-birthing, occasionally emitting a low growl directed at a more-than-usually daring dustbunny, the bonedog's acutely articulated leathery wings reflexively snickersnacking in stifled pursuit.

Three times daily Motherway got his walkies. Down the four flights of badly lit, incongruently angled stairs Jack and his pet would clomber, Motherway's cloven chitin hooves scrabbling for purchase on the scarred boards. Last time down each day, Jack would pause in the lobby and check for mail. He never got anything, barring his moonly check, but it was good to clear the crumblies out of his wall-adherent mailsack. Dragoman Mr Spiffle wouldn't leave the mail if contumacious crumblies nested within Jack's fumarole-pocked personal mailsack. And Jack didn't blame him! One or two migrant crumblies a day could be dealt with—but not a whole moonly nest!

Outside on Marmoreal Boulevard, Jack and Motherway always turned left, toward Newspaper Park. Marmoreal Boulevard paralleled the Isinglass River, which gurgled and chortled in its high-banked channel directly across the Boulevard from Jack's flat. The mean and treacherous slippery river was further set off from foot and vehicle traffic by a wide promenade composed of earth-mortared butterblox and a rail of withyweave. Mostly, the promenade remained vacant of strollers. It didn't pay to get too close to the Isinglass, as more than one uncautious twitterer had discovered, when—peering curiously over the rail to goggle at the rainbowed plumduff sluicejuice pouring from the Stoltz Refinery pipes—he or she would be looped by a long suckered manipulator and pulled down to eternal aquatic slavery on the spillichaug plantations. GAWPERS AND LOOKYLOOS, BEWARE! read the numerous signage erected by the solicitous Drudge City Constabulary.

(Boating on the Isinglass held marginally fewer risks. Why, people were still talking about the event that quickly came to be known throughout Drudge City and beyond as "Pale Captain Dough's Angling Dismay," an event that Jack had had the misfortune to witness entire from his own flat. And he had thought the squeaky pleas of the tiddles were hard to dislodge from his mind—!)

Moving down the body- and booth-crowded sidewalk with a frowsty and jangly galumph that was partially a result of his fossilized left leg and partially attributable to the chunk-heeled, needle-toed boots which compressed his tiny feet unmercifully, Jack would enjoy the passing sights and sounds and smells of his neighborhood. A pack of low-slung Cranials surged by, eliciting a snap and lunge from the umbilical-restrained Motherway. From the pedal-powered, umbrella-shielded, salted-chickpea cart operated by Mother Gimlett wafted a delectable fragrance that always convinced Jack to part with a thread or two, securing in return a greasy paper cone of crispy steaming legumes. From the door of Boris Crocodile's poured forth angular music, the familiar bent notes and goo-modulated subsonics indicating that Stinky Frankie Konk was soloing on the hookah-piped banjo. Jack would lick his bristly nodule-dotted lips, anticipating his regular visit that evening to the boisterous Beanery and Caustics Bar, where he would be served a shot of his favorite dumble-rum by affable bartender Dinky Pachinko.

On the verge of Newspaper Park, beneath the towering headline tree, Jack would let slip Motherway's umbilical, which would retract inside the bonedog's belly with a whir and a click like a rollershade pull. Then Motherway would be off to romp with the other cavorting animals, the gilacats and sweaterbats, the tinkleslinks and slither-sloths. Jack would amble over to his favorite bench, where reliably could be found Dirty Bill Brownback. Dirty Bill was more or less permanently conjoined with his bench, the man's indiscriminate flesh mated with the porously acquisitive material of the seat. Surviving all weathers and seasons, subsisting on a diet scrounged from the trash can placed conveniently at his elbow, Dirty Bill boasted cobwebbed armpits and crumbly-infested trousers, but was nonetheless an affable companion. Functioning as a center of fresh gossip and rumors, news and notions, Dirty Bill nevertheless always greeted Jack Neck with the same stale jibe.

"Hey, Neck, still wearing those cellbug togs? Can't you afford better on your GGGB?"

True, Jack Neck's outfit went unchanged from one moon to the next. His ivory- and ash-striped shirt and identically patterned leggings were the official workwear of his union, the MMMM, or Mangum Maulers Monitoring Moiety, and Jack's body had grown accustomed to the clothes through his long employment. Of course, the clothes had also grown accustomed to Jack's body, fusing in irregular lumpy seams and knobbly patches to his jocund, rubicund, moribund flesh. That was just the way it went these days, in the midst of the Indeterminate. The stability of the Boredom was no more. Boundaries were flux-prone, cause-and-effect ineffectual, and forms not distinct from ideations. You soon got used to the semi-regular chaos, though, even if, like Jack, you had been born 'way back in the Boredom.

With the same predictability exhibited by Dirty Bill (human social vapidity remained perhaps the most stable force in the Indeterminate), Jack would consistently reply, "Happens I fancy these orts, Dirty Bill. And they fancy me!"

With a chuckle and a snaggletooth snigger, Dirty Bill would pat the bench beside him and offer, "Sit a spell then, neckless Jack Neck—not too long though, mind you!—and I'll fill you in on my latest gleanings. That is, if you'll share a salty chickpea or two!"

"Gladly, you old plank-ass!" Diverting as the perpetual Motorball Tourneys on television were, Jack relished simple human intercourse. So while Motherway chased six-legged squirrels (all four of the mature bonedog's feet an inch or two off the ground; only bonedog pups could get much higher), Jack and Dirty Bill would confab the droogly minutes away.

After his supper each night—commonly a pot of slush-slumgullion or a frozen precooked bluefish fillet heated in the hellbox, whichever being washed down with a tankard of Smith's Durian Essence—Jack would leave Motherway behind to lick doggy balls and umbilical while the bonedog's master made his visit to Boris Crocodile's. There on his reserved barstool, while empty-eyed Nori Nougat danced the latest fandango or barcarole with beetle-browed Zack Zither, Jack Neck would nod his own disproportionate head in time to the querulous squeegeeing of Stinky Frankie Konk and affirm to all who would pay any heed to the elderly GGGB-er, "Yessir, assuming you can get through the rough spots, life can turn out mighty sweet!"

But all that, of course, was before the advent of the Worrybird.

* * *

That fateful morning dawned nasty, low-hanging hieratic skies and burnt-toast clouds, an ugly odor like all the rain-drenched lost stuffed-toys of childhood seeping in from the streets. Upon opening first his good left eye, then his bad right ('twasn't the eye itself that was dodgy, but only the nacreous cheek-carbuncle below it that was smooshing the orb closed), Jack Neck experienced a ripe intestinal feeling telling him he should stay in bed. Just huddle up 'neath his checkerboard marshmallow quilt, leaving his beleathered feet safe in the grooves they had worn in the milkweed-stuffed mattress. Yes, that seemed just the safest course on a day like today, so pawky and slyboots.

But the allure of the common comforts awaiting him proved stronger than his intuition. Why, today was a Motorball matchup made in heaven! The Chlorine Castigators versus Dame Middlecamp's Prancers! And then there was Motherway to be walked, Dirty Bill's dishy yatterings, that Dinky-Pachinko-poured tot of dumble-rum to welcome midnight in. Surely nothing mingy nor mulcting would befall him, if he kept to his established paths and habits. . . .

So out of his splavined cot old bunion-rumped Jack Neck poured himself, heavy hump leading Lady Gravity in an awkward pavane. Once standing, with minor exertions Jack managed to hitch his hump around, behind and upward to a less unaccomodatingly exigent position. Then he essayed the palpable trail midst the debris of his domicile that led to the bathroom.

As soon as Jack entered the WC, he knew his vague forebodings had been spot on. But it was now too late to return to the safety of his blankets. For Jack saw with dismay that out of his chipped granite commode, like a baleful excremental spirit, there arose a Smoking Toilet Puppet.

The rugose figure was composed of an elongated mud-colored torso, sprouting two boneless and sinuous claw-fingered arms, and topped by a rutted warpy face. The Puppet's head was crowned by a small fumey crater, giving its kind their name.

"Ja-a-ack," wailed the Puppet. "Jack Neck! Step closer! I have a message for you."

Jack knew that although the creature might indeed have a valid and valuable delphic message for him, to heed the Puppet's summons was to risk being abducted down to the gluck-mucky Septic Kingdom ruled by Baron Sugarslinger. So with an uncommon burst of energy, Jack grabbed up a wood-hafted sump-plunger and whanged the Puppet a good one on its audacious incense-dispensing bean.

While the Puppet was clutching its abused noggin and sobbing most piteously, Jack stepped around it and flushed. Widdershins and downward swirled the invader, disappearing with a liquidly dopplering "Nooooooo—!"

Jack did his old man's business quickly while the runnels still gurgled, then lowered the heavy toilet lid against further home invasions. He stepped to the sink and the sweatcrusted mirror above it, where he flaked scales off his reflection. He shaved his forehead, restoring the pointy dimensions of his once-stylish hairline, plucked some eelgrass out of his ears, lacquered his carbuncle, and congratulated himself on meeting so forcefully the first challenge of the day. If nothing else adventured, he would be polly-with-a-lolly!

Back through the bedroom and out into his sitting sanctuary, where Motherway lay snoozily on his fulsome scrap of Geelvink carpet. Approaching the dirty window that looked out upon Marmoreal Boulevard and the Isinglass, the incautious and overoptimistic Jack Neck threw open the wormy sash and shouldered forward, questing additional meaning and haruspices from the day.

And that was precisely the moment the waiting Worrybird chose to land talon-tight upon the convenient perch of Jack's hapless hump!

Jack yelped and with an instinctive yet hopeless shake of his hump withdrew into the refuge of his apartment, thinking to disconcert and dislodge the Worrybird by swift maneuvers. But matters had already progressed beyond any such simple solution. The Worrybird was truly and determinedly ensconced, and Jack realized he was doomed.

Big as a turkey, with crepe-like vulture wings, the baldy Worrybird possessed a dour human face exhibiting the texture of ancient over-waxed linoleum, and exuded a stench like burning crones. Jack had seen the ominous parasites often, of course, riding on their wan, slumpy victims. But never had he thought to be ridden by one such!

Awakened by the foofraraw, Motherway was barking and leaping and snapping, frantically trying to drive the intruder off. But all the bonedog succeeded in doing was gouging his master's single sensible leg with his hooves. Jack managed to calm the bonedog down, although Motherway continued to whimper while anxiously fidgeting.

Now the Worrybird craned its paste-pallid pug-ugly face around on its long sebaceous neck to confront Jack. It opened its hideous rubbery mouth and intoned a portentous phrase.

"Never again, but not yet!"

Jack threw himself into his slateslab chair, thinking to crush the grim bird, but it leaped nimbly atop Jack's skull. By Saint Foraminifer's Liver, those scalp-digging claws hurt! Quickly Jack stood, prefering to let the bird roost on his hump. Obligingly, the Worrybird shifted back.

"Oh, Motherway," Jack implored, "what a fardelicious grievance has been construed upon us! What oh what are we to do?"

Motherway made inutile answer only by a plangent sympathetic whuffle.

* * *

The first thought to form in the anxious mind of bird-bestridden Jack Neck was that he should apply to the local Health Clinic run by the Little Sisters of Saint Farquahar. Surely the talented technicians and charity caregivers there would have a solution to his grisly geas! (Although at the back of his mind loomed the pessimistic question, perhaps Worrybird implanted, *Why did anyone suffer from Worrybird-itis if removal of same were so simple?*)

So, leaving Motherway behind to guard the apartment from any further misfortunes which this inopportune day might bring, Jack and his randomly remonstrative rider ("Never again, but not yet!") clabbered down the four flights of slant stairs to the street.

Once on Marmoreal (where formerly friendly or neutral neighbors now winced and retreated from sight of his affliction), Jack turned not happy-wise left but appointment-bound right. At the intersection of the Boulevard and El Chino Street, he wambled south on the cross-street. Several blocks down El Chino his progress was arrested by the sloppy aftermath of an accident: a dray full of Smith's Durian Essence had collided with one loaded with Walrus Brand Brochettes. The combination of the two antagonistic spilled foodstuffs had precipitated something noxious: galorping mounds of quivering dayglo cartiplasm that sought to ingest any flesh within reach. (The draft-animals, a brace of Banana Slugs per dray, had already succumbed, as had the blindly argumentative drivers, one Pheon Ploog and a certain Elmer Sourbray.)

Responding with the nimble reflexes and sassy footwork expected from any survivor of Drudge City's ordinary cataclysms, Jack dodged into a nearby building, rode a Recirculating Transport Fountain upward and took a wayward rooftop path around the crisis before descending, all the while writing a hundred times on the blackboard of his mind an exclamation-punctuated admonition never to mix internally his favorite suppertime drink with any iota of Walrus Brand Brochettes.

Encountering no subsequent pandygandy, Jack Neck and his foul avian passenger arrived at the Health Clinic on Laguna Diamante

Way. Once inside, he was confronted with the stern and ruleacious face of Nurse Gwendolyn Hindlip, Triage Enforcement Officer. From behind her rune-carven desk that seemed assembled of poorly chosen driftwood fragments, Nurse Gwendolyn sized up Jack and his hump-burden, then uttered a presumptuous pronouncement.

"You might as well kill yourself now, you old mummer, and free up your GGGB for a younkling!"

Jack resented being called a mummer—a mildly derisive slang term derived from his union's initials—almost more than he umbrigated at the suicidal injunction.

"Shut up, you lava-faced hincty harridan! Just take my particulars, slot my citizen-biscuit into the chewer, and mind your own business!"

Nurse Gwendolyn sniffed with bruised emotionality. Jack had scored a mighty blow on a tender spot with his categorical comment "lava-faced." For Nurse Gwendolyn's scare-making and scarified visage did indeed reflect her own childhood brush with a flesh-melting disease that still occasionally plagued Drudge City. Known as Trough'n'Slough, the nonfatal disease left its victims with a stratified trapunto epidermis. Nurse Gwendolyn forever attributed her sour old-maidhood to the stigma of this pillowpuff complexion, although truth be told, her vile tongue had even more to do with her empty bed.

Snuffling aggrievedly, Nurse Gwendolyn now did as she was bade, at last dispatching a newly ID-braceleted Jack to a waiting area with the final tart remark, "You'll surely have a long uncomfortable wait, Mr Neck, for many and more seriously afflicted—yet naytheless with a better prognosis—are the helpseekers afore you!"

Coercing his fossil leg into the waiting room, Jack saw that Nurse Gwendolyn had not been merely flibbering. Ranked and stacked in moaning drifts and piles were a staggering assortment of Drudge City's malfunctioners. Jack spotted many a one showing various grades of Maskelyne's Curse, in which the face assumed the characteristics of a thickly blurred latex mold of the actual submerged features beneath. The false countenance remained connected by sensory tendrils, yet was migratory, so that one's visage slopped about like warm jello, eyes peeking from nostrils or ears, nose poking from mouth. Other patients showed plain signs of Exoskeletal Exfoliation, their limbs encased in osteoclastic armor. One woman—dressed in a tattered shift laterally patterned blue and gold—could only be host to Dolly Dwindles Syndrome: as she approached over months her ulti-

mate doll-like dimensions, her face simultaneously grew more lascivious in a ghoulish manner.

Heaving a profound sigh at the mortal sufferings of himself and his
fellows, Jack sat himself saggingly down in a low-backed chair that
permitted the Worrybird to maintain its grip upon Jack's hump, and
resigned himself to a long wait.

On the 749th "Never again, but not yet!" Jack's name was called.
He arose and was conducted to a cubicle screened from an infinity of
others by ripped curtains the color of old tartar sauce. Undressing was
not an option, so he simply plopped down on a squelchy examining
table and awaited the advent of a healer. Before too long the curtains
parted and a lab-coated figure entered.

This runcible-snouted doctor himself, thought Jack, should have
been a patient, for he was clearly in an advanced state of Tessellated
Scale Mange, as evidenced by alligatored wrists and neck poking from
cuff and collar. Most horridly, the medico dragged behind him a long
ridged tail, ever-extending like an accumulating stalactite from an
infiltrated organ at the base of the spine.

"Doctor Weighbend," said the professional in a confident voice,
extending a crocodile paw. Jack shook hands happily, liking the
fellow's vim. But Doctor Weighbend's next question shattered Jack's
sanguinity.

"Now, what seems to be the matter with you, Mr Neck?"

"Why—why, Doc, there's an irksome and grotty Worrybird implacably asway upon my tired old hump!"

Doctor Weighbend made a suave dismissive motion. "Oh, that. Since
there's no known cure for the Worrybird, Mr Neck, I assumed there was
another issue to deal with, some unseen plaque or innervation perhaps."

"No known cure, Doc? How can that be?"

Doctor Weighbend cupped his dragonly chin. "The Worrybird has
by now slyly and inextricably mingled his Akashic Aura with yours.
Were we to kill or even remove the little vampire-sparrow, you too
would perish. Of course, you'll perish eventually anyway, as the
lachrymose-lark siphons off your vitality. But that process could take
years and years. 'Never again will you smile, but not yet shall you die.'
That's the gist of it, I fear, Mr Neck."

"What—what do you recommend then?"

"Many people find some small palliation in building a festive
concealing shelter for their Worrybird. Securely strapped to your torso

bandolier-style and gaily decorated with soothing icons, it eases social functioning to a small degree. Now, I have other patients to attend to, if you'll permit me to take my leave by wishing you a minimally satisfactory rest of your life."

Doctor Weighbend spun around—his massive tail catching a cart of instruments and beakers and sending glassware smashing to the floor—and was gone. Jack sat wearily and down-in-the-dumpily for a few long minutes, then levered himself up and trudged off down the aisle formed by the curtained wards.

Almost to the exit, Jack's attention was drawn between two parted drapes.

On a table lay the Motorball Champion Dean Tesh! Bloodied and grimacing, his signature cornucopia-shaped head drooping, sparks and fizzles spurting from his numerous lumpy adjuncts, Jack Neck's hero awaited his own treatment. Assuredly, that day's game had been a rumbunctious and asgardian fray! And Jack had missed it!

Impulsively, Jack entered the Champion's cubicle. "Superlative Dean Tesh, if I may intrude briefly upon your eminence. I'm one of your biggest fans, and I wish to offer my condolences on your lapsarian desuetude."

Dean Tesh boldly smiled like the rigorous roughrider he was. "'Tis nothing, really, old mummenschanz. Once they jimmy open my cranial circuit flap and insert a few new wigwags, I'll be right as skysyrup!"

Jack blushed to be addressed by his union's highest title, in actuality undeserved. "Your magnificent spirit inspires me, lordly Dean Tesh! Somehow I too will win through my own malediction!"

Dean Tesh's ocular lenses whirred for a better look. "Worrybird, is it? I've heard Uncle Bradley has a way with them."

"Uncle Bradley! Of course! Did he not design your own world-renowned servos and shunts? If medicine holds no answers to my problem, then surely Uncle Bradley's Syntactical Fibroid Engineering must!"

And so bidding Dean Tesh a heartfelt farewell replete with benisonical affirmations of the Champion's swift recovery, Jack Neck set out for Cementville.

*　*　*

Soon Jack's trail of tiny archless footprints—outlined in fast-growing sporulating molds and luminescent quiverslimes—could be traced through many an urban mile. Behind him already lay the evil precincts of Barrio Garmi, where the Stilt-legged Spreckles were prone to drop rotten melons from their lofty vantages upon innocent passersby. Jack had with wiles and guiles eluded that sloppy fate. The district of Clovis Points he had also cunningly circumnavigated, wrenching free at the last possible moment from the tenebrous grasp of a pack of Shanghai Liliths, whose lickerish intention it was to drag innocent Jack to their spraddle-skirted leader, Lil' Omen, for the irreligious ceremony known as the Ecstatic Excruciation. For several blocks thereafter he had dared to ride the Henniker Avenue Slantwise Subway, disembarking hastily through his car's emergency exit and thence by escape-ready ladder-chute when he spotted a blockade across the tracks surely erected by the muskageous minions of Baron Sugarslinger. Luckily, Jack had had the foresight to obtain a transfer-wafer and so was able to board the Baba Wanderly Aerial Viaticum for free, riding high and safe above the verdigrised copper-colored towers and chimney-pots, gables and garrets of Doo-Boo-Kay Flats.

At last, as a pavonine dusk was o'erspreading the haze-raddled, swag-bellied firmament, Jack Neck and his endlessly asseverating Worrybird—its face like a hairless druid's, its folded wings gloomy as a layoff notice from Krespo's—arrived at the premises of Uncle Bradley. The largest employer in gritty Cementville, the firm of Bradley and His Boyo-Boys, experts in SFE, ran round the erratic clock all thirteen moons a year, turning out many and many a marvelous product, both luxuries and essentials, the former including Seductive Bergamot Filters and the latter notable for Nevermiss Nailguns. Renowned for accepting any and all engineering challenges, the more intractable the more alluring, Uncle Bradley represented Jack's best hope in the Worrybird-Removal Department.

At the towering portal to the lumbering and rachitic nine-storey algae-brick-fronted manufactory that occupied ten square blocks of Dimmig Gardens, Jack made free with the bellpull: the nose of a leering brass jackanapes. A minidoor opened within the gigundo pressboard entrance, and a functionary appeared. As the employee began to speak, Jack noted with dismay that the fellow suffered from Papyrus Mouth: his words emerged not as ordinary vocables but as separate words printed in blearsome bodily inks upon shoddy scraps of organic-tissue paper.

Jack sought to catch the emergent syllables as they spelunked buccally forth, but some eluded him and whiffed away on the diddling breezes. Nervously assembling the remaining message, Jack read: *Business state Bradley please with.*

"I need to solicit dear Uncle Bradley's genius in the area of invasive parasite disengagement." Jack jerked a thick split-nailed thumb backward at his broodsome rider.

A gush of flighty papyri: *Follow Bradley Uncle free see if me.*

Most gladfully, Jack Neck entered the dynamic establishment and strode after the Papyrus Mouther. Through humming, thrumming offices and sparky workshops—where crucibles glowed with neon-tinted polymeric compounds and, under the nimble fingers of Machine Elves, transistors danced the Happy Chicken Trot with capacitors and optical-fluid valves—Jack and his guide threaded, until at last they stood before a ridged and fumarole-pocked door with a riveted steel rubric announcing it as UNCLE BRADLEY'S CARBON CAVE.

Wait here.

Alone, Jack hipper-hopped nervously from toe to toe. He prayed to all the Saints whose names he could remember—Fimbule and Flubber, Flacken and Floss, Fluffie and Farina—that Uncle Bradley possessed the secret of his salvation—and at a price he could afford.

After an almost unsquingeable wait, the Papyrus Mouther returned.

with Bradley will now you Uncle meet.

"Oh, thank you, kind underling! A myriad blessings of the Yongy-bongy-bo descend upon you!"

Into the fabled Hades-embered Carbon Cave now, whose inward-seeming rattled Jack's sensory modes. The walls and ceiling of the vasty deep were layered with snivelling encrustations of Syntactical Fibroid Engineering at its most complex. Flickering readouts and mumbling speaker-grilles obtruded their cicatrice-bordered surfaces from amongst switches and pulls, toggles and knife-throws, fingering-holes and mentation-bands. Innumerable crystal monitors studded all surfaces, displaying upon their garnet and amethyst faces scenes from across Drudge City. For a briefer-than-brief second, a shot of Marmoreal Boulevard—right in front of Boris Crocodile's!—flashed acrost one, and Jack nearly wept for the nostalgic past of mere yester-day!

In the middle of the Carbon Cave, on his numinous, numbly throne, sat Uncle Bradley. Almost totally overwhelmed with layers of SFE extrudements, a helpful carapace of gadgetry, the master of the Boyo-Boys showed bare only his snaggle-toothed and wildly inventive face, and his two striped arms, one of which terminated in chromium piratical hook. Dangling all around inspiration-eyed Uncle Bradley were speakers and microphones, mini-monitors, telefactored manipulators and sniff-sources, allowing him to run his many-branched enterprise without leaving his cozy sanctum.

As Jack approached tentatively across the wide checkerboard floor, he could hear from Uncle Bradley a constant stream of queries, advice and commands.

"Lay on ten thousand more karma-watts to the Soul Furnace! Process Violet-Hundred is failing? Six hundred kilograms of Charm Catalyst into the mix! Eureka! Start a new assembly line: personal Eyeblink Moderators! Has the Bloodwort stabilized yet? No? Lash it with the Zestful Invigorators! Cancel the Corndog Project, and feed the experimental subjects to the Hullygees! How are the Pull Hats selling this season? That poorly? Try them with claw-tassels in plaid!"

Jack and his momentarily silent Worrybird had reached the base of Uncle Bradley's seat of power, and now the Edisonical eminence took notice of the supplicant. Before Jack could even state his need, Uncle Bradley, laying a machicolated salesman's smile upon him, was offering a concise prix fixe of options.

"Worrybird, correct? Of course! Obviousness obtrudes! Here are your recoursical tactics, in order of cost and desirability. For five thousand crones, we inject the bird with a Circuitry Virus. In three days the bird is totally roboticized. Still unremovable, of course, but its lethality is slowed by fifty percent. For three thousand crones, we attach a Secondary Imagineer to your cerebrumal interstices. You promptly forget the bird is there for the rest of your allotted span. For eight hundred crones, a simple cable allows you to share the bird's own mentation. Thus you enjoy your own death, and feel it to be Darwinically mandated. Lastly, for a piddling three hundred crones, we remand one of our novice Boyo-Boys to stay by your side till you succumb to the inevitable wastage. He plys you with personalized jest and frolic, and remonstrates with anyone who dares to offer you contumely!"

Jack could barely conceal his dismay. "Those—those are my only choices?"

"What more could a sensible man want? The Worrybird is an incorrigible opponent, and no one besides the recondite and rascally Uncle Bradley dares even to tamper with one! Be quick now, old gansel! Which will it be?"

Jack wimbled and wambled pitifully. "I have not even the three hundred crones for the humblest palliation. I was hoping for more triumphalist affronts and easier terms—"

"What! You dare to waste Uncle's invaluable chronospasms without funds in reserve! And then to derogate my nostrums as if you were a fellow engineer at a throwdown session of the Tinkerer's Sodality! Away with you, laggardly old momerath!"

Suddenly, the Papyrus Mouther was by Jack's elbow. Without pleasant hostly ado, Jack was spun about and frog-marched from the Cave of the SFErical Monarch. Just before the heavy door slammed behind him, Jack could hear Uncle Bradley resume his litany of savantical willfullness: "Engage the services of ten thousand more Glissandos, and another dozen Kriegsteins!"

Summarily and insultively ejected onto the cheesily porous cobbled terrace before the SFErical Emporium, true night pressing down from above like a corpulent lover, Jack knew himself at the end of both his abilities and the universe's possibilities. The weight of the Worrybird seemed suddenly Atlasian. At the first "Never again, but not yet!" every nerve in Jack's poor frame thrilled with galvanic imbroglication. He hung his head, able to focus only on the snailslick cobbles.

Three tags of papyrus skittered by just then, and without much hope Jack used the last of his scanty vigor to retrieve them.

Seek Saint Fiacre.

* * *

Now was veracious and lordly midnight come without fear of fleering misrecognition to occupy Drudge City like a famously conquering cubic khan. Much too low in the sky hung a sherberty scoop-hollowed partial moon like a slice of vanilla ice cream-sheened cantaloupe half-eaten by a finicky godling. Stars shown in the space between the tips of the errant satellite's horns. Insect-seeking sweaterbats, their calls of "stitch-stitch!" leavening the mist, thronged the curvaceous canyons formed by the tottering towers of home and office, both kinds of hobbledehoy establishment darkened as their inhabitants blissfully or troubledly slept. Only meeps and monks, strumpets and troubadors, witlings and mudlarks were abroad at this hour—at least in this dismal section of Drudge City. Perhaps among the delightful theaters in the district known as Prisbey's Heaves, or in the saucer-slurping cafes of Mechanics' Ramble, good citizens yet disported themselves without fear of encountering lurking angina-anklers or burrow-bums. And surely—most sadly of a certainty—at Boris Crocodile's Beanery and Caustics Bar, ghosty-eyed Nori Nougat was even at this moment frugging with ledge-browed Zack Zither, while Stinky Frankie Konk tortured banshee wails from his hybrid instrument.

But out here, where putrid Ashmolean Alley and rancid Rotifer Gangway ranked as the only streets of distinction, no such gaiety could be found. There lolloped only a besmirched and bedaubed and bedemoned Jack Neck, bustedly dragging himself down block after block, in search of Saint Fiacre.

The last Jack had heard—from Dirty Bill Brownback, in fact—rumors of a Saint sighting had recently wafted from out Ubidio way. No guarantee that said sighted Saint was named Fiacre, or that he was even still present. Saints had a disconcerting propensity to phase-shift at random. Yet poor Jack Neck had no other phantom to pursue, so thitherward he now leathered.

Two hours past the night's navel, Jack Neck emerged from encircling buildings onto bare-tiled Pringle Plaza. In the middle of the civic space ruminated an eyelid-shuttered naked Saint.

The Saint had once been human. After much spiritual kenning and abstemious indulgences, making the choice to give him or herself up entirely to the avariciously bountiful forces of the Indeterminate, the human had morpholyzed into a Saint. The Saint's trunk had widened and spread into a bulbous heap, from which sprouted withered legs and off-kilter arms, but no visible generative parts. Instead, out of the trunk at queer angles protruded numerous quasi-organic spouts and intakes similar to rusty gutter-pipes. The Saint's neck was a corded barrel supporting a pointy-peaked head on which the features had wandered north, south, east and west. Overall, the creature was a pebbled mushroom-white, and three times the size of Jack. Around this living interface with the Indeterminate, the air wavered whorlfully.

Humble as a wet cat, Jack approached the Saint. When the Worrybird-carrier was within a few yards of the strange being, the Saint opened his eyes.

"Are thee Fiacre?" nervously intoned Jack, who had never cozened with a Saint before, nor ever thought to.

"Aye."

"I was sent to thee. This bumptious bird I would begone."

The Saint pondered for a chronospasm. "You must perambulate round the Inverted Stupa for three hours, reciting without cease, 'Always once again, and perhaps now.'"

"This will cause the Worrybird to relinquish its hold?"

"Not at all. The procedure will simply give me further time to peer into the Indeterminate. But nonetheless, you must attend with precision to my instructions, upon pain of rasterbation."

"As you say, oh Saint."

Luckily, the Inverted Stupa was only half a league onward. Hurrying with renewed hope, Jack soon reached the famous monument. In the middle of another peopleless plaza, lit fitfully by torches of witch's hair, was a railed pit of no small dimensions. Looking down over the rail, Jack saw the vertiginous walls of the Inverted Stupa, lighted windows stretching down to the earth's borborygmus bowels, deeper by far than even Baron Sugarslinger's realm.

Without delay, Jack began his circular hegira, chanting his Saintly mantra.

"Always once again, and perhaps now. Always once again, and perhaps now. . . ."

The Worrybird seemed in no wise discommoded by Jack's croaking exertions. Jack tried not to lose his resurgent tentative cheer. At long last, just when Jack's legs—both good and bad—felt ready to snap, a nearby clock tolled five, releasing him to return to the Saint.

Saint Fiacre sat unchanged, a yeasty enigmatic effigy with a face like an anthropomorphic cartoon breadloaf.

"You have done well, old mockmurphy. Come close now, and cover my sacred Intake Number Nine with your palm."

Jack sidle-stepped up to the Saint, entering the zone where his vision burbled. He raised his hand toward the properly labeled body-pipe, then capped the opening with the flat of his permanently work-roughened hand.

Instantly, the insidious and undeniable vacuum-suck of ten dozen black holes!

Jack's hand was quickly pulled in. Before he could even gasp, his shoulder was pressed to the treacherous Intake Number Nine. Then Jack felt himself drawn even further in! Oddly he experienced no pain. Only, he was sure, because he was already dead.

Soon Jack was ingulped headwise up to both shoulders. His hump delayed his swallowment slightly, but then, thanks to a swelling surge of pull-power, even his abused hump was past the rim.

And the Worrybird too? Apparently not! Peeled off like a potato skin was that manfaced mordant! But what of their commingled Akashic Aura? Only Gossip Time would tell. . . .

Within seconds, Jack was fully through Intake Number Nine. Then began a journey of sense-thwarting intricacy. Through a maze of bloodlit veiny pipes Jack flowed like the slorq at Krespo's, until he finally shot out of a funnel-mouth into ultracolored drifts of sheer abundant nothingness that smelled like a bosomy woman and tasted like Shugwort's Lemon Coddle. Here existence was a matter of wayward wafts and dreamy enticements, so connubially unlike the pestiferous hurlyburly of mundane existence. Time evaporated, and soon Jack did too. . . .

Early morning in Pringle Plaza, sunlight like the drip of candy apple glaze. Sanitation chimps were about their cleaning, sweeping litter and leaf into the open mouths of attendant roadhogs. A traveling preacher had unfolded his pocket altar and was preaching the doctrine of Klacktoveedsedsteen to a yawning group of bow-tied office dandies. Saint Fiacre, having just given a lonely little girl the second head she had requested, suddenly quivered all over as if stricken by Earthquake Ague, then decocted a real-as-mud, sprightly-as-fleas Jack Neck from Outflow Number Three.

Jack got woozily to his tiny feet. "Saint Fiacre, I thank thee!"

"Say twenty-seven Nuclear Novenas nightly, invoking the names of Gretchen Growl, Mercy Luna and the Rowrbazzle. And do not stick your foolish mummer's head out any more windows without forethought."

And then Saint Fiacre was gone.

* * *

Having polished off his supper and seen the merry Motherway lickily attending to his bonedog privates, mawkly old Jack Neck now commonly got to Boris Crocodile's a little later each night. Those Nuclear Novenas took time, and he did not trust either his tongue or his pledged determination after a shot of Dinky Pachinko's dumble-rum. Neither could his saviorology be allowed to interfere during the day with Jack's ardent eyeballing of the exploits of the mighty Dean Tesh, Motorball Mauler! So postprandial were his doxologies.

But despite the slight change in his schedule, Jack still entered the Beanery and Caustics Bar in mid-stridulation of hookah-banjo, still found his favorite reserved barstool awaiting him, still feasted his rheumy eyes on the flirtsome gavotteners atrot, and still affirmed to any and all who would lend an ear, "Yessir, assuming you can get through the rough spots, life can turn out mighty sweet!"

This story was inspired by the paintings of Chris Mars. For more information, contact Chris Mars, P.O. Box 24631, Edina, MN 55424.

STEALING HAPPY HOURS

The wedding reception could have been mistaken for a wake.

I had never attended a gloomier celebration. The courtroom proceedings for my own divorce—as rabid and rancid a ruckus as any since the days of Henry VIII—would have passed as a Saturday night during the pinnacle of Studio 54, when juxtaposed with this dreary affair.

At my table, reserved for unmated oddball friends of the bride and groom, a middle-aged woman on my left was endlessly stubbing out the same dead cigarette in the remains of her potatoes au gratin. The trim elderly gent to my right had taken to polishing his eyeglasses to invisibility with a corner of his napkin. And across the littered expanse of tablecloth a twenty-something gal—hair gelled sharp and colored like a tetra's scales—chewed her drearily painted fingernails like a cougar gnawing its own trap-bound leg. And as for myself, I wallowed in an orgy of long, deep sighs, foot-tapping and wedgie-level squirming.

And the biggest scandal of the whole day was that there was absolutely no reason for this pall.

Stan and Andrea were a wonderful couple: witty, young, energetic and generous. Everybody loved them. The vibe in the church had been one of overwhelming joy. Any tears had been consecrated with pride and pleasure. Every part of the ceremony had gone off without a hitch. Even the weather had cooperated, the June sunlight like some kind of photonic champagne.

But as soon as everybody had settled down in the lush banquet hall—bang! Complete morbid ennui descended inexplicably like soot from a smokestack over the entire party. The band, much touted, began to play. They sounded as leaden and lackluster as an unprogrammed drum machine. The waitpeople circulated like bit players from a George Romero film. At the head table, the bride and groom and their attendants wore smiles as wan as those of felons who had just been spared the death sentence but gotten life plus ten.

And it wasn't as if people weren't still *trying* to have fun. You could see it in their faces and postures. They were straining to enjoy themselves, having anticipated this day for months. The collective amount of energy being exerted by the crowd could have powered an Arctic icebreaking cutter. People grinned painfully and tried to chat throughout the meal. Forced laughter brittled the room. Much liquor was consumed. Couples strove to put some zip in their dancing. But all their efforts died on the vine. It was as if some invisible wet blanket an inch above our heads smothered all the excitement as soon as it was born.

When I saw Stan excuse himself, probably to go to the john, I got up too. I figured I'd catch him in the men's room and broach the problem to him, get his ideas about what anyone could do, even at this late hour, to liven things up. Also, I wanted to make sure he didn't hang himself with his bow tie.

Strangely, in the lavatory I felt a little better. Stan nodded to me, and we peed at adjacent urinals without conversing, just relishing the psychic and physical relief. Then, zipping up, I spoke.

"Why's everyone on such a sudden massive downer, guy? Something happen I don't know about? Favorite uncle of Andrea's die between the church and here maybe? Stock market went down the tank? Nuclear war declared?"

"Jesus, Mitch, how should I know? I can't explain it. This was supposed to be the happiest day of my life, and instead I feel like I just got a ransom note for my unborn daughter. I've been racking my brain, but I can't come up with an answer. Food poisoning? Sick building syndrome? Roofies in the champagne? Maybe it's some weird fluke of the seating arrangements. But the majority of these people have known each other for decades. All hatchets have long been buried. I just can't come up with any reason that makes sense."

We started back toward the main room, and the closer we got, the more lackluster I felt, as if I were a balloon man leaking his precious helium. My unease caused me to blurt out precisely what I was thinking.

"I sure hope your honeymoon doesn't suffer from this same mysterious malaise."

Stan got a look on his face like someone had dropped an anvil on his head. "Oh, Lord, this gloom and doom couldn't last past the reception, could it? Andrea's been dreaming about Hawaii for a year now."

"No, no, of course not."

We reentered the hall, and that was when I saw him.

The one person enjoying himself.

An innocuous fortyish fellow, utterly average-looking, he sat alone at the worst table in the place, near the exit and half-hidden by a pillar. Brimming glass in hand, he was nodding his head and tapping his foot in time to the morose strains of the band. Unlike most other dinner plates, his had been totally cleaned, apparently with zeal, and he seemed to have consumed three pieces of cake, judging by the stacked dessert plates. A smile like the Great Rift Valley split his bland face, and his eyes gleamed.

I nodded toward the anomalous celebrant, and whispered to Stan. "Who's that?"

"I don't know. Must be from Andrea's side. I'll ask her."

Curious, I accompanied Stan back to the head table to learn the man's identity. But Andrea couldn't provide a name based on our Identikit description, and so she came back with us to eyeball him.

But he was gone, vanished.

And at that very moment the party began to take off. The music grew sprightly, the talk scintillated, the laughter ignited happy echoes, and Stan's ninety-five-year-old Aunt Bertha hit the dance floor to illustrate the Charleston for all us youngsters.

* * *

I met Lorraine at a party some years after the memory of Stan and Andrea's weird wedding was nothing more than a dark blot on my mental landscape. Possessed of middling Mediterranean good looks and an average body, she nonetheless stood out from the bunched partygoers for the sheer amount of fun she was having. More so, since no one else—myself included—seemed to be having a very good time.

But Lorraine, seated on the floor by the CD player, bobbed her head in blissful rhythm to the music, pausing only to sip her tall drink with evident satisfaction, and never failed to give a bright big "Hi!" to anyone who happened to glance her way. Most of the people singled out returned only a desultory grunt, the affair having reached such a desperate sump of surly unease.

I made my way across the room to this bubbly woman whose name I did not yet know, and dropped down beside her. Instantly, I felt immensely happy. I now recall wondering, Was this love at first sight?

"Hi! My name's Lorraine!"

"Mitch." We shook hands. "Where can I get a glass of whatever you're drinking?"

"What do you mean?"

"You seem the be the only person here enjoying yourself. It must be the booze."

"Silly! It's only ginger ale. Here, taste."

I did, conscious of the intimacy of the shared drink.

"Anyway, I never touch alcohol."

"What's your secret then?"

Lorraine shrugged, and I thought it the most charming shrug I had ever seen. Her gesture seemed to light up the room.

"Oh, I don't know. It's just a talent. The right mix of brain chemicals. I just seem to enjoy myself wherever I go."

"Life's too short, right?"

"Something like that."

"Think you could enjoy yourself if you left here with me?"

"Sure! I had you spotted first, though."

We grabbed our coats, and stepped out of the apartment.

Behind me, I could hear a surge of reborn ecstasy, almost feel a wave front of relief, as if a thousand fat matrons had discarded their whalebone corsets simultaneously.

Eight months later, Lorraine and I were married.

Relations never went bad between us. We were always happy at home, when only the two of us were present. Contentment was the rule, for over a year of unruffled domesticity.

But during that same year, I began to lose all my friends. One by one, they fell away from the tree of my life like desiccated autumn leaves. Invitations to dinners, movies, sporting events, parties—they all dried up. One-on-one, my buddies still seemed amiable and unchanged, joshing, confiding, treating me as they always had. But about half a year into my marriage, they all simply stopped inviting Lorraine and me as a couple anywhere. Conversations at work actually became quite awkward.

A coworker would ask, "Hey, folks—anyone want to catch that concert on Friday with me?"

"Lorraine and I'd love to!"

"Uh, on second thought, I don't think I can make it myself."

Affairs finally reached the point where I braced Stan on the subject, one day after work at our favorite bar.

"Stan, I have to know. What does everyone have against me and

Lorraine? We're pariahs! I feel like a goddamn leper. Did we do something so hideous that we've fallen into some kind of social black hole?"

Stan studied the depths of his beer as if the Delphic Oracle hid at the bottom of the glass. "No, Mitch, it's nothing specific I can point a finger at. It's just, it's just—" He looked up and caught my gaze. "It's just that Lorraine's such a bringdown."

Out of all the accusations anyone could have leveled against my wife, this was the single one I was completely unprepared for. The charge made no sense at all, given Lorraine's zesty sociability.

"Hello? Are we talking about the same person here? Lorraine's the life of any get-together! When everyone else is wearing a long face, she's got a thousand-watt smile shining. She talks to anyone, acquaintance or stranger. I always feel like a million bucks when I'm with her, and you should too."

"But nobody else *does*, Mitch. It's just a fact. No one wanted to admit it at first, but the pattern eventually became too obvious to ignore. Whenever Lorraine shows up, the good times fall to ashes. She's some kind of—I don't know—some kind of jinx. It's like she's got an invisible albatross tied around her neck—just like that guy at my wedding."

Mention of this ancient incident snapped a trap in my brain. "You mean that happy stranger we could never identify? I don't see the connection—"

But I did. Painful as the revelation was, I could no longer deny it. If I were to believe my friend—and the suppressed evidence of many memories—then both Lorraine and that uninvited guest served as some kind of happiness sink, sucking all the ambient joy into themselves. I was immune only because I resided somehow in the sphere of her influence.

Stunned, I stood up from my stool and started to leave.

"Mitch, don't go. You're not hurt, are you?"

I was very hurt, in some deep, foreign way I couldn't quite identify. Until this moment, I had believed I loved Lorraine deeply. But now I began to fear that what I had identified as love was only some kind of shared spillage from her unnatural ration of happiness.

Bereft of friends, Lorraine and I took to spending a lot of our recreational time in public places: restaurants, coffeehouses and bars. And in these venues I witnessed with growing horror the exact phenomenon Stan had described.

Whenever Lorraine and I entered a place, the level of joy dropped like a shotgun-blasted duck. It never happened to me alone, either, only when we were together. So it had to be Lorraine who was cursed.

From this point two feelings warred within me: grief and remorse at these impossible disruptions, and an unending surfeit of unwarranted happiness.

And of course, I never said a word about any of this to Lorraine.

How could I? She was always so *happy*. It would have been a crime against nature to shatter that placid lake of tranquility.

From the first day of our marriage, Lorraine had insisted on having one night out alone every week. I couldn't object, since I reserved the same right for myself—even more so as our social status deteriorated, and I sought lone relief. Lorraine never really got too specific about these solo excursions of hers. I was led, I now realize, to make vague, unconfirmed assumptions about evenings with old girlfriends, hospital visits, spinster aunts, bowling leagues, health club appointments—whatever plausible reason might suit me. Still, how could I possibly protest? Lorraine always returned home at a reasonable hour, fresh as a corsage, no trace of carnal infidelity about her. Her affectionate attitude toward me and her desire for lovemaking remained unaltered. Curiously, though, her homecoming after a night out never brought with it the same degree of happiness I felt when, say, I re-encountered her after a day at the office.

I don't remember exactly when I resolved to follow her on one of her nights out. I suspect I reached that dire decision after we emptied a Starbucks one night in a quarter of an hour flat. But once the notion had taken root, it soon flowered into action.

*   *   *

The house I trailed Lorraine to that night was an unremarkable suburban homestead, some miles outside the city. Once she had parked, I drove past her as she strode happily up the walkway to the front door. Completely unsuspecting, she never looked back to see me. After parking my own car a block away, I scurried through a series of unfenced backyards printed randomly with oblongs of lights from kitchen windows and TV screens, until I reached the lot that held the house Lorraine had entered.

Shrubs bordered a flagstone patio accessible by sliding glass doors. Curtains were drawn nearly all the way across the doors, but one panel of glass had been drawn back several inches for ventilation. Through this slit I could see a tiny slice of the room—nothing more than a corner of a couch and a seated man's trousered legs—but I could hear speech quite plainly.

Drugs. The answer hit me with the force of a punch. Lorraine had fallen in with a bunch of high-class heroin addicts. But then the absurdity of that easy solution struck me. She exhibited no symptoms of drug use, no needle marks, no cravings, no secret expenditures. And no drug I knew of could explain Lorraine's effect on others.

Without a clue regarding what was about to happen, I settled in behind the foliage and began to concentrate on the conversation. The plummy, clotted voices of those inside the house bespoke a bloated satiation mixed with an undercurrent of still unsatisfied avarice.

A woman said, "Now that Lorraine's here, we can begin. Who'd like to start?"

"I'll share first," said a man. "I have something very piquant for you. Try a taste of this."

A vague sense of happiness leaked out of the house and tickled my mind. The sensation was as familiar as the pleasure I felt in Lorraine's daily presence. Impossibly, horribly, I found myself smiling, despite the rotten atmosphere of corruption I also sensed. Inside, a chorus of *mmms* and *ahhhs* followed the man's proffered "taste." The wordless sighs and moans were almost sexual in tone, yet I was somehow certain that no conventional orgy was in progress.

"Any ideas on the source?" the man asked after the sounds of appreciation had subsided.

"Give us a hint."

"Young."

"Oh, come on now—anyone could tell *that* much!"

"Well, how about young and outdoors?"

"A kid flying his first kite?"

Now Lorraine spoke. Her voice held that same note of jaded anticipation. "I sense the sea."

"Exactly, Lorraine! What a nose! I snatched a toddler's first dip in the ocean! You should have seen his mommy and daddy wondering why he wasn't more excited!"

Laughter greeted this telling detail, and I felt the gorge rise in my throat.

Now began the trading in earnest of stolen happy hours, pilfered from their rightful perceivers.

The audience at a circus when the clowns tumbled out. The viewer of a sunset as the clouds began to burn. The author of a book typing a period at the end of the final sentence. The winner of a footrace as the tape broke against her chest. The new owners of Detroit's latest model as the dealer handed them the keys. The parents gazing through a maternity ward's windows. The student receiving a higher grade than expected. The bum finding a quarter in the gutter. The politician winning a legislative victory. Lovers in bed.

Serially, like gourmets at a leisurely wine-tasting, the happiness vampires exchanged stored samples of other people's joy.

And I, outside in my hiding place, experiencing the merest inebriatory edges of this awful communion, wanted only to vomit.

At the same time I admitted a growing, unmasterable desire for more.

After an unknown interval guiltily swallowing the crumbs from the thieves' table, I finally tore myself away.

*   *   *

When Lorraine entered our living room that night with a big "Hi!" I did not greet her in turn, but instead asked her a single question.

Someone else might have demanded, "How could you?" or "What are you?" But I only said, "Are you happy, dear?"

"Of course."

"That's too bad."

My hands were around her throat before she knew what was happening.

As I throttled her, I began to weep at the imminent death of all I had loved.

And to laugh with manic joy.

For in a reflex of survival, Lorraine poured out at me all the charge of exuberant stolen hours she still retained.

This close, the recorded sensations hit me like the blast from a fire-hose.

I was a horse eating my hard-earned oats, and a dog having its stomach scratched. I was a kid playing hooky, a scientist tabulating ground-breaking research. I sailed a yacht on gleaming waters, and piloted a plane I had built for myself. I roared at a touchdown, and hit a brilliant serve across the court. I was a supermodel on the catwalk, and a monk in my cell. Glory and exaltation burnt down my nerves like fire down a fuse.

But my grip on my wife's throat never slackened.

I knew she was dead when the happiness stopped.

When I left our home for good, Lorraine's corpse sprawled across the rug, I took nothing but my wallet. At a gas station outside the city I filled my car's tank, as well as a jerry can.

The front door of the house where the happiness vampires convened had been left ajar, even though it was 3 A.M. Despite intact furnishings, the house radiated a deserted feeling, and I knew no one would be returning. Its owners, with their greater sensitivities, must have felt Lorraine's dying burst all the way from the city, and fled, the coven scattering to new identities, new haunts, new victims.

I torched the place anyway.

And then I fled too, carrying nothing except the American dream.

Life, liberty, and the pursuit of happiness.

SINGING EACH TO EACH

Black-bordered, this innocuous modern picture-postcard offers to the eye a mostly white canvas partially occupied by a window of comber-sudsed sea, a sprawling figure, and some text. One-quarter of the sea-portrait hosts a stripe of hazy blue sky. In the upper left corner of the card, adjacent to the boxed-in seascape, the word "Mermaid" runs aslant in cursive; in a different yet equally frilly font, "Greetings from Southern New England" parallels the card's lower border. The partly human figure meant to represent the lone prominent noun cuts dominantly across the entire middle of the card.

Starting on the left, the card's border trims off a small portion of fish tail, glossy black, orange and silver. The ribbed tail narrows into the scaly body, where a troutlike pointillism of umber and ivory begin to dominate. Now the fish body widens, forming the "hips" of the figure. (Curiously, a small nugatory fin sprouts here, a feature of mermaids not discerned in most mythological representations.) As the "hips" narrow again toward the waist, the archetypal transformation occurs. Golden scales diffuse and melt irregularly into human womanflesh.

The woman is nude, visible upwards from just below her navel. Her human portion is curved skyward, torso arching away from her fishy nether region, not exactly as if to deny that morphological impossibility, part and parcel of her nature, but rather as if to signal aspiration and playfulness. Ample breasts are partially concealed by strong arms folded across her chest. (Does a slight arc of areola show on the right one?) Her left hand curls protectively around her ribs, while the other maintains a strange mudra, index finger pointing downward like some arcanely admonitory medieval saint. Her skin is not overly tanned, but as the shading-to-white slope of her gravity-sloshed breasts reveal, her epidermis is still somewhat duskier from exposure to the sun than any hypothetical winter hue.

The mermaid's wavy long hair glows a seemingly natural copper, pulled back and away from her three-quarters-profiled face and one visible ear, secured by a plain white fabric tie. Her bold chin is uplifted, pulling cords in her throat taut. Her painted lips part not precisely in a smile to reveal her bright upper teeth, and her heavy-lashed eyes are held either closed or narrowly slitted, concealing their color.

She is not overyoung, this mermaid, nor hardbodied like current supermodels. (Her age might accurately be pegged somewhere between twenty-five and thirty-five.) Her belly pouches tenderly, her upper arms are plump, although the lines of her throat are sharp. Yet she is alluringly glamorous, carnal in the archaic manner of Bettie Page, her piscine femininity undeniably potent, despite its banal, generic setting. From her image courses a kind of rude yet knowing vigor and pleasure in sheer existence.

This card came to me in an auction lot a little over a year ago, among a hundred others. Unused, its obverse bore no stamp nor message. Originally, I considered myself lucky to have won the bidding on this lot, since it contained many fine specimens for my collection.

But that was before I found myself—unaccountably, and, I initially thought, harmlessly—bemused by this mermaid and then—more disturbingly, more compulsively—fascinated, enamored, hypnotized by her silent siren song, by an unquenchable longing to meet, to hold, to have her, in whatever way she might allow.

*   *   *

Driving northward under louring late-autumn skies bland as skim milk, attending with half my mind to the moderately trafficked freeway that was taking me further and further from my home, I wondered for the hundredth time about the wisdom of my current trip, and even once again started to question my basic sanity. Hot, tropical emotions surged confusingly through me like a school of fleeting fish, hard enough to identify and classify in their blurred passage, much less corral or catch among the coral of my heart.

I had never wanted or intended to fall in love—if love was what I was feeling—with the impossible photograph of a nameless stranger. Had anyone propounded such a hypothetical plight to me before my own misfortune, I would have laughed the notion away as an adolescent's jejune folly. But gripped in the selfsame predicament, I could only pine for the object of my fantasies and chastise myself for a fool, all without altering my feelings a whit.

Logically, I realized I was chasing the faintest of ghosts, attempting to track down the living model for a kitschy artifact from another era. I rode now in search of a woman who might no longer even exist, and who, if she still walked this earth, certainly did so on two human legs, not atop a squelching, bent, slab-muscled fish tail. (And would encountering the desired woman and finding her merely mortal from the waist down produce the same sensations in my gut as the undismissable notion of meeting the depicted mermaid?)

My current course was plotted on the thinnest of clues, equivalent to a dying pirate's mumbled death-mutterings: a line of tiny print on the otherwise blank obverse of my postcard that read "Distributed by Book & Tackle Shop, P.O. Box 1462, Westerly, RI 02891."

And what real excuse, I continued to belabor myself, did I have for dragging my fantasies into action in the real world? That I was a fifty-two-year-old bachelor, retired prematurely from teaching, with nothing better to do with my small sufficiency of time and money? That I was simply extending, from the library and internet into the non-virtual world, the research that had long satisfied my collector's soul? Or perhaps I could nobly cast my motives in terms of another person. The mermaid, despite her undeniable elan and vitality, seemed also to exude a kind of world-weariness, a certain weighty sadness or mortal angst. And why not? Would this not be exactly the expression such a chimera would wear, forever suspended between two worlds, neither of which she comfortably fit into, yet neither of which she could happily relinquish?

And surely, I must have crazily thought at the time, I could help her be happier, as if melding our two sorrows would birth one joy.

I stopped after the first hundred and fifty miles for breakfast at a roadside McDonald's. Getting out of the car, I was forced to favor my stiffened lame left leg more than usual. Limping to the restaurant, I fancied myself some wooden-legged sailor just off his whaler.

The posters inside the McDonald's coincidentally touted a recently reissued Disney animated film whose heroine synchronized so ironically with the object of my quest that I felt compelled, after using the toilet and ordering, to take my breakfast meal out to my cramped car, rather than eat it under that mockingly tawdry cartoon gaze.

Having begun my drive before dawn, I crossed the state line into Rhode Island not long after one o'clock in the afternoon.

Westerly was a border town, lying hard on the coast, and its exit came up quickly. Driving into the town's compact center, I immediately felt more at ease. The small well-tended community evinced a quaint charm, an old-fashioned grace. Mammoth old stone civic buildings flanked a village green where the grass was still defiantly verdant in the face of impending winter. With the exception of a Starbucks (whose ironic cartoon logo I pointedly ignored), all the stores were non-franchised and exhibited a commercial well-being; the few citizens out strolling on this Wednesday afternoon appeared easygoing and happy. Far from being a cliched hoary Lovecraftian sump, this town radiated normalcy. Everything appeared prosaic, rational, without the smallest trace of oddness or superstition. This reassuring environment where I hoped to discover—at the very least—more information regarding my mermaid served to remove my delusions from febrile inner twilight into commonsensical sunlight, rendering them simply whimsical.

Without leaving downtown, I parked outside a diner, heaved my reluctant limbs out of the car, and limped inside. The warm, peopled interior immediately fogged my glasses and filled my nostrils with a wealth of odors: bacon, coffee, wet wool, maple syrup, frying hamburger meat, tobacco. I stopped, removed my glasses, polished them, then found a seat at the counter.

A white-haired, ruddy-cheeked, apron-clad man immediately approached with steaming glass coffeepot in hand, righted a cup that had been inverted in its saucer before me, and self-assuredly poured me a mug of dark brew.

"What'll it be, chief?"

I picked an item off a hand-lettered placard. "The roast beef dinner sounds good."

"Got that right."

He turned to leave, but I detained him with a tentatively phrased question.

"I'm looking for a certain book and tackle shop . . . ?"

"That'd be Ryecroft's place, in Watch Hill."

"Watch Hill?"

"Part of the town right on the shore. Just head east on Sulky Street."

"Thanks."

Another fellow, younger and wiry, turned from a seat further down. "You might not find Ryecroft in his shop. After Labor Day, he keeps it open pretty much only as he pleases. But anyone in Watch Hill can point you to his house."

"Thank you. You're very considerate."

"No problem."

I had always disliked that modern substitute for "you're welcome," but I chose not to let this lapse of etiquette irk me. I felt both queasy and confident, somehow certain that I had not come so far merely to hit a dead end, yet leery of what I might discover about my dream maiden.

The old man returned shortly with my meal.

"Noticed you've got a bum leg. That stool comfortable enough?"

"Sure."

"Hard to get old. I got plenty of aches myself."

"I'm used to it. My leg's been bad since I was a child. Touch of polio, just before the vaccine came into use."

"Lucky enough then."

"I suppose so."

The tender gravied meat and homemade mashed potatoes and canned carrots went down pleasantly enough, although once in my car again, I couldn't recall ever tasting them at all.

*   *   *

Past fine homes and lesser ones, motels closed for the season and ice cream and produce stands shuttered tight, beyond an elementary school noisy with recess-rampant children, the queerly named Sulky Street carried me toward the sea. Cresting a rise, I caught sight of the brooding Atlantic, laminated in aluminum. Hard by the water, a small collation of stores defined the neighborhood nucleus of Watch Hill, and I saw that I could drive no further, the road looping back on itself in a circular cul-de-sac.

I parked in a legal spot on the curve, with no competition for spaces, as my car was the only one present. I stepped out into a bracing breeze, heavy with marine scents and a peppering of fine sand from the beach beginning only a few yards away. A small weather-boarded carousel hunkered down between sidewalk and strand, the ghost of its summertime tinny music almost audible, like a lonely dowager humming to herself. Like all summer resorts beset by winter, Watch Hill radiated a melancholy somnolence, as bracing in its own way as a dignified old age. Most of the stores, all visibly catering to tourists, were closed. Almost immediately, I spotted the Book & Tackle sign on a weathered building, and crossed the empty street directly for it. My heart was thumping uncommonly fast, but I attributed it to the diner's strong coffee.

A creaky wooden porch held a dangerously canting bookcase whose sloping boards exactly matched the pitch of the shabby porch roof. The case was stuffed with cheap paperbacks and hardcovers. A sign advised any patron to take what he wanted and stuff the appropriate money through the mailslot. Dusty windows half-obscured with piled material showed only darkness.

Disheartened, convinced by these tokens that the store was closed, I nonetheless tried the doorknob. Much to my surprise, it yielded, and I stepped quickly inside, out of the cold wind.

The familiar musty smell of old books congregating enveloped me. I moved a few paces down a narrow aisle hedged by haphazard stacks of books, and into the unheated twilight interior of the store, careful not to dislodge any of the precariously heaped volumes. I turned a corner, and confronted across the width of the store a flyspecked display case filled with fishing lures—their chrome gone rusty in spots—and spools of monofilament line: the "tackle" portion of the shop. Behind the jumbled counter sat a wizened, grizzled elderly fellow wearing a green plastic eyeshade and a tattered archaic lumberman's plaid jacket.

"Help you?"

"No thank you, just browsing."

I had noted the wire spinner rack full of postcards next to the owner's—Ryecroft's—perch, but decided to avoid it for the moment. I turned at random to the nearest shelf, and found myself facing the poetry section. My eye fell on a Faber edition of Eliot, and I took it down. The price penciled inside was much too high, but it was an edition I didn't own, and so I retained the book as I moved about the cramped store.

After what I supposed was enough time spent playing the idle customer, I approached the counter and laid my find down. Within Ryecroft's personal space, I could smell whiskey and pipe tobacco and unwashed hair. "I'll take this one, please."

Gnomishly intent, Ryecroft picked up the book. "Hmph. Not too popular anymore, this oldster."

"I've always had a fondness for his Prufrock."

The bookseller brightened at the prospect of some literary banter. "Dry wearisome codger, that one. 'Shall I part my hair behind? Do I dare to eat a peach? I shall wear white flannel trousers, and walk upon the beach. I have heard the mermaids singing, each to each. I do not think they will sing to me.'"

Ryecroft finished his recitation proudly, but I was too distressed by his accidentally apposite allusion to properly applaud him. Instead, as if suddenly noticing the postcards, I turned to the rack. Spinning it creakily, I instantly spotted my card, a thick stack of dozens. The sight of my familiar mermaid duplicated for the uncaring and undeserving masses raised a feeling of disorientation in me. I plucked a lone, sun-bleached sample of the card and dropped it atop the book.

"As long as you've raised the subject of mermaids, I may as well take this too. I can use it as a bookmark. Rather striking image, isn't it?"

Ryecroft glowed. "Ain't it, though? Big seller, that one. I had that card done up personally."

"Really?" I felt on the verge of fainting as I asked my next question. "Who was the model? Someone local?"

Ryecroft scratched his dandruffy scalp through the ring of his eyeshade. "Lord, I can't rightly recall. That there photo's thirty, thirty-five years old, you know."

My heart convulsed at the confirmation of my worst suspicions. "Oh. So your mermaid would be at least my age by now."

"Yup."

Desperation urged words out of my constricted throat. "What about the photographer? Might he still be around?"

"Nils Standeven? Sure, he's getting on, like all of us. But he still keeps his studio going. I bet he'd remember the gal he used for this shot." Ryecroft winked luridly and tapped the postcard with a dirty fingernail. "Probably had good reason to, if half of what I hear about the young Nils and his models is true."

I wanted to choke the old man for his vile insinuations, but restrained myself and simply asked, "How much do I owe you?"

We settled up, and then, as if voicing an afterthought, I said, "Whereabouts is Standeven's establishment? I might look him up."

Without any apparent further interest in my motives, Ryecroft gave me the directions I needed. (Standeven's place was only a few miles away.) Turning to leave, I noted the westering sun outside — it was past three — and suddenly felt the full weight of my long day. My investigations would have to wait till tomorrow.

"Is there a nearby motel open at this time of the year?"

"Not rightly a motel, but there's a bed-and-breakfast out on Route One, the Mirror and Comb."

After learning the way to the B&B, I left Ryecroft's.

The owners of the Mirror and Comb, Pete and Nicky Crow, were also Watch Hill's doctor and druggist. Mr. Crow was responding to a mother in labor, but I caught his pharmacist wife just as she was heading out to open up her store for an emergency prescription. She kindly paused long enough to get me registered and settled.

Stretched out on the comfortable bed with a cup of tea and some biscuits, I picked up Eliot's poems, but found myself unable to focus my mental powers sufficiently to read them. Instead, I switched on the television to a random channel, and caught the opening minutes of a Jim Carrey movie, half-recognizing it as a remake of some older film starring Don Knotts. After only minutes, my mind revolving a hundred jumbled thoughts, I fell deeply asleep, shoeless but still dressed, lying atop the coverlet, and didn't wake till eight the next morning.

*　*　*

Standeven Studios—"Portraits a Speciality"—occupied a small converted church in a mixed residential and business zone. Unpruned bare trees clustered closely around the building, and overgrown evergreen shrubbery encroached on the walkway to the front double doors. The clapboards of the steeple were practically bare of paint, while the lower reaches of the building—about as high as a man on a stepladder might reach—were hued a rich blue that seemed to sublime at its edges into today's bright sky.

The hour was eleven. I had lingered over a good breakfast at the Mirror and Comb, reading a local newspaper that induced a foreigner's disorientation with its obscure issues and personages, while subliminally puzzling over my emotions. I realized that playing the detective yesterday with Ryecroft had left me feeling foolish. What was I doing here, haunting this faded resort town like a restless ghost? I almost set out for home, then. But in the end, although I did check out of the B&B, thanking the Crows for their service, I drove not south but merely a mile or so west to Standeven's.

Knocking on the church doors, I tried to imagine the scene—confrontational or pleasant—that might follow. But nothing prepared me for the sight that met my eyes as the left door swung open under someone's hand.

I was looking directly into the unpartitioned nave, flooded with sunlight both unfiltered and also tinted from several stained glass windows. But although there were no interior walls, the space was hardly empty. Quite to the contrary, it was jam-packed with hundreds and hundreds of oddball items, arrayed on cabinets and shelves and tables—props no doubt for the photographer's trade, a cabinet of curios enlarged beyond sane bounds.

In the span of a few seconds, I registered several stuffed animals (a gull, a raccoon, a fox, a ferret), dozens of vases, old machine parts, a pile of textile bobbins, antique farm tools, old milk bottles, heaps of horseshoe-crab shells—and these were just the nearest items. The unexpected bazaar seemed endless in its variety and extent.

On the raised dais of the chancel area, an upright Japanese folding screen partially shielded a rumpled bed which stood next to a sloppy-topped bureau.

The man on the other side of the door spoke. "Can't say I like this damn cold one bit, and it's only early December. Don't just stand there, friend. Come in."

I entered, and Nils Standeven shut the door.

The photographer was barefoot, dressed in beltless loose-fitting jeans and faded flannel shirt. At least ten or twelve years older than I, he nonetheless still flaunted the vestiges of what must have once been a startling square-jawed handsomeness. Like the well-kept ruin of many a Hollywood star—Mitchum, say, or Heston—he exuded a self-confidence tempered only slightly by the ravages of age. Additionally, an insouciant insulation—derived from what I assumed was a lifelong bohemianism—seemed to protect him from the standard indignities of his years.

Standeven regarded me with neutral blue eyes. "How can I help you? If you want to book my services for a wedding, I have to tell you right off that I'm busy every weekend between now and New Year's. Lord, these local kids are mating like swans! Even got a couple of dates involving old duffers like us. But it's never too late for love, right?"

I opted for a truthful approach. "No, no, it's not a wedding. I'm interested in a postcard you once did."

Presented with the card I had purchased yesterday, Standeven narrowed his eyes. "Should've known. Out of all the cards I made up for Ryecroft over four decades, that's the only one anyone ever asks about. Just my fate to be remembered for a stupid damn cut-and-paste job, rather than all the beautiful work I've poured my heart into."

Talk of other interested parties worried me, but I focused instead on the mention of artifice. "Cut-and-paste?"

Standeven laughed heartily. "Hell, you didn't figure she was real, did you? Would I be living in goddamn Westerly, Rhode Island, if I had discovered a real mermaid? Her back half's a trout. I hand-painted the scales where they join her belly."

I must have looked crestfallen or disbelieving, because Standeven immediately hustled off to rummage among his disordered props. After a minute of muted grumbling and cursing, he returned with a whole mounted fish whose body, although worse for the years, was plainly identical with the image in the postcard.

I felt the need to sit down, but no chair presented itself. My gimpy leg trembled, but all I could do was stammer, "And—and the woman? Just some anonymous model clipped from the skin magazines, I suppose?"

Standeven laid down the trophy and regarded me solemnly. "No sir, she's real enough. A local gal. Happens I know her quite well."

"Could—could you tell me her name?"

"What's your interest in her?"

"Nothing untoward. I'd just like to meet her."

"I don't know—"

Inspiration struck. "I'm a collector. I'd like both you and her to sign the card. It will increase its value considerably."

"Collector, huh? Where was the Teich Company headquarters?"

"Chicago. Founded 1896, closed 1974. I've been to the museum that holds their archives, in Wauconda, Illinois."

Standeven remained silent for a long moment, until I was convinced I had lost him. Certain of defeat, I almost failed to comprehend his approval.

"Her name's Margot, Margot Tench. She lives just outside the town, on Cliffside Road. Margot don't see so many people nowadays that I suppose she'd mind a visit from a fan."

"Thank you, thank you so much." I turned to leave, and Standeven stopped me.

"What about me signing your souvenir?"

"Oh, of course!"

I was halfway back to my car when the photographer called out to me.

"Treat Margo kindly, you hear! She's had a hard life."

* * *

Cliffside Road incarnated its name, winding along the top of a substantial bluff bordering the surging sea. Wind-warped cedar pines and riotous stands of bayberry bushes and beach roses were the only landscaping. In spots, the land closest to the sea was crumbling under the patient assaults of the environment: on the fractional portion of one house lot, the broken half of a sagging foundation protruded into the air, precariously balanced over the wave-washed rocks below. I supposed that this geological instability explained why the houses here were mainly ramshackle affairs, despite the incredible views, which otherwise would have commanded top dollar.

Could my beautiful mermaid really live in such a neighborhood? I tried to reconcile her youthful proud demeanor, the bold vitality that had first attracted me to her picture, with the shabbiness and poverty I saw around me, but failed.

Driving slowly, I scanned each widely separated mailbox for her name. The sky had gone gray as ominous clouds moved in to occlude the blue. So intently was I focused on each approaching letterbox that when the one bearing Margot Tench's hand-printed name appeared, I needed an awkward moment to correlate the dwelling I saw with the anticipated mailbox.

In the center of a quarter-acre lot strewn with threadbare tires, a shopping cart and other debris, an old rust-patched Airstream trailer rested on cinderblocks, tethered to civilization only by a drooping power line running from the streetside pole. A few dried stalks of vegetation spiked futilely into the hard ground outside the trailer's jury-rigged wooden steps recorded the passage of that summer's sparse flowers. Twin propane tanks huddled against the trailer's flank like the faulty booster rockets on a doomed space shuttle.

I pulled into a short gravel drive and shut off the car's engine. My mind had gone blank with despair, and only a crude automatism carried me from the car to the trailer's flimsy door.

My hesitant knock was answered in reasonable time by the shambling mortal remains of my mermaid.

Margot Tench had not gotten obscenely fat with middle age, just typically, hopelessly stocky. Whatever phantom curves she might have retained were now hidden beneath a cheap shapeless dress and a pilly synthetic cardigan. But the thickness of her calves and ankles—feet shoved into dirty crushed slippers—argued against any concealed treasures of shapeliness. Her distinctive sharp facial features that had once smiled into oceanic infinity had collapsed much like the surrounding cliffs, pillowing downward in crevassed folds. A wild kelp forest of gray hair exhibited a strand or two of fugitive sullen copper amidst the drabness. And whatever height Margot Tench might have once attained in her youth (I realized now for the first time that the addition of the fish tail in the photograph had left me with an impression that she would stand quite tall), she now came up barely to my shoulder.

"What's your business?" she demanded, in a rough voice coarsened by cigarettes and drink.

"I—I wanted to meet this woman."

She did not flinch from the sight of the postcard, glancing unblinkingly at what had to be a hauntingly painful image before pinning me with wrinkle-cupped eyes that were a deep marine green.

"You're thirty years too late. But you can come in anyhow, if you still got a mind to."

The interior of the trailer was lit by a naked fluorescent fixture flickering in the low ceiling. A metal-topped table paired with two stark chairs took up a lot of floor space near a small sink and countertop hot plate. A spavined recliner faced a TV; a bunk folded downward from the wall. The space smelled like boiled cabbage and mold.

Margot Tench shuffled about. "Let me pump the heat up a little. There. The place leaks air like a goddamn sieve! I was just gonna have myself a beer. Want one?"

"All right, please, I will."

From a dorm-sized fridge, she withdrew two cans of Golden Anniversary beer. No glass was offered, so I popped my tab and tasted the drink tentatively. It was truly awful.

Margot dropped heavily into a wooden chair. "Have a seat."

I took the chair opposite her. Beneath the table, our knees nearly touched.

She pushed a chapped, reddened hand through her snarled hair. "Not what you expected, huh? Sorry to let you down. But you might say life let me down first."

"Would you care to tell me about it?"

She slugged her beer from the can, and then looked wearily at me. "Not a lot to tell, but why the hell not? You look friendly, and talk kills some time, right?

"I met Ben Tench in 1965. He was a cod fisherman out of Galilee. That's a local town up the coast. Awfully handsome guy—nice to women, too. We got married not long after he heard me sing one night at a little party. We had three good years together, before his ship went down with all crew lost. Poor Ben. He didn't leave me any savings, and I had never even had a job before. I lost our house, and bought this trailer secondhand with a little life insurance money from the fishermen's co-op. Headed south with some notion of reaching Florida, but my old heap died in Westerly. Been here ever since."

She lit up an unfiltered cigarette, and I noticed the overflowing ashtray between us. Exhaling a foul cloud, she continued her story.

"What could I do? I set up as the town whore. It wasn't a bad life, till my looks went. The men were mostly decent—I got this land deeded to me by a customer—and even a few of the local womenfolks liked me well enough. Oh, there were the usual reformers, preachers and cops and the like, but I mostly ignored them. Then there was Nils, Nils Standeven."

"I've met him. He seems like a gentleman."

Margot's eyes hazed over. "Oh, that he was. He showed a real interest in my welfare. Set me up with a few modeling jobs, but I never took to that life. I found out you had to mostly screw someone first to get a posing job, so I said, 'Hell, this is *double* the work for the same money!' and I just cut out the posing. Let me see that card."

I passed over the postcard, and Margot studied it intently. I assessed her tilted face with a grim fascination, but couldn't begin to fathom the depths of what she might be thinking or feeling.

"Lord, I sure enough was a sweet little piece, wasn't I? I think I was high on some killer weed Nils shared with me during that shoot. Explains that weird look I had." She flipped the card back at me, and I let it land atop the table. "If I had just a lousy nickel for every one of these sold, I sure wouldn't be here today. But all I got was a hundred bucks, and I called Nils generous at the time. Shit."

I got clumsily to my feet, my rotten leg throbbing.

"Hey, where are you going? We're just getting to know each other. You look like a classy guy, stay awhile. I haven't forgotten everything I once knew."

Horribly, the old woman began to unfasten the top buttons of her dress.

I knocked over my full beer in my haste, and scrabbled blindly at the door handle. Outside, my mind ablaze with shame, self-pity, horror and disgust, I trotted lopsidedly away from my car. I was in no shape to get behind the wheel; I'd have an accident for sure. A short walk in the open air would clear my mind and senses, I felt, allow me to accept my failure and become reconciled to the horrible travesty my mermaid had become.

Across the road, some hundred yards from the trailer, I slowed down and risked a glance over my shoulder.

Margot Tench stood forlornly in the door of her trailer, watching me.

The sky had begun to let down an intermittent drizzle. I flipped up my coat collar and increased my pace.

Something drew me to the edge of the bluff. Perhaps I imagined the clean sight of the innocent sea would restore my heart to me.

Looking back nervously, I saw that Margot had put on a coat and was walking toward me.

The edge of the cliff was capped with brown grass. As I spun about, intending to distance myself from the approaching woman, the wet grass and my weak leg both betrayed me, and I went flying over the edge.

I don't suppose it was more than thirty feet down. But my impact with the deep freezing water felt as if a giant had picked me up by the heels and slammed me against a concrete wall. My right shoulder smashed into a boulder, but luckily the rest of me encountered no rocks. Stunned below the water, I knew I had to struggle or drown, so I battled my way back to the surface.

I was just in time to greet a huge wave with my face. I choked and flailed, but the undertow sucked me further out.

When I came up for the second time, I caught a wild glimpse of Margot Tench standing fixedly atop the cliff. I dragged up enough strength to yell: "Help! Help!"

She didn't run to summon rescuers, and I recalled with a vivid pang her lack of a phone. Instead, to my utter amazement, she opened her mouth and began to sing.

The husky voice of the old woman was miraculously replaced by a supernal, dulcet sweetness. Wordlessly, the strange entrancing melody lanced out above even the crash of the surf.

But I heard no more. My bad leg cramped then, so severely that it bent me ineluctably in half. The waters swallowed me as I frantically tried to ease my calf and thigh muscles by massaging them with frozen hands I could not even feel. My lungs threatened to explode, and I realized I had lost track of which direction was up.

And that was when I saw the pair of them, with the hyperacuity of panic, despite the gloomy, turbulent underwater scene resembling planes of fractured green glass.

Powerful golden tails, bountiful buoyant breasts, streamers of bronze hair, cryptic smiles, eyes protected by a transparent membrane, small useless fins on their hips.

Two powerful arms fastened around my sternum from behind and pumped my lungs empty of dead air. But before I could inhale water, a mouth pressed against mine. I clawed wildly, but my wrists were pinioned by irresistible hands.

The air that I desperately drew in from the mermaid's donor lungs tasted of brine and raw shellfish and saltwater taffy. Her tongue met mine, and then she pulled back.

Seconds later, I lay half out of the water, safe on a pebbled strand.

I listened for Margot's song, but she must have stopped singing once her sisters arrived, as she realized her summons was successful. Instead, I heard only the common siren of an onrushing ambulance.

My right hand was clenched, I realized. With effort, I forced it open.

Several strands of beautiful red hair curled across my palm.

But even as I stared at them they changed in my sight to Margot's gray.

RARE FIRSTS

Mamoulian sweated ink. Or so it first appeared in the dim light of the hot slope-ceilinged attic. As generationally undisturbed strata of chimney soot, coal dust, airborne grit and greasy cobwebs mingled with the perspiration on his furrowed brow and bare hairy arms, the stained rivulets came to resemble the flow from a press's founts, as if the heavy-set laboring man were striving in vain to mint books epidermically.

Surrounded by tottering stacks of unlabelled, crumple-cornered cardboard cartons, by immigrant steamer trunks and old cedar chests, by sad broken toys too memorious to be discarded and musty vintage clothing redolent of dead dreams, Mamoulian resembled some Minotaur in a junk labyrinth. And like the Minotaur of legend, his flaring temper seemed easily provoked.

An old fruit crate laden with Eisenhower-era *Reader's Digests* (the mailing labels addressed to "Burton Hollis") blocked his access to deeper boxes. He shifted the crate to a precarious new position, and triggered a small avalanche of photo-stuffed shoe boxes onto his loafer-shod foot.

"Goddamn it!" He kicked at the spill of Polaroids and Kodaks, sending sheaves of photos skittering across the attic floor. The impact hadn't really hurt that much, but the incident served as a useful trigger for Mamoulian's impatient and growing sense of being personally affronted. Look at all this trash! What made people regard the trivial and generic possessions of their lives as so precious? What made them feel they could waste the valuable time of an expert such as himself on such slight pretext? "Please come inspect my dear dead Burton's books, Mr. Mamoulian. I'm sure he owned something you'd be happy to purchase. Perhaps one or two items are even rare enough that they'll help stretch out the insurance settlement . . ."

Playing on his sympathies, that's all such talk amounted to. Trying to get something for nothing. His hard-earned money for their useless shit. Look at all this crap. Back issues of *Time*. Book club editions of old novels no one had remembered six months after publication. Mountains of the local newspaper. Grocery-store encyclopedias. That's what most people thought of as a "library." God help him, he might die of shock if he ever encountered a real library. He couldn't recall the last time he had been privileged to handle a bona fide collection. Usually the big dealers with connections got to the rich troves first, leaving Mamoulian to scavenge such dungheaps as this. And his professional sense of pride, reduced and diminished though it might be, would force him to examine every last box, in the slim hope that a real treasure might be lurking, despite all outward signs.

Huffing, dripping black droplets onto the lace of an old wedding dress, Mamoulian uncovered a final box. Anticipating more gratuitous crap, he peeled back the interleaved flaps of the top.

What was inside stopped his laboring breath.

Gaudy paperback covers bright as the day they first hit the drugstore rack caught the spotty luminance from the dusty skylight like a heap of dragon's gold. Mamoulian picked one up tenderly, with utter disbelief. The spine was uncracked, the cover unfoxed, the pages bright white. And more germane to his monetary pursuits, this was a first edition of Jim Thompson's *The Alcoholics*, published by Lion Books, worth easily two hundred, two hundred fifty dollars.

Mamoulian set the treasure down gently, and examined the rest of the box's contents. All Thompson first editions. So hidden from daylight were these books that the dead husband, dear old Burt, must have had a secret noir jones he didn't want his wife discovering. Chances were she didn't even know these books existed. Twenty-five-cent paperback originals were now worth a couple hundred each. Over three thousand dollars of profit here.

Quickly, Mamoulian layered a few *Reader's Digests* over the trove. Carrying the box as if it contained his hypothetical firstborn, Mamoulian worked his way out of the maze and back to the attic stairs. He banged his head on a rafter at one point, but made no vicious exclamation. He barely felt the blow, such hunter's elation filled his veins.

Down in the kitchen, the aproned and bespectacled widow Hollis stood at the stove, tending a pan of boiling water. She smiled tentatively at Mamoulian and his burden, causing him to feel like some comic strip character soliciting cookies from the old lady neighbor.

"I'm just making us some instant coffee, Mr. Mamoulian. I see you found something. . . ."

"Just a box of old magazines. Generally, these things are a dime a dozen. But I culled a few issues with articles on various celebrities— DiMaggio, Marilyn, James Dean. I can always sell those for a dollar or two. How about twenty-five dollars for the whole box?"

The widow's smile wavered, then bravely reset itself. "Whatever you think is fair, Mr. Mamoulian."

Mamoulian rested the box on the kitchen table, hurriedly wrote a check, then picked up the concealed rare firsts and turned toward the door.

"Won't you be staying for coffee?"

"No thanks. Nervous stomach. Gotta run."

In his swiftly accelerating old Buick, Mamoulian allowed himself a small smile that quickly broadened into a large grin and then transformed to full-blown laughter. He powered down his window and reached across the seat to the treasure box. He picked up one of the crappy *Digests* and hurled it out the window, watching it arc like a crippled bird. One after another the worthless magazines flew out to die like literary roadkill on the highway's shoulder, reading matter for the wind alone.

That sight should really give the widow something to puzzle about next time she drove into town.

* * *

The phone at Mamoulian Rare Books rang, and Mamoulian snatched it up.

"Alex, it's me. Can I come over?"

Mamoulian sighed at the unexpected sound of his brother's voice, the nasal whine tempered only slightly by a shred of unwonted humility. "Lev, I run a shop that's open to the public. How could I keep you out?"

Lev Mamoulian remained quiet a moment, then said, "I've had more gracious invitations—"

"Where to? The drunk tank?"

"—but I'll come over anyway."

"There are ten bars between your house and here. Do you think you'll show up sometime today?"

"I'll be there in fifteen minutes."

"I'm not holding my breath."

"Goodbye, Alex."

Mamoulian hung up the phone and returned to his study of several of his competitors' impressive catalogues. Every one boasted a cyber-address. More and more, his peers seemed to be moving their book-selling enterprises to the Web. Mamoulian knew nothing about the Internet, but suspected that it would soon supersede the old way of doing things, if it hadn't already. Where such a phenomenon would leave him and other old-fashioned booksellers was not in doubt. Even more in the gutter than he already was, subsisting on scraps, if not out of business altogether.

Slapping down the catalogues onto his desktop, Mamoulian made a silent resolve to do something about getting online. He was too middle-aged and otherwise talentless to change careers now. Evolve or die, that would have to be his motto. Businesswise, he had been stagnating for too long. Surely his wiles and cunning would translate intact to the computer world. There had to be a reasonable profit margin somewhere in cyberspace for the guy with a sharp eye for bargains and more hustle than his peers.

The bearish Mamoulian stood up and, in the absence of any customers, began tidying his already neat store. Two small rooms on the fourth floor of an old office building in a fading downtown, a space about as big as your average ice cream stand. Mamoulian could recall when his neighbors in the building had consisted of an assortment of professionals—dentists, lawyers, architects, jewelers. Now most of the offices served as storage space, holding old files belonging to an insurance company that remained as the sole major tenant. One office was bloated with bags of Styrofoam peanuts—property of the Wrap-and-Pak franchise on the first floor—like some kind of dormitory prank. If his rent hadn't been frozen decades ago (Mamoulian had earned the undying gratitude of his now elderly landlord by tracking down a copy of *St. Nicholas* magazine the man had fondly recalled from his child-hood, then offering it as a gift), Mamoulian would have moved long ago.

Circulating among the shelves of fiction and nonfiction, the boxes of plastic-enveloped ephemera, Mamoulian dusted the familiar titles, many of which had sat on his shelves for so long that they had become more fixture than stock, foster children meant to be housed temporar-ily, yet now immovable graybeards ensconced in their rockers. He polished the glass front of the locked cabinet that held his unsold rare firsts, pausing as always to admire the spine of the gem of his stock. But today he felt a need to actually fondle his baby, and so he unlocked the cabinet and removed the priceless glassine-jacketed book.

The entire print run of Doubleday's edition of Ballard's *The Atrocity Exhibition* had supposedly been pulped before distribution, under orders from the morally offended publisher. Yet in his reverent hands, Mamoulian held a copy from that legendary printing. He had obtained it for a dollar from an anonymous street vendor on the Bowery during a New York City buying trip in 1979, but its authenticity was not in doubt. No one but a madman would have forged to utter perfection such a dubious title. No doubt some sticky-fingered pressman or warehouse employee had carelessly swiped it without anticipating its subsequent value. Mamoulian knew that he could sell the apocryphal book in an eyeblink, but he had never even done so much as hint at its existence to anyone else. Owning it somehow validated his whole crummy shop.

Like a furtive Ali Baba, Mamoulian restored the treasure to its cave, and returned to his makework. He shuffled a stack of new orders—distressingly small—into ranking by date of receipt. He penciled the price of one dollar into a couple of loser titles recently acquired in an auction-lot, modern self-help crap. Then Mamoulian opened the door to the corridor where he kept a shelf of cheap stuff designed to entice inside any hapless soul lost enough to end up here.

Down the corridor, the antique elevator bonged and ratcheted open. Lev Mamoulian stepped off and turned to spot his brother Alex. Older than Alex, Lev resembled his brother enough to cause both of them the pain of being forced to confront one's living semblance, a truth-telling fetch sent to embarrass and chastise.

Mamoulian waited impatiently by the door to his store while his brother shambled closer. (A pane of frosted glass bore the store's chipped gold-painted name). Surprisingly, despite Lev's damaged gait, the older man seemed sober and halfway respectable looking, his rumpled clothes unpatched by vomit or blood.

Lev held out his hand to shake Mamoulian's, who responded warily.

"Can I come inside?"

"You're here, aren't you?"

Behind the closed door, Lev scanned the interior of the store for potentially eavesdropping customers, then dropped wearily into the only chair, the one behind Mamoulian's desk. He knuckled his temples and grimaced.

"God, my head hurts."

"Sorry, I don't have any booze in the store."

Lev dropped his fists into his lap but kept them clenched. "I don't want any stinking booze. I'm checking into a clinic today. That is, if you'll help."

Mamoulian balanced on the desk's edge, near the cigar box that held his change-making cash. "I don't believe you. What brought this immense change of life on?"

"Roberta. She's going to leave me this time, for real, and take Avram with her, unless I dry out. I can't live without my wife and son. I've got to do it, no matter how hard it is."

"But you don't have the cash."

"No, I don't have the cash."

"And you want a loan from me. Another one."

Lev banged the desk. "Don't make it sound so sleazy! I'm not pouring it down a rathole. This time's different, damn it!" Lev's bravado ebbed as swiftly as it had flared, and he slumped in his seat. Mamoulian considered his broken brother for some time, then spoke.

"How much?"

Lev lifted his head. "Two thousand for two weeks. After I get discharged, I keep right on with AA. Wilkins has promised me a job once I dry out. He said I was the best model-maker he ever saw, until my hands started to shake. Can you help me, Alex?"

"Get out of my chair."

Lev rose in defeat and began to shuffle toward the door.

"Where are you going? I just need to dig out my checkbook."

After Lev had folded the check into his pocket, he asked Mamoulian, "Is there anything I can do for you, Alex?"

"Get sober."

"I'm doing that for myself. Nothing else?"

"You don't know any cheap computer guys who could set me up on the Web, do you?"

Lev brightened. "Avram's a whiz with that stuff. He'd do it for free just for the fun of it. He's bored as hell sitting at home this summer."

Mamoulian pondered the offer. "I'll pay him something. I don't want him feeling like he's working off his old man's debt."

"There's no danger of that." Lev patted the pocketed check. "You'll see this money back soon. You just made the best investment of your life."

"I'd like to believe that, Lev. I really would. Listen, you'd better get going now. I've got to try to earn the rent on this dump."

At the door, Lev said, "How are you and Mona doing these days?"

"Mona and I are no longer an item. She claimed she could never envision signing her charge slips 'Mona Mamoulian.'"

"That's one useful excuse for breaking up, I suppose. Well, thanks again, Alex. Good luck with your book hunting."

"Luck is only half of it, my friend. Only half of it."

*　　*　　*

The quiet, underpopulated river valley spread lazily across three states. Once a hotbed of industry and commerce, its mills humming, its cities bustling, its casually polluted waterway boldly shouldering freight and travelers, the region now slumbered, generally ignored by cultural and business trendsetters, existing in a semi-detached fashion from the rest of the country. Pastures and farms had reverted to new forests. Cities had hollowed out, suffered for decades, then been either partially revived or left to rot, to greater or lesser degrees, by civic and private capital. Like collapsing stars, the area's smaller towns had either compacted to denser matter or fallen entirely down black holes. The region's roads were second-rate, the last in the tristate area to be plowed after winter storms, but its river was cleaner than it had been a century ago. The pace of life was easy, and the valley's residents exhibited a certain despondent charm, having learned how to survive in such diminished circumstances. Overall, the forgotten land seemed not such a bad place to live. And from Mamoulian's viewpoint, the place represented his secret seam of gold: a small, twisty lode hard to work, but just rich enough to sustain him.

The junk shops and Salvation Army stores of the valley would often be salted with collectible books going for just cents on their real dollar value. The contents of the sleepy and musty used-book stores were hardly any more expensive, and frequently just as rare. Generally located in the most decrepit neighborhoods, run mostly by crotchety elderly men and women (half of them seemingly Libertarians, to judge by the piles of anti-government bumper stickers stacked on their counters), these stores usually rewarded Mamoulian's searches, despite the annoying heaps of Harlequin romances and survivalist series novels he had to fight past. Then there were the antique-heaped barns and hastily arranged estate sales to consider, both of which often offered troves of books acquired by Victorian and Edwardian robber barons whose lineages had now gone extinct. (Once, Mamoulian had discovered dozens of Wodehouse first editions in the office of a machine shop undergoing a bankruptcy sale.)

Taken all in all, the valley served as Mamoulian's private preserve, continually restocked by fate and changing circumstances with exotic species.

Yet for some reason, on this buying trip he kept coming up empty-handed. It had been six months since he had visited the region, plenty of time for its contents to churn in the mysterious fashion arranged by birth, death and economics. But they simply hadn't. For some freak reason, from one store to another he encountered only trash. His biggest find so far, a week into the trip, a week of crummy motels and junk food, had been a complete run of *The Spirit* reissues done by Harvey Comics, purchased at a yard sale for a dime each from a pimply adolescent, and worth over twenty-five dollars apiece. Not too shabby, but Mamoulian hated dealing comics. They seemed declasse and louche, offensive to his sensibilities, not the kind of trade he wanted to conduct under the banner of Mamoulian Rare Books.

If he hadn't had someone minding the store, he would have cut this futile expedition short. But with Avram tending the premises, Mamoulian felt he could hold out a little while longer, in expectation of a big hit just around the next corner.

As Lev had predicted, Mamoulian's sixteen-year-old nephew had jumped at the offer to help his uncle establish a foothold in cyberspace. Together, man and boy had first gone computer shopping. The chosen hardware now bulked alienly on Mamoulian's desk. Avram had chosen a host server for the Website, one that boasted the capacity for secure credit-card transactions. The kid had built a very handsome website, promising to add the bells and whistles later. To Mamoulian, the gleaming image on the screen looked just fine as it was. Now Avram sat daily in the shop doing the data-entry on Mamoulian's stock and dealing quite competently with the odd walk-in customer.

On the day of his departure, Mamoulian had given the kid a fifty-dollar bonus in cash. Avram exhibited a sheepish grin, raising a fore-finger to push back nonexistent slipping eyeglasses, until he remembered that he now wore contacts (thanks to Roberta's care; the boy would probably be in rags if his welfare had been left solely to Lev at his worst).

"Gee, thanks, Uncle Alex."

"You earned it, boy. If I have a good trip, I'll sweeten up your next paycheck too. Well, I gotta hit the road now, before traffic gets too bad. Hold the fort against the goddamn Indians for me."

Avram walked his uncle out to the rented van Mamoulian used on such trips.

"Thanks for what you did for Dad, too, Uncle Alex."

"Purely selfish, kid. He owes me for loans back to 'eighty-six, and I figure this was my only chance to get repaid."

"Whatever you say."

Driving down a stretch of crumbling asphalt, eyes shaded by drugstore sunglasses against the August glare, Mamoulian shook his head ruefully. What he had told Avram had been pure sugar frosting on an unpalatable cake. He might just as well have set fire to a pile of his hard-earned cash, for all the chance he had of seeing it again. After a few weeks of sobriety at most, his brother would go off on a binge, and the whole downward booze-lubricated spiral would commence again. Mamoulian chided himself for being such a witless soft touch. What had he been thinking that day in the office? Flush from the big Thompson score, face to face with his pathetic older brother, he had plunged two grand on a nag hobbled from birth. And now here he was, forced by the rotten circumstances of his own senseless life (had he actually made any more of his opportunities than his brother had?), out on the merciless road again, cadging a nickel of profit here, a dime there, just to stave off the human creditor wolves circling Mamoulian Rare Books as if it were a busted sleigh mired on the goddamn tundra.

Despair and disgust washed over Mamoulian like slops thrown from a fishwife's window, leaving him feeling weary and filled with bilious sludge. Suddenly, the prospect of arriving at the little down-at-the-heels city that was his immediate destination, of crossing the worn thresholds of the too-familiar stores and seeing the same hostile, ennui-engraved faces of the race of trolls that rolled up the steel shutters of such places, of spotting the same worthless titles he had seen in the last broken village— This scenario struck him as a veritable hell on earth. He just couldn't face it.

At the next junction of roads, Mamoulian took an arbitrary turn away from his abandoned destination. He did the same at the next three crossroads until, after forty-five minutes, he found himself in a part of the valley completely unknown to him. He paused by the side of the road to consult a map, but he could only locate himself within a vague circle of territory. He shrugged, stuffed the map into the glovebox, and drove onward.

A shabby roadside diner beckoned ahead just as Mamoulian's stomach was reminding him that another delivery was scheduled, the morning's hash, eggs and toast being only partial payment for his continued existence. Mamoulian swung the van across the gravel lot, parked and locked it. Little chance that any larcenous rube would want the eccentric contents of this particular van, but why risk it?

At the counter of the busy restaurant, Mamoulian ordered up coffee, a steak sandwich and fries. He latched onto a rumpled copy of the local paper—*The Newbery Gazette*—and scanned the classifieds for rummage sales and the like, but came up blank. Typical of this whole trip. Why had he imagined that a few impulsive gestures would be sufficient to change his bad luck? Might as well expect a copy of the Gutenberg Bible to drop out of the skies into his lap. . . .

Working on a superlative piece of flaky cherry pie that went some small way toward brightening his mood, Mamoulian caught a stray phrase from one of his rural countermates:

"—book sale."

Mamoulian turned to the local. Like so many of the valley's residents, the man looked like some outdated funny-pages character, a homely archaic figure out of *Gasoline Alley*, *Terry and the Pirates*, *Polly and Her Pals* or *The Katzenjammer Kids*, as if the declining fortunes of the region had arrested the century's transfiguring hand, leaving the natives in a pristine state of American innocence. Mamoulian's prospective interlocutor resembled, of all people, Andy Gump.

"Did someone mention a book sale?"

"Sure did. Started a couple of hours ago, out at the Caxton Daye Academy. They're looking to raise some money for renovations to the gym."

"Whereabouts is this school?"

"Just head west when you leave here. You'll see the sign."

Mamoulian instantly paid his bill and departed without finishing his pie or coffee.

The road west of the diner trunked out into a leafy channel, and Mamoulian almost missed the shrubbery-concealed sign for the Caxton Daye Academy at the mouth of a badly paved drive. He swung a sharp left just in time, and motored up half a mile of degraded asphalt until a broad lawn opened up before him. The academy seemed to consist of a single large multistoried mansion at least a century and a half old, valiantly but ineffectively maintained, as well as several impoverished outbuildings. At this time of the year, no students roamed the grounds. Only three or four cars occupied the parking area. At least one of those had to belong to the person running the sale, making Mamoulian's immediate competition look minimal—assuming some other dealer hadn't arrived first thing and cleaned the place out.

The odors inside the building twanged chords within Mamoulian

long unstrummed: decades of paste, wet galoshes, chalk and construc-
tion paper, not to mention the signature scent of old books.
Unerringly, Mamoulian nosed along the strengthening scent gradient
straight to the room hosting the sale. Presiding over boxes and card tables
full of orderly ranks of books, three locals sat behind a long folding table,
sipping coffee, chatting and eating donuts. A hand-lettered sign
announced the sale's prices: hardcovers, one dollar; paperbacks, fifty
cents or three for a dollar. A lone old lady with purple hair rummaged
among the cookbooks. Otherwise, Mamoulian was the only customer.

Mamoulian suppressed an impulse to chortle and rub his palms
together like Snidely Whiplash. Jeez, a week in this Land That Time
Forgot was starting to unhinge his mind! No matter what he found
today, he'd have to head back home tonight, cut his losses and come
up with some other money-making options.

With an expert's eye, Mamoulian began to filter through the offer-
ings like a whale sieving krill. A lot of the books were ex-library, bearing the stamp of the Caxton Daye Academy, which lowered their
values considerably, but he nonetheless found quite a few good items
among these discards, including, astoundingly, a copy of the first UK
printing of Ballard's *Empire of the Sun* ($75 if fine, half of that in this
condition). This odd synchronicity with his prized volume back home
confirmed Mamoulian's initial sense of his luck turning. Maybe his
spontaneous departure from routine had been inspired after all.

A fair percentage of the volumes seemed to be donations unmarred
by institutional stamps or card pockets. Among these, Mamoulian
found a pleasing array of desirable stuff, including some Photoplays
(but unfortunately not the *King Kong* one worth $1,500), the Armed
Services paperback of Lovecraft's *The Dunwich Horror* (at least $65),
and—whoa, Nelly!—the Random House first edition of the John
Holbrook mystery, *The Man in the Cage* ($400). Within half an hour,
he had accumulated two boxes of material worth at least twelve
hundred dollars. His retail cost: thirty-five smackers.

Mamoulian lugged his purchases to the table where the organizers
sat: two old gents wearing bowties and, despite the heat, sweater vests,
flanking a trim middle-aged woman. His lust for books temporarily
sated, Mamoulian spared some cursory attention for the woman.
Despite her tightly pinned mousy hair, high-buttoned collar, Betty
Crocker skirt and fuddy-duddy shoes, she wasn't half bad-looking. Her
pixyish face radiated a genuine pleasure in the simple act of reigning
over this backwoods fundraiser. For a brief moment, Mamoulian actu-

ally envied her poise and serenity, her seeming happiness with her simple lot in life. Then he grimly pushed the feeling aside as she began to unpack the contents of his boxes in order to total his purchases. If she recognized any of these books as valuable and tried to jerk him around on the prices, she'd hear such a squawk about bait-and-switch tactics—

But the woman only smiled as she counted the spines, seemingly oblivious to titles, and said, "Quite a reader we have here."

"Yeah, I spend a lot of lonely winter nights by the fireplace, just me and my Dickens."

The old gents nodded sagely, and the woman's smile broadened. "Oh, you love Dickens too! So do I! We have one of his first books in the Hemphill Collection. It's not for sale, but if you'd like to see it, Mister—?"

"Mamoulian. Sure, I'd be happy to take a look." Might as well humor the gal, now that he'd cleaned out her sale. Thirty-five dollars should buy at least a few shingles for the gym roof, right? Anyhow, she was probably inordinately proud of some tenth printing of some twentieth edition of A Christmas Carol, but Mamoulian would lay on the praise. Who knew, but this sale might become one of his regular stops. . . .

After money changed hands and Mamoulian's books had been reboxed, the woman said, "Arthur, Fred, will you watch Mister Mamoulian's purchases and handle the sale while we step away for a moment? Thank you so much."

The woman led Mamoulian out a different door and down a dim corridor deeper in the academy. "My name's Emily Lerner. I'm the librarian here. Have been for the past twenty years, and will be until I retire, I suppose. The job's very satisfying, except of course for the lack of money."

Growing impatient and not a little unnerved by the eerie quiet of the old building, Mamoulian was only half listening. "Yeah, salary's always a bitch."

"Oh, I wasn't complaining about my wages. It's true they're low, but it doesn't cost quite so much to live here in the valley as it does elsewhere. No, I was lamenting the relative lack of funding for new book purchases. Caxton Daye doesn't exactly attract the children of privilege and their parents' endowments. But that's an old story. In fact, that's how the Hemphill Collection first came about."

Mamoulian made no reply to this gratuitous information, but

simply followed Emily Lerner impatiently as she ushered him through another door—

—and straight into paradise.

*   *   *

Paradise was a small airless shadowy room where dust motes danced above a worn floor of wide wooden planks, the whole interior poorly illuminated by a series of porthole windows high up one wall.

Obviously, Mamoulian first observed, his awestruck brain working with some desperate attempt at objective precision, the single wall of shelves in the time-lost room held their contents not in alphabetical order, but in chronological sequence. The relatively drab books on the upper shelves were jacketless, leather-bound and gilt-lettered, as comfortingly bulky and solid as most other pre-twentieth-century arti- facts—cast-iron stoves, say. As Mamoulian's eyes traversed the shelves, left to right, up and down, straining to capture intriguingly suggestive names and titles, the books morphed sequentially into modern, more colorful shapes: trimmer, bejacketed, potentially lighter in heft. Eventually, after his stunned yet still avaricious gaze had raced over roughly a thousand books, he stopped at a couple of terminal volumes that might have come straight from the "new arrivals" table of a Barnes & Noble.

Like a sleepwalker, Mamoulian crossed the room to the shelves. As he got closer, names swam randomly into focus: Thackery, Eliot, Collins, Fitzgerald, Hawthorne, Stein, Poe, Colette, Twain, Faulkner, Alcott, Mailer, Kerouac, Hemingway— Dimly, he sensed the librar- ian of the Caxton Daye Academy, Emily Lerner, trailing him without speaking, as if respectful of his bibliogenic trance.

Mamoulian reached out for a volume spaced about midway on the shelves. He pinched it delicately and withdrew it reverently from its niche as if handling either a vial of nitroglycerin or the governor's commutation of his death sentence. Where were his cloth curator's gloves? Back in the van, of course, useless now. But he couldn't tear himself away long enough to retrieve them. Cradling the handsome, well-preserved book as if it were a premature baby or the withered hand of his dying grandmother, Mamoulian opened its cover.

The inner pages confirmed this to be a Shakespeare and Company first edition of James Joyce's *Ulysses*. That wasn't a complete surprise, for Mamoulian had suspected as much from first sight of the book's exterior, which he'd once seen in a Sotheby's catalogue. But the presence of Joyce's autograph below an inscription—"To Miss Rosemary Charcroft: long may you Bloom."—was definitely not foreseen.

This single book was worth at least $150,000.

Mamoulian began, uncontrollably, to weep. But unlike his sweat, his tears ran clear, no ink leaking from his dazzled eyes.

Wafting a scent of lavender, Emily Lerner stepped past him, oblivious to his distress, or at least pretending not to see his tears. She blithely plucked a single book from near the beginning of the Hemphill Collection and offered it to Mamoulian.

"Here's that Dickens I mentioned."

Gently, Mamoulian reshelved the Joyce, wiped his cheeks with the backs of his hands, wiped his hands on his pants, and took the Dickens.

It was the 1836 Macrone first printing of *Sketches by Boz*, worth a paltry twelve hundred dollars. A minute ago, Mamoulian would have trembled to hold such a find. Now, faced with a whole wall of what must have been rare firsts, he could only nod like a spring-necked dashboard doggie and murmur, "Very nice. Very fucking nice."

*   *   *

When Mamoulian shouted, every diner in the Golden Goose—that pleasantly old-fashioned restaurant offering a serene view of the church-dominated village green forming the center of the town of Newbery—turned to look. Mamoulian realized he had half-risen out of his seat, and that his own dining companion, the inestimable Emily Lerner, had instantly flushed at becoming the center of attention. With an exercise of extreme self-control, Mamoulian lowered his rear into his chair and also lowered his voice.

"I'm sorry. I just can't believe that you let the kids handle those books."

"Only the honors students. They're very respectful and mindful. Caxton Daye attracts that kind of child. And I always stress the age of the books to them."

"The age, the age—what about their goddamn *value*?"

Emily sniffed dismissively at Mamoulian. "That was never a consideration in my mind or the minds of my students. We are interested in literature alone, Mister Mamoulian. That is the only reason for the existence of the Hemphill Collection."

Mamoulian picked up his wine glass and slugged back a hearty mouthful, then poured himself another generous portion. "Tell me you don't let the kids take the books home."

"I let them take the books home, yes."

Before he could speak again, Mamoulian had to refill his glass twice more. "Jesus, Emily, do you realize what your goddamn Hemphill Collection is worth? Let me give it to you straight from the shoulder, no dealer-style bullshit. This find is too big for me to play games. Pay close attention now. Easily, no hype, I'm guessing a million. Maybe more. I'd have to examine each book individually to firm up the figure."

Mamoulian studied the librarian's relatively unlined, lightly cosmeticized, heart-shaped face for a reaction. Demure, that was the word he had been searching for. Yet subtly complex, with depths not easily plumbed. Was she as naive as she seemed, or really a sharp player? Mamoulian hadn't been this flummoxed by anyone on the other side of the bargaining table in a long while.

For the first time in their short acquaintance, the woman's face betrayed some signs of agitation. "Oh my goodness. I hadn't realized the collection had accrued such value. I wonder what Amy would think of such an outcome?"

"Amy?"

"Amy Hemphill, the first librarian at Caxton Daye."

"Oh, right." Mamoulian's stomach nudged him not to entirely neglect his meal, and he wolfed down a buttered roll. "Would you run the whole story by me again? I still can't quite believe it."

Emily's smile bore a keen edge. "Are you asking me to be a boring pedant on our first date, Mister Mamoulian?"

"Huh? Date? Oh, you're making a joke, right? No, just lay the history on me informal like."

Her smile dimmed. "I'd be happy to."

As Emily began to talk, Mamoulian sliced into his steak and listened more attentively than he had a few hours ago back at the school, when he had immediately demanded to know the origin of all the rare firsts, and then cajoled Emily into dining with him that very night so that he might present a business proposition that would benefit the school immensely.

"In 1827," Emily Lerner dispassionately lectured, "Caxton Daye, a wealthy merchant and trader, founded the school that bears his name in order to implement his rather stern ideas about vocational instruction. One of the first teachers he hired was Amy Hemphill. Her ancillary duties included the post of librarian. Unfortunately, the small library she presided over was composed almost entirely of ponderous tomes on farming, blacksmithing, weaving, and other practical arts. About the lightest confection Daye permitted the school to buy officially was *The Pilgrim's Progress.*

"A dedicated reader of borrowed novels herself, Amy felt that her young charges would benefit from exposure to contemporary literature. She began to acquire a few books on her own, using whatever small portion of her wages she could spare. She kept these books separate from the academy's holdings, and loaned them out at her own discretion.

"Amy held her job for the next thirty years, until her death. By that sad but inevitable date the collection was approximately one hundred and fifty books large. Amy willed it to her successor—whom she never actually met—a woman named Virginia Norton. Amy's will also enjoined Virgina to continue the tradition of extracurricular purchases, which Miss Norton gladly did.

"Virgina saw the collection reach the turn of the century, and approach the five-hundred-volume mark. By then, of course, the academy had become a more typical liberal-arts institution, and the main library offered its own share of popular fiction. But the tradition of librarians purchasing a few additional high-quality books continued. Virginia's successor was Rosemary Charcroft—"

"The gal mentioned in the Joyce volume?"

"Yes. Amy had established a tradition of securing inscriptions from many of the authors she selected, dealing with them through the mail. While not every book in the collection is signed, the majority of them are."

Mamoulian moaned incoherently, but Emily politely ignored him and continued.

"Rosemary passed on the collection to Helen Castelli around 1935, and I took it over from Helen in 1979. During my tenure, I've added approximately twenty-five books per year. That's a higher average than my predecessors maintained, but I don't claim any extra devotion to the collection. It's just that books are cheaper nowadays than they were at many points in the past. Helen, for instance, had an awful time during the Depression. I think she managed only three acquisitions a year during the worst of that era. Buying all of Dos Passos nearly bankrupted her."

Mamoulian's groans simulated the painful calls of an unfed hyena. Finished with her account, Emily turned efficiently to her meal, pasta with shrimp. They ate silently for a while, Mamoulian trying to ingest both words and food.

"Okay," Mamoulian finally said, "I can accept five do-gooders amassing a private library over the course of nearly two hundred years. But what gets me is the *quality* of it. Every book in your frigging collection is a literary masterpiece. The lowest lowbrow item I saw was *Gone with the Wind*—worth roughly thirteen hundred nowadays, by the way."

"That was Helen's first purchase. She debated long and hard before she plunged on that one, she told me before she retired. She loved the book herself, but worried that it might be too racy for her students. In fact, she wasn't entirely happy with some of Rosemary's daring choices. Joyce and Hemingway, primarily."

"All right, so there were some minor disagreements among you. But still, you all seem infallible in your own way. I mean, what're the chances you five would pick nothing but winners? How come there's no F. Marion Crawford or Bulwer-Lytton crap in the goddamn Hemphill Collection? For instance: how'd you personally decide to snag the first edition of *Angela's Ashes* before there was any buzz about it? It's fetching five hundred bucks now, you know."

Emily dabbed at her lips with her napkin and considered the question. "I can't really speak for the others, but I suspect that my motives were also theirs. First off, we were all educated women from similar backgrounds with a certain level of taste who bought what we liked. Isn't that the first rule of collecting, Mister Mamoulian?"

"Alex, for Christ's sake. Mister Mamoulian is my father."

"And second, Alex, we all held the enlightenment of our students paramount. We were determined not to buy ephemeral trash."

Now it was Mamoulian's turn to ponder. He shook his head uncomprehendingly after a few minutes. "It's still uncanny. It's like you all had some sixth sense for literary horse races. If you won that consistently in a casino, you'd be out on your ass for cheating."

"Fortunately for us, the headmasters of Caxton Daye Academy did not follow casino rules."

His expression earnestly overwrought, Mamoulian laid down his utensils and leaned toward Emily. She awaited his speech with seemingly sincere interest.

"The books in that room are being wasted, Emily. You realize that now, right? You could replace all of them with nice reading copies for a few thousand dollars total, and your honor students wouldn't know the difference. The texts would be the same, the kids wouldn't give a— They just wouldn't care. Believe me! And the sale of the collection would bring in a million bucks for the school. You're hoping to renovate the gym, right? You could buy gold-plated dumbbells with that kind of money!"

"And what do you get out of all this, Alex? Are you an altruist?"

"No! I admit it! I'm a sharper, a hustler. I've always got my own interests foremost. But money's not the issue here. Didn't I play it straight with you about the collection's real value right from the start? Pardon me, but the way I cleaned out your crummy book sale shows I could've pulled the wool over your eyes on this deal too. Now, I can't buy the collection off you and resell it on my own. I don't have that kind of capital. But with your consent, I *can* take the credit for discovering it, and I can oversee the auction. That kind of publicity could vault me into the big leagues. My reputation would be made, and my business would take off like the goddamn space shuttle! Oh, if you wanted to give me a commission of a few percent on the sale, I wouldn't fight you. But the main thing is that I get the kudos for the discovery. What do you say? Can we work together on this?"

Mamoulian reached out and grabbed Emily's left wrist (no ring graced the elegant tapered fingers of that hand, he noticed). She let him hold her for a moment before disengaging. Her expression registered genuine confusion.

"I don't know, Alex. You make a plausible case. But the children *do* appreciate the first editions, I think, at least on some level. They represent a continuity to the school's history, and to the history of literature."

Mamoulian sank back in his chair. "Hell, Emily, if you're determined on throwing away this once-in-a-lifetime opportunity, just tell me and I'll be on my way. Or maybe you don't like me as an individual. You think another dealer would be more savvy, classier, maybe do a better job."

"I didn't say any of that."

Mamoulian allowed a look of sudden shocked awareness and dismay to alter his face. "Maybe you're planning to cut the academy out of the deal altogether? Is that it? I suppose the books *are* legally yours, since they've been willed from one librarian to another. I don't blame you for giving in to temptation, Emily. You can still set yourself up pretty well with a million these days. But the ethics of such a sneaky-pete move— Well, Emily, I never would have suspected—"

"I don't need a lecture on ethics from you, Mister Mamoulian. All I'm trying to say is that I need time to sleep on my decision."

Mamoulian shifted to an optimistic grin. Considering her naked ring finger, he almost suggested that sleeping with someone might hasten the decision-making process, but ultimately decided that perhaps he had better not push his luck.

"I respect that, Emily. I really do."

❊   ❊   ❊

Mamoulian had rented a room at an old-fashioned motor court on the edge of Newbery named Teepee Lodge. The chenille-covered bed proved comfortable enough, but Mamoulian never slept in it. During what remained of that night, he alternated between lying down wide-awake in his sleeveless T-shirt and boxer shorts—fantasies of his fabulous future racing through his head—and pacing the floor barefoot in the mellow light from a yellow-papered lamp whose glazed ceramic body was shaped like a stag being torn by hounds. He had bought a six-pack of some local brew to keep him company, but after finishing two cans he saw a vivid image of his brother drying out in the clinic, and poured the rest down the toilet.

As early as consonant with decency, Mamoulian phoned Emily Lerner at her home. She spoke before he could even employ any of his carefully formulated courtesies.

"Yes, I'll sell them, for the sake of the academy. But just don't ask me to be happy about this."

"Happiness is generally not a prerequisite to making some serious money, Emily. But I don't think you'll regret this move. Maybe the school will even give you a bronze plaque or something. Now, when can I come in to catalogue the books?"

"Why not start today? 'If it were done, then 'twere well it were done quickly.'"

"That's a quote. Shakespeare. Am I right?"

Emily sighed. "Yes, you're right."

"Stuff rubs off on you in this business, Emily. You'll see."

"I wish you hadn't promised me that."

The door to the dusky, book-redolent room housing the Hemphill Collection opened to Emily Lerner's key. Mamoulian and the librarian stepped inside, and Emily switched on an overhead light Mamoulian had not noticed yesterday. The heightened clarity of the miraculous vision staggered him again almost as deeply as the original encounter. Regarding the rows of rare firsts was like looking at his own name in lights fifty feet high. Get ahold of yourself, man, Mamoulian advised himself. Remember your professionalism.

"Have you eaten yet, Mister Mamoulian?"

"No, not since last night. But I couldn't stomach anything right now. I've got to get to work. I'm going to be making extensive notes on titles and conditions. Should take me about three long days if I really push. When I get back home, I'll type up a catalogue that we can use as bait to snag a big-name auction house. The books themselves can stay with you until we have a solid agreement with someone. They've been safe here for a couple of centuries, so I guess a few more months won't put them at risk. Unless, that is, you intend to blab to everyone about what we've got here. Then I can't guarantee anything."

Today Emily wore a white blouse, plaid skirt and penny loafers, almost as if she were in schoolgirl uniform. This woman could do with a makeover for sure. "No, I won't say a word to anyone." She walked slowly to the shelves and ran her fingertips lightly along a few feet of spines, producing a skritching noise that made Mamoulian wince.

"I know the children will miss these old books," Emily said wistfully. "I wish you could see their faces the first time they earn entry here. The reading experience isn't just words, you know. It's feel and smell and typefaces and bindings. Everything will be different with new editions."

Mamoulian almost yelled at her not to treat his books so cavalierly, but bit his tongue. Instead, he pulled on his soiled curator's gloves ostentatiously. Emily paid no mind to his silent rebuke, but instead lifted out a book from near the end of the collection.

Her voice was thick with dreams. "Raymond Carver. He was one of my firsts."

Mamoulian took the book away. "*What We Talk About When We Talk About Love*. Knopf, 1981, fine in dustjacket. Two hundred and fifty bucks, minimum." The dealer shook his head in wonderment. "Damn! How did you *know* back then?"

"I can't say. I just followed my heart."

"I wish my goddamn heart had that kind of savvy. I'd rent it out to Wall Street."

Emily turned away, but not before Mamoulian saw a tear crawling down her cheek. "If you want anything, I'll be in my office. School starts soon, and there's plenty for me to do there."

"Yeah, great, we'll both keep busy."

Mamoulian had intended to approach the Hemphill Collection

systematically, but his eye kept getting snagged by random titles. For the first couple of hours he couldn't resist taking down anything that intrigued him, and just marveling at its rarity.

Trollope's *Can You Forgive Her?*, Chapman and Hall, 1864: $850.

Kerouac's *On the Road*, Viking, 1957: $3,700.

Mailer's *The Naked and the Dead*, Rinehart, 1955: $1,000.

Longfellow's *Evangeline*, in a special presentation edition limited to fifty copies, 1848: $4,500.

Collins's *The Moonstone*, Harper and Brothers, 1868: $300.

Thoreau's *Walden*, Ticknor and Fields, 1854: $7,500.

Burroughs's *Naked Lunch*, Olympia, 1959: $1,000. (First Mailer, then Kerouac, now Burroughs. That Castelli woman who had balked at *Gone with the Wind* must've gotten more radical in her old age.)

Banks's *The Wasp Factory*, Macmillan, 1984: $125. (Another surprise. Mamoulian wouldn't have pegged Emily as a Banks reader. Those depths he had sensed in her yesterday must conceal some strange currents. . . .)

Mamoulian spotted a book whose unique spine instantly and improbably evoked a childhood memory: Barrie's *Peter Pan*. He took the book in hand. It was the first U.S. edition, Scribner's, 1906, worth over nine hundred dollars. But save for its superior condition, it was identical to the beat-up copy Mamoulian had read and reread as a child. His mother had inherited it from her mother, and Mamoulian had discovered it by himself on the family shelves. Until this very moment, Mamoulian hadn't realized he had been handling the first edition as a kid—

He had been a bright ten-year-old, a voracious reader, eager to explore the world through books. The Disney *Peter Pan* had just been released, and Mamoulian had gotten "hooked" on the Edwardian fantasy. Falling into the novel had proved an even more rewarding experience, offering a crisp and thrilling mental movie Disney could never bring to the screen.

Jesus, where had that retarded bookish kid disappeared to? Swamped somewhere in Mamoulian's ponderous flesh, he supposed. When was the last time he had actually *read* a book?

Mamoulian shook his head as if to dislodge invisible cobwebs. The motion, combined with his lack of sleep and food, made him dizzy. Oddly, the echo of Emily's fingertips straying across the bindings and a whiff of her lavender scent seemed suddenly to fill the room. On a whim, his heart racing unaccountably, Mamoulian opened the novel to its first page and began to read:

> *All children, except one, grow up. They soon know that they will grow up, and the way Wendy knew was this. One day when she was two years old she was playing in a garden, and she plucked another flower and ran with it to her mother. I suppose she must have looked rather delightful, for Mrs. Darling put her hand to her heart and cried, "Oh, why can't you remain like this forever!" That was all that passed between them on the subject, but henceforth Wendy knew that she must grow up. You always know after you are two. Two is the beginning of the end.*

And that was the last Mamoulian knew of the common world until he came to himself hours later behind the wheel of his van, barrelling down the highway at ten miles over the speed limit, a sign informing him that he was already halfway home.

*   *   *

The pile of unopened orders on Mamoulian's desk reared higher each day since his return, but he let them sit untended. The blank screen of his new computer monitor was filmed with dust. The shelves of his shop needed dusting as well, but he couldn't summon up the energy. He sat all day behind his desk, trying to fathom what had happened to him in Newbery. He might have perpetuated such a daily stasis forever had not his brother walked in unannounced one afternoon, and dropped a pile of cash on the desk.

Mamoulian bestirred himself. "What's this?"

Lev beamed, but Mamoulian refused to mirror the expression. "Part of the money I owe you."

"You're really working again?"

"You bet. And me and Roberta are getting along really good too."

Mamoulian poked at the money disinterestedly. "Well, that's a first. Good for you—I guess."

Lev frowned. "Shit, Alex. Are you actually disappointed that I didn't screw up again?"

"No, no, I'm glad you got back on your feet. It's just— Listen, when you were hitting the bottle hard, did you ever blank out? Maybe go through a few hours you couldn't remember afterwards?"

"Of course. All the real alkies experience that. Why do you ask?"

"Something like that happened to me recently. And it scared the fuck out of me."

"Were you drinking?"

"No. That's the scariest part. I was stone cold sober, and in the middle of the best experience of my professional life."

"Sounds like overwork to me. I've heard about that happening to type A guys. Some stockbroker on the edge walks out of his office and wakes up in Peoria a week later. You work too hard, Alex. You should think about taking a vacation. Come with me and Roberta and Avram next time we go to the shore. You can bring a friend if you want."

Mamoulian snorted. "Yeah, sure. Me and Mrs. Palm."

Turning to leave, Lev said, "Think about it, Alex. I'll be back next month with the rest of your loan."

After the door had closed behind his brother, Mamoulian took out his prized rare Ballard from its cabinet. He turned it this way and that, but the book roused no feelings of pride or pleasure in him. He propped it up by the keyboard as a reminder. Next time Avram stopped in, he would have the boy show him how to post sale entries to his Website, using the Ballard as the first instance. Sell the damned chimera and forget about it, let the scholars debate its existence.

The next thing Mamoulian did was find his checkbook and, after consulting his records for the relevant name and address, write out a thousand-dollar check to the widow Hollis. On the memo line he wrote: *Sold those magazines for more than I planned.* He sealed the check in an envelope, stamped and addressed it.

About to step out for lunch, Mamoulian was halted by the ringing of his phone.

"Mamoulian Rare Books."

"Mister Mamoulian. One of us had to call, and it seemed that someone wouldn't be you."

Mamoulian dropped into his chair. "Emily. How you doing?"

"Just fine. More to the point, how are *you* doing?"

"To level with you, not so great. I seem to have lost the thrill of the chase somehow. My job isn't what it used to be. I can't get excited about rare books anymore."

"That's too bad. What's going to happen to the Hemphill Collection now?"

"That's totally up to you. I'm out of the picture."

"You know, when you vanished so inexplicably, I have to confess that I thought you might have purloined the choicest items and bolted. But a quick glance showed me nothing was missing. That left me very puzzled. I still am. Would you like to help relieve my confusion at all?"

"Boy, Emily, I sure would. Then maybe I'd feel better too. But I can't explain what happened to me. I just fell into some kind of crazy fugue. You and your goddamn million-dollar library just sent me round the bend. Now every morning when I wake up, the first thing I do is check to see if I've gone nuts during the night."

Emily remained unspeaking for a moment. "And so far?"

"So far I seem okay. But I can't risk getting close to your Hemphill Collection again. It's too full of spooks."

"Literature is powerful, Mister Mamoulian."

"Is that a quote?"

"No. But maybe it should be. Well, I guess I won't bother selling the collection now. My heart never advocated such a sale. Only my brain kept insisting the money could do the academy some good. But money for the gym renovations can accumulate through bake sales. The books will remain here, just where they've always been, if you'd ever care to visit them again."

"Maybe I'll take you up on that offer someday, Emily."

"I guess our association is at an end then. Goodbye, Mister Mamoulian."

"Emily—"

"Yes?"

"Uh, what new authors do you like these days?"

Emily's voice registered a rare vitality. "Oh, there are quite a few undiscovered wunderkinds out there. For instance, do you know the name—"

Nodding sagely, pen in hand, Mamoulian took very careful notes.

RETURN TO COCKAIGNE

The pretty, nervous-looking woman—thirtyish, dark hair in bangs, long cloth winter coat concealing her taste in clothes—entered the Kirby-Ditko Extended Care Residence hurriedly. She brushed past the bored attendant at the reception desk, rode the elevator to the third floor, turned left familiarly down the long, disinfectant-scented corridor, and hastened to a private room. Inside she carefully closed the door, then grabbed a handy chair and wedged it under the knob.

"Westbrook, Calla—sorry I'm late. Do you think jamming the door will give us enough time?"

On the high-tech bed centerpiecing the room lay a comatose man, hooked to various supplemental machines and assorted drips. The sheets neatly drawn up to his neck failed to conceal the lines of his wasted form: limbs like rope-wrapped poles, chest a set of wax-paper bellows. Grapes under blanched rose petals, his closed eyes punctuated a sunken, expressionless face.

Two earlier visitors, a man and a woman both of an age with the newcomer, sat in ugly institutional chairs beside the patient's bed. The finely suited man possessed the brutish handsomeness of a troll, ameliorated by an impish grin. Legs crossed, he jogged his raised leather-shod foot impatiently. The other woman—plain-faced, wearing a drab blouse and skirt, oversized prescription glasses buffering watery blue eyes—remained intensely focused on the unconscious man and seemed content to wait as such forever.

"Our old friend just underwent a bath and massage," replied Westbrook, the male visitor. "Mealtime, of course, to use one of the patient's own favorite phrases, is a non-issue. I doubt he'll receive any more attention for the next several hours, at least. That should give us plenty of time for us to get in and out. With luck, no suspicious or dutiful helper will even so much as jiggle that knob. But I appreciate your concern, Hazel."

The seated woman, Calla, looked up grimly. "Plenty of time if nothing goes wrong."

Hazel's nervous expression deepened. "What could go wrong? Do either of you anticipate something going wrong?"

"You can look at Pike and still wonder what could go wrong? We never anticipated losing him this way."

Westbrook intervened between the women. "Now, now, ladies. Pike's condition owes nothing to the drug and everything to his own megalomania, overconfidence and greed. We three should experience no problems, especially considering we're all two decades wiser than the last time we did this."

Hazel expressed her dissent with this character analysis by a snort. "Speak for yourself. Some days I feel I know even less than I did at fifteen. I'm less certain about the meaning of it all, that's for sure."

Westbrook's grin resembled a crag fissuring. "But can you really ever be sure about uncertainty?"

Calla stood up. "Enough talk. Let's go rescue Pike."

Westbrook also rose to his feet. "Rescue him from himself, you mean."

"Yes. From himself, from the allure of the Land. And don't forget the starostas."

Hazel shivered. "I *hate* the starostas. Almost as much as the lumpkins do. But I suppose we're committed now."

With this last remark, Hazel shrugged out of her coat. Naked beneath except for shoes, she appeared at ease with her body on display before these two particular witnesses.

Westbrook bowed appreciatively. "You look as beautiful as you did in your teens, my dear. How I've missed seeing you thus."

"We're not kids anymore, Westy, going skinny-dipping on a dare. We all have our own lives now. Our own families, our own jobs—our own lovers."

Westbrook replied, "Too bad, don't you think? Who knows what would have developed among us four, had the Tetrad retained access to the Land? But such idle speculation is fruitless. As always, Hazel, you cut directly to the chase." The burly man tossed his suitcoat aside and began loosening his tie.

Calla turned her back to unbutton her shirt. "Shouldn't Pike be naked too?"

"I doubt it's necessary. He's firmly in the Land already. I debated even wasting a dose on him, but in the end I felt such a measure couldn't hurt."

As her friends continued to undress, Hazel asked, "This is the real supraliminal stuff, isn't it? The same as twenty years ago?"

Westbrook pulled his pants down. "But of course. Iatros handed it to me himself."

"I still don't understand. Where did he come from after all these years? Why did he cut contact with us back then? How did he find you? Why now?"

Naked knobby spine toward her companions, Calla peeled off her panties, then turned defiantly around. "You're asking all the same questions we never had the answers to in the first place! Where did Iatros ever come from? Why did he leave us high, dry and hurting? How did he ever find us? Why then?"

"Now, now, ladies. Are you forgetting the Compact of the Winetree Grove?"

Both women appeared humbled. Westbrook nodded approvingly at their contrition, then added, "All I can tell you is that our mysterious friend looked not a day older than when we last saw him. I have no reason to distrust his gift, and I look forward to nothing beyond this one unexpected visit. He might show up again tomorrow—or in another fifty years. Who can say? Now, allow me."

Westbrook removed a thumb-sized squeeze bottle containing a barely discernible amount of clear liquid from the pocket of his chair-draped coat. He uncapped it to reveal a pinhole outlet. "A different delivery system this time, you'll notice. Please, take your seats and put Pike in the circuit."

The women took up stations on either side of the comatose man and each gripped a withered hand beneath the sheets. Westbrook moved to Pike's nutrient line, where he added a drop from his bottle directly into a feed-valve. Then he hastened to each woman and decanted a drop apiece upon their tongues. He established himself in a chair at the foot of the bed, squirted the final drop into his own mouth, then grabbed the free hands of the two women.

"Cockaigne, our Dreamland—at last we return!"

*   *   *

The weird adult had been hanging at the fringes of the high school grounds for the past several days. Mornings and afternoons, as the students flowed in and out of the school, he maintained his innocuous yet disturbing stakeout. Sitting in his luxury sedan on a public street under the shade of a sycamore, reading some kind of strange magazine printed in a foreign language, sipping occasionally from a cardboard cup of coffee, the guy made no illicit or innocent overtures to anyone, male or female. But although the magazine seemed to claim his whole attention, his eyes shifted subtly from time to time toward the adolescents.

The principal and the school custodian had gone to talk to the man on the third day, but whatever explanation or identification the guy offered must have satisfied the authorities in charge of student safety, since no higher security procedures were invoked, and the stranger was allowed to maintain his lazy vigil.

Pike was the first member of the inalienable foursome to suggest speaking to the stranger.

Megawatts of energy surging through the thin copper wire of his fifteen-year-old body, the glimmer-eyed Pike often led his three friends down back roads of adventure they might not have otherwise ventured on. Calla, Westbrook and Hazel both appreciated and feared their nominal leader's wild bravado.

They sat now on the deserted bleachers at the edge of the football field behind the school, the last class of the day half an hour behind them.

"Turn that noise down a minute, Westy," Pike ordered. "I want to suggest a little game."

The rough-featured boy bent to the huge Panasonic boom box at his feet and cut the volume, reducing Blondie's "Call Me" to a background drone.

"I don't know why you don't get yourself one of these," said Pike, displaying a Sony Walkman big as an abridged paperback dictionary.

"I like to share my music. Your gizmo makes it too private."

"I'm into being private, okay?"

"Sure. And I'm into sharing."

Pushing her clunky glasses further up her small nose, Calla leaned over to inspect the Walkman. "It's got two headphone jacks, doesn't it, Pike? You could still share your music." Without asking, she popped the tape out. "Devo. I like them."

Hazel rocked backward and laughed. "I can just picture the two of you walking side by side leashed to the same little box. What happens if you spontaneously go around opposite sides of a telephone pole?"

"Kerchung!" Westbrook mimed a jerky fall.

"That's a non-issue. I've only got one set of headphones."

Calla sat back disappointedly.

"But I didn't want to talk about this kind of theoretical crap when I asked Westy to turn his box down. I wanted to propose a little adventure. Let's have some fun with Chester the Molester."

Westbrook objected. "The magazine guy out front in his car? I don't know . . . He's really creepy."

"What did you have in mind?" Hazel asked.

"Let's try to get him to do something really evil. Then we can turn him in to the cops and be big shots."

"Why hassle the lousy pervert?" Calla said. "He's just pitiful. You're only lowering yourself to his level."

"I'm bored. And who says I'm living on some level higher than this guy to start with?"

"I'd like to think—" began Calla, but she was interrupted by Pike's abrupt leap to his feet.

"I'm doing it now! Whether you guys are with me or not."

Pike gained a lead of a few yards before the others caught up with him. Rounding the building, they saw the stranger apparently slumbering in his car. His seat semi-reclined, he lay back with his glossy magazine covering his face. All the school buses had long departed, and no other kids lingered.

Slowly they approached the car. A yard away, the stranger's voice—accented, dark and bitter as Aztec chocolate mixed with heart's blood—halted them dead.

"Children of Cockaigne, I have been waiting for you."

*   *   *

They arrived in immortal Cockaigne as always, transitionlessly, startlingly, opening their eyes first and eternally upon Piebush Meadow, near the edge of the Winetree Grove.

Three gods regarded each other joyously, with clear-eyed intimacy. Caparisoned in elaborate greaves, gorgets, and gauntlets, caped and cowled, plumed and prinked, laced and leathered, booted and buckled, the trio—two Junoesque women and a Herculean man—stood tall as the lower limbs of the remote winetrees, those branches themselves a good ten feet above the licorice-moss carpeting the Meadow.

"Aniatis."

"Dormender."

"Yodsess."

So they named themselves, and broke into roiling laughter at the splendid sound of their own immense plangent voices.

215

"How marvelous to be home again!" said the man. "I feel as if shackles have been struck from my wrists and ankles!"

"Dormender, you name the sensation exactly!" The woman who had addressed Dormender whipped off her winged casque and released banners of thick red hair. "The eagle of my spirit soars high once again!"

The second woman smiled also, but fatalistically, and did not remove her own shining headgear, keeping all of her corvine tresses captured, save for a stray curl or two. "Yodsess, I too experience delight at the return of the swelling passion and supernal vitality that form our birthright. But I would advise you to redon your armor. Have you forgotten the starostas? Likewise, what of our mission to rescue our lost comrade, Theriagin? There is no telling what foul manifestations in the Land may have arisen from his perverse and overlong tenancy in Castel Djurga."

Yodsess replaced her helm upon her noble brow, but could not resist twirling around. "Aniatis, as of old, your counsel is wise but over-sober. Let all evil crawlers crawl, all ghastly ghaunts gibber, all starostas shamble! Our function is to exult! Look at the firmament that your earthly eyes have not beheld for much too long! Marbled with sherbert clouds! Smell the odors of the pepper shrubs and squab roots! Let the warm winds arriving from their long journey across the Berryjuice Sea caress your cheek!"

Dormender grinned, as much at Yodsess's paean as at Aniatis's obvious attempt to leash her own natural exuberance. "One an inebriate, one a clerk, and only I providing the voice of moderation. Ah, well, the middle path is a fine road for Dormender to travel. Come, ladies, let us leave Piebush Meadow behind, in quest of Castel Djurga."

So urging, Dormender adjusted the long sword yclept Salvor that was slung across his back and strode off. The women followed, and before they reached the marge of the grove they had all availed themselves of sustenance from the bushes that gave the meadow its name. Once under the trees, meaty gravy running down their chins, they snapped gourds full of heady beverage from the lowest branches and drowned their lunches in tart wine.

"Remember you the Pact made here?" Dormender asked jokingly.

Aniatis and Yodsess blushed at the thought of their old conflicts, and in what pleasant manner they had been resolved. Then the latter answered, "I remember."

"Yes, I too," said Aniatis. "I remember everything."

＊   ＊   ＊

Pike could not restrain his elation at the incriminating words spoken by the foreign creep. "You heard him guys, he offered us coke! Man, your ass is grass now, weirdo! C'mon, let's go call the cops!"

Much to their surprise, the burly man seemed unruffled by the gleeful threats of the children's leader. He removed the magazine from his face, revealing in profile an olive complexion, chubby cheeks, a splayed, blemish-pitted nose and a goatee. Far from frightening, he most closely resembled an opera impresario in a Bugs Bunny cartoon. Out of sight, his hand maneuvered the seat control to power himself upright. He turned to face the four teenagers fully, captivating them with his dark eyes.

"Have you never felt the wrongness of your lives? Do you not all experience the odd sense of being exiled? Isn't this world deeply unsatisfying somehow, a pale parody of what might truly exist? Yes, people turn to sense-numbing drugs to escape just such a feeling of emptiness. But you misperceived my speech. I named not the crippling white powder cocaine, but the peerless realm of Cockaigne."

Pike hesitated a moment in the face of the man's assurance and subject-changing tactics, but recovered enough bravado to insist, "You can't get out of this with a lot of fancy double-talk, mister. You're nothing but a lousy drug pusher, and you're going down."

"True, I do intend to offer you a drug. But it's a drug not of this world. Liberating, enlightening, transporting—"

"That's what all the pushers say! I've heard everything I need to hear now." Pike whirled toward his friends. "Guys, let's—"

His companions obviously failed to share his certainty. Silent till now, they exchanged timid glances among themselves before Westbrook spoke.

"Pike, admit it—we've all felt exactly the feelings he's describing. None of us truly belongs here. And that name, Cockaigne—it means something to me."

Hazel gripped Pike by the wrist, nailed him with her ardent gaze. "I can almost picture the place he's talking about."

"Me too," said Calla.

Pike shook his head in confusion. "This is too weird. He's hypnotized you three and now you're all trying to hypnotize me. Somehow you're putting pictures in my brain—"

"No," said the stranger, "those are memories."

Pike lurched a few feet away, then halted. The man levered open his door and emerged. Squat, wearing a wool suit, he held an old-fashioned satchel in his left hand. He extended his right hand, and Westbrook shook it.

"My name is Doctor Iatros. Take me to a quiet, unfrequented place where we might talk. Quickly. Cockaigne needs you as soon as possible."

* * *

Many staunch words of comfort from Dormender and vast quantities of reassuring petting from Aniatis and Yodsess had been needed to calm the lumpkin enough to secure speech from the creature. At first, when encountered in the foothills of the Sugar Mountains, the quivering, frightened little furball (when standing, only as tall as the shins of the godlings) had retracted all its limbs and tried to hide behind an outcropping of pink-veined rock candy. Prodded from its niche, the lumpkin had deliberately rolled toward the nearby Great Gravy River as if to drown itself. Rescued from this fate, the timorous citizen of Cockaigne had required fully an hour of coaxing to reach the point where it could sensibly converse.

"Now, lumpkin," cajoled Dormender, "speak truly of what drove you to fear us, the legendary protectors of your race."

The lumpkin's voice piped bitterly. "Many and many a century have passed since any of your kind walked the Land to offer a shield or sword on our behalf. The only one of your breed remaining never leaves Castel Djurga. And he is no friend to any who dares trespass on the Jumbles."

"The Jumbles?" queried Aniatis. "What unknown territory do you name?"

"For hundreds of parasangs around Castel Djurga, the Land has been rendered fulsomely and morbidly rebarbative. No feature of the landscape offers solace or nourishment, the rude denizens affright, and the very sunlight that falls heavily there abrades the skin."

Yodsess smacked her mailed fist upon a cinnamon gumdrop big as a hassock. The sweet boulder absorbed the force of her blow, but not the sting of her words. "The Land bordering Castel Djurga was always the fairest spot in this paradise, a harmonious precinct of laughing waters and succulent pasturage! How could it now be so perverted?"

Dormender frowned. "Only through the madness of our comrade Theriagin, I fear."

Aniatis quizzed the lumpkin further. "You cite unkind inhabitants of these Jumbles. Are they the starostas?"

"No, worse! Even the starostas are affrighted of the Jumbles-dwellers, and venture not within their grasp. If I may be so bold, these dreadful beings resemble—they resemble you, your worships! But primitive, cloddish, puny travesties of your divine features."

None of the three divinities had any response to this puzzling information, and after a small amount of additional interrogation, they bade the lumpkin to bounce off on his way.

"Too much vilely sweet and egocentric solitude has rendered poor Theriagin a pustule of sickness upon the Land," Yodsess declaimed.

"Judge not our fellow too harshly," Dormender urged. "Any of us might have fallen into the same trap."

"Righting this wrong upon the Land must be our primary duty," Aniatis reminded them. "Rescue and rehabilitation of Theriagin comes second, if at all."

"I recall the dark labors we faced when first we arrived in the Land," Dormender said reflectively. "Those lessons will stand us in good stead now."

Yodsess raised her sharp labrys called Insight. "Onward then to Castel Djurga!"

❊   ❊   ❊

Pike chivvied out the two younger kids who had been using the space under the gymnasium's back stairs as a lovers' lane. Arranging several plastic milk crates in a rough semicircle on the greasy gravel, he fumed silently while his companions stared worshipfully at the weird Doctor Iatros. The intriguing stranger had refused to answer any of their questions until they were all settled down on their hard waffle-bottomed stools, shielded on three sides by graffiti-scribbled damp concrete. From the mildewy shadows, they could look down a long open slope of sunlit grass and spot any intruders long before they themselves could be surprised.

Once arranged in this manner, with two children to either side, Doctor Iatros began to spin his tale.

"Ten million years ago, I created a world—"

Immediately Pike interrupted with a derisive exclamation. "Shit, man! I thought the dope spiel was lame, but now we get fairy tales on top of it!"

Paul Di Filippo

"My words are indeed deemed myths in my pocket universe, by those who know no better. Here they are literal facts. But even as myths, they contain much truth. Fairy tales too are instructive, but not in the same manner. Now, shall I continue?"

The other three choroused yes, and Pike was forced to consent grudgingly as well.

"Ten million years ago, I created a small universe and named it Cockaigne. It was intended to be an Edenic place, offering its inhabitants an easy life, yet one not without its heroic challenges. Unfortunately, due to my extant immature skills, my universe contained an inherent flaw. A coarseness in the quantum weave allowed all higher intelligences to leak out into the ambient multiverse. I watched with intense dismay as the souls whom I had intended as the guardians of my Land evaporated after only a short existence and pinwheeled away, indestructible but lost, across the cosmos, finding unnatural homes in a myriad of other forms.

"Without sentient guardians to help shape Cockaigne, my creation began to degenerate. Mourning, I left it behind to seek out the original lost inhabitants wherever they might be in the cosmos—a laborious quest, believe me—and offer them the chance to return and help me repair my beautiful world. I cannot transplant you permanently to your native Land, for the congenital flaw remains, irreparable without destroying the place and starting over. But I have found a way to insure that your visits are frequent and extensive enough to be wholly satisfying and productive and beneficial, both for the Land and for your own souls."

Doctor Iatros fell silent. Westbrook ventured, "Are you, like, God?" The doctor laughed and patted his stomach. "With this body? Hardly!" Hazel said, "Do you have any pictures of Cockaigne?" "No," replied Iatros, "for your kind of cameras do not work in the Land." Ever practical, Calla asked, "How do we get there and back?"

As his answer, Iatros reached down to the satchel at his feet, opened it, and withdrew a square of blotter paper about the size of an index card. The paper was printed with smeary blue watercolor lines dividing it into four cells; inside each cell a different blurry symbol shone with a faint indigo radiance: sword, spear, double-bladed axe, and flail.

Pike jumped up, nearly banging his head on the underslant of the stairs. "That's acid! LSD, pure and simple."

Iatros paid no heed to the accusation. "These tabs have been soaked in a supraliminal drug of my own devising, tailored to the physiology of your species, which allows your souls to awaken fully and travel astrally to Cockaigne, where they will automatically manifest bodies out of the templates I have installed there. Once embodied, all will come naturally to you. Your return is likewise automatic, upon the timely waning of the drug in your mundane veins. I recommend taking the drug in unison, while maintaining physical contact of some sort. Ideally, to facilitate your temporary abandonment of this world, your psychic rebirth, you should also be naked."

Pike was beside himself. "Naked! Naked! Now we're taking orders from a sex pervert too! Have you guys all gone totally nuts?"

"I will not be present when you use the drug. But might I suggest that you make your first experiment soon? I have many light-years yet to cover in my quest, and I would like to leave you with a supply of the drug while I'm away. But not before you satisfy yourselves as to its use."

"Right, right," Pike ranted. "Hook us now for free, then make us pay in blood and sex games. Well, I'm not biting, Doctor Asshole! Let's just see what the cops have to say about all this."

Bent over, Pike scuttled for the exit. Halfway there, Iatros called out, "Pike! Recall Castel Djurga!"

Pike stiffened, then collapsed to the gravel. His friends hastened to his side and helped him up, laying him down across several crates. Within minutes his eyes fluttered open, and he reached toward Iatros.

"Hand that stuff over, Doc. Cockaigne needs us."

*   *   *

Aniatis pulled her begored and steaming spear named Caritas from the guts of the starosta, and the hideous creature, formerly pinned to the trunk of a broadcloth tree, fell to the turf. The mortally wounded yet still belligerent monster whipped its many suckered tendrils in vain, lisped chthonic obscenities from its psittacine beak, shook its riotous green mane, exuded venom from all its stingers, fangs and barbels, and madly clawed scales off its own teated belly. Darting gracefully in and out of the circle of its lashing mace-like tails, Dormender and Yodsess employed sword and axe to amputate and eventually decapitate the evil being. Upon final expiration the creature released a noxious cloud of puce bodily gas; but knowing the eventuality of this ultimate assault, the three practiced attackers had already retreated.

Cleaning their weapons with swatches plucked from the broadcloth trees, the godlings regarded their fallen prey with mixed satisfaction and concern.

"This marks the tenth starosta we have slain twixt the Diamond Lanes and Firewater Creek," noted Dormender, "a region where once their vile kind were extinct. I thought we had battled long and hard in ages past to confine the feeble remnant of their race to the Sherbert Polar Floes."

Yodsess slung the gleaming Insight over her brawny shoulder. "Cockaigne has slid inevitably a long way back toward the chaotic conditions reigning when first we regained our home."

"To think that the starostas once cruelly ruled over all the Land," said Aniatis. "Why Lord Iatros ever created them in the first place, I shall never understand."

At the mention of Iatros's name, all the trees bent and the grasses murmured, though no breeze passed.

"Unriddling the ways of our Creator concerns us not," Yodsess chided. "Our mission must be to reestablish the critical balances we once so carefully engineered."

"We are more than halfway to Castel Djurga," Dormender said, pointing with pristine Salvor toward the east. "Soon, if the lumpkins spoke accurately, we will cross into the misshapen Jumbles. But at the moment, if memory serves, a covey of Roast Fowls is wont to nest nearby, hard upon a patch of Mead Gourds. Let us refresh ourselves, then make hard march."

They sallied forth in high spirits then, while the elephant-sized carcass behind them slowly deliquesced into the scorched turf.

* * *

Eagerly the four sweaty teens shucked their daypacks and fell with near-unanimous exclamations of relief onto the coarse grass of the clearing.

"Ow!" complained Hazel, "I landed on some kind of pricker!"

"Better than landing on some kind of prick," Calla dryly observed.

Pike reacted to the bawdy comment unmercifully. Since his fainting spell, he had switched from being the biggest detractor of Cockaigne to the biggest defender of Iatros and his message.

"Shut up, Calla. This has nothing to do with sex. We're here to find our true home and save it from decay."

Westbrook shrugged. "We'll know the truth of it all for sure in a few minutes, won't we?"

Hazel said, "I still don't see why we couldn't stage this test inside."

Pike patiently explained. "Zonked out in somebody's bedroom, we'd be more likely to get discovered by horrified adults. But no one ever comes up here, except maybe some other kids once in a while. If anybody stumbles on us, they'll think we're just on some kind of nut and berry nudist trip."

"Trip is the right word," said Calla. "Despite everything, I'm still half expecting this stuff to be nothing but acid."

"And if it is plain old LSD—something you've talked about trying more than once, Calla—this setting should be safe and pleasant enough to give us a good trip. Okay, enough talk. Everybody strip."

Westbrook, Hazel and Pike undressed swiftly enough, but Calla hesitated, three-quarters turned away from her friends.

"Oh, come off it, Calla. I've seen you naked plenty of times in the locker room already, and you've got nothing to be ashamed of."

"I can't help being modest, Hazel."

"Modesty won't cut it where we're going," admonished Pike. "When I was out of it under the stairs, I saw vague shapes of the things we have to fight, and they won't care whether you're naked or not before they try to rip your head off."

"Which poses an interesting question," Westbrook said. "Can our bodies here be hurt by whatever happens to us in Cockaigne?"

"Don't know. But if we ever manage to shut up and do it, we'll learn that too."

Naked, the foursome found comfortable spots in the wild pasture in which to sit. A vagrant breeze riffled the fine down on the girls' arms and tightened the boys' scrotums. Pike held the blotter paper. Once settled, he ripped it into quarters and passed the emblemed squares out. Regarding each other with fervent determination, the teenagers placed the chalky papers on their tongues, then linked hands.

Within ninety seconds, their souls were loosed.

The sun climbed across the sky, reached its height, then began to fall, while clouds raced or ambled and wind pimpled the insensate flesh of the immobile, softly breathing adolescents. Finally their errant spirits returned, relighting their visages.

"Pike, you were *awesome!*"

"That canyon!"

"Those rapids!"

"The way those leopard-deer things ran!"

Paul Di Filippo

"What did we call them? I can't quite bring up the name now."

"But there's so much wrongness there to put right!"

Calla held forth her arm. "Feel the spot where the stained-glass thorn went in."

Her friends took turns pressing an area above her wrist.

"So cold, so very cold," Westbrook said.

"All right, all right," Pike admitted. "So we have to be careful. But didn't you feel more or less invincible? Powerful too! What could stand against us in Cockaigne, once we get our bearings?"

"Nothing—so long as we stick together."

* * *

Upon first beholding the mad unnatural sprawl of the Jumbles, the trio felt their souls truly quail, for the first time since their return to Cockaigne.

"Can it be that here once stretched the Chocolate Vale?"

"And what of Lemonade Lake and the Doughnut Isles?"

"I bring to mind the gay flocks of Marzipan Macaws that used to darken the skies."

From a promontory they surveyed the cankerous conglomeration that cordoned Castel Djurga, that distant towered and buttressed manse just visible on its own isolated mesa at the center of the abominable territory. Even the firmament above the Jumbles appeared tainted with smoke and ashes.

A grid of hard-surfaced black streets divided the landscape into harsh lines. Flanking the streets without so much as a blade of grass between them, one tall glass and steel box after another revealed their hive-like interiors, lit with actinic lights. The residents of the Jumbles—small simulacra resembling the godlings, dressed in drab uniforms, their faces dull, their voices reedy—rushed into and out of the buildings, clutching rigid cases and small, ear-braced deities to which they ceaselessly prayed. Down the streets, in obedience to colored signals, raced noxious self-powered carriages.

Dormender spat upon the outcropping of marbled bacon rock on which they stood. "This obscenity touches some dim nightmare in the recesses of my brain."

Aniatis said, "Ever unhappy with his surroundings, Theriagin seeks to recreate what we all willingly left behind."

Yodsess exclaimed, "Ah, of course! Despite his stated dream, to possess all Cockaigne forever, he quickly reverted to a facsimile of what he had deliberately abdicated."

The three titans hefted their weapons: Salvor, Insight and Caritas.

"Further speculation avails us naught. Let us wade through these vermin now, and confront our errant brother."

With seven-league strides they descended into the Jumbles. At the sight of the giants, whose heads topped the second story of each building, the deformed and mindless inhabitants of the Jumbles panicked like ants. Above the sounds of their synthetic screams and the crumpling of metal and crashing of glass, the laughter of the three conquerors rang like rolling thunder, as Caritas spitted, Salvor cleaved, and Insight hewed.

*   *   *

"I don't understand why we can't divide the doses into four sets, and each keep our own."

Westbrook had obviously been brooding on this topic for some time. Confronting Pike now, the homely-looking boy could not hide the indignation in his voice. Pike ignored the provocative tone, and replied matter-of-factly.

"First, Iatros handed the sheaf of hits directly to me, remember? 'Theriagin,' he said, 'I entrust these to you.'"

Supportive of Pike, Calla chimed in. "True. That's what the doctor said. Just before he told us he'd be gone for a short time."

Pike nodded smugly. "Second, by having a single guardian of the drug, no one can be tempted to make a solo trip to Cockaigne."

"No one but you, that is."

Pike turned on Hazel. "What are you saying? Are you accusing me of visiting Cockaigne alone? Where's your proof?"

"I don't have any proof. Just a suspicion. The last time we were all there, the Land felt different somehow, as if—I don't know! It's so hard to retain impressions and memories from Cockaigne, or even to find the words for them back here on Earth."

"What if I swear to you all by the stones of Castel Djurga that I haven't been cheating? No solo trips. Would that satisfy you?"

Westbrook tentatively said, "I suppose it would have to. . . ."

Calla moved closer to Pike. "I don't know why you two are ganging up on Pike, but I don't like it. We all need to trust each other. Do you want to suspect the comrade guarding your back when a pride of poppyfaces or a school of basikores is attacking? I certainly don't!"

Hazel agreed. "There's no way the Tetrad can succeed in rehabilitating Cockaigne if we don't all work together."

Pike clapped his hands as if gavelling a motion closed. "It's settled, then. I'll hold on to the doses."

"How many do we have again?"

"Fifty four-part blotters. At two trips a week, that's roughly six months' worth. Doctor Iatros will certainly return by then."

Calla shivered. "Six months from now is November. I don't plan on being butt-naked outdoors by then. We're going to have to figure out some other jumping-off place."

Hazel said, "I wish we could afford to go more than twice a week. The time differential between Cockaigne and here cuts two ways. One of our excursions lasts a long time in Cockaigne's frame. But between trips a lot of time continues to pass. I hate going back and seeing stuff we worked so hard on wrecked by the starostas. Just look at the mess they made of Bugtown."

"True. But twice a week is a good compromise. Spacing out the trips this way actually allows us to gauge the long-term effects of our actions. Aren't you glad we got to see the consequences of nearly eliminating the Sewing Needles, before we totally exterminated them?"

Westbrook grimaced. "Major screwup! None of the Turkey Trees got pollinated."

"It's hard to be a god," Pike said.

"Gods," said Hazel, frowning. "Hard to be *gods*."

*　　*　　*

They paused, breathing stertorously, to lean upon the gore-slick machicolations and crenellations of Castel Djurga. In this brief lull from carnage, there was no time for such niceties as cleaning of nicked steel or bold asseverations of justice. The sole task the three tattered and wounded warriors could focus on was filling their laboring lungs with air enough to battle anew.

Reaching the foot of the bluff upon which loomed Castel Djurga had presented no real challenges. The puny mock-citizens of the Jumbles had offered no substantial resistance, fleeing madly or at the most hurling small harmless pebbles from noisy hand-throwers. At the base of the bluff, Aniatis, Yodsess and Dormender had halted before setting eager feet upon the Adamantine Stairs. Halfway up they had met the first line of Theriagin's inner defenses, a barrage of razor-headed hoopsnakes tumbling down the narrow way. Upon sighting their foes, the snakes had loosened teeth from tail to arrow futilely at the armored bosoms of the invaders. Meeting that assault successfully, the trio hastened forward, reaching the pastille-tiled top of the butte, only to encounter wave after wave of enslaved malignant beings. In a frenzy of slaughter, the godlings dispatched spike-tailed, acid-dripping, scalpel-toothed beasts by the bloody scores, amidst a furious storm of shrieking, scratching, and snarling. All the while they wept at seeing Castel Djurga—where many and many happy, peaceful years had been passed with song and laughter and sensual dalliance—so besmirched.

Their goal was the Council Chamber on the highest level, where they intuitively sensed Theriagin had closeted himself.

Now, interrupting their hard-fought recess, a last-ditch wave of defenders sought to whelm them. More in the nature of domestic servitors than soldiers, these imps and halflings nonetheless brandished implements of potential harm. Tearful yet determined, the godlings perforce slayed them all.

At the wide brass-studded double doors of the Council Chamber, they hammered defiantly. Her flaming hair clotted with alien matter, Yodsess shouted, "Theriagin, your long-delayed bane arrives! Open for your doom!"

The doors swung soundlessly apart under no man's hand, and the three avengers entered.

A stalwart figure, brawny of torso and wry of lips, Theriagin confronted them from the far wall of the tapestried, raftered room. They halted, and Aniatis said, "Advance, traitor."

"Alas, I cannot greet you properly, old friends. My situation is rather, ah, inflexible."

Moving cautiously closer, all quickly realized what Theriagin meant.

Their comrade of yore formed a living bas-relief, integral with the wall of Castel Djurga. Soul melded to stone, only the frontward third of his body, including his entire arms but not his legs, retained an independent existence from the marmoreal stratum.

"Only thus," said Theriagin, "and at such price, did I insure my solid anchoring in this realm throughout all these lonely centuries."

Dormender cursed. "And so you chose perpetual tainted exile over any sane return! Now you can only die!"

Heeding Dormender's decisively voiced declaration even before it ceased ringing in the air, Yodsess broke from the others and, ululating wildly, with axe upraised, plunged toward the tethered villain.

Theriagin's right hand, concealed in shadow till this fatal moment, swung up, bearing Success, the flail. Yodsess either failed to see the threat or cared not for her own safety.

The barbed chains of the flail wrapped around the woman's neck, and Theriagin yanked.

The sound of Yodsess's axe cleaving the mortal breastbone of the granite-backed godling coincided with the sharp crack of her own snapping spine.

*   *   *

Amidst the debris of a small New Year's Eve party, the four teenagers, alone together, unsupervised by adults, huddled mournfully after all their cheerful peers had departed.

"What are we going to do now?" Hazel moaned. "He's overdue by two months."

"I don't know about the rest of you, but I'm really hurting," said Westbrook. "Without Cockaigne, the rest of my life seems like a joke."

Calla's hand sought Pike's. "That's just how I feel too. What good is the future, if we can never return to the Land? How can we grow up without Cockaigne? The whole experience is already fading, like some kind of wonderful, impossible dream."

Pike patted Calla's hand, then released it. "Have faith. Doctor Iatros will come back sooner or later."

"But till then—how do we go on?"

No one had an answer. And after a short silent time of being alone with their thoughts, Westbrook strode off with Hazel into the empty new year.

Calla fell into Pike's arms. He cradled her with a certain remoteness. "If only the four of us had just one more dose apiece," she murmured.

"I have one more dose. For myself."

Calla shot out of his tepid embrace. "What!"

"You heard me. I kept a dose aside. Several sheets, actually. But they've all been used up except for one last hit. I'm going into Cockaigne tonight, Calla—and I'm not coming out."

"But, but—that's impossible!"

"No, it's not. On my earlier solo trips, I learned how to get around the inherent flaw of Iatros's creation. There's a price to pay, but it will all be worth it. The sacrifice is a non-issue."

"Caitiff bastard!" Eyes leaking behind her glasses, Calla balled her fist and raised it as if to strike Pike. He awaited her assault patiently, until, quivering, she finally dropped her unclenched hand and threw herself on him.

"Pike, don't go! Wait with us, please. Iatros will return soon, I know it. Pike, if you stay, I—I'll sleep with you!"

Delving beneath her shirt, Pike said, "Oh, really?"

Calla made no reply, but lowered her eyes and began to unbutton her blouse.

When they had finished having sex, after Calla had fallen asleep in his arms, Pike, still naked, disengaged himself without waking her, took out his wallet, removed a tab of blotter paper, and slipped it beneath his tongue.

*   *   *

The lugubriously droning equipment revealed that all of Pike's vital signs had flatlined, his twenty-year coma ended. Unbreathing also, Westbrook, spine shattered, lay contorted like a broken doll upon the linoleum floor.

Donning their clothes quickly yet without any signs of agitation, Hazel and Calla failed even to flinch when the banging started on the jammed door of Pike's room. What terror could such mundane assaults hold?

After shrugging into her coat and slipping on her shoes, Hazel bent to kiss Westbrook's cooling brow. "Always did fiery Yodsess exhibit more bravery than caution."

"The Land will enshrine her name forever."

As an ethereal gleam faded from their eyes, the women hugged each other, then moved toward the door.

"If he found Westbrook after so long—" began Calla.

"Then, Dormender, plainly Iatros can find us," finished Hazel.

"And when he does, Aniatis?"

"What else? Would you have all this death among the Tetrad be for naught? We return. We return to Cockaigne."

THE SHORT ASHY AFTERLIFE
OF HIRAM P. DOTTLE

The head of the spike bites deep into the hard substance of my body, and the man's blunt teeth grip the lower part of my anatomy with compulsive, fearful force. The spike supports me, while my body in turn supports the man's entire weight. He's a small, dumpy fellow, to be sure, but still the strain on me is considerable. Relying thus on a small piece of rusty hardware for our lives, both of us dangle over five stories of empty space, the cobbled street far below us a rain-slick bumpy surface lit by a few dim streetlights casting golden pools of lumi just then the gunshot rings out.

*   *   *

My name is Hiram P. Dottle, and once upon a time I enjoyed a quiet easy life, full of cerebral and sensual pleasures of a mild nature. No guns or danger intruded into my reclusive private sphere. But all of that security and somnolence ended with the arrival of Sparky Flint.

But I rush ahead of my story. More of this temptress soon enough.

Although not born to great wealth, at the time my tale commences I was living comfortably on a guaranteed income, having retired in early middle age from my career as an accountant. I owed my good fortune to the demise of an elderly and well-off maiden aunt in Crescent City: Denise K. Sinkel, formerly of the Massachusetts Sinkels. Her will left everything to "my nephew, Hiram, the only one who always remembered his lonely old aunt at Christmas."

This statement was accurate, even down to poor Aunt Denise's famous self-pity. My contribution to Aunt Denise's good cheer was, I fear, minimal, and offered me as much pleasure as it did her. I always saw to it that Aunt Denise's house was graced with several handmade wreaths and garlands, as well as a few poinsettia plants during the holidays. Riding the bus myself from Central City to its urban neighbor, I kept careful watch over the homemade wreaths and personally cultivated plants resting securely in overhead stowage, never relaxing my vigilance until the cabbie deposited me safely at Aunt Denise's.

Horticulture and flower arranging, you see, were my hobbies. You'd probably never guess it from looking at me, but accounting was never my real love, merely a safe and reliable means of earning my income. Mother and Father both insisted that I turn my adult hand to some low-risk mode of employment promising a small but steady return. So I reluctantly discarded my typical childhood fascination with such icons of daring exploration as Lowell Thomas, Frank Buck and Richard Halliburton—why, today I can hardly believe the youthful dreams I had, involving travel to exotic climes and battle with wild animals and savage natives!—and when I reached my early maturity I enrolled at Keating's School of Accountancy.

Thirty years later Mother and Father had long since passed away, deeding me the ancestral home where I still occupied my boyhood room. The property consisted of a well-kept but fading Victorian manse set on five acres of land in a neighborhood rather fallen, if you'll permit the pun, to seed. This surprising legacy descended on an asocial bachelor who in the morning mirror seemed undressed without his green celluloid eyeshade and sleeve garters. Having perused enough ledgers and balance sheets to build a tower to the moon—had I cared to indulge in such fanciful behavior—I was more than ready to leave my career behind and plunge more deeply into my passions.

The redeeming moments in what most people would call a boring life occurred in my garden. In the suburbs of Central City, my property, through diligent and loving application, had been ultimately turned into a miniature Versailles, replete with espaliers, pollarded aisles and substantial fountains. I venture to say that not even the immaculately landscaped grounds of Idlewhile Cemetery (I am naturally excluding that spooky and mysteriously overgrown portion in the northwest corner) could compete on a foot-by-foot basis with my land. Why, the neighborhood children, dirty urchins all, frequently congregated at my fence to gape in awe. At least I assumed their emotions were respectful, although several times I sensed an out-thrust tongue swiftly withdrawn when I turned to face them. No matter, though, for I was content.

After Aunt Denise's independence-granting demise, I enjoyed four whole luxurious years of complete devotion to gardening. My joyful days were filled with propagating and repotting, grafting and staking, double-digging and turf-laying. I managed the funds that had so unexpectedly become mine with care and wisdom, investing them in U.S. Treasury Bonds at a solid 1.5 percent annual return. Combined with my own personal savings, this interest income satisfied all my simple needs. Although I admit I did once boldly dip into some of the capital to secure a new wheelbarrow, a toolshed, and some fine hand-wrought British tools.

Including, in a magnificent example of life's irony, the well-honed axe that killed me.

You will have gathered by my small clues that an unexpected climacteric occurred in my life shortly after my inheritance. That deadly turning point consisted of my meeting the irresistible Sparky Flint.

I can't now say what came over me that fatal night. Some imp of the perverse took hold of my lapels and whispered evil urgings into my ear. To be short about it, I developed an instant but avid craving for a spot of sherry.

Aunt Denise had always treated me to a small annual glass of sherry upon my completion of decorating her house. After ten years of the ritual I grew accustomed to the taste, and actually came to look forward to the uncommon indulgence. Now, four years without tasting a drop of sherry, and my quiescent desires suddenly came to life. I felt an unquenchable thirst that only strong drink could satisfy. So I set out with grim determination for a saloon.

The trolley dropped me off downtown. Walking the unfamiliar nighttime streets of Central City, I tried to gauge which establishment might prove most suitable for a gentleman of my retiring nature.

Unfortunately, my instincts were flawed. I ended up entering a most ungenteel "dive."

The "joint" was packed with smoking, sweating, cursing, laughing humanity, their voices echoing off the garish walls and grimy ceiling. I felt like a frightened cow amidst his ignorant bovine peers on the abattoir walkway.

Nonetheless my unnatural compulsion for the fruit of the vine still held sway. I worked my way toward the bar, past lap-seated trollops hoisting foamy mugs of beer to their lips and brawny laborers knocking back "boilermakers."

At the bar I secured my drink, enduring a sneer or two at my uncommon choice of beverage from my immediate neighbors and even from the bartender himself, an ugly bruiser. I rested one foot on the brass rail, in imitation of my fellow imbibers, but the stance felt too unsteady, and I moved off to a small empty table.

And then the singing began.

Supernal, sirenical singing like nothing I had ever heard before, as if hundreds of calla lilies had suddenly taken voice.

I suppose the mode employed by this diabolically angelic female voice might have been termed "torch song." If so, the metaphor was apt, since my whole soul was enflamed by the unseen songstress. No doubt the alcohol coursing wildly through my veins played its part as well.

I stood up instinctively in an attempt to spot the singer and was rewarded by sight of a small, lighted stage. And there she stood, microphone in hand.

Sparky Flint.

Her hair a tumbling mass of poppy-red curls, her cosmetic-enhanced face brazenly sensuous, her Junoesque figure wrapped in a tight jade evening dress, the singer caressed each syllable of her lustful song in a way that delivered the words like vernal osmosis straight to my heart.

I remained standing for the exotic chanteuse's entire hypnotic performance, learning her name only when a coarse emcee ushered her off the stage.

Collapsing back into my seat, I downed the remaining inch of my sherry in one dynamic swallow. And as I set the glass down, my eyes confronted the satin-swaddled bosom of Sparky Flint herself.

"Mind if I pull up a chair, honey?"

"Nuh—no, nuh—not at all."

She took up her seat so closely to mine that our knees almost touched, and I could see the very weave of her silk stockings where they caressed her ankle above the strap of her shoe. Conquering the reek of spilled ale and tobacco and human musk, a whiff of her sharp synthetic floral scent carried to my nostrils. The barroom seemed to spin in circles about me.

"Care to buy a girl a drink, sport?"

"I—that is—why, certainly." I tried to adopt a dapper manner. "I fear I must have misplaced my manners in my other suit."

I summoned a barmaid and Sparky ordered a cocktail unfamiliar to me. Once she had refreshed her tired vocal cords, she fixed me with an inquisitive yet friendly stare.

"I never had no guy stand up for my whole show before. Most of these bums wouldn't know if the management had a hyena cackling up there. You musta really liked my singing, huh?"

"Why, yes, most assuredly. Such dulcet yet thrilling tones have never before laved my ears."

Sparky drained her drink and began toying with a toothpick-pierced olive. "You're a regular charmer, fella. Say, what's your name?"

"Hiram. Hiram P. Dottle."

"Well, Hiram, let me let you in on a little secret. A lady likes to be appreciated for her talents, you know. She can get mighty friendly with the right guy, if he shows a little gen-u-wine interest. And even though I've got a swell set of pipes, that ain't all the assets Sparky Flint's got hidden. Say, speaking of assets—why doncha tell me a little more about yourself."

I gulped, swallowing some kind of sudden lump big as an iris corm, and began to recount my life history. Sparky brightened considerably when I described my home, and became positively overwrought when I detailed the clever way I had invested Aunt Denise's money. By this point she was practically sitting in my lap, and I confess that I had indulged in two more glasses of sherry.

"Oh, Dottie, you've led such a fascinating life! You don't mind if I call you Dottie, do you?"

No one had ever employed such a diminutive variant of my name before. But then again, never had I established such a quick bond with any female of the species. "Why, I—"

"I thought you'd be jake with that! You're such a broad-minded character. Did anyone ever tell you that your mustache is so attractively wispy, Dottie? I bet it tickles just like a caterpillar when you kiss."

And then to test her proposition, she planted her lips directly upon mine, in the most thrilling moment of my life, comparable only to my success in breeding a pure-white pansy, a feat written up as a sidebar in *Horticulture Monthly*.

We were married one month later. Only upon securing the marriage license did I learn Sparky Flint's birth name. Christened Maisie Grumbach, she had been raised in Central City's orphanage, and possessed no kin of any kind.

"A girl on her own's gotta be fast on her feet, Dottie. I learned that early on at the orphanage. When it's slopping time at the hog trough, the slow piglet goes to bed hungry. The main chance just don't linger. Grab what you can, when you can—that's Sparky Flint's motto."

The first six months of our marriage offered all the connubial and domestic joys imaginable. Sparky lavished her affections on me. If I could blush in my present state I certainly would, to recall how she twisted her "little Dottie-wottie" around her slim fingers, with honeyed words and lascivious attentions. And all the while, behind her facade of love, lurked a heartless viper of greed and treachery.

The first rift in our romance developed when I proposed to spend one thousand dollars to put in an elaborate carp pond. I realized this constituted a large sum, but I felt justified in devoting this amount to my harmless hobby. After all, hadn't I given Sparky the elaborate wedding she desired, spending liberally on her gown and jewelry, as well as providing a feast for those few guests we could summon up between us? (I found Sparky's friends rather unsavory, and spent as little time with them as possible.)

"Ten Ben Franklins on a fishing hole!" shrieked Sparky, abusing her nightingale's throat most horridly. "And I haven't had a new pair of shoes in a month! What the hell are you thinking? Do I look like the kind of dame who prefers sardines to high heels?"

"But Sparky, dear—"

"Fuhgeddaboutit!"

Our marital situation deteriorated rapidly from that point on, as if a plug had been pulled on a greasy water tower full of ill feelings that now drained over us. Accusations, vituperations, insinuations—these replaced whispered endearments and fond embraces on Sparky's part. My share of these increasingly frequent arguments consisted of silence and a hangdog expression, followed by contrite agreement. Nevertheless, unplacated, my wife began spending inordinate amounts of time away from home, frequently returning only after I had finished my nine o'clock snack of milk and common crackers and turned out the lights for sleep.

The final straw apparently came with a most unwise and unannounced expenditure on my part. I had learned by now not to advertise my horticultural expenditures. Consequently, the delivery of lumber, cast iron fittings and sheets of glass sufficient to construct a charming Edwardian greenhouse took Sparky completely by surprise.

She had the tact to wait until the delivery men left before laying into me, although judging by the mottling of her complexion, the restraint had nearly caused her to burst a vein.

"What the hell *is* all this, buster! Are you out of your everlovin' mind? Your wife is walking around in rags, and you're blowing through my inheritance like a dipso through free muscatel!"

I tried to divert her anger by joshing. "Oh, come now, dear. You have a sturdy and healthy husband not much older than yourself. Surely it's premature to be speaking of my unlikely demise and your grieving widowhood."

A look of pure vicious hatred such as I had never before seen on a human visage passed fleetingly across Sparky's beautiful features, to be replaced by a composed mask of indifference. "Oh, too early is it? Maybe—and maybe not. . . ."

Her words and expression alarmed me to such a degree that I shrugged quickly into my ratty old puttering-about cardigan, murmured something about attending to a fungus problem, and hastened outside.

Kneeling at the base of a large, mistletoe-festooned oak tree, I was delicately aerating the soil around its roots with a small tool when I heard someone approaching. I looked over my shoulder and saw a horrifying sight.

My loving wife Sparky, hoisting high my fine British axe in her gloved hands.

Struck mute, paralyzed, I could only listen helplessly to her insane rehearsal of some future speech for an unknown audience.

"This is an absolutely *awful* neighborhood, officer. I've noticed tramps and vagrants and petty thieves lurking around our estate ever since my poor dead husband brought me here as his blushing bride. One of them must have finally broken in. I'm sure my husband died defending my virtue."

"No, Sparky, no!" I finally managed to croak.

Too late, for the axe was already descending.

In my fading eyesight, filled totally with a close-up landscape of bark, I watched my own blood jet and pool in a hollow formed by two intersecting oak roots.

Then all went black.

*   *   *

The astonishing return of my consciousness at first brought with it no sensory data, aside from a sense of well-being and wholeness. For an indefinite time I basked in the simple absence of the shattering pain that had accompanied Sparky's treacherous assault. The utter blackness and lack of sound in my current environment failed to frighten me. I felt too much at ease, too peaceful. I could only conclude that some good Samaritan had rescued me from my wife's attack in time to save my life, and that now I rested in a cozy hospital bed, guarded by watchful nurses and doctors, my eyes and ears bandaged, my healing body suffused with morphine.

The closest I came to worrying about my old life was a vague feeling that certainly some drastic changes would have to be engineered in my spousal relations, once I fully recovered. Perhaps even a trial separation.

Then, after this period of idle, happy musing, odd, subliminal sensations began to filter into my consciousness. I seemed to register light striking me, but in a new fashion. Sunlight seemed to be impinging upon my "skin" and "face" in a whole-body manner, as if I were—horrors!—utterly unclothed at the beach. Discordant, jagged images swept over me. Likewise, I perceived the ambient soundscape in a novel, jumbled manner. Oddest of all though were fresh tactile impressions. I experienced a contradictory feeling of compression and extension, as if I were stuffed into a closet, yet simultaneously stretched on a not uncomfortable rack.

Likewise, my sense of time's passage had altered. Objective minutes, gauged by the fragmentary movements of the sun, seemed to drip by like hours.

I used this extended realm of time wisely, and by the end of what must have been a single day, I had thoroughly integrated my new senses so that I could see and hear and feel in a coherent way.

From my new immovable vantage I enjoyed a 360 degree omniscient view of some very familiar landscaped grounds. And when I focused my "sight" in one particular direction, I saw my ancestral home standing forlorn and dark. Triangulating my position by landmarks, I could no longer deny the obvious conclusion.

My soul now inhabited the very oak tree at whose foot I had been slaughtered. I was now a male dryad, if such a creature were possible.

Acknowledging this impossible truth, I directed my vision and other senses downward. My human body had been carted away, but my sticky blood still filled the hollow where it had gushed. Alarmingly, I experienced a feeling of oakish satisfaction at this extra-rich watering, as if grateful for my pagan due. Apparently the original spirit of the oak still to some degree overlapped mine, offering its old perceptions.

Well, this was a fine fix, I thought. My old life had reached a premature conclusion, and such comforting rituals as milk and common crackers availed naught. But questioning the miracle would be futile, and I would simply have to learn to inhabit my new body and enjoy this mode of existence.

Surprisingly, the transition came quite easily.

By dawn of the next day, approximately forty-eight hours after my murder, I was already happy in my arboreal magnificence.

All my nurturing of this tree had prepared a veritable temple for my spirit. My roots stretched deeply down and out into nutritious, stable soil, while my crown of efficient leaves reared high into the welcoming sky. My inner flesh was strong and healthy, my limbs proud and free of disease. Birds and squirrels nested in my niches, providing gay company, while sun and rain stoked my slow engines. Ants crawling up and down tickled and massaged me and warred with insidious insects that would have harmed me. Like some Hindoo holyman, I experienced an absolute contentment with my condition, free of unsatisfied desires, my mind at one with ancient cosmic imperatives.

But then came a disturbing incident that awoke my human side.

Out of my old house stepped Sparky Flint, my murderous wife.

And with her was a man!

Tall and impressively muscled, clad in a dark suit and crisp fedora, the fellow strolled alongside Sparky with a sober yet irrepressibly jaunty air. I instantly assessed him as ten times the physical specimen I had ever been (although of course he was pitiful compared to my current girth and strength), and I felt complete jealousy toward this new suitor.

But then as the pair approached and I spotted the small mask guarding the stranger's identity, I recognized him and my feelings flip-flopped instantly.

This was the Shade! Central City's daring crimefighter, champion of the oppressed and wronged, had come personally to investigate and avenge my murder!

I focused my "hearing" on Sparky and the Shade, a small matter of forming a parabolic cone with certain of my leaves.

"I wish I had returned from my affairs in China a day or two earlier," said the Shade, "before Klink and his boys completely obliterated this lawn. Look at this mess! Those flatfoots might've been playing a duffer's round of golf, the lawn's so hacked up. Any clues to the identity of your husband's killer are long gone."

For the first time I noted the terrible condition of the lawn. What the Shade had observed was true. I regretted I would not be able to roll out and reseed in my current state.

Attired in widow's weeds, a veil floating across her devilishly beautiful features, Sparky sniffled with touching, albeit insincere sympathy. "Poor Dottie! He was ever so prideful of his whole garden. Sometimes in fact I think he loved it more than me. . . ."

Not so! I wanted to shout. *Well, perhaps . . .* , honesty instantly forced me to amend.

The Shade regarded Sparky with a natural compassion, tempered, I thought, only by those common suspicions that attach to the spouse of any murdered husband. "There, there, Mrs. Dottle. I know it's small comfort, but we'll eventually catch the fiend who did this."

"That's what I pray for each night before I climb into my lonely empty bed, Mister Shade, where I writhe and squirm feverishly until dawn." Sparky gripped the Shade's right bicep in an overfamiliar manner and fluttered her long lashes at him.

The Shade appeared a trifle flustered. "Ahem, yes. Now, let me just have a look at this tree."

Crouching at my base, the Shade produced a magnifying lens and examined my bark. With one gloved finger he took up a few flakes of my rain-washed and sun-dried blood. He cogitated a moment, then stood.

"I would've thought a man startled by an axe-bearing assailant might have made a dash for his life, or at least clawed at the tree where he kneeled in an attempt to scramble upright. Yet he died without a scuffle right where you earlier saw him working."

Unwisely perhaps, Sparky vented her residual hatred. "Dottie was a meek little shrimp!" Hastily, she recovered. "That is, my husband had a mild disposition. He must've fainted straight away when the awful thug came on him."

"Yes, that's one explanation. Well, Mrs. Dottle, there's not a lot I can do here. I'll be going now."

"Oh, please, Mister Shade, just walk me back to the house. I can't stand to be alone near this tree. There's something creepy about it now, since my husband died."

As the Shade and Sparky retreated, she cast a dire look back at me, almost as if she could see her husband sheltering inside his oaken suit.

Once the pair was out of sight, I found myself sinking down into blissful vegetal somnolence again. The happy sensations of being an oak completely wiped away any mortal cares left over from my prior life. Why should I trouble myself about human justice? My old life would never be restored through the courts. Let the fleshly ones squabble among themselves. Their little lives had no impact on mine.

My arrogant invulnerability lasted for roughly a year. Through summer, fall and winter I gloried in the magnificence of my being, experiencing each turning season with new joy.

But then in the spring came my comeuppance. I had been much too cavalier in dismissing Sparky's ability to do me further harm.

One day near the anniversary of my murder, a second set of killers arrived to slay me once again.

I witnessed the truck from Resneis Arborists pass through the gates of my small estate and down the drive. Improbably and most uncivilly, it actually continued up onto my prize lawn, the turf now looking less than perfect due to lack of attention. Rough-handed workers tumbled out, and a foreman began to shout orders.

"Okay, you jokers, get a move on! We've got to take down every tree on this property plenty pronto, if we want that bonus. And the big oak goes first!"

Horrified, I watched two men pull a huge saw from their truck and start toward me.

I could feel the big sharp teeth placed harshly against my barky skin.

The first rasping cut produced a dull agony. The second, deeper stroke sent fiery alarm signals down my every fiber.

I could feel my consciousness pulling instinctively back from the pain. I had an impulse to gather myself into the deepest core of my being, to escape the torture.

But before I lost touch with the outer world, I caught the arrival of Sparky and a brutish-looking stranger dressed in a suit with roguishly wide lapels. I forced myself to focus on their *sotto voce* dialogue, as they conversed in what they deemed utter secrecy.

"I gotta hand it to ya, Sparky baby," said the thug. "This land is gonna make a swell spot for Central City's new casino. But ain't'cha being a bit, well pre-ma-tour with the choppin' an' the bulldozin' an' all? The permits an' licenses from City Hall ain't exactly a shoe-in. Mayor Nolan ain't too keen on gamblin'. And her copper daddy'll bust a gasket if he finds out who your backers are."

"You just leave Commissioner Nolan and his brat in City Hall to me, big boy, and concentrate on what you do best."

"Lovin' and killin', right?"

"Right, Jules."

The conniving pair went into a clinch that violated every element of the Hays Code, but I could spare no further attention for their reprehensible licentiousness.

Loud creakings and groanings were issuing from my numb nether regions, which had self-protectively lost all sensation. With grave misgivings, I noticed that I was beginning to cant and tip.

My ultimate downfall followed swiftly. The final fibers holding me upright parted, and I crashed toward the ground. The thundering impact was titanic, and I lost consciousness for some time. When I came to, I could feel my proud branches being lopped. In short time I was hoisted by a newly arrived crane onto an accompanying flatbed truck and carted off.

Huddling deep inside myself, I realized then that my fate most likely involved a quick trip to the sawmill and a swift transition into planks.

But such was not the case. Apparently I was destined for stranger ends.

Whether subconsciously or not, Sparky had chosen a fate for my wooden corpse meant to humiliate. Even in death I would be denied utilitarian dignity.

When I felt a cessation of motion, I pooled my dwindling organic energies and tried to apprehend my destination. I saw a sign that read CENTRAL CITY SCHOOL OF ART AND DESIGN, and quickly intuited my ignominious lot: to become practice billets for budding, ham-fisted sculptors. The best I could hope for was to grace a tobacco shop as a lopsided wooden Indian.

Sure enough, I was trundled into the school's carpentry shop and, once callously stripped of my bark, rapidly dismembered into several largish sections of trunk. With each cut I pulled my ectoplasmic bits of mental being out of the severed section, retreating and retreating, until finally, with the last slice, I found all my fading identity concentrated in one portion of trunk.

For a long time I existed in a state of hibernation, as I cured in a storeroom. What became of my nonsentient bits I cannot tell. After an unguessable duration, the portion housing my ghostly self, roused by motion, eventually rode a dolly to the atelier of a youth possessed of handsome Mediterranean looks and clad in leather apron and work gloves. I heard him addressed as "Gino" by the delivery men.

Gino wrestled me upright into position on a platform, then stepped back to survey me. "Hmm, I see hidden in this dumb wood a straining heroic figure, fighting against injustice. Perhaps I'll call this masterpiece *Samson Rages against the Philistines.*"

Much as I appreciated Gino's noble goals for my desiccated flesh, I still cringed to imagine the first blow of his chisel. Trying to avoid his blow, I concentrated my essence far away from his anticipated strike. But then, at the last moment, he shifted positions and cleaved off that very block of matter containing all my soul!

I fell to the floor, ignored in the white heat of artistic creation.

But at day's end, to my surprise, Gino picked me up and carried me home.

The young sculptor lived in an Italian slum on the far side of Central City. Apparently he shared his dismal cold-water flat only with his father, a cheerful old fellow with an aura of deep wisdom about him.

"Poppa, look," Gino called out as soon as he entered. "Some raw material for your hobby."

Gino's father took me in his rough hands. How humiliating, I thought. From Hiram P. Dottle, bookkeeper, botanist and husband, to mighty oak to hunk of kindling. The old man turned me over and over, examining me with a keen eye before finally speaking.

"It's-a not fine Algerian brier, Gino, like-a what-a we had back in Napoli. But the grain, she's a-fine. Maybe Mario Deodati can make-a one nice pipe out of this scrap."

"Thataboy, Pop! Go to it!"

Thus began my final metamorphosis, under the magically skilled hands of Mario Deodati. Pared away with patient cunning, the block revealed the shape hiding within it. And amazingly, as Mario lavished attention and craft and even love on me, I felt my identity taking renewed strength.

At one point, holding my still-chunky form, Mario spoke to me. "I see a face in-a you, Mister Pipe. I'm a-make your bowl into a smiling head."

Good as his word, Mario carved facial features into his creation. I had no mirror to observe myself in, but I could feel from inside that my new visage was perhaps overly jolly and gleeful in the manner of a Toby jug. Mario's sensitivity to my true nature extended only so far.

One day in late winter, when the winds rattled the loose, rag-stuffed windows in the apartment, Mario and Gino had a terse, painful discussion which I observed and listened to from my perch on a shelf.

"It's no use, Pop. I'm going to have to quit school. We don't even have the money for coal and groceries, never mind my tuition."

Mario banged the table with the hand that had birthed me. "Did me and your sainted Momma teach-a you to be a quitter! You gonna stay in school, boy!" He struggled to his feet and snatched me down off the shelf. "Go sell this! And get-a the best price you can!"

Wrapped in an old piece of flannel, I left my latest home.

I surmised that it was now nearly a year since I had been felled, and my fate once more loomed obscure.

Five stores later, a deal was consummated. I changed hands for the princely sum of one hundred dollars, enough to keep the Deodatis afloat for several months, and I silently bade farewell to Gino.

My new owner was a portly, bearded, punctilious gentleman in vest and suit. The tip of his tongue protruding absentmindedly from the corner of his compressed lips, he inked a price tag in the amount of two hundred dollars, tied it to my stem with string, and placed me on a velvet cushion in a display case. That night, when the shop lights clicked off and only stray glints from street lamps illuminated my new home, I tried to communicate with my new neighbors. But they failed to respond to the most vigorous of my psychic efforts, and I realized I was the only sensate pipe amongst them. Internally, I shed a self-pitying tear or two as I contemplated my sad lot.

The next few weeks established a boring routine of shop-opening, commercial traffic, shop-closing and a long night of despair. I was handled and admired several times, but never purchased.

But one day my salvation arrived, in the form of two famous customers.

The well-dressed and decorously glamorous woman with her twin rolls of blonde hair pinned high atop her head appeared first in my field of vision. Lowering her half-familiar happy face to the glass separating us, she spoke. "Oh, Shade, look! Isn't that model with the carved face just darling?"

The masked visage of the Shade appeared next to the woman's. In context, I recognized her now as Mayor Ellen Nolan. The Shade did not seem to share all of Ellen Nolan's enthusiasm. His manly features wrinkled in quizzical bemusement.

"Gee, Ellen, I've seen better mugs on plug-uglies from the Gasworks Gang! And two hundred dollars! Do you realize how many orphans we could feed with that money?"

"Don't be such a wet blanket, Shade. Spending a little more of my personal money on Daddy's birthday won't send any orphans to bed hungry."

The Shade lifted his hat and scratched his scalp. "Are you sure this is a good idea, Ellen? How are you going to get Nolan to give up his favorite old stinkpot in favor of this one, anyhow?"

"Simple. I'll hide it."

A whistle of admiration escaped the Shade's lips. "And the newspapers say *I've* got guts! Well, I leave it all up to you."

"A wise decision. Sir, we'll take this one. And wrap it nicely, please."

Into a dark box I went. The crinkle of folding gift-paper and the zip of cellotape from a dispenser was followed by careful placement into what I presume was a shopping bag. I could tell by the long stride I then shared that the Shade carried me home to Ellen's house. I heard the smack of a kiss upon a cheek, then felt further lifting movements, ending up, I supposed, hidden in a closet.

The routine of the house for the next day or so quickly became aurally familiar. The gruff yet loving Commissioner Nolan arrived home and left at odd hours of the day, while the perky but forceful Mayor Nolan held to a more regular schedule. The Shade popped up unpredictably.

Finally one special morning, muffled in my closet, I could hear Ellen's father ranting, turning the air blue with his curses.

"*Where* could that dangblasted, consarned *pipe* of mine have *gotten* to! Ellen! Ellen! ELLEN!"

"Yes, Daddy, whatever's the matter?"

"My favorite pipe! I can't find it! I'm certain I left it on the bed stand when I went to sleep, but now it's missing! How can I go to work without it?"

Footsteps approached me, a door creaked open, and I was lifted down in my package. Ellen's sweet voice soothed her father. "Well, I haven't the foggiest notion of where you've mislaid that awful thing. But luckily enough, I have this little gift right here. Happy birthday, Daddy!"

My wrapping began to rip. "Grmph. Hmph. Frazzleblast it!"

"Let me give you a hand, Daddy dear."

The light of day made me metaphysically squint. I found myself face to face with a choleric, jaw-grinding Commissioner Nolan. The three patches of white hair on his otherwise bald head were mussed and flyaway.

He scowled at me, and I knew we had not hit it off.

"Is this a kid's bubblepipe? What am I supposed to pack it with—cornsilk?"

Ellen began to tenderly stroke her father's hair into better order. "Come on now, don't be a gruff old bear. This pipe has a hundred times more class than your old one. Won't you at least try it, please—for me?"

Nolan turned me around so I faced away from him. Then for the first time I felt the curiously intimate sensation of his blunt teeth biting down on my stem. His irritation caused me to waggle furiously up and down almost in time to his thumping, agitated pulse, so much so that I feared for his dangerously high blood pressure.

"Feels strange," Nolan said. "Not like my old one."

"New things take some getting used to. Here's your tobacco pouch. Smoke up a bowl or two and you'll see how lovely it is."

Nolan stuffed my wooden head full of pungent weed, tamping the plug down with a blunt, nicotine-stained thumb. Then I heard a match scrape and felt the small flame singe my crown. The pain was less than if I had tested my human flesh with a match, and I resolved to be stoic in my new role.

Puffing furiously, Nolan seemed to relax a trifle. "Draws well enough," he cautiously admitted. "But that simpering little face on the bowl—"

"Shush now! Off to work with you!"

Nolan snatched up a battered old leather satchel and exited. A police car and driver awaited him outside, and we set off.

Well, I cannot begin to describe the tremendous excitement of the subsequent several weeks. I experienced firsthand the glamorous crimefighting life of the Shade and Nolan in a way no one else ever had, not even the Shade's loyal Negro sidekick, Busta! Never absent from Nolan's pit bull-like mandibular embrace, I found myself swept up in innumerable thrilling confrontations with the forces of evil. Shootouts, chases, last-minute rescues! Threats, torture, mysterious clues, exotic locales! Villains, henchmen, mad scientists, *femmes fatales*! Why, once I remember we slipped quietly through the slimy, drip-plopping sewers on the trail of the Crustacean, only to discover the archfiend in his lair with—

But I ramble. I'll never reach the end of my personal tale if I recount all the wild adventures I experienced. Suffice it to say that out of my three existences to date, being Commissioner Nolan's trusty pipe has proved by far the most invigorating!

Of course, I had to endure many boring meetings as well. Politics played a part in crimefighting, as it did in everything connected with the civic life of Central City. Whenever one of these tedious events was scheduled, I fell into an absentminded reverie. I confess to being in one such fugue at the start of that fatal evening.

The clock in the mayor's shadowy office struck midnight when the

Shade and Ellen walked in, causing my owner to hastily remove his feet from his daughter's desk and leap up from her ornate office chair.

The Shade looked shamefaced. "Sorry we're late. I thought I spotted the wily spy Pola Fleece down by the docks, but it turned out to be only a fashion magazine shoot. It took a while to settle up damages with the photographer and models. Are those slimy business partners here yet?"

Nolan knocked my head on the edge of a trash can to remove my dead embers, then restuffed me with shag and lit up. I was quite used to the flickering flame by now, and paid it no mind as Nolan began to puff furiously.

"Not yet. I don't like this, Shade—not one little bit."

Ellen chimed in. "I agree. That Flint woman gives me the willies. What a cold-blooded witch! Only a few months until the second anniversary of her husband's murder, and she's already taking up with another man. Why, I hear she's even carrying his *lovechild!*"

Ellen blushed charmingly upon uttering this remark, and the Shade coughed as if he had swallowed a fly.

Sparky? Were they speaking of Sparky? A twinge of mixed affection and hatred passed through my wooden frame, and I woke into greater alertness.

"And she hasn't snagged just any beau," the Shade added. "Jules 'The Fife' Reefer has a history of misdeeds as long and bloody as the Carnivore's."

Nolan said, "Still, we've never been able to pin anything on him, and this request of theirs to build a casino seems on the up-and-up."

"I agree they're following legitimate channels," said the Shade, "but the big question remains. Do we want to let Reefer construct such an efficient money-laundering enterprise for his other illegal rackets?"

"Of course not," Ellen said. "But we've stalled them in every legal way we can. There's no way we can avoid giving them the permits for their casino any longer."

The Shade pushed his hat back on his head and smiled. "That's the purpose of tonight's meeting. We've gotten them so frustrated that they're bound to offer you a bribe. Why else would they schedule such a late-night get-together? I'll be in the next office with the door ajar. Once the money is out in the open, I'll bust in and put the cuffs on them. End of story."

Nolan scowled. "I suppose it's the only way. But I don't like putting Ellen at risk."

Ellen straightened up proudly. "I'm the mayor, Daddy. Don't I deserve my share of the bribe? In fact, I think you and I will have to split it seventy-thirty."

"Hmph! Sixty-forty," joshed Nolan, "and that's my final offer."

Outside in the empty City Hall corridor the elevator bell chimed, signaling the conveyance's arrival on our floor.

The Shade darted for the connecting door. "Stations, men!"

A few seconds later, my ex-wife and her new lover walked in.

Clutching her purse demurely, Sparky looked more desirable than ever, with her tumbling Titian curls framing her adorable face. Recalling Ellen's catty gossip, I thought I saw a slight swelling of her tummy, heralding the bastard child, substitute for the offspring we had never managed to conceive. I felt myself falling in love with her all over again—until I recalled with a shock the murderously contorted lines of this same visage as she swung the axe at my back.

Her companion—the same thuggish man I had seen her with while still a tree—I paid little attention to, deeming him beneath my mature consideration. Besides, it was hard to consider myself his vigorous rival while wearing the semblance of a pipe.

Reefer hailed us as if meeting buddies at an amusement park. "Howdy, Mayor, Commissioner! Hope we ain't kept you up past your bedtimes. But the deal we got in mind needs a little privacy, heh-heh, if you get my drift."

Sparky kicked Reefer's ankle and took over the pitch, her dulcet voice achingly familiar.

"What my partner means is that we intend tonight to put an end to all delays. Twelve months of red tape have left us feeling very antsy. If there's any way we can, um, grease the wheels of progress, we are quite willing to—"

"Just spit it out, baby. We're ready to put down some serious mazuma to get this project under way. Whatta we talkin'? Ten thousand? Fifteen thousand?"

I quivered menacingly between Nolan's choppers. If only Sparky and Reefer had been able to read the language of my jiggling, they would have turned tail and run. But they were blind to Nolan's rage.

"Let's see the color of your money, Reefer."

The mobster reached into his suitcoat's inner pocket and hauled out a sheaf of bills weighty as one of my prize cabbages. All eyes except mine were magnetized by the bundle of large-denomination bills. Thus only I witnessed the Shade sneak cat-footedly up behind Reefer and tap him on the shoulder.

"Jig's up, Reefer. Will you come quietly, or do I have to use force?"

Everyone had forgotten Sparky. Until they heard in the stunned silence the click of the hammer on her .45, loud as my former oaken body crashing to the ground.

Sparky's eyes were hard as her stage name, her face taut with rage. "Jules ain't going nowhere. It's you three that are gonna take a little trip."

Even Reefer seemed stunned by his paramour's steely determination. "Put the rod away, baby. We can beat a little bribery rap. It's just their word against ours."

Sparky swung her gun toward the Shade, but addressed Reefer. "Sometimes I swear you've got less spine than that mousy dirtgrubber I married! Win a case against the Shade? Are you crazy? He's got this town sewed up!"

"It's simply a matter of being on the correct side of the law, Miss Flint. Now if you'll just do as your boyfriend advises—"

"Shut up, you! Now, head for the staircase!"

The trio of captives shuffled out—under two guns now—while I was still fuming over the insult Sparky had paid my memory. Once in the stairwell we climbed steadily upward, emerging onto the roof. The summer sky hosted an infinity of stars, as likely to offer us useful help as anyone else in the city.

"Go over near the edge," Sparky commanded. "There's gonna be a little accident here tonight. Three clumsy stargazers are gonna take a little dive. Maybe the papers will even figure the Shade was somehow responsible. When our crew takes over City Hall, we won't have a care in the world."

We now stood at the low parapet protecting us from five stories of oblivion. I could see the Shade tensing his muscles for a lunge. But Sparky anticipated just such an action.

"Jules, grab the girl." Once in Reefer's clutches, Ellen suffered the muzzle of the pistol jammed against her stomach. "Try anything funny, and your girlfriend gets gutshot. It's not as easy a death as a broken neck, believe me."

With surprisingly acrobatic ease, the lumpy Nolan jumped atop the parapet. "Don't shoot her, Flint. I'm going first."

And with that he jumped, taking me with him, of course.

Nolan's blunt fingers gripped the ledge and interrupted our fall. I deduced his plan: to lure Sparky and Reefer over for a look, then make a surprising grab at them with one hand, thus breaking the stalemate. But even in the dim light Sparky must have seen his efforts.

"Reefer, he's holding on! Turn the girl loose and go whack the old coot's fingers."

I witnessed Reefer above us hefting his own gun, reversed. He smashed the butt down.

Nolan grunted, fell a foot with uselessly waving arms—

—and that was when the protruding spike intercepted my bowl.

Nolan's teeth bit into my stem like a crocodile's.

Reefer called out, "He's hanging on by his damn pipe!"

"Shoot the pipe out of his mouth then!"

Reefer took careful aim—

*　　*　　*

And just then the gunshot rings out, simultaneously with the sound of a scuffle on the rooftop, the thud of fists on flesh, of muffled grunts and screams.

The bullet pierces my stem, severing it completely. The pain of my mortal wound wracks me with titanic agonies. I try to hold onto consciousness, but feel it ebbing swiftly. In my last seconds of full awareness, even as my two halves tumble into the void, I thankfully witness the Shade lunge three-quarters over the edge of the parapet to grab Nolan by his wrist.

Then a familiar mortal darkness descends.

Curiously, unexpectedly, my soul is not completely extinguished. Although split in two, my human essence remains connected by a dormant thread of ectoplasm. Patiently, able to do nothing else, I await the reinvigorating reunion of my halves, a repair I am somehow confident will arrive in due time.

At last the blessed event comes. Jagged lower stem intersects with upper fragment and bowl, firmly secured with a spot of Elmer's glue. Although certainly unfit to be smoked, I can still exercise thought and perception.

I find myself stapled to a plaque, hanging on a wall beneath an odd circular skylight. Weirdly, the view through the cross-barred aperture reveals not mere sky, but an eerie nighttime landscape of canted tombstones.

I am underground! And where else but in the Shade's fabled but never pinpointed sanctum, its location now disclosed to me alone as the haunted corner of Idlewhile Cemetery!

The Shade himself steps back from hanging me up on his trophy wall. Beside him stands the short, lumpish, wide-eyed figure of Busta, that faithful son of Ham who assists the Shade and drives him about Central City in his yellow cab.

"Well, Busta," confides the Shade, "yet another relic of a case well-solved. Not only did we jail Sparky Flint and Jules Reefer for bribery and multiple attempts at homicide, but, thanks to her confession, we cleared up the old murder of her husband, poor chap." The Shade patted me affectionately. "Unfortunately, Dottle had no lucky talisman such as this pipe to save him, in the manner it saved Nolan."

The Shade turns to a set of blueprints spread out on a table. "But enough of past glories, Busta. Let's direct our attention to this diagram of Fort Knox. I expect the Gasworks Gang will strike next month, during the annual ingot dusting—"

Safe, protected from the elements, privileged to share a vicarious life of crimefighting, I settle cozily down on the wall to listen to the Shade's brave scheming.

There are worse fates for a broken pipe. And for a man as well.

SLUMBERLAND

The Candy Kid

"Wake up! C'mon, Gramps, rise and shine! It's a new century now, don't wanna miss any of it. And today's special, real special. I got word from your floor nurse that you hit one hundred today. Ain't everyday one of Slumberland's residents notches up the big one-double-oh."

The irreverent, irrepressibly careless young voice ended the old man's uneasy slumber. Accompanied by a waft of peppermint breath, this morning call for attention boomed annoyingly close to his hairy, flaccid-lobed, aged ear, shattering his shallow anxious dreamless sleep.

He opened his rheumy brown eyes to a placid nebula of sunlight, to the smell of bacon grease and the rattle of dishes on a wheeled trolley. He strained to focus on the blurry pink male face pulling back from his.

"Glasses. Get me my glasses, please."

The kitchen aide declined. "Naw, I ain't messing with no glasses. Let the nurse's aide handle that. You don't need no glasses anyhow just to drink *your* kinda breakfast. Nice can of vanilla Enfamil. Mmm-mmm! Look, I'll power up the top half of the bed so you don't choke, then I'll put the straw right 'tween your lips. Here you go—"

The hospital bed motors whined, and the elderly occupant of Room 1905 of the Slumberland Extended Care Facility felt his withered torso being levered creakingly upward.

"Enough, enough."

"Okay, don't blow a fuse, centennial dude. Here, sip."

The man weakly sucked some of the over-sweet nutritious slurry up through the plastic tube, while the kitchen aide watched approvingly, all the while clicking around an omnipresent breath mint between his upper and lower teeth, as if to accent the old man's own toothless condition.

"Everything cool now? 'Cuz I got lots more breakfastses to deliver."

The old man feebly spat out the tip of the straw. "Fine, fine."

The kitchen aide turned to leave, but the old man stopped him with a question.

"Is it really a new century?"

"Yeah, sure, why would I say so if it wasn't?"

"And it's my birthday today?"

"That's what your babysitter in uniform tells me."

"Then I am a hundred now."

"Cool. Well, save me some birthday cake, Pops."

The aide left, whistling what sounded improbably like some old Broadway show tune from the man's youth.

The old man lifted a trembling hand toward the fuzzy image of his breakfast tray, which was positioned over him on the extensible arm of a wheeled bedside platform, then he altered the course of his motions to smooth the few wisps of white hair trailing across his bald, spotted skull. Sinking down deeper into his pillows, lowering his eyelids, spurning his insulting breakfast, the old man thought:

One hundred years since I was born.
Ninety-five since the dreams began.
Nearly ninety years since they ended.
And just that long have I been searching for a way back into them.

Impie

Every Sunday the dreams had come like clockwork, beginning when he turned five years old and continuing for the next six years.

Like nothing else in his life before or since, the dreams had come to lend his whole juvenile existence deep meaning, rich excitement. More vivid than reality, they had cast his mundane life under a shadow, rendering the mortal world's diurnal colors less bright, its successes less joyful—but also, in partial compensation, its failures less painful. All his waking experiences had paled against the memories of his Sabbath dreams. And only when his weekly excursion into that magical otherworld arrived did he feel truly alive.

At first, the dreaming had come hard. For several sequential weeks he had known the worst sort of frustration. Each week's dream started and ended on repetitive notes, unvarying in their clunky monotony. (Although what occurred between the entrance and exit points shifted fantastically, a constantly changing canvas of wonders.)

He entered his dream each time by appearing to awaken in his own bedroom (a false virtual renouncement of sleep that paradoxically betokened a deeper immersion into those very waters of the unconscious). He would bolt up in bed at some disturbance, whether noise or motion or visitor. Sitting up curiously in that dream analogue of his familiar bulky bed, he would confront the miraculous: clowns, sprites, animals, fairies, once the smiling visage of the moon, all come to summon him to the realm of dreams, where further wonders—and the companionship of a certain princess—were promised to await him as his natural reward, his secret birthright as it were.

He would leave his bedroom behind then with whatever guide had manifested that week, ready and eager to cross the changeable fantastical terrain separating him from the veritable kingdom of dreams. But disaster of one sort or another always intervened. Landscapes collapsed or fragmented around him, due either to his clumsiness or incapacity, or to some uncontrollable natural calamity. Often his own dream death aborted his quest. Then he would be plunged out of the bizarre geography of his pilgrimage, back into his cold sheets, usually to tumble awkwardly upon the hard floor, his flesh-and-blood postures mimicking the contortions of his astral form.

His parents would rush in then to see what all the commotion was about. His mother, robustly beautiful as a Gibson Girl; his father, all mustachioed Ben Turpin bluffness. Or perhaps some relative spending the night would be delegated to check on the restless boy, doting aunt or dotty uncle.

His mother. Dead these fifty years now, all her golden piled tresses first turned gray, then white, then boxed away below the ground. His father, dead even longer, from frantic overwork during the Depression, when their family had lost the big Edwardian house where the dreams had visited him. But by then the dreams themselves had been absent for decades.

That was how my personal golden age ended, though. Remember rather how it began.

Week after week this truncated sleep charade continued. He accepted all the humiliations and frustrations, however, after some initial puzzlement. The characters who cajoled him were so convincing! Invitation, strange travel, impassable barricade or physical failure, then a sharp jolting exit. And how some of those exits had hurt! Falling onto the spiky thorns, pierced by arrows, gripped in the claws of a monster crab—

It hurt! It hurt! Now, nearly a century later, those assaults still hurt!

"Mistuh, what's wrong? Where's it hurtin'? You want me to call the nurse? Use your call-button, that's why you got one."

The old man opened his eyes and muzzily discerned, close by his pillows, the familiar black face of the janitor assigned to the nineteenth floor. Half-hopeful, half-fearful, the janitor's broad face seemed to the old man a dark sun radiating some kind of supernatural warmth. In one hand the janitor held a broom; in the other, he offered the patient the call-button dangling from its cord. A feather duster stuck in the janitor's rear pocket and some rags tucked into his waistband made him appear to be wearing a plumed loincloth.

The old man suddenly realized that his pain was actual, not illusory, not a memory. Something was wrong in his chest. He scrabbled for the call mechanism, and the janitor helped him wrap his fingers around it.

"Yes, thank you, young man. I'll call the nurse."

The Princess

While he awaited some response from the overworked and generally uncaring staff, the old man tried to forget the battering ram beneath his ribs by concentrating on his memories.

How had he finally surmounted those harsh barriers separating him from that mystical, sidereal domain that beckoned him so strongly? How had he gotten past the gates and locks and labyrinths? Only with the advent of the Candy Kid. That gaily gentle psychopomp had done the trick, bringing the mortal boy for the first time into the actual proud avenues and grand chambers of his appointed dream country.

Suddenly the steady assault from the invaders besieging the castle of his heart faltered, then redoubled, forcing a gasp from the half-upright man. He tried to calm himself with a massive injection of nostalgia.

All the glories he had seen with his eyes closed.

The people.

The places.

The incidents.

And the way they had made him feel.

Consider the people first, then; and among those, the lesser before the greater.

For unknown reasons, circus life had been the dominant theme among the unearthly crowds and retainers in his new home. Clowns, mummers, harlequins, Pierrots by the score. Faces painted, necks ruffed, legs outlined by spangled tights, feet cased in pointy-toed or comically overbroad shoes. Hats conical, tufted, pom-pom'd and feathered. Then came the leopardskin-cloaked strongmen and aerialists, tumbling acrobats and dauntless animal tamers. A gaudy perpetual Barnumscape, those background mobs.

Other colorful figures always hovering namelessly around him seemed drawn from Ruritanian courts and pseudomedieval tapestries. Knights, dukes, earls, admirals, generals, countesses, grandees, diplomats, ladies-in-waiting, jesters.

Then came the impossibles from myth and legend: Father Time, giants, Santa Claus, dragons, Uncle Sam, mermaids, Neptune, wizards, witches, trolls, Mercury, pirates, Jack Frost, Martians even!

Finally, for balance, a few familiar figures from his waking world: Keystone Kops and bad boys and winsome orphan girls, mostly.

Yet somehow the whole outrageously heterogeneous mix had cohered into a well-sorted citizenry, a true community. Was it just the surreal logic of the dreaming, or had there really been some ordering principle at work, a governing deity shaping the chaos into living art?

Of course in theory, King Morpheus, stern and expressionless and rotund, ruled over all. Name him first among those with whom the young visitor had grown intimate. But ultimately King Morpheus seemed ineffectual, more blustering figurehead than domineering tyrant, happier when departing for a vacation in his floating summer palace than when seated on the throne. And no one else occupied a plausible position of omnipotence. Doctor Pill, Uncle Dawn, Granny Hag, the Professor, Mr. Gosh— They were all minor players, each with their powers and provinces, but none capable of ruling the whole infinite sphere.

But what of the three people closest to him? Could any of them have been the secret governor? This question had plagued him for decades.

Impie the savage buffoon? Certainly not!

Flip? Green-faced, cigar-smoking Flip? Well, Flip was an enigma beyond plumbing. Yes, it could have been Flip, nephew of the Dawn Guard—

And the princess?

His first, best, and, ultimately, his only love, asleep or awake? Could she have been pulling the strings all this time? Could it be her inexplicable spontaneous boredom or displeasure that had exiled him from his dream sanctuary?

No! They had been too much in love.

Children both, they nonetheless adored each other with an adult passion, innocent yet deep and complete. The princess's longing for him had been the catalyst that brought him over the borders of sleep. Together every possible minute, they walked hand in hand through the dreams, clad in fanciful brocades and plumed hats, or bathing suits, or ballgown and tuxedo, or Eskimo gear. When, as often happened, they became separated by the unpredictable circumstances of that garish, hectic empire, they longed fervently for each other, wept and strove to reunite. (Although admittedly he had strayed from time to time, gotten swept up in events, taken bad advice, even stolen a cheating kiss or two from paper dolls or glass beauties.)

No, if the princess had indeed been the unacknowledged ruler of the world of his dreams, then surely she would not have forsaken him, her beloved, never have exiled him, cast him out forever. Powers beyond her control must have brought about their long painful separation. And certainly all would be different, if she knew now what he was undergoing—

"Bed 1905A! What's the problem here now?"

The blurry female face above a dirty white blouse, swimming angrily into view, held no sympathy. The nurse gripped his wrist and took his pulse.

"Jesus, you're off the charts. Did you get your meds last night?"

"No. Yes. I think so."

She dropped his arm back rudely. "What a bunch of screwups they've got on that night shift. More effin' work for us. Well, I suppose I'll have to get the doctor now."

"Yes, please. Get Doctor Pill—"

Doctor Pill

Of course his parents had taken him to physicians and alienists when the dreams showed no sign of dissipating after several months, but instead grew stronger and more dominant. Alarmed by their son's constant references to his "imaginary" world (and by the way the hallucinations affected his school work), disturbed by his deteriorating relationships with his peers and with his loving relatives, his mother and father had appealed to various authority figures for an explanation and

banishment of his delusions. All in vain. Nothing anyone could say—
from school teachers to priests to medical specialists—could convince
the little boy that his dreams were unreal.

And so after a time, he wised up. Said nothing more about his weekly
visits to another realm, beyond a blurted phrase or two when he invari-
ably tumbled with a start from his nocturnal sheets. He tried to re-engage
with ordinary life, with the dull routines of school and home and church.
He exerted himself but failed to find much charm in the shabby appur-
tenances and tinsel attractions of the waking world.

But how could he, really, after all he had seen? Oh, he had learned
how to fake an interest in what occupied everyone else, especially
after the dreams had ended. (And what a painful transition that had
been, into and through his dreary blank adolescence and young man-
hood.) But the sights presented to his opened eyes were washed-out
and bland compared to those viewed from behind lowered lids every
Sunday night.

He had ridden impossible animals across turbulent skies and from
sun to sun across the Milky Way. Boats and cars and airships of every
conceivable stripe had ferried him from one locus of wonder to
another. He had visited the Moon and Mars. He had swum with the
sirens and helped any number of demiurges mismanage the diurnal
workings of the cosmos. Seething jungles, tropical archipelagos,
canyons with walls high as continents, sherbet-colored polar wastes,
spiky caverns measureless to man: he had plumbed a vast range of
strange climates and elastic geographies.

But most remarkable had been the abundant architecture of his
dream civilization. Never had the greatest empire of any earthly paradise boasted its like.

The builders worked big in Morpheus's kingdom. And in what
exotic materials! Porphyry and travertine, sandstone and marble, onyx
and jade, chrysoberyl and ivory. Embellished with gilt, mosaics, scrollwork and mother of pearl inlays. Prinked out in a pastel palette or with
pyrotechnic panache. Cyclopean ceremonial structures whose glitter-
ing, shadowy arcades and architraves, lintels and loggias, roofs and
rafters, columns and corridors, porticos and patios, towers and tun-
nels, all stretched to infinity. (Once he had climbed a staircase all the
way to the Moon.) But the sizes and textures and hues, although
impressive, were the least of the attractions—and frights—of this
world. The changeability of the constructions outweighed by far their
grandiose dimensions.

Everything was mutable: roads could become caves, fireplaces open onto stairwells, floors become ceilings. Buildings—entire cities—sank into the soil, fell from the sky, dwindled and disappeared, or sprang from nowhere. It took a flexible mind to accept such a continuum, and the boy had prided himself on his adaptation to the dream universe (although of course he could still be shocked, right up to his final dream, a dire event whose significance had been betrayed by no grand conclusion or apocalypse.)

And the distinction between organic and inorganic hardly counted there: snowmen cavorted, beds sprouted legs, a boy became rubber, buildings tore themselves up from their foundations and ambled about. Nor did conventional rules of physics apply. Gravity was abolished, inertia coerced, cause-and-effect confounded.

How then could even a Coney Island roller coaster or the Central Park zoo be expected to entrance or delight?

Or, later, women, song, or wine?

The doctor's breath smelled of alcohol, and his high hat dislodged a shiver of snow onto the old man's sheets, where the slush began to melt.

A cold stethoscope coined a minor discomfort against his chest, to match the greater one within. "You'd better not be malingering, old man. I was at lunch, you know."

"No, I think it's my heart—"

The doctor withdrew in alarm. "Nurse, nurse, can't you recognize a goddamn myocardial infarction when you see one! Call the ambulance!"

Ambulance? What did they need an ambulance for? (Although truth be told, that was one vehicle he had never yet ridden, asleep or awake.) Just give him the wonderful wand he had wielded in Shantytown, and he'd cure himself—

King Morpheus

In his early twenties, he had finally admitted the truth of his sorry condition to himself.

The dreams were never going to return. At least not with the vividness of their original run.

And the succeeding years had proven his sad suspicion correct. During a couple of brief unpredictable intervals separated by decades, some paltry semblance of the dreams had actually recurred. But all the actors therein seemed mere lifeless simulacra, all the colors of the land beyond sleep now pallid and dull, all the events a rehash of the originals. And, worst of all, when he entered these frustrating reiterations, he entered as a five-year-old, not the adult he now was. The actual bodily reversion did not trouble him; that condition was probably a predicate of gaining his dream empire. But the fact that he also reverted *mentally* truly dismayed him. This shearing away of any wisdom or experience he might have gained over the years indicated to him above all other clues that these were not true mystical experiences, for they lacked any eruptions of grace or glory, but rather mockeries sent to him by some malignant counterforce.

So he had attempted to become a good, productive, functioning member of society. He had taken a job almost at random. What job it was he no longer even recalled, for at age one hundred he had been retired almost as long as he had been employed, and the job had never held any more of his attention or concern than was absolutely necessary to perform it with minimal competence. After the death of his father and the loss of his childhood home, his mother had gone to live with one of her sisters (the old man was an only child), and he had found lodgings for himself in a cheap boarding house, the first of many before his eventual consignment—because of failing health— to this cheap and tawdry nursing home called Slumberland.

Of course, he had never married. Never even courted.

To betray the princess? She of the winsome sighs and unstinting devotion? Unthinkable! And besides: what flesh-and-blood woman could compare to that fabled child bride of his spirit?

Recreations he had none. What could substitute for the sparkling attractions of his dream life? Incomparable parades, festivals, parties, dinners: he had played the guest at more grand affairs than the richest, most popular terrestrial socialite. Games? He had ridden sleds down glaciers, dived to the bottom of the sea, and drifted in a dirigible around the world, visiting the dream doppelganger of every state of his nation and every country of the globe. Dinosaurs and dragons had carried him through forests of giant mushrooms and entire cities built of children's blocks.

Really, what kind of travel could lure him from his lonely tenement hermitage? He had been a giant in microworlds, and an ant in macroworlds. Tropical islands full of cannibals had known his step. He had helmed naval destroyers across jade seas of miracles.

And all the love and adulation he had received! Those dream affections had been the most painful birthrights to lose. In his dreams he had always been the center of attention. People fawned over him, catered to his every whim. He was pampered and petted, cossetted and consulted. Even when thwarted by his primal antagonist, Flip, he had felt himself honored by the magnitude of his opponent's efforts. And if this universe of sleep did not revolve entirely around him— there was always a disturbing sense of ongoing agenda and schemes much, much larger than his small self—then at least he always felt that he was one of its most privileged citizens.

And never had he experienced this sensation more keenly than when he visited Shantytown, that ghetto precinct of King Morpheus's realm, where, with his miraculous wand, he served as savior to its suffering inhabitants, easing their pains and tribulations like Christ himself.

Of course, awake, he occupied no such exalted position. No savior amidst the mortal dust of existence, he was just one more of the faceless millions, another atom in the uncaring cosmos. How deeply that pained him, to the core of his soul!

Anxiety had burned away the booziness in the doctor's voice. "Where are those goddamn beta-blockers? Have those freaking junkies we call aides raided the pharmacy again? Didn't we get a new supply? Christ, I can't lose another old fuck! I'm already under review. At least get me some goddamn aspirin for his rotten heart!"

The old man wanted to tell the doctor not to bother, but he couldn't quite find his voice. The pain had transcended itself to become a vacuity, a hollow at his center. And the hollow was rapidly expanding to empty the old man from the inside out.

"What's going on here?"

The owner of Slumberland resembled a bloated plutocrat of yore, a figure out of editorial cartoons from the old man's youth. Seen in detail through the old man's glasses on previous visits, the owner recalled no one so much as Nast's indelible image of Boss Tweed.

Now, waddling like King Cole, his plummy cheeks visibly flaring, his waistcoat straining against his girth, the owner had rushed in to take command.

In the midst of the uselessly fluttering workers and gawpers, the old man rediscovered his voice, enough to croak out a single name, a name that surprised him as much as it baffled the listeners.

"Flip. Please, Flip. Help, please, Flip—"

Flip

They had torn off his shirt and pressed abrasive paddles against his chest, but not yet triggered the Frankenstein jolts that might convince his balky pump to labor uselessly on, prolonging a life that should have ended ninety years ago, for all the utility or joy or good deeds the old man could realistically chalk up.

A choir of blurry faces hung about his bed: the Candy Kid, Doctor Pill, King Morpheus, the princess, Impie—

But no Flip! Where was Flip? Flip would save him, sure he would, that rascal. . . .

That green-faced, unblinking, cigar-smoking amalgam of Penrod, Jiggs, and Moon Mullins, who had first appeared in pure ornery envious opposition to the young visitor from the realm of wakefulness, yet who had become, in some strange fashion, his best friend among the dreamfolk (though still inherently prone to causing disruptions, detours and disasters galore). Often and often had Flip extended a saving hand when danger threatened. Wouldn't he trump death now, darting in from offstage during the crisis of this final act?

The paddles crackled to life, and, under their misplaced harshness, the old man's heart burst.

Waves of crimson occluded his dying eyes. The shimmering red draperies boiled for an infinite moment, then were sucked down as into a whirlpool, pooling into a single red knot—

—the ember on the tip of Flip's cigar.

"Feelin' kinda punk there for a minute, hey, kid?"

The old man took stock of his bodily condition first: no pain, an effortless vitality flowing through his limbs, his wrinkled, palsied hands smoothed to youthful elasticity and steadied by confidence, his head full of wavy brown hair.

His surroundings? A white canvas, untouched by artist's brush or pen.

His clothing: a soft flannel suit of footed pajamas.

His sole companion? Flip, in red-and-white striped pants, garish weskit with buttons the size of dinner plates, billowy yellow cravat, insouciant top hat.

The reborn boy stuck out his hand, and Flip gripped it with his typical rude vigor.

"Sorry to take so long fetchin' ya back, kid, but we had a busy night here at the palace since we last saw each other. Rogue herd of gogglemops got loose in the pantry. Devil's own work corralling them. Chef fell in the birthday cake batter too."

"One night? Was that all it was?"

"Yeah, just a single night. How come ya ask? Time kinda drag for ya?"

"A little, yes. It seemed like years."

"Well, you're too many for me, pal. But ya know ya won't have that kinda headache here. Plenty to keep ya busy. Almost too much sometimes, ya ask me. Now let's get movin'. Lotta folks waitin' for ya— including one special little lady, if you get my drift. You don't wanna miss yer own birthday party. Hope ya don't mind if yer cake tastes a little like the chef."

"How do we get there?"

Flip smacked his forehead. "Wotta lunkhead! After all this time, ya gotta ask me! Use yer wits, peabrain!"

The boy thought a moment, then gripped twin handfuls of the canvas and pulled, tearing open a wide jagged split, to reveal—

The real Slumberland at last.

MEHITABEL IN HELL

well boss it s me archy again
your cockroach pal
transmigrated free versifier
bulletheading on your office
typewriter once more
after a long silence
open parentheses
the dull roots of which we will not
trifle with close parentheses
bringing some big news both sad and
miraculous beyond belief
and i don t know
whether to laugh or cry

and by the by are you the last old fashioned
newshound in this new millennium
still using an ancient underwood question
mark what i wouldn t give for uninterrupted
access to a computer keyboard with
its easy action keys soft on the chitinous
noggin floating cursor delete capabilities
et cyber cetera but your office is also
the last one to keep a supply of white paste handy
on which i subsist so qed

anyhow don t mind my griping
the news i got is more important
than personal complaints

mehitabel
she always at the heart
most of my news question mark

now you know the history of this
bad cat what she has done or what
hasn t she done in her long
scroungy irresponsible life
of racketing up and down the alleys
and boulevards of this mean old town
plus paris france and other environs
from past lives even when she claimed
to be cleopatra and sundry other
high class gals who weren t around anymore
to refute her outrageous claims
and in every situation her motto has been
open quote toujours gai close quote
which she has never been slow
to back up with a sharp set of claws and
matching razor teeth

but mehitabel finally met her predestined
nameless fate which not even high spirits
or a sneaky one two punch could defeat
and that is namely to buy the farm
if by farm you mean a dumpster
behind the ming gardens restaurant
down in chinatown
where radish curls formed her only wreath
and leftover chow mein her bier

that is how i encountered mehitabel
for what i thought was surely the last time
during a little expedition of my own
double dash looking for some cockroach
love if you must know double dash
and i felt like hell at the sight of her
bloody corpse and i cursed all the gods
who had led her to this unseemly end

and who had made me an insect who
couldn t even cry for his best friend
physiologically speaking because i
sure was weeping inside

needless to say the next few weeks were
pretty miserable and grim all
the life seemed to have fled this lousy
burg with mehitabel s untimely exit
i got so down i couldn t even eat paste
and was on the point of withering away
to mayfly weight why not die i said to myself
and maybe get reborn as something better
if not a human poet again then at least
a journalist ha forgive me ha

but nearly on the point of expiring i bethought
me of a pal who might be able to lift
this load of blues off my wings
and that was clarence the ghost

clarence i figured with his access to
astral realms beyond the styx and
unto the farthest starry spheres
might have some comforting dope
on mehitabel s progress in the great hereafter
so i hastened to get in touch with
my spectral pal through a ouija
board inside the games room
of the west side ymca one night
after hours pushing the planchette around
like sisyphus shouldering his boulder and
sure enough clarence materialized
before too long dripping ectoplasm
onto a pile of convenient towels

clarence i yelled without even making
polite noises because after all
the dead are really immune to

such chitchat tell me what you know
about the soul of mehitabel
exclamation point

clarence replied archy i was just
waiting for you to call so i could share
with you the biggest news from hell
since the kaiser kicked napolean s
keister from pit to pit
mehitabel is down there causing
the sweetest stink i ve ever seen
unlike all the other humbled and despairing souls
who capitulate immediately upon finding
themselves in the land of brimstone sulfur and flames
she refuses to kowtow to old nick and his minions
raking her claws across the faces and
flabby behinds of all the lesser demons
assigned to corral her and once
when old nick himself intervened
even scoring a nice set of stripes on his gross gut
she just won t take her licks like he had planned
for her something about being buried
up to her neck inside a ring of catnip
placed just out of reach of her questing
tongue and unless she submits to her
allotted punishments then she will
never get a chance to be reborn

boss i can t tell you how this lifted
my heart knowing mehitabel had maintained
even in hell her indomitable courage
and piss pardon my french
but at the same time i was worried
because who wants to be an eternal rebel
in hell when with just a little
submission
contrition
and endurance
over a subjective eternity or two
you can be reborn into this sad yet delightful

old world of ours maybe as a persian
lapcat gangster s moll or nautch dancer
any one of which roles i could easily
envision mehitabel filling and excelling in

clarence i inquired further what will happen
to mehitabel question mark must she give in
or is there another way out for her question mark

the ghost paused and wavered an indication
i knew of deep thought and in fact i could see
firefly neurons firing inside his transparent
head in elaborate cascades of reasoning
well clarence finally said there is me

you i queried

yes me a ghost obviously
i died yet was not reborn
into a mortal carcass
that is an option for some
an escape clause in the celestial
infernal contract inked eons ago
between adam and eve and pinch me
to leave behind either heaven or hell and
stalk the earth in less substantial form
for an indefinite time

i cogitated myself on this option
for a time but something just didn t
jibe between this possibility
and mehitabel s essential nature
then of course it hit me colon
mehitabel was such a carnal creature
a thing of sinews and hormones
juices and bones that existence
as a ghost among mortals double dash
herself airy and nontactile yet
perpetually taunted
with the pleasures

of the flesh double dash
would be a punishment
more cruel than anything old nick
had in store for my friend

i explained all this to clarence and after
some more luminous pinball style mental
efforts on his part he volunteered that there
were other kinds of boggles than ghosts

enumerate i ordered and he did

stop i yelled when he uttered a term
i recognized from my poetaster days
a term we bards were fond of using
for certain super seductive inamoratas
that s perfect exclamation point
clarence can you intervene as mediator
between old nick and mehitabel
for friendship s sake and try to strike
this deal i think they'll both agree
happy to be out of each other s hair

sure said clarence and i ll report back
tomorrow night

boss that twenty four hours crawled by
like a beetle down an endless drain
but somehow i survived the anxiety
and made it back to my planchette
and when i got clarence all focused
on our earthly plane i held my breath

it s a done deal he said

and so you see boss
i am ultimately the one responsible
for all those spooky headlines in your own
newspaper lately to wit colon
devil cat alarms midnight frolickers

epidemic of missing felines
dogs frightened barkless
et demonically cetera
for mehitabel you see is now a feline
succubus as corporeal as they come
her fur is lush and seductive her eyes
burning garnets her sleek haunches
perpetually raised high in lordosis
luring tomcats everywhere into
frenzied matings impossible to resist
which leave them pitiful shells
of their former tough yegg selves
and when she s not sexing it up
mehitabel is happily raising cain among all her
old enemies such as phonies swells canines
politicians and cheapskates

Oh yes one final thing colon
the oddest feature of succubi wombs is that
they gestate really quickly
like in about a day so that mehitabel is
regularly dumping half mortal half infernal kittens
by the bushel basket full
and so i would be very careful
boss if you go to adopt any strays
in this town better check first
for a certain sparkle in the eyes
and a tendency to spit acid
                              archy